COPPER KINGDOM

COPPER KINGDOM

IRIS GOWER

REISSUED 1987

CENTURY

LONDON   MELBOURNE   AUCKLAND   JOHANNESBURG

First published in Great Britain in 1983 by
Century Hutchinson Ltd
Brookmount House, 62–65 Chandos Place,
London WC2N 4NW

Century Hutchinson South Africa (Pty) Ltd
PO Box 337, Bergvlei, 2012 South Africa

Century Hutchinson Australia Pty Ltd
PO Box 496, 16–22 Church Street, Hawthorn,
Victoria 3122, Australia

Century Hutchinson New Zealand Ltd
PO Box 40-086, Glenfield, Auckland 10,
New Zealand

Reprinted 1987

ISBN 0 7126 0062 0

Printed in Great Britain by
St Edmundsbury Press Ltd, Bury St Edmunds, Suffolk

*To Tudor
and our family
with love*

Chapter One

The sounds, repetitive and ominous, echoed through the squat, whitewashed cottage, reverberating from the sparsely furnished parlour and along the cold flagged passageway. Hammer upon nail, pausing and continuing, penetrating the thick, drystone walls to the kitchen where the scrubbed table gleamed like raw bones in the shaft of winter light probing the dusty glass of the single window.

The rhythm, like a pulse gone awry, brought father and daughter together in an unexpected slant of January sun that washed over the cobbled yard at the rear of the building. The two stood as though frozen in a moment of heavy stillness, eyes refusing to meet over the stark shape of the coffin that stood between them.

Both were dark and vital but David Llewelyn was a bull of a man and everything about him was large from the breadth of his shoulders beneath the leonine head to the hands that wielded the hammer with more strength than skill.

As he crouched now over his task, his thighs bulged hugely beneath the coarse flannel of his trousers. His entire body seemed coiled like a spring. There was a tension in him and a deep sadness that was reflected in the lines around his mouth.

Mali had her father's darkness. Her hair, thick and abundant, fell like a cloak to below her trim waist. But her features were more delicate, beautiful even now with fatigue and despair etched into them. And her most striking resemblance to her father was in her eyes, which were clear green, large and luminous.

She was almost seventeen but might have been taken for

7

little more than a child for she was small boned, with tiny hands and feet. And yet her carriage was upright and she had an air of dignity that belied her youth.

Mali breathed in the scent of pine shavings that lay strewn like bright curls over the yard, and a great pain filled her as she remembered Mam's hair, so fair and silky even to the end.

The grating sound of metal against stone brought Mali's attention back to where her father was sorting nails, his big fingers so clumsy that she knew he was not concentrating on his task. His head was bent, his big neck exposed so that he seemed very vulnerable. He turned to look at her questioningly and sweat ran from his face into the open collar of his striped shirt, dampening the springy dark hair on his chest. He was persevering with a job that was foreign to him in every way and suddenly she was achingly proud of him.

The long box was almost finished. The wood, clean and sweet with fine patterns of grain running its length, had somehow taken shape. She caught his glance and knew he did not like her watching and yet she longed to help him so that their grief might be shared.

'There's some hot tea brewed, Dad.' The words came out harshly and not at all in the way she'd intended. Her father shook his head, resuming his efforts to strike home the nails, and Mali turned away, feeling that she was dismissed. Her eyes were suddenly bright and her throat ached with the effort of holding back her tears.

Indoors it seemed dark and gloomy after the brightness outside. She glanced towards the steep wooden stairs and to the bedroom door above, a door that was firmly closed.

'Mammy.' Her voice was a strangled cry to which there could be no answer, not ever again. Mali hurried into the warmth of the kitchen, shivering. A fire burned brightly behind the blackleaded bars of the grate and she crouched before the flames, feeling as though she would never be warm. It was here in the kitchen that she felt most alone, for the room had once been the hub of the house in Copperman's Row.

Now Mali must work alone. This morning she had been up from bed early, unable to sleep. And the brass fender glowed with reflected light from the fire for she had worked fiercely, rubbing the metal with an abrasive made from ashes and water.

Restlessly Mali rose to her feet; the hammering seemed to be within herself and her head began to ache. She stared around her, wondering what she could do to keep her thoughts occupied but water had long since been fetched from the pump in the yard. Dishes were washed and dried, the plates set out neatly on the dresser, the cups hanging in uniformity from the brass hooks on the shelf. The mundane tasks that had always been part of the pattern of her life had offered a sort of solace but she had worked at them too eagerly and now there seemed nothing left with which to fill the silent, aching void.

She would pour herself tea from the brown earthenware pot, she decided, and watched the fragrant liquid spill into the cup. She bit her lip, worrying about Dad. He had eaten little, for he was bent on continuing with his job of making the coffin. Not that he confided in her at all, rather he was dumb and silent in his sorrow.

The tea warmed her a little but her hand shook and drops of liquid patterned the blue slabs of slate underfoot and they gleamed briefly, spots of gold caught by the glare of the fire.

The outer door opened and her father was in the kitchen, filling it with his size and presence. His great hands pushed back the dark curls from his forehead and his eyes looked hauntedly about the room as though he was searching for somebody.

'I'll have some of that tea now, girl.' He spoke harshly and she knew that it was not anger that coarsened his voice, but pain. And yet in spite of her concern for him, she felt irritated because even now when they were alone, he did not use her proper name. She wanted to tell him that she was a person, not simply the girl child he had got from love for his wife. He sat down, resting his arms on the scrubbed wood of the table, and sighed wearily.

'A cart,' he said. 'I must have a horse and cart.' He did not look up. 'You will have to go and ask Tom Murphy for a loan of Big Jim.'

Mali trembled as protests rose to her lips. Mam could not go to her rest with such a lack of dignity.

'Mr Murphy's cart is for fish, Dad,' she said reasonably.

Davie did not reply but his fingers were suddenly twisted together so fiercely that his knuckles showed white. With swift insight Mali realised that the cost to her father's pride in asking for anyone's help was great indeed.

'You can use a scrubbing brush, can't you, girl?' He shook his head from side to side like a wounded beast and Mali longed to go to him, put her arms around him, lean against his broad shoulders, but she knew she would be rebuffed for Davie was not a man to make a show of his grief.

She took a deep shuddering breath and moved woodenly towards the back door. There, with her hand on the latch she paused for a moment, struggling for words of comfort, but her own hurt was so hard to bear that she was afraid the tears might come.

'I won't be long, Dad,' she said hoarsely. In the bleakness of the yard she stood for a moment, breathing in the cold air. The sun had gone and shadows lay thick and heavy beneath the shallow back wall. Mali clenched her small hands into fists, it was going to be hard to ask anything of the rough-hewn Irishman for he had always put the fear of God into her. Sometimes in the night, his voice would ring out in anger, sending the rats scurrying into the crevices between the walls, and in her bed Mali would shiver.

The Murphy house, although joining the cottage where Mali lived, was not part of Copperman's Row at all but was the beginning of Market Street where the small traders of the area lived. Willie the Bread occupied the tall building next door to 'Murphy's Fresh Fish', which sounded grand but was only a house with the front room turned into a shop, and Dai End House lived at the corner of the dusty lane running behind the cottages.

As Mali opened the gate facing the Murphys' back kitchen her heart was beating so loudly within her that it seemed to echo the knocking of her knuckles against the door. She stumbled so badly over her request that she was forced to repeat her words several times before Tom Murphy could make sense of them.

He drew her inside, his hand warm on her shoulder, his pale eyes probing her small breasts beneath the cotton of her high-necked blouse. He frowned and a jutting shelf of ginger brows drew together over his large nose.

'Go on ahead into the kitchen with you,' Tom said amiably enough, but his tone changed as the crying of the baby echoed loudly throughout the building.

'For love of the Blessed Virgin shut that infant up, woman, and leave the gin alone, for sure it does you no good.'

Mrs Murphy sat in a low rocking chair, the newest child held close in her arms. She fumbled in her bodice and the baby fell into a soft quiescence, sucking sleepily at the meagre breast.

'Our Katie's not in, bless you.' She brushed back her tangled hair with thin fingers. 'But sit down and have a drop o' gin and don't go listenin' to my Tom, he likes a drop of the hard stuff well enough himself.'

Tom Murphy shook his head at his wife as though in despair as, ignoring him, she poured a liberal measure of gin. The sweet sickly smell of it drifted towards where Mali stood in embarrassed silence.

'She's not here to see Katie, not at a time like this. Have a bit of sense, woman. It's the cart she's come for.' As though reminding himself of his task, Tom left the kitchen and Mali could hear the tinkle of horse brasses as he gathered the tack together.

'Sit down, Mali, Tom will not rush himself, you may as well be comfortable while you wait.'

Obediently, Mali seated herself on the shabby artificial leather chair, and glancing round saw that the two older Murphy babies were lying side by side in an old pram body that had no wheels but rested on a rag mat on the floor. There was little more than a year between the children and they slept alongside each other like two peas from the same pod.

'Our Katie's out courtin',' Mrs Murphy volunteered. 'Though to be sure my Tom does not know of it, nor likely to, not from my lips. Shake the very heavens he would with his anger if he knew his only girl was out with a man.'

Katie was the eldest of the Murphy family, the only surviving child of the first years of the marriage. For a time it had seemed as though many miscarriages had left Mrs Murphy barren, but quite suddenly and in quick succession she had brought forth three fine sons. Yet it was Katie who remained the apple of her father's eye and it was no wonder, for she was a beautiful girl and gifted with a fine sense of humour.

For as long as Mali could remember she and Katie had been friends. They had giggled together, confiding their hopes for the fine marriages they would one day make. It was no surprise to Mali that Katie, with her lovely red-gold hair and creamy skin, had been the first to realise her dreams.

William Owens was a copperman, young and dark and vital. His skin was bronzed, coloured by slow impregnation from the metal which he worked. He was handsome and intelligent and Mali had been tonguetied when she had first met him.

'Katie's a very lucky girl.' It was as though Mrs Murphy was reading Mali's thoughts. 'Will spends his fat wages on her, always buying her some frippery or other.' She sighed. 'And sure doesn't she love him as though he was the only man in the world?' Her eyes clouded. 'I fear for her sometimes, she's that trusting.'

Tom Murphy's return saved Mali from making any reply. He rested his hand on her shoulder, leaning too close for comfort.

'Cart's out the back lane and I've hitched up Big Jim. Don't you be afeared of the creature, he's docile enough in spite of his size.'

Mali followed him outside, wishing he would take his hand away; it felt moist and warm against her neck and she moved uneasily. As the huge, liver-coloured horse turned as though to look at her, Mali breathed in the pungent odour of fish with distaste. She wondered if it was ungracious of her to wish for something finer than a fish cart to carry Mam's coffin. She felt Tom Murphy glance at her.

'Goin' to do it up a mite, I expect.' He frowned. 'Shall I not come wid ye then, give you an' your dad some help?'

'No thank you, Mr Murphy, we can manage.' How could Mali explain that Dad was a private man who hugged his grief to himself, not even allowing his own daughter to share it with him?

Tom Murphy handed her the reins and clucked his tongue, urging the great horse into movement. Spurts of dust were raised by the animal's hooves but Mali did not notice. The residents of Copperman's Row fought a constant battle against the fine particles of copper, so abrasive that they scored the glass in the windows.

Mali heard the Irishman return to the cottage and close the door behind him and as though released, she leaned her head against the warmth of Big Jim's wiry mane, clucking to the creature softly, finding the animal's nearness comforting.

She tied the reins to the scratched woodwork of the gate leading into her own yard. There was dimness now, creeping over the cobbles and the heavy shape of the coffin crouched menacingly in the deep black shadows against the ground. For a moment Mali stood still, gathering her courage for the moment when she would enter the kitchen where Dad would be sitting lost and alone.

But there was work to be done, the cart must be scrubbed clean while some vestige of light remained.

'There's a good boy,' she said as Big Jim nuzzled her hand with a soft mouth. 'Wait by here, I won't be long.'

Davie was still leaning on the table. Now that his bout of activity was over, he seemed drained and empty. His head was sunk low onto his big chest, his hands lay, palms upwards, calloused fingers curled. Tears formed a lump in Mali's throat, she wanted to cry out her pain but the habits of a lifetime were hard to break and the Llewelyns had never been given to shows of emotion.

She reached beneath the stone sink and drew out a bag of soda and a scrubbing brush. Her father did not even look up as she poured water from the kettle into the zinc bucket. The flow drummed against the ridged bottom, sending steam into Mali's face, and the beads of moisture felt like the tears she could not cry.

The bucket was heavy but she managed to haul it out into the yard. She skirted the spot where the long box lay and pushed at the creaking gate. The wood of the cart was old and splintered and scales of fish gleamed silver in the dim light. A jagged splinter caught Mali's soft palm and she winced with pain, sucking at the blood before continuing with her efforts.

At last, she flung the remainder of the swiftly cooling water over the cart, satisfied that it was as clean and fresh as she could make it. She watched the rivulets stream from the boards, dropping into the dusty ground to be immediately soaked up. She hoped that the timber would dry quickly for she must set about making the cart look more presentable.

She remembered that in the old tin trunk under her Mam's bed there was a square of dark silk so old that the violet colour was almost black. It had once been intended to make a shawl with a silk fringing decorating the edges, but that had been before Mam's sickness had taken hold.

She returned to the kitchen, pushing aside thoughts of her mother. She washed the soda from the bucket and placed the cleaning materials behind the curtain beneath the sink.

'It's done, Dad,' she said at last. He looked up at her as though just realising that she had returned, his eyes were green and luminous as though they had been washed in a mountain stream.

'There's still the smell of fish,' she said desperately. 'It's in the wood, nothing will shift it.'

Davie rose to his feet, like a man about to go to his doom. 'Don't fret about that, girl.' His voice held bitterness. 'There's no one to notice, 'cept us.'

The silence was heavy, a coal moved in the grate and the room was full of shadows. 'I'll just be a minute, Dad,' Mali said. 'I'm going to cover the cart with a piece of silk.'

In the room upstairs, the window stood open and a rush of cold January air swept over Mali, but it was not from coldness she shivered. She would not look towards the double bed but rummaged beneath it, dragging out the trunk, selecting the material from sense of touch rather than sight, for the room was almost dark.

She left the place quickly, closing the door with a sigh of relief. She knew that Mam would not hurt her while she was alive so why should she fear her in death? Yet she was glad to reach the warmth of the kitchen once more.

She paused to catch her breath before going towards the back door. 'I won't be a minute, Dad.'

Outside, she heard Big Jim breathing gently as she covered the rough boards with the silk.

'It's all right, boy, I won't keep you standing here much longer,' she said reassuringly.

'Come on girl, time you were dressed.' Her father was

calling to her from the doorway. 'Go on, your job is finished, it's all up to me now.'

In her small room, Mali leaned against the windowsill, sighing deeply. She listened to the heavy tread of her father's footsteps as he entered the next bedroom and she closed her eyes, not wanting to imagine his task.

She pressed her hands to her face, wondering how her life could have changed so much in the space of a few short months. Now the very cottage in which she had been born was no longer hers. The copper boss owned it and would want it back, for yesterday Dad had been dismissed from his job.

Mali flung off her damp apron with the smell of soda still clinging to it. It was good to feel anger against someone and the owner of the Richardson Copper company would do very well indeed.

It had been wrong of him to give Davie his marching orders when he had worked all his life at the furnace mouth. It was so unjust that because Davie had been forced to spend time with his sick wife these last weeks, he was to be no longer employed by the richest family in Sweyn's Eye.

Her anger faded as panic began to beat within her. She could vividly imagine how it would feel to have their new possessions put out of the house into the dust of the lane, for she had seen such a thing happen when she was a child. Once the copper had done with you it was out into the streets and no going back.

She dressed quickly, the cold bringing goose bumps to her flesh. Her crisp blouse with its Peter Pan collar was quickly buttoned over her woollen chemise. She drew her one good flannel skirt up over her boots and stood for a moment, hands against her cheeks, summoning up the strength to face the coming ordeal.

Her father's voice rang out harshly in the stillness, calling to her that he was ready. She pulled on her shawl and hurried down the stairs, ignoring the trembling of her limbs.

Davie's only concession to the occasion was that he had slicked down his hair with water in a vain attempt to tame the unruly curls. His shirt sleeves were rolled up above the elbows and only his waistcoat offered any protection from the chill of the evening air.

'You'll be cold, Dad,' Mali said, and her tongue felt thick in her mouth. He shook his head without replying and, silently, she followed him outside.

The cart drew Mali's eyes and she saw that the dark silk now covered the coffin. The horse had been standing in patient submission and jerked into movement at the clicking of Davie's tongue. Mali walked behind, head bent, staring down into the dust of the lane without really seeing it.

'We'll go down past the pluck, girl,' her father's voice drifted back to her. 'It's more private that way.'

Though Mali did not look left or right, she was aware of the silent neighbours standing in doorways, paying their last respects the only way they could. Mali's dark hair drifted across her face, blown by the cold wind, and she was thankful to be hidden from curious stares, however kindly.

The waters of the pluck nestled in the valley, a natural lake formed from many hillside streams and now they gleamed richly copper, illuminated by the flames that flew forth from the forest chimneys above the works. Mali glanced around her as though she was witnessing the spectacular display for the first time rather than being born and bred amid the copper.

Smoke trailed upwards, green and thick, pouring from the tall stacks to mingle with the sky's grey clouds. The sun was dying now and had small chance of competing with the rich cauldron of colour that lit the banks of the River Swan.

The cart shook precariously as it moved across the wooden struts of the bridge spanning the swollen waters. Mali seemed to be walking in a dream, not thinking or feeling but keeping her emotions tightly in check.

Above her loomed the twin slopes of Kilvey and the Town Hill, large and black against the sky. Mali stumbled a little and forced herself to concentrate on the pitted track that was leading her around the mountain side and away from the works. The dusty roadway curved gently, sloping down towards the graveyard. The effects of the copper dust did not reach this far and Mali wondered suddenly why the smoke should kill everything beautiful in its path.

'There it is, Dan-y-Graig Cemetery.' Davie spoke softly. Mali saw him pause in mid stride and his shoulders stiffened as he lifted his hand to his eyes, straining to see into the distance.

16

'It seems the Richardsons are burying their dead too, girl,' he said huffily, as though affronted. 'See there are six fine horses and an elegant hearse and God knows how many carriages. There's no justice.'

The cemetery was divided into two parts by a low, thick hedge that formed a barrier. On the one side along the path which Davie took was a piece of ground bristling with wooden crosses while the other part of the graveyard was resplendent with gracious marble headstones.

Mali, watching the carriages roll by, saw that the one nearest her was occupied by a stately woman wearing a black fur cape and a hat that sat hugely on glossy dark hair. And then the cortege was past and Mali became aware that Davie was drawing Big Jim to a halt.

'This is the spot I've picked out for my Jinny,' he said sombrely. 'Just here underneath the trees with the wall running alongside.'

The gaping hole that was Mam's last resting place was all ready to receive the coffin, for Davie had worked off and on as a gravedigger during the last weeks. He had spent several hours a day at the cemetery, toiling so that his wife could have a decent resting place at very little cost.

Davie struggled to slide the coffin from the sloping cart, easing it into the ground. His strength was great but even he felt the strain, for after he had put Jinny into the earth, he leaned panting against the tree trying to recover his breath.

After a time, he took up the spade and filled in the grave. Mali bit her lip, wishing there was a minister from the chapel present, just so a few holy words could be read over Mam. Mali stared up into the branches of the tree that was barren now but in spring would be heavy with blossoms, and her grief was almost too much to bear.

Davie had finished filling in the grave and was mopping his brow. With an uncharacteristic gesture, Mali moved forward and slipped her hand into her father's strong fingers, which were still grimed with earth.

'I'll say a prayer, Dad.' She spoke softly and after a moment, Davie nodded and bowed his great head.

Her voice, lilting and small in the silence, asked the Good Lord to look down on Jinny Llewelyn and to be with her always. Mali moved away then, sensing that Davie wanted to be alone.

'I'll come after you in a minute, Mali,' he said softly, and it was as though they both recognised that she had become a woman.

As Mali walked past the lines of wooden crosses, she shivered a little and drew her shawl closer around her shoulders. The sound of hooves clopping along the pathway drew her attention and looking up, she saw that the procession of mourners from the Richardson funeral was returning along the path towards the gate.

Suddenly a dark shape loomed up out of the twilight, bounding towards her. Mali had cried out in alarm before realising that it was only a large dog, coming to a halt before her with tongue lolling as though waiting to be patted.

'Sam, to heel boy!' The voice was strong and masculine, fine and English. Mali stood with her hand on the dog's head as the tall figure approached her.

'Sorry if Sam startled you.' He was much taller than Mali, with a proud set to his shoulders. He stood with easy grace and yet there was a quality of litheness in his stance that suggested whipcord strength. Even in the gloom she could see the gleam of his bright hair.

'I'm all right,' she said selfconsciously.

The clouds moved across the sky and a late shaft of light pierced the dimness, the last flare of the dying sun. Mali caught her breath as she saw clearly now the clean-cut line of the jaw and the level brows framing piercing violet eyes. The mouth beneath the golden moustache was strong and sensual, curled upwards at the corners as though in amusement.

He was regarding her steadily. 'Do I pass muster?' he asked lightly, and Mali felt the rich colour suffuse her cheeks as she realised she had been staring. She turned to move away but he caught her arm.

'Don't run off.' His voice was assured and he spoke with such authority that Mali stood obediently still.

He was the one staring now; his eyes moved over her with

such an intense scrutiny that Mali almost felt he was reaching out and touching her.

'Mr Richardson!' The voice calling through the stillness broke the spell and the man holding her in such an arbitrary manner glanced over his shoulder.

Mali froze. She tugged her arm away and stood staring up fiercely.

'Are you Mr Richardson,' she demanded, 'boss of the copper works?' Suddenly she longed to hit out at the handsome face, of course he was Mr Richardson, who else would he be?

'So you're the one who gave my Dad the sack.' She heard her voice strike at the silence like hard stones. 'Punishing a man because he takes time off to look after a dying wife, that's your way isn't it? Well I hate you, Mr high and mighty Richardson, and I hope you rot in hell!'

Mali turned and ran back to where her father stood over his wife's grave. He did not notice her presence. She leaned against the flank of the patient horse and Big Jim turned and nuzzled her arm. Suddenly tears were in her eyes, trembling on her lashes and running into her mouth. 'Oh, Mammy I miss you!' she whispered and the cold wind lifted her words and carried them away.

Chapter Two

The small township of Sweyn's Eye huddled round the basin of the harbour, encroaching insidiously on the surrounding hills. Shops crouched on grey cobbled streets, glassy-eyed windows bearing gaudy advertisements for Sloan's Liniment and Pears Soap.

The outer edges of coffin-shaped doorways sported strings of highly polished boots from which emanated the tangy smell of leather. Brisk scrubbing brushes lay, like a plague of over-turned bugs, in wide-mouthed zinc buckets.

Set between twin hills, Sweyn's Eye faced the seas of the Bristol channel, a small, South Wales town grown fussy and important by involvement in the business of copper smelting. Once graceful barques had sailed into the wide, natural harbour but now steamships brought bustling activity to the proud new docklands. Chinamen walked with easy familiarity along the narrow, stone-built quays while Indians in fine bright clothing bartered with Welshmen over the price of a chicken.

To the east of the town lay the copper works, diminished in number now for the foreigners from Chile had learned the art, kept secret so long, of extracting pure blister copper from crude ore. And yet the smoke and stench still lingered on and some of the eastern hills were desolate and barren, sporting only a show of bleached camomile flowers resting like skulls against the brownness of the earth.

Around the headland to the west sat fine villas with gleaming windows facing clean golden beaches and rolling seas. All were elegant but the most magnificent of them was Plas

Rhianfa, a tall, turreted house supported with pillars like a Grecian temple. This was the home of the Richardson family, come from Cornwall a hundred years before to build an empire.

Sterling Richardson was now the head of that empire and at twenty-six years of age, he was man enough, he felt, to do justice to the task before him. He sat in his bedroom, staring into the fire and thinking about the funeral earlier that day. It had all seemed strangely unreal, and rather than grief he had felt only relief that his father had slipped so painlessly from life. He closed his eyes and the image behind his closed eyes was of a young girl with tousled dark hair and large, trusting green eyes.

He had been chasing after Sam; the damn dog had spotted some small creature in the grass and had run away from the funeral cortege. Truth to tell, Sterling had felt relieved to be given an excuse to leave the long faces behind him for a moment. Perhaps that was why the girl had provided a pleasant diversion, at first.

He had been amused at her scrutiny of himself and more than willing to oblige her with a tumble in the hay at some future date but then, once she'd known his name, she had treated him like a leper.

He had watched as she'd run away from him, skirts flying, and had seen her join her father beneath the shelter of the trees.

Sterling knew David Llewelyn of course, a strong man and a fine ladler. What he didn't know was that the man had been dismissed, for Ben the manager dealt with matters of that sort. But there was no great difficulty, he would reinstate Llewelyn as soon as possible. Not that he cared a damn about the opinions of others, certainly not some little wench from the poorer quarter of the town. But Llewelyn was too good a worker to lose, especially as the man had a reasonable excuse for his many absences from work.

Workers were easily dealt with but Sterling was not too sure about his partners. Both James Cardigan and Dean Sutton were older than he was and might well resent the fact that he was now in charge. What they didn't know was that Sterling had taken the burden of work from his father's shoulders, albeit discreetly, for some time now. But if the partners chose to remain distant, as they had done, then they must accept decisions that were made without their knowledge.

Some months before, Sterling had cornered his father in his study. 'Look Father,' he had held out a sheaf of papers. 'You can see from these trade figures that Chile is manufacturing enough copper to supply all demands. They have their own mines while we need to import ore.'

His father had waved him away. 'We have developed the finest method of smelting in the world, son, there will always be the need for Welsh copper.'

Sterling had sighed. 'But we are too slow, Father, it takes six operations to bring out the blister copper. Why not change to steel? Just consider it, that's all I ask.'

But Arthur Richardson had been adamant, change was unwelcome to him and he would not hear of it.

Sterling rose to his feet and moved across to the window. Outside, a pale wintry moon was shining across the sea; he could just make out the headland of Gilfach with its lighthouse sending out intermittent signals warning ships to steer clear of the craggy reef that reached with long fingers out into the channel.

Cuts would have to be made. He would pare the workforce down to a minimum, streamline the existing copper sheds before beginning to explore the possibilities of introducing steel and tinplate.

A chain of lights shone into the sea, colouring the water. Sterling smiled, thinking once more of the girl at the cemetery. If he was not mistaken, she was a blossom ready for plucking.

Victoria Richardson sat alone in her room. Soon she must go downstairs to the dining room, sit with her sons, talk with them, make a pretence of eating. No doubt any suspicion of vagueness on her part would be taken as a sign of her natural grief over the loss of her husband. And of course she would miss Arthur badly, he had been solid and dependable, always there when she needed him.

She rose to her feet and stared at her reflection softened by the gas lighting. At forty-five she was still an attractive woman, she thought a trifle complacently. Her glossy hair, brushed wide on her forehead, held only a few streaks of grey. Her round face above the high collar of her dark velvet gown was scarcely lined at all. Jet beads, a gift from Arthur's mother and a sign of mourning, hung over her full breasts. She turned from the mirror abruptly, there was no one to admire her looks now and her eyes misted with tears of self pity.

But she had been loved in her time, oh how she'd been loved. She sat in her chair and stared into the coals. She had been young and her blood had run singing through her veins. She had given herself to James Cardigan with complete abandon, meeting him secretly wherever and whenever she could. It had been difficult to escape from the vigilance of her parents but she had been cunning, stealing an hour from a visit to one of her friends or meeting him in summer on the outskirts of her parents' estate while she was walking her pet dogs. No one had ever suspected, not until she had conceived James's child.

Marriage was impossible for he already had a wife and a baby daughter, and James had turned her love for him into despair when he had told her there was nothing he could do to help her.

'My advice is to marry as soon as possible.' His eyes had been dark, unfathomable, and she had longed to throw herself at his feet and beg him not to desert her when she needed him most.

Arthur Richardson had been the means of her salvation. A man twenty years her senior, he had outlived one wife who had left him no issue and he had become a constant visitor to Victoria's home, a close friend of her parents.

He had always indulged and pampered her and when Victoria turned to him for comfort, he had arranged the marriage between them with surprising speed. To this day, Victoria never knew how much Arthur understood of the situation but certainly he had accepted Sterling as his own.

She had always been grateful to him, respecting him even while she could not give him the passion she had spent upon James; and Arthur had loved her dearly, his possessiveness a balm to her broken spirit.

It was a relief when, some time later, she had brought forth a son who was the image of Arthur in every way except one. Where Arthur was steadfast, Rickie was wild. He seemed to

23

grow up with a strange grudge against his elder brother, almost as though he knew that his rightful place as heir to the Richardson fortune had been stolen from him.

Victoria moved towards the window and stared out into the darkness. How many times had she stood here this way thinking about James? She had been unfaithful to her husband in her mind many times but never once in fact.

And James had continued to be involved in her life though she had thought it strange at first when he had decided to buy into the copper company. But in those early years, his quick mind and his flair for a good purchase had made him an asset.

After a time, he had lost interest in the business, leaving the bulk of the work to Arthur. It seemed to Victoria then that once he was satisfied that his son's future was secure financially, James was content to keep his distance.

She realised that it must have been difficult for him over the years, seeing Sterling growing up to manhood, especially after his wife had died leaving him with only one daughter and no son to bear his name.

And now they were good friends. James was almost fifty years of age and just as handsome as he had always been. Victoria's heart lifted a little, was it not possible that some time in the future they might come together again?

Dreamily, she moved to the desk that stood to the left of the white marble fire place. Her fingers searched in the small niche beneath one of the drawers and she took out the tiny key, staring at it speculatively. There was no need for secrecy now that Arthur was dead.

Within the drawer lay a dark oak box, flat and smooth, decorated with gilt hinges and inlaid with ivory. The lock was small but intricate and it was with difficulty that Victoria opened it; her eyes were no longer as sharp as they had once been. She fingered the smooth lid in anticipation, she would read the letter again, just once, and then she would destroy it. Arthur's death had made her aware of her own mortality and no one must be allowed to read the contents of that letter.

It had been James's one indiscretion, written after the birth of their son, smuggled to her by her most trusted maidservant. It spoke in graphic terms of their union and told of his undying gratitude for the gift of a son. She had forgiven him then totally and unconditionally for his weakness when she had first told him of her dilemma. She made many excuses for him in her mind and the years had done the rest.

She pushed back the lid and looked down into the satin-lined box. A wave of nausea swept over her as she saw that there was no letter, only emptiness. She tried to stem the panic that flared through her and her fingers feverishly probed within the drawer. It must be there, she reasoned, breathing deeply in an effort to calm herself, no one knew of its existence, it could not have simply vanished.

She drew open cupboard doors, feeling within the dark interior of the desk, desperate now. She pulled out drawers and felt behind them, even kneeling upon the floor to try to see behind the solid piece of furniture.

At last, she sank down into a chair and dabbed distractedly at the beads of perspiration on her forehead and upper lip. Dumbly, she stared at the scene of disarray before her. Tortoise-shell combs lay among perfumed linen handkerchiefs and the long leg of a pale silk stocking hung grotesquely over the edge of the desk.

'Oh, why didn't I burn it years ago?' she mumbled, closing her eyes in anguish. The letter was a potential weapon of destruction, one that could entirely ruin the life of her elder son. She thought of hostile eyes reading the words that were imprinted on her mind, and suddenly she felt cold.

Forcing herself into activity, she went through the tall, dividing doors into Arthur's room. The bed was neatly made, the covers turned down as though it would be occupied as usual that night, and Victoria felt suddenly bereft and alone. He had been more to her than she had realised, her rock, a man to lean upon even though many times she had chided him for his unbending nature.

Victoria was calmer now; she began to search systematically through her husband's belongings. His gold watch in its bed of rich red velvet was silent now and she stared at its ornate face as though she would find an answer to her problem in the gleaming gold numerals and the slender, motionless hands.

She pushed the large handkerchiefs back into place; her search was fruitless, the letter was not here. She stood in the silence battling with an unfamiliar feeling of fear and tried to be rational: who could have taken the letter and why?

She returned to her own room just as there was a knock on the door. Sterling looked in at her, his smile changing to an expression of concern.

'Mother.' He quickly crossed the carpet and drew her into his arms. 'You are such a stoic always that I forget you must be grieving for Father.'

Victoria's heart went out to her son. She had always loved him the best, his welfare had come before his brother Rickie's and Arthur's, though she prided herself on her ability to hide her feelings.

'I've just got a tiny headache.' She patted his cheek reassuringly. 'Nothing that won't pass.'

'Can't I get you anything?' he asked, moving away from her, thrusting his hands deep into his pockets. He was so handsome, she thought, so like his father.

'No, I'm all right, Sterling.' She forced herself to smile though her mind was still on the letter. Why had she not destroyed it all those years ago, what perverse vanity had caused her to keep it locked away?

'Well, you don't look all right to me,' Sterling said abruptly. 'Father's sickness was harder on you than on any of us.'

Victoria sank into a chair. Her son was right, she had sat with Arthur day and night, knowing instinctively that this last bout of fever would prove too much for him. He had aged rapidly over the past months, had taken to drinking a little more wine than was good for him and yet, ironically, she had not been with him when he had breathed his last.

She was aware of Sterling poking the fire with quick, restless movements, and her eyes softened. He was so tall, but thin yet. Soon he would become broad of shoulder and thigh, just like James. She almost wished he was a child again so that she could feel his arms warm around her neck and know that she was the centre of his universe. But those days had vanished for ever.

She wondered if her son had known yet the joy of a woman's love. Passion he had surely experienced for there was a pent-up sensuality in his nature that showed in the strong lines of his mouth. In that too he was following his father. And yet there had always been a strange antagonism between them; even as a

26

small boy, Sterling had pulled away whenever James had attempted to make friends with him.

'I'm thinking of moving in to an establishment of my own.' Sterling spoke casually and Victoria's heart plummeted like a stone. 'It's high time, Mother.'

'I expect you are right.' Her tone was even but she longed to cry out to him to stay with her for just a while longer, she did not want to be alone.

'You'll still have Rickie.' Sterling must have guessed something of her thoughts. 'He's finished with college for good now and I can't see him wishing to come into the business, he's always hated it, so he claims.'

Victoria had an overwhelming desire to be alone. How could Rickie ever take Sterling's place? The boy was a stranger to her, always had been from the moment she had looked into his tiny, red, newborn face and wondered if she had been presented with a changeling.

She had felt nothing but relief when a few years later Arthur had suggested that the boy attend boarding school back in Cornwall, so that her second son had been more out of her life than in it. She rose to her feet.

'Go on out with you, I must prepare myself for dinner,' she said to Sterling in mock reproof. 'You'll keep me talking here all night, go along off with you.'

But he was not deceived by her pretence of lightheartedness. He stood looking back into the room at her for a long silent moment, then he smiled and the admiration in his eyes was like a balm.

'See you at dinner then, Mother.'

Victoria stared at the closed door, feeling suddenly drained. Her son imagined that it was her grief at Arthur's death that was fretting her and of course, that was part of it. She pressed her fingers against her eyes and saw behind closed lids every word of the letter James had written to her.

'Fool!' she said to herself in sudden anger. She moved towards the bed and sank down onto the soft silk of the counterpane. She felt suddenly very alone and terribly vulnerable, she who had always imagined herself to be strong. But she would not cry, what good were tears? And yet her spreading fingers were suddenly moist.

27

Later when she entered the dining room, Sterling and Rickie were seated opposite each other, staring across the candlelit table as though they were adversaries. Almost absently, Victoria noted that Arthur's place had been set; she must speak to the servants about it. Her attention was caught by Rickie's voice raised in triumph.

'I just knew it, you're taking on the man at the cemetery, the one with the fish cart. Do you really want such riff-raff in the works?'

Victoria took her place, resisting the impulse to leap to Sterling's defence. He was a man now, well able to speak out for himself.

Sterling leaned back easily in his chair, shaking out the immaculately white napkin.

'David Llewelyn is an experienced copper man,' he said goodnaturedly. 'He was dismissed because of some lack of communication and I intend to reinstate him.'

Rickie gave a short laugh. 'And I suppose you didn't even notice the pretty wench with him.' His tone was heavy with sarcasm. Staring at him, Victoria wondered how she could feel such antipathy towards her own son; perhaps it was because she could see her own failings written so clearly into Rickie's nature.

Sterling shrugged without answering and Rickie, obviously piqued that his barb had missed its mark, leaned forward, elbows resting on the pristine damask cloth.

'You are so above it all, so high and mighty, aren't you Sterling?' His voice shook with anger. 'But remember, pride comes before a fall.' He rose quickly and strode towards the door.

'Rickie!' Victoria called, 'come back here at once, how dare you be so rude as to leave the table that way?' But the door had slammed shut and Rickie was gone.

'What on earth's wrong with him?' Sterling asked thoughtfully. 'He must be taking father's death more badly than I thought.'

Victoria fought back the wings of black panic that beat at her. Rickie must have a very good reason for behaving so abominably and she did not think that it had anything to do with Arthur's demise. A terrible suspicion began to take shape in her mind, she remembered the empty box with vivid clarity and she gripped her hands tightly together in her lap.

'Let's have dinner,' she said with forced calmness, and no one would have suspected that her world was falling to pieces around her.

Chapter Three

The green smoke lay low over the row of cottages, penetrating the crevices in the stonework, filling the cobbled roadway with a stench that caught the breath and burned the eyes of the children playing there.

Mali stood in the doorway staring into the dimness of the evening. Her heart was heavy within her, loneliness a burden she could scarcely bear. From the corner of Market Street came the sound of Dai End House playing the accordion. The plaintive melody rose and fell on the still air like a lament. Mali's throat tightened. Behind her the cottage was empty and silent and she was reluctant to return to the kitchen's warmth. She drew her shawl more closely around her shoulders, listening to the screams of delight from the children as they chased a rat into the canal.

Her father had left the house almost an hour ago. He had pulled a cap on his unruly hair and wound a scarf around his bull neck and Mali, watching him walk down the row, his big shoulders slumped, did not begrudge him the relief he would find in a jug of ale at the Mexico Fountain.

Abruptly the music died, even the children were silent, watching as a tall figure made his way easily along the cobbled street. It was as if he was being drawn towards Mali by an invisible thread as inexorably he moved forward.

She stepped back a pace into the light of the kitchen and the man followed her without so much as by your leave.

'Mr Richardson!' She heard the disbelief in her voice but even through her anger, she could not help but feel the magnetism of him. He closed the door and Mali swallowed hard.

'I don't know what you think you're doing here,' she said. 'If it's to put us out into the street, then don't bother, we know well enough that the cottage is yours.'

He took off his black hat and his hair gleamed brightly in the warm glow from the lamp. He smiled easily and seated himself in a chair, staring up at her, and his dark blue, almost violet eyes seemed to be undressing her.

'I haven't come to "put you out into the street" at all,' he said smoothly. 'On the contrary.' His eyes continued to gaze at her with disconcerting frankness and Mali became aware that her hair was hanging in untidy curls upon her shoulders and that she was wearing one of her oldest skirts that had been patched and mended many times.

'Then what do you want?' she asked hotly. She folded her arms around her waist, drawing the shawl closer. It was a gesture of self protection and she saw by his quick smile that he understood it.

'Don't worry.' He leaned forward in the chair, his eyes warm with laughter. 'I won't ravish you.'

Mali bit her lip in anger. 'Dad would give you a hammering if you so much as touched me,' she said quickly and then felt very foolish as his smile widened.

'I don't know what you find so funny!' she said. 'But say your piece, whatever it is, and go.' She moved towards the fire and absently pushed the large kettle onto the flames.

'Ah, good, you're about to make me some tea.' He spoke evenly and Mali took a deep breath, searching her mind for something scathing to say to him but then he was on his feet, standing beside her.

'I've come to offer your father his old job back.' He was so close that she could smell the clean soapy scent of him. She felt small and insignificant against his tallness and once the meaning of his words sunk in she was bereft of speech.

He leaned towards her and before she knew what he was about, he had taken her face between his hands.

'You are a very pretty girl,' he said lightly, and for a breathless moment she thought that he meant to kiss her.

Suddenly she came to her senses. 'Get away from me!' She pushed at him fiercely and smiling, he moved away from her. She felt shaken but as Sterling resumed his seat he seemed to be

31

completely in control of the situation. Mali tried to compose herself and spoke without looking at him.

'I don't know if Dad will want the job, he's a proud man.' She was angered by the way her voice trembled but there was nothing she could do about it. 'I'll tell him you called. Now leave me, please.'

'Very well.' Swiftly he rose to his feet. 'Tell your father that I will expect him to start first shift in the morning.' All at once he was again the great Mr Richardson, copper boss. It was as though he had never taken her face between his hands and looked into her eyes.

'I'll tell him.' She held her head aloft for he had come specially to the cottage in the row to ask Dad to return to work and it was a good feeling.

She stood in the doorway and the gas lights were lit now along the cobbled roadway, casting shadows into the canal, but her eyes were on the tall figure disappearing into the distance. The sharp sudden turmoil within her made her catch her breath. Her skin seemed to tingle where he had touched her and she felt again the strength of his long, sensitive fingers. But men like the copper boss were not to be trusted and she would not lose her head over him, she told herself firmly.

Quite abruptly huge drops of rain began to fall cold and sharp, beating up from the cobbles. Children were running into the cottages and doors began to close so that in a moment the row was empty. Mali sighed and moved back into the kitchen, about to close her own door when a light voice called to her.

'Mali don't shut me out, 'tis me, Katie.'

The Irish girl hurried inside, her hair swinging damply against her shoulders and her pale skin holding a radiance that had nothing to do with the coldness of the night air.

'I've just left me William.' She spoke breathlessly. 'I'm in love so I am.'

Mali smiled, 'Sit down have some tea, *ti'n disgwl yn oer*.'

Katie laughed and flung back her hair. 'What strange words you speak Mali, but soft and beautiful so they are.'

'I only meant you must be cold,' Mali explained, stirring the coals beneath the kettle. 'Bring me some cups from the dresser and tell me all about your William.'

Katie did as she was told and her high boots patterned the slabs of the floor with dampness.

'Oh such a buck you've never seen in your life,' she said, her eyes shining. 'Always wanting to kiss and cuddle so he is but it don't do to give in right away.' She sank into a chair, crossing one slender leg over the other and lifting her skirts to the fire's warmth. 'I shall hold out against his coaxing so I will,' she asserted. 'Tell him no until he makes me an offer of wedded bliss all proper like.' Her eyes were suddenly misty.

'But it's so hard to refuse the man when 'me insides tell me he's mine and I'm his and nothing between us can be wrong.'

Mali warmed the brown teapot. 'Be careful Katie,' she said soberly. 'If you end up full with child your dad will throw you out into the street.'

Katie seemed unperturbed. 'To be sure an' don't I know that? But I won't have no babe, I know better than to be caught.'

Mali laughed sceptically. 'Aye, so that's why your mam and dad has four of you is it? Told them how to do it proper like did you?'

Katie sighed softly in exasperation. 'Me ma and dad is supposed to have a babe whenever they lay together, that's our religion and for sure you've know us Murphys long enough to understand that much, Mali Llewelyn. Course it don't always happen 'cos I've heard them often enough rollin' around in that creaky old bed of theirs.' She leaned forward, her elbows on her knees, her slender hands cupping her chin.

'Don't go on for long though, Ma cries and Dad starts to snore and it's all over and done with like a dog and a bitch in the street.' Her voice held a trace of disgust and Mali shook her head at her.

'You're a cat, do you know that? Talking about your mother and father that way, you should be ashamed, mind.'

Katie shrugged her slim shoulders. 'Maybe I should but I pray to the Blessed Virgin that it won't ever get like that for me and Will.' Her smile became soft and she seemed to be dreaming of experiences that were beyond Mali's understanding.

'But then Will loves me.' She sat back in her chair as though ashamed of her own tender words. 'An' we do know how's not to have a babe, so there.' After a moment's silence she relented.

'Want me to tell you about it?'

'Aye, I suppose you will anyway.' In spite of herself, Mali was curious to know more. Katie seemed to be so much older than she and infinitely wiser in the ways of the world. But not for anything would she show that she was impressed.

'Now don't you be after tellin' anyone.' Katie made a wry face. 'I don't know what Father O'Flynn would say if he knew. Not that I care a shamrock leaf for him, he has a side-piece himself so he has.'

'Katie, for shame!' Mali could hardly believe that the young open-faced priest who visited Katie's house with unswerving loyalty could be so deceitful.

''Tis true!' Katie was indignant. 'And who can blame him? He's only human after all.'

Mali poured the tea. 'Well get on with it, soon you'll be saying you must get off home and I still won't know any more than I did when you came in through the door.'

Katie leaned forward with the air of a conspirator. ''Tis like this, the boy, when his moment of crisis comes, casts his seed to the ground just as it says in the Bible.' She giggled. 'It can't do no harm there for sure enough you never see babies growing in Clover Meadow do you?'

A coal shifted in the grate and Mali rose to mend the fire. Outside the rain had ceased and the streets glowed dull grey in the lamplight except when the shooting, upward sparks from the works turned the wet cobbles the colour of blood.

Katie sighed. 'Well, I'll tell you this, me and my Will shall be wed as soon as there's enough dibbs to pay the priest.' She hugged herself and her eyes were alight. 'I'll have a fine cottage and keep it like a new pin, so I will.'

Mali made a wry face at her friend. 'That's just like you telling me all your news and not asking about me.'

Katie looked at her sharply. 'Why, what have you been up to, miss sly boots?'

Mali savoured her moment of triumph, she knew that Katie did not really believe anything exciting could have happened to shatter the dullness of her life.

'Mr Richardson copper boss came to see me,' she said importantly. 'Walked into this very kitchen, large as life.'

Katie smiled. 'And twice as handsome and I know, for sure

haven't I seen him with me own eyes?' She paused and stared at Mali with a look of disbelief. 'But then what for would Mr Richardson come to see you? Tis tales you're tellin' me, makin' it all up so you are.'

Mali smiled. 'Well that's all you know.' She tweaked her skirt into place and smoothed out a crease, aware that Katie was waiting impatiently for her to continue.

'He came to ask Dad to go back to the works because they can't do without him. Best copperman in the row he is and everyone knows it.'

Katie's eyes were wide. 'Well go on, what else happened, did he try to smarm around you?'

'No he did not, he's too much of a gentleman for that sort of thing.' Not even to herself did she admit the disappointment of his sudden leavetaking. Something of her feelings must have shown in her face for Katie was suddenly serious.

'You watch him with both eyes, Mali,' she said softly. 'His sort has only one use for girls like us and that's to have our skirts above our head as soon as tis possible.'

'Trust you to spoil it all for me.' Mali spoke furiously. 'He's a real gent, I tell you, he's not at all horrible like you try to make out.'

'Sorry I opened my trap,' Katie said stiffly. 'Just trying to warn you so I am.' After a moment she relaxed.

'You are such a babe on times, Mali and I don't want to see you getting into trouble. Let's forget Mr Richardson, shall we?'

Mali sat in silence for a long moment and at last she looked up at Katie, her eyes appealing. 'It's a job I want,' she said. 'I just can't sit around here all day, now that Mam's gone.' She tried to smile unwilling to admit how near to tears she felt.

Katie stared at her doubtfully. 'And do you want me to ask at the laundry for ye? Tis like the cauldrons of hell in there sometimes with the steam ruinin' your hair and the smell of dirty washing making you sick to your stomach.' She shook her head. 'Your mam showed you how to be clever with figures and you write your letters real fine, the laundry's no place for you.'

Mali stared at her imploringly. 'Please Katie, I need to earn

35

money of my very own.' Her shoulders slumped. 'In any case, I can't remain at home, sitting in here by the fire like an old lady, I'll go out of my head.'

Katie nodded. 'All right, I'll be after askin' for you first thing in the morning but tis no promise I'm making, remember, just puttin' in a word I am.' She brushed back her long hair, drying now into bright curls.

'I'd best be goin' or Dad will be bawlin' for me all along Market Street and down Copperman's Row. When he starts they all hear him, sure they do.'

Mali did not relish the thought of being alone, she wanted to reach out to Katie and beg her to stay but she could not expect her friend to risk Tom Murphy's anger. At the door, Katie paused.

'Now, I'm goin' to give you good advice me girl, don't you go lying with any man in Clover Meadow for you're the sort who falls for a babe straight off.' A smile illuminated her face, softening the sternness of her words. Without waiting for a reply, she let herself out into the street.

Mali made a face at her reflection in the brass of the fender. It was unlikely that she would ever be asked to go to Clover Meadow, she thought ruefully. And yet there was a fluttering inside her as she felt again the touch of Sterling Richardson's hand upon her own.

Restlessly, she clicked open the latch on the door and stared out into the cobbled street. The rain had vanished as quickly as it had come and from an open doorway further along the row she heard the sound of the accordion played with more vigour than skill. Dai End House was in one of his festive moods, as he often was at closing time. Soon, he was likely to be joined by others coming home from the public bars and perhaps an impromptu dance would take place.

Mali took her old grey coat from the peg on the back of the door and on an impulse stepped out into the night. She left the door ajar so that light spilled warmly onto the cobbles. No one needed a lock, not in Copperman's Row.

'Evening, girl.' Dai End House was a chimneysweep but now he looked strangely clean, with his hair slicked down from a middle parting and his face fresh over the collar of his striped shirt. He sat in the doorway, his accordion moving

36

restlessly between his fingers as though picking out a tune of its own volition.

''Evening, Dai.' Mali nodded her head to him. 'Just going for a little walk, perhaps meet Dad coming home from the public.'

'A man needs his ale at times like this,' Dai said softly and the music he played was like the mournful sound of a woman crying.

The haunting strains of the accordion followed Mali as she turned the corner into Mexico Street. The large bulging windows of the Mexico Fountain stared down at her, the gaslight falling softly onto the roadway. On tiptoe, Mali strained to see within the smoke-filled room.

A long bar of polished wood dominated the taproom. It was covered with heavy glass bottles and tankards of ale. Six brass handles sprouted from behind the bar, and the landlord, a bluff man in a stiff collar, was still drawing up foaming beer from the barrels below in the cellar.

It was some minutes before Mali could make out the figure of her father and she recognised him in the crush of people by his abundance of thick, springy dark hair. With a shock, Mali realised he was not alone, his head was bent as he talked to a woman who was wearing a cheap fur around her neck and a dingy feathered hat upon suspiciously bright hair.

Mali's heart sank like a stone. Davie was falling into the hands of a no good, a woman of the streets who would rob him blind and doubtless give him the pox in return. Before she could stop to think, Mali pushed open the doors and strode into the heat and stink of the bar. Davie saw her and dropped the bottle he had been holding; it splintered in the sawdust to the cries of derision from the bystanders.

'I've come to fetch you, Dad,' she said, putting her hand on his arm. 'There's something important I've got to tell you.'

'Get off home, girl,' he said roughly, and Davie's green eyes looked at her as though he didn't know her. 'Go on, this is no place for the likes of you.'

'Nor you, Dad,' she said fiercely. 'Come home, please.' She tugged at his arm once more but he resisted her easily.

'There's bossy you are.' The woman turned towards Mali, hands on hips. She was quite young, Mali realised, though her

37

heavily floured face and the dark lines drawn over her eyebrows gave her an appearance of hardness. 'Go on, run off home like a good girl as your dad wants you to.'

'Leave me be, Mali,' Davie urged, his face red with embarrassment. 'Go on now, don't make a show of yourself and of me too.'

'Your dad is big enough and man enough to make up his own mind, so push off home.' She leaned closer to Mali. 'I won't tell you again.'

'Now, now Rosa.' Davie put a restraining hand on her arm. 'She's not meanin' any harm.'

Anger burned white hot inside Mali. 'I've got something very important to tell you Dad,' she said clearly. 'But if you don't want to hear it then stay with your whore, see if I care!'

She ran out into the darkness just as a shower of sparks rose high into the sky, turning the heavy clouds to a bright vermilion. The smell of sulphur permeated the streets and Mali coughed, her hand pressed against her mouth. She hurried past Dai who was still playing his accordion, and once inside the cottage she closed the door with a bang.

Her hands were shaking as she pushed the heavy kettle back onto the hob, away from the last of the fire's warmth. She poked down into the coals, riddling the ashes, knowing they would soon fade and turn into grey dust. She sank into a chair, staring at the dying embers, her mind numb. She still could not believe that her father would take up with a street girl so soon after Mam's death, it seemed like a nightmare. Surely he could not care for this Rosa? And yet he had looked down into her face as if she was beautiful and good just as Mam had been.

Mali still held the poker between her fingers when the door opened and her father entered the kitchen with Rosa at his side. Davie appeared hangdog, refusing to look to where Mali now stood but the woman with him stared around her insolently.

'He says I can stay here tonight.' Her red lips curved in triumph. She edged Davie into a chair and then straightened the fur collar around her thin neck.

Fury such as she had never known before rose within Mali. How could Dad bring home this whore so soon after Mam's death? She moved forward menacingly.

'You'll stay under this roof over my dead body, slut!' She heard the words, clipped and hard, force themselves from between her clenched teeth. This was a part of her self she did not recognise and furthermore did not like.

'Davie, your girl wants to chuck me out into the streets.' Rosa pouted, seeming a little uncertain of herself now. 'And after all the comfortin' I've done an' all.'

Mali stared at her. 'And after all the drinks you've had on him. Your sort doesn't do anything for nothing.'

Rosa turned on her. 'And what do you know about my sort?' she shouted. 'You with your nice warm kitchen and enough food to go in your belly every day, you make me sick! Look at you, never done a hand's turn in your life and you a woman grown, there's a pity you aren't married with a string of kids around your neck, you might know a bit then.'

'And you'd have the coast clear to move in with my Dad, is it? Well I'm telling you once, get out of this house while it's still decent and respectable before I put you out.' She waved the poker in the air and Rosa fell back a step or two.

'I'm going,' she said. 'But I'll be back, Miss hoity toity, and then we'll see who's got the upper hand.'

She flounced through the door, pausing to look back at Davie who was hard put to keep his eyes open. His great hand was slumped on his chest and his cheeks were red, a heat caused by the ale, Mali reasoned, for the fire had gone down into grey ash now and the cold draught from the doorway chilled the room.

'I'll be seeing you, Davie boyo,' Rosa said and with an angry tweak at the brim of her dingy hat, she clattered away down the cobbled street.

Mali subsided into a chair. She had won but how permanent the victory would be she could not say. Rosa seemed an uppity sort of person and she would not let go easily, not once she had her hooks into a fine man like Dad.

Davie was suddenly awake, his head raised as he stared unseeingly into the blank fireplace. His big hands clenched together and his lips made a straight line of self disgust. Mali went to him, kneeling beside him, putting her arms around his neck, ignoring the scent of cheap perfume that clung to his clothing.

'Good news, Dad,' she said softly. 'Mr Richardson called when you were out, you're to have your old job back, can't do without you, it seems, best ladler in Sweyn's Eye, you are.'

Davie was silent for a long time and at last, Mali looked up into his face. As she stared at her father, her entire being seemed to dissolve for there were tears glinting on his rugged cheeks.

'It's going to be all right, Dad.' She buried her head against the warm hollow of his neck. 'Don't cry, no need for crying mind, everything is going to be just fine and dandy, you'll see.'

Chapter Four

The early morning light cast a pale glow over the town as Sterling rode his horse down the hill and away from the gates of Plas Rhianfa. Ahead of him lay the works, crouched along the dull, metallic line of the river, the chimneys already sending flames high into the sky. Sterling shivered and it was with a feeling of relief that he rode in through the gates and slid from the saddle, handing over the reins to the young stable boy before striding across the frosty cobbled yard.

It was warm in the office after the biting cold of the street outside and Sterling made his way towards the tall stove, drawing off his gloves, eager to warm his hands. The works manager sat in his customary seat near the old stained desk, tweaking the ends of his waxed moustache, looking as though he was a permanent fixture in the works, part of the furnishings.

'Good morning, Ben, damned cold out,' Sterling remarked conversationally but the old man did not reply and when Sterling glanced sharply in his direction, Ben was staring down at the pen in his hands.

'What's wrong?' Sterling asked at once and Ben raised his head.

'Reversing engine's broken down again,' he said gloomily. 'Can't roll any copperplate until it's fixed.

Sterling concealed his impatience. 'Had anyone to look at it?' he asked and Ben shook his head.

'Twill cost a pretty penny, can the firm stand the expense?'

Sterling shrugged off his topcoat.

'It's a case of needs must when the devil drives,' he said

grimly. Damn it, did everything have to go wrong at once?

'What else?' he asked and Ben brushed back his thinning grey hair moodily.

'Two of the furnaces are choked up, need a good clean out, they do, haven't been seen to these many months. Another thing, this last batch of ore is nothing but gangue.' He ran a finger inside his stiff collar as though it was suddenly too tight for him. 'Travers is to blame, no eye for copper, no feel for it.'

Sterling seated himself in the straight-backed leather chair and tapped the desk with his fingers. 'What you are saying is that Glanmor Travers is no good at his job, Ben.'

The old man pursed his lips as though unwilling to allow the words to spill forth, his face reddened and his pale eyes behind his glasses stared intently into the flames of the stove.

'He's no good at his job,' he said at last. 'Not half the man his old dad was. Too keen on swilling down ale at the dockside taverns if you ask me. Comes in here late, he does, parading around the office as though he owned the place and all because he's in thick with young Master Rickie.'

Sterling rubbed his jaw thoughtfully. Old Ben did like to grumble and he wondered how much of his complaint was justified. If it was true that Glanmor Travers was failing in his job then something would have to be done about it.

'See, old Joss Travers was a genius when it came to choosing ore,' Ben continued. 'Not a bit of rubbish did he buy in all the years he worked for Mr Richardson, God rest his soul.' He paused. 'But his son is no chip off the old block, he thinks that college can teach a man to sort out good copper from dross but that's his first mistake.' Ben hid his face in a large spotless handkerchief before taking off his glasses and polishing them with quick, nervous movements.

'Where are the figures for last month, Ben?' Sterling waited patiently while the old man sorted out the dusty red ledger from a pile of books on the shelf.

'It's bad enough without the likes of Travers making it worse,' Ben said. 'See, once we'd have got ninety pounds a ton for the copper, now we're lucky to get twenty.'

In silence, Sterling looked over the pages. It seemed that over the last six months, sales of copper vessels to the brewing industry had slumped.

'How long is it since we signed Glanmor Travers on?' he asked, already knowing the answer. Ben frowned in concentration.

'Just after your father took real sick, it was,' he said. 'Let me see now, summer wasn't it? Yes, six months I'd say.'

'I see, then we're going to have to let him go, make up his wages Ben, give him a month in lieu of notice.'

'He won't like it,' Ben said and there was a gleeful light in his eyes. 'He won't like it one little bit. *Duw*, I can't wait to see his face.' He was silent for a moment.

'You do know that your father gave the man's brother a loan, don't you?' he asked. 'Not that I agreed with it. Too soft you are, Mr Richardson, I told him, but he wouldn't be swayed.'

'No, I didn't know about it, Ben, tell me.' Sterling sat back in the chair, tipping it onto the sturdy back legs, thawing out a little as the heat from the stove permeated the room.

'Mr Joss Travers approached Mr Richardson,' Ben said. 'It was all done legal and proper, mind. It appears that the other boy, Alwyn Travers, was in difficulties, his mine was losing money though the Lord knows why, the price of coal today. In any event, your father made Alwyn Travers a substantial loan, holding the deeds of the property as surety.'

'I see.' Sterling shrugged. 'Well, I have nothing against this man and so long as he continues to meet his obligations, repaying the loan regularly, I shall honour the agreement.'

Sterling suppressed a smile, he could see by Ben's face that he thought the young Mr Richardson as soft as his father. Ben rubbed at his glasses once more before settling them upon his nose.

'Well you're the boss right enough, Mr Richardson,' he said reluctantly. 'But them two boys are not a credit to old Joss Travers, wasters, the both of them, drinking and brawling in the publics and afraid of a bit of work as well.'

Sterling was too deep in his own thoughts to answer the old man. It surprised him that his father had digressed from the usual run of business procedures and made a private loan even to please an old friend and a loyal employee. One thing was sure, now that Joss Travers was dead and his wild sons were left without a steadying hand to guide them, Sterling intended to keep an eye on things. The copper company was not in the business of subsiding loafers.

'Shall I get a man in to look at the reversing engine, Mr Richardson?' Ben's voice penetrated Sterling's thoughts. He glanced up and nodded.

'Yes, right away Ben, we can't afford to lose any time, not with Chile and Cuba to say nothing of Australia exporting large quantities of blister bar.'

Ben looked glum. 'Sink us they will,' he said bitterly. 'These foreigners, taking good Welshmen and getting the secret of the smelting process out of them one way or another. *Duw* it's not right, not right at all.'

Sterling looked carefully through the pages of the ledger resting on the table before him; it was clear that drastic action was needed if the business was to survive.

'We have problems, Ben,' he said. 'You've worked in the copper all your life, what do you think is going wrong?'

Ben whistled through his teeth. 'Mainly it's them old calciners,' he said at last, 'most of them are cracked, should have been replaced these twenty years since.'

Sterling nodded. 'I agree. I've been looking at some Gerstenhofer furnaces which have the advantage of utilising the copper smoke, converting it into sulphuric acid.'

Ben pinched at the end of his moustache. 'No good, you'd need to have alkali and phosphate plants right alongside the works.'

'That settles it then, I must forget about trying to make the copper more viable and turn to some other source of income.' He smiled and if Ben had gained the impression that this was what Sterling had been leading up to all along, he was not wrong.

'Zinc,' Sterling said firmly. 'I've been looking into the manufacturing of zinc very carefully and it seems the only solution.'

'Very different it is to copper,' Ben said with maddening slowness. 'Most of the works round here have tried the English method of production and damned expensive it is too.' He coughed and rubbed at his glasses. 'The ores are reduced in vertical retorts inside a circular furnace, seen it done many

44

times and it's a process that only yields about one ton of zinc a week.'

Sterling smiled. 'But there are other forms of processing available now, the Belgian method of extraction for example. It is done by using fireclay about three feet long and six to eight inches wide, closed at one end and arranged in tiers within a cast iron frame.'

Ben looked impressed. 'You've certainly made it your business to find out all about it,' he said. 'But do you know that the consumption of fuel in these zinc furnaces is most extravagant?'

Sterling shook his head. 'No more coal is used than in the smelting of copper.'

Ben shrugged as though bowing to Sterling's superior knowledge. 'I may be a little old-fashioned,' he said, 'but these newfangled ways are not proven, not like the copper process which has been a secret to the family for over a hundred years.'

Sterling sighed. Ben did not have to speak of his resistance to change, he lived in the past, remembering the glory that had once been the Richardson Copper company. There was a time when the works prospered and flourished so quickly that the word copper was almost synonymous with gold. Well he intended the company should one day in the not too distant future be rich once more. He had examined other companies, seen that change however small had brought increased profits. If he did not move ahead then the firm would go bust, nothing was more certain.

Ben coughed nervously. 'Do you think you should consult with Mr Cardigan or Mr Sutton before you commit yourself?' he asked a trifle diffidently. Sterling shook his head.

'I don't really think they are interested Ben,' he replied, 'and I can't say I blame them. My father made sure that the company was always firmly under his control and all his partners really did was to put up money, funds that should have been used then for expansion but which have merely subsidised our losses thus far.'

He closed the ledger with a bang. 'Anyway, I shall have the calciner furnaces replaced.' He gave a wintry smile. 'We shan't lose sight of the copper altogether, don't worry.'

Ben took out his handkerchief and mopped his brow. 'I'm

glad about that,' he said, 'for copper's in my blood Mr Richardson and I can't imagine the works given over entirely to spelter or the coldness of steel, losing us the good name we've got for copper.'

Sterling looked at the older man curiously. 'Did my father never think of making changes, Ben?' he asked, and the older man smiled ruefully.

'Joss Travers tried to persuade him once. Told him that some sort of manure could be made from the smoke, almost got his head blasted off for his troubles.' Ben gave one of his rare smiles.

'*Duw* your father was angry, you should have seen his face. "Manure", he said, "what's wrong with good old horse droppings?"'

Sterling could well imagine that his father's remarks had been far more pithy than that and were modified now by Ben's ingrained sense of the proprieties.

There was silence for a moment in the small office, both men lost in their own thoughts. The stove, warming the room, made soft noises like the breathing of an animal and outside, a cold breeze ruffled the feathers of the birds clinging to the bare branches of the trees.

Sterling sighed. 'Well we should get an engineer to look at the reversing machine and as soon as possible,' he said. 'See to it, will you, Ben?'

As the older man left the office, a cold rush of air lifted the papers on the desk. Sterling shivered and moved across to the stove, lifting the top to place the canteen of coffee over the blaze. He stood beside the window staring out at the corrugated waters of the river swept into swift movement by the wind. A sailing ship moved gracefully downstream, masts pointing to the sky. It was a sight that was growing rarer with each passing day, soon steam would take over entirely and the picturesque barques would vanish for ever.

Sterling's eyes roved to the huddle of buildings in the yard. The gatehouse stood near the cobbled street and the small window that was manned by a watchman most of the time was empty and staring like a blank cyclops eye at whoever came into the premises.

To the rear of the office block and just visible from where

Sterling stood was the mass of the works. The sloping roofs of the sheds slanted against the dark sky and the forest of chimneys sent out the stench that was like eggs gone rotten.

This, Sterling thought, was his inheritance, and he would build it up into the greatness it had once known. He thrust his hands deep into his pockets, determination eating at his gut like a fire. The Richardson Copper Company would not die, not if he could help it.

The inside of the sheds was something Mali could never have imagined. It was a shimmering, steaming, sulphurous place where the air was hot and acrid, almost unbreathable. As soon as she entered the doors, she felt perspiration break out on her brow. She pushed back the shawl that suddenly felt unbearably heavy on her shoulders and stood for a moment looking around her.

She seemed to be in some nightmare world where men did not appear as humans at all but as strange, ill-shapen devils, arms and legs swathed in canvas and caked with mud their only protection against the fierce heat.

Tentatively, she moved forward, her gaze drawn to the nearest open, roaring mouth of the calcinating furnace. A copperman was pushing a long green sapling into the boiling metal which gushed and spewed forth smoke.

It was a dragon, Mali decided, a beast devouring everything in sight. The red-gold liquid grew agitated as the tree was swallowed up, appearing like an exotic stew composed of gold and fire and gushing gases.

'Mali, what are you doing here, *cariad*?' Davie's voice at her side startled Mali and she stared at him anxiously.

'I've brought your grub pack, Dad.' She found it difficult to breathe, it was as though her throat was on fire. She blinked rapidly and stared up at Davie, trying to see through the haze of heat. His chest was damp with sweat and the muscles of his upper arms bulged hugely, the sinews standing proud. Mali wanted to take him home with her to the safety of the house in Copperman's Row.

'I didn't know it was going to be like this, Dad.' She watched as he dipped his arms in a bowl and slapped mud over the faded canvas around his wrists and hands.

'It's not as bad as it looks, mind.' He smiled at her. 'Lucky you are to see it, the secret of the smelting is passed on only from father to son but there's no reason girls can't know it too, I suppose.' He continued to plaster his arms with clay as Mali watched fascinated. 'See the copper is roasted for more than a day, takes six furnaces to bring out the real rich heart of the copper. Long job it is but worth it when the metal is rolled out as sweet as silk.'

Mali brushed her hair from her forehead and coughed a little and Davie stared down at her in concern, his task of covering his hands completed.

'Come on, now Mali, off home with you, the other men in my tew gang will be after my guts if I don't pull my weight.'

Mali stared at him questioningly. 'Tew gang, Dad, what's that?' Davie waved her away impatiently. 'Something like a chain gang it is, now go on home, will you?'

Outside, the air was so cold after the heat of the sheds that Mali shivered, drawing her shawl more closely round her shoulders. As she hurried over the cobbles of the yard, she saw the door of one of the buildings open and a tall figure stepped out in front of her.

'Mr Richardson.' Mali felt guilty as though she'd been doing something wrong. She squared her shoulders, discomfited by the cool lift of his brows and the scrutiny of the eyes that were so dark a blue that they appeared almost violet. He took in her appearance in a swift glance that encompassed her from head to toe.

'Trespassing?' he said lightly. 'Perhaps I should send for the constable.'

He folded his arms, barring her way and she felt foolish as though he was making fun of her.

'I'll walk with you to the gate,' he said, taking her arm firmly. 'I don't think my manager would be very pleased to find that someone had slipped past him, Ben prides himself on his vigilance where the works are concerned.'

She listened to his strong, masculine voice as he talked to her. She knew he was being polite, making conversation with the daughter of one of his coppermen, but he spoke pleasantly and she was happy to listen.

There was a pause and she looked up at him, suddenly aware that he had asked her a question. Flustered, she waited for him to repeat it. He smiled slowly and his eyes seemed to look deep inside her.

'I was wondering if you had another name, apart from Miss Llewelyn,' he prompted pleasantly. She felt her colour rise.

'Mali,' she said quickly, 'but I know it's a strange name, Welsh you see.'

'Mali,' he said and the sound of it was magic on his tongue. They were amid the huddle of the buildings now, hidden from sight. Here there seemed to be quietness and Mali felt conscious that she was alone with Mr Richardson. She glanced up at him, her heart beating uncomfortably fast and he returned her gaze with disconcerting openness.

'You are very pretty, Mali,' he said and he seemed to move a little closer to her. Suddenly Katie's warnings loomed large and threatening in her mind and she backed away from him, stumbling a little in her haste.

He caught her in a steadying grip but she pulled away from him quickly as though his touch burned.

'Leave me be, you think I'm some cheap little flossy don't you? I know your sort. I'm a respectable girl and I don't care if you are the copper boss, I wouldn't touch you with a barge pole.'

He gave a short laugh. 'I don't think you are a – flossy, was it? Indeed, I don't think of you at all. There's the gate.' His tone was dry.

Humiliated, Mali retaliated the only way she knew how – her booted foot shot out and caught him a sharp blow on the shin. Then she was running, through the gate and along the street, wanting only the sanctuary of her own hearth.

Once indoors, she stoked up the fire and pushed the big kettle onto the flames. Her hands were trembling and she knew deep within her that she was beginning to take too much interest in Mr Richardson. He was a boss, a rich, handsome man and doubtless he would want nothing to do with a girl of her sort except for a quick tumble as Katie had said. And yet the pleasant way he'd made conversation with her and the

49

coolness of his eyes as they'd looked into hers were all imprinted on her mind.

A strange feeling uncoiled within her and she wondered desperately what was wrong with her judgment. Here she was, a silly little fool, fancying a man she scarcely knew. The sooner she put him out of her mind the better.

She sat in the rocking chair wishing Mam was here to advise her but Mam was lying beneath the trees in Dan-y-Graig Cemetery. And those last days had been so hard to bear, with Mam coughing her life away, afflicted by the Dolur Ysgyfaint that stole the breath and burnt out the lungs.

There was a sudden rapping on the door and Katie's voice calling from outside. 'Let me in afore I catch a chill.'

Mali realised that in her haste she had pushed the bolt in place as though she could shut out her very thoughts.

'What's wrong Katie?' she asked as she flung open the door, 'why aren't you at work?'

Katie shrugged. 'Been sent home,' she said with maddening calm. 'Big Mary said I could have some time off.' She looked casually at her hands, as though examining her nails and Mali stared down at her friend with a smile stretching the corners of her lips upwards.

'Come on Katie, there's a good girl, you've got news for me haven't you?'

Katie pouted. 'You're no fun so you're not, guessing what's in me mind like that. Oh, all right then, I might as well tell you, there's a job for you in the laundry and you start today, right now if you've a mind to.'

Mali sat down abruptly in her chair, excitement and apprehension warring within her; she was going to work for the first time in her life and suddenly, she was afraid.

Chapter Five

Bea Cardigan sat in the conservatory, her sewing lying idle on her lap. A pale winter sun shone in through the windows, shedding a slant of light over the glossy aspidistra plants that rose stoutly from thick china pots. A feeling of discontentment pulled down the corners of her full mouth and her dark eyes held a dreamy faraway expression, for her thirtieth birthday was fast approaching and there was no sign of marriage anywhere on her horizon.

Her father seemed content to keep her at his side indefinitely and who could blame him? In his daughter, James Cardigan had a convenient hostess and companion, the roles she had undertaken on her mother's death ten years ago now almost to the day. She was beginning to think that her father did not wish her to marry, ever.

It was true that he had occasionally brought home some presentable young man for Bea's inspection but she had always been indifferent, the would-be suitor had invariably been immature and somewhat gauche and she had begun to doubt the true sincerity of her father's intentions. She smiled softly, wrapping her arms around her body as though hugging the secret, kept to herself these many years, that of her love for Sterling Richardson.

He had been part of her life ever since she could remember and the mere sight of his strong clean features and his thatch of golden hair was enough to set her heart fluttering. She believed that he cared for her too for he was always kind and considerate and yet thus far, he had not seen fit to approach her father and ask his permission to court her.

At that moment, James Cardigan entered the room. He

moved towards her smiling, a big handsome man with a strong nose and a high intelligent forehead. He leaned forward and kissed the top of her head.

'Day dreaming again, Bea?' he asked goodhumouredly, holding out his hand to take hers. She looked up at him, suddenly concerned.

'You look tired, Daddy,' she said softly. 'Is anything wrong?'

He sat down beside her and pinched her cheek playfully. 'Of course nothing's wrong.' He rested his arm lightly around her shoulders. 'I'm just wondering what will happen to the company now that old Arthur Richardson is gone. I haven't played a very big part in the running of things these last years but then I felt I wasn't needed, perhaps now I am.'

'Everything will be all right,' Bea said lightly. 'I'm sure Sterling is very capable, he did help his father a great deal, you know.'

James looked at her thoughtfully and Bea felt the colour rise to her cheeks. Had she betrayed her true feelings for Sterling? But her father was engrossed in his own thoughts and did not notice her discomfort.

'I expect the boy's capable enough,' he said. 'And yet he's still so young and there are wolves in the business world only too ready to dupe someone inexperienced.' He sighed. 'Well, I've invited Sterling to take tea with us, so I suppose I'll soon learn all about his plans for the company.'

Bea rose to her feet, suddenly flustered. The thought of seeing Sterling was like wine to her senses. She looked down at her dull tweed skirt and bit her lip in vexation. She felt a momentary impatience with her father for not warning her of Sterling's visit sooner but as she looked at him, slumped on the hard-backed oak settle, her ill humour dissolved in a rush of love.

'Everything will be all right, Daddy, you'll see.' She wound her arms around his neck and kissed his cheek, laughing as the coarse hair of his sideburns tickled her nose.

'I'm going to my room to change, I refuse to be seen looking like a frump,' she said in mock reproof. 'You really should let me know when anyone is coming to call, you know I want to be a credit to you always.'

She was aware of her father's quick look. 'You don't have to make any special effort for Sterling,' he said gruffly. 'You played together as children, if you remember.'

'Well there's no harm in me wanting to look pretty, is there?' Bea asked lightly and at last, James shook his head. 'I think you look perfectly well as you are but go and change if you must.'

Bea blew him a kiss and hurried through the hall and up the wide staircase towards her room. Once inside, she closed the door and went directly to the window and looked down into the gardens. The grounds were swathed now in misty rain and far below, she could hear the wash of the sea against the shore.

She rested her face against the cold of the glass pane, closing her eyes, picturing Sterling's sensitive, handsome face. She wondered, as she did frequently these days, how it would feel to have his lips capturing her own. She moved impatiently from the window and looked at the bare third finger of her left hand. Marriage to Sterling had been a dream that had sustained her for some time now. He was the only man she would ever want but he had never said anything to make her believe her dream would one day become a reality.

Bea opened the heavy door of the wardrobe and drew out a soft velvet skirt and a jacket of baby blue angora. The blouse she was wearing was of thick, creamy lace and would do very well, she thought.

She was a woman who had come to full maturity. Her mouth and the droop of her heavy-lidded eyes revealed a sensuality of which she was not entirely unaware. Her hair was glossy and dark, drawn away from a high intelligent forehead. About her was an air of waiting, like a bud before it comes to its full-blown glory.

Bea had just finished dressing when she heard the chiming of the doorbell. Quickly, she slipped on her soft leather shoes with their small, baby Louis heels and hurried downstairs.

Sterling's face shone with cold and his bright hair was diamonded with droplets of rain. He brought into the hallway with him the feeling of the outdoors, of air fresh and balmy. He smiled down at her and absurdly, Bea felt suddenly shy.

'You look very lovely today.' He spoke lightly but his eyes rested on her with such approval that Bea felt breathless with happiness. He was so close that she could have reached out and touched him and yet it was as though a great divide separated them.

'Thank you, Sterling.' The words sounded stilted even to her own ears and she wondered where the easy relationship they had enjoyed in their childhood had vanished.

'Come into the drawing room,' she added quickly, 'Daddy won't be long – I left him in the conservatory.'

Together, they moved into the warmth of the spacious room where a huge fire roared and crackled in the ornate hearth. A carpet of rich Indian weave covered the floor and a grand piano occupied pride of place near the large window. Against one wall stood a high-backed sideboard upon which rested a set of lead crystal decanters and matching glasses.

'Would you like some brandy?' Bea asked, her face turned away from him. 'Please, Sterling, sit down, don't stand on ceremony with me.'

As she approached him with the glass, he patted the sofa beside him and she felt it would be churlish to refuse.

'I'm very fond of you, Bea,' he said softly. 'But I'm sure you know that already.'

'Do I?' She wanted to cry to him that she was growing older, that friendship was no longer enough. She longed for him to speak to her father to ask for her in marriage but treacherous thoughts such as these could not be spoken.

He rose to his feet, thrusting his hands into his pockets, staring down at her, seeing not Bea's questioning eyes but some far-distant notions of his own.

'The time has come for me to settle down,' he said at last. 'I need a place of my own for Plas Rhianfa will be my mother's home while she is alive.' He smiled, 'And I do believe I've found just the house for me.'

Bea felt her heart begin to thump, she scarcely dared hope that Sterling was hinting at marriage and, even as her hands trembled, she tried desperately to appear composed.

Sterling stared down at her for a long moment in silence, as though lost in his own thoughts. Was he, she wondered, as nervous as she?

'Sterling, it's all right,' she said. 'I think I know what you're trying to say.' Her voice was light and triumph bubbled inside

54

her so that she thought she would explode into a hundred sparkling fragments, but her eyes were demurely downcast.

He sighed in relief. 'I knew I could count on you to help in any way you could,' he said. 'Mother is determined to put up fussy drapes and decorate the place like a woman's bedroom and that's something I don't intend to put up with.' He smiled and Bea blinked rapidly, trying to assimilate the meaning of his words.

'You have such flair,' he continued. 'I've always admired the way you've kept this house so light and airy.' He came towards her and took her hand.

'You know something, Bea? You're like the sister I've never had.'

The pain was almost a physical one. She sank back against the hard sofa, trying to fight the waves of hysterical laughter that washed over her. Sterling thought of her as a sister, he wanted her help in furnishing his house but he most certainly did not consider her for one moment as being mistress of it.

The door opened and James Cardigan entered the room. He came forward, hand outstretched, a hearty note in his voice that struck Bea as being false.

'Sterling my boy, happy to see you, got a great deal to talk over haven't we?'

Sterling's smile was nothing more than polite. 'Yes, indeed.' Briefly, he shook hands.

'Well, shall we leave it until we've had tea?' James's smile included Bea. 'What are we having dear, some of those delicious scones you have made your speciality?' His pride in his daughter was evident but Bea felt herself flush with embarrassment; trust father to extoll her virtues at exactly the wrong moment.

'I haven't done any cooking today,' she replied a little impatiently. 'You'll just have to manage with whatever Mrs Bevan has prepared.'

James seated himself in the chair nearest the fire and though he leaned back against the cushions he gave the impression of being anything but comfortable.

Bea did not listen to the conversation between the two men for they spoke of nothing of importance. The words seemed forced and stilted and Bea retired into herself, sinking back against the hardness of the corded velvet sofa, the hurt within her almost too much to bear. At her side Sterling sat stiffly upright, his back and shoulders revealing his tension. Looking at the hair so crisp and bright resting against the darkness of his jacket collar, she longed to reach out and touch it.

She bit her lips, trying to comfort herself with rational excuses about his behaviour. He did not mean to offend her by telling her his interest was purely sisterly. If that was how he did truly see her then it was about time she changed his mind for him.

Hope began to grow within her, after all he had invited her into his home and there, she would have ample opportunity to try to impress him. There was no other woman in his life, of that she was sure, for Sweyn's Eye would have been buzzing with gossip by now.

The afternoon seemed to draw on so slowly that Bea felt like screaming. Darkness came down early and the gas lights hissed and popped in the many silences that fell between the two men. At last, Bea rose to her feet.

'If you will both excuse me.' She forced herself to speak lightly. 'I will leave you to your business talk.'

Sterling rose to his feet and opened the door for her, smiling down in a way that made her heart turn over.

'Don't forget your offer to help me with my house,' he said, his eyes warm. 'And if you need me for anything, I have taken a suite of rooms in the Mackworth Arms, just as a temporary measure.'

She smiled up at him as though he'd offered her the most wonderful gift.

'I shall need to see you,' she said definitely. 'I must consult you about colour schemes and that sort of thing.'

He inclined his head as though bowing to her superior knowledge of such matters and then the door was closed and Bea was in the hallway alone.

She stood for a moment, staring down at the polished wood of the floor without really seeing it. She felt weary, drained of all her spirit and tears were ready to slip down her cheeks.

In her room, she drew her chair closer to the fire, she was shivering and the flames did nothing to warm her. She closed her eyes, wrapping her arms around her body, trying to imagine herself in Sterling's arms. She longed to be held close in the embrace of a lover but perhaps even more than she needed passion, she wanted tenderness and love.

Dean Sutton was a big man and what some might call ruggedly handsome. His features were large but regular and when he smiled, his teeth were white and even. He stood in the doorway of his home and stared around him; the rain had ceased and a pale sun illuminated the few acres of land that were his. It was a far different cry from his home in South Georgia where the ground rolling away as far as the eye could see belonged to the Suttons.

He had left America under a cloud, the black sheep of the family. He gambled and drank far too much for his father's liking but then Grenville Sutton had been a religious man, carrying his faith to extremes and his eldest son had always been an anathema to him.

At last, inevitably, Dean had gone too far, he had seduced Mary Anne Bloomfield, his brother's bride to be.

Dirk was younger than Dean by almost ten years, the spoilt baby of the family. Such an act of betrayal by one brother to the other was more than Grenville Sutton would tolerate. Dean was banished, ejected bag and baggage from the Sutton home with only the small inheritance left him by his mother to pay his way.

It had been his own decision to travel to Britain and for a time, he had roamed the small country from coast to coast. At last he had settled in Sweyn's Eye, attracted as much by the rugged coast and sloping hills as by the business of the copper-smelting industry.

It had not taken Dean very long to build a house of his own, a splendid place with marble pillars and many windows. It had taken a little longer to become accepted by the local people and Dean knew full well that it was the large amount of capital he had offered Arthur Richardson, that had opened the doors for him to be drawn into the social life of the town.

He was not as interested in the copper as perhaps he might have been and just lately, the copper shares had yielded very little profit. He had begun to wonder if this was an expedient time to pull out of the company. It was just as well that after living in the town for almost ten years, he had managed to consolidate his small fortune by investing in a diversity of business ventures.

The groom brought round his horse from the stable and Dean mounted the animal with the ease born of long practice. Not for him these newfangled automobiles, nothing could ever replace the exhilaration of being seated high in the saddle with the fresh sea breeze blowing across the hills.

His journey was a short one. He was making for the home of James Cardigan; it might be just as well to ask his partner what he felt about the future of the copper industry. Dean smiled to himself, knowing it was merely an excuse, what he really wanted was to see Bea's beautiful eyes looking up at him with melting sweetness.

He recognised that it was about time he found himself a bride. He was thirty-five years of age and needed to put down roots. Four fine sons, that's what he wanted from life, and Bea looked strong and healthy enough to give him as many children as he desired.

It was about time he broached the subject of the marriage to James. Dean felt certain that the older man would welcome the suggestion with open arms for Bea was past the first flush of youth. But still beautiful enough to stir the senses of any man, he thought wistfully.

The maid who answered the door to Dean looked up with glowing eyes, her wide smile revealing her pleasure at seeing him. As Dean handed her his hat and riding crop, he winked at her. Bertha did not need telling in which direction his affections lay. She was sensitive to anything that affected her beloved mistress and had a closeness with her that was only usually found between sisters.

'Fine day it's turned out to be, Mr Sutton,' Bertha said warmly. 'Brought the sunshine, you have.'

Dean rubbed his hands together. 'A little too cold for my liking, Bertha, but fine enough for all that. Is Miss Bea at home?'

Bertha nodded. 'Yes, sir, she's in her room, I'll call her at once.' She hesitated. 'Mr Cardigan is in the drawing room, he has company, perhaps you'd like to wait in the conservatory?'

Dean stared around him, stifled by the plethora of plants. Everything here was so small and so confining, perhaps one day he would return to his homeland and maybe take with him a wife and family.

He turned as he heard a sound in the doorway. 'Bea, as lovely as ever.' He took the hand she held out to him and gently kissed her upturned palm. She smiled warmly at him, her wide, generous mouth curving upwards so that her face was transformed.

'This is a pleasant surprise, Dean.' She seated herself in a chair and spread the soft blueness of her skirt around her small feet with a gracious movement of her small hands. He would be the envy of all American society if he took home with him such a prize.

'You seem so serious, what is it, Dean?' Bea held her head on one side in a charming gesture and Dean resisted the impulse to sweep her into his arms. He had found from experience that these people liked to move slowly and with decorum.

'I am serious – about you,' he said and as her eyes widened, he realised with a sinking feeling that she had never thought of him in the role of suitor.

'I've startled you,' he said, watching in fascination as the rich blush suffused Bea's face and throat. He longed to put his mouth where the tiny pulse beat in the hollow of her neck, he just knew that behind that controlled exterior was a passionate woman.

She looked down at her hands, avoiding his eyes. 'I suppose I am a little surprised,' she said softly and Dean could have smiled at such understatement if he had not been feeling so disappointed.

The door to the drawing room opened and James Cardigan appeared in the hallway, his arm around the shoulder of Sterling Richardson.

'Come again, any time, my boy.' James spoke warmly and then both men were looking in through the open doorway of the conservatory.

'Dean, hello there, I didn't expect you see you today.' James came forward, hand outstretched. 'It's always a pleasure to have a visit from you.'

Dean was suddenly aware of Bea catching her breath raggedly at his side. He glanced and saw that her gaze was fixed on Sterling Richardson's young handsome face. Rage and jealousy burned in Dean's gut. He wanted to reach out and snap the younger man in two with his bare hands.

So that was how the land lay. Well, he would not give up easily, Dean told himself. He would convince Bea that she was better off with him than with this young pup who had nothing to offer but his youth and a decaying copper company.

Chapter Six

It was a dull morning when the light fell yellowish grey across the cobbles; heavy clouds swirled over the rooftops and the waters of the canal ran misty bronze.

As Mali stepped out of the cottage, she clutched her shawl more closely round her shoulders and was thankful that she had worn long thick woollen stockings with her good boots buttoned up around her ankles, for the ground was cold underfoot.

The door of the Murphy house swung open and light spilled out, seeming to carry with it the sound of the baby crying. Katie emerged rubbing her eyes sleepily, her mouth a dark circle in her pale face as she yawned hugely.

'Sure an' I'll never get used to bein' out this time o' mornin',' she said, staring at Mali sourly. 'I don't know why you're looking so pleased with yerself and you with eyes wide open as though it's mid day instead of barely six o'clock.'

'I'm excited,' Mali explained. 'There's at least a dozen butterflies inside me whirling around, it's my first job and I really am a working girl now.'

They fell into step, side by side, Katie silent as she hugged her shawl around her thin shoulders. She was shivering a little, her clothing worn, the boots upon her feet shabby, lacking the attention of the polishing brush.

'Sean's about to cut a tooth,' she said dourly. 'Cried all night, so he did, I swear me dad will hammer the boy if he keeps us all awake again tonight.'

Mali remained silent, she had heard the baby's pitiful wails and even though she had put the pillow over her head the sound had been difficult to drown. And yet she had woken refreshed, this morning, giving Dad his breakfast, making up his grub and mixing sugar and tea in a twist of greaseproof paper, and a tin of milk so that he could make himself a brew. Some of the workers in the copper sheds drank beer to quench the terrible thirst that was caused by too much sweating but Davie liked his tea and for that Mali was thankful.

'Saw your dad so I did.' Katie spoke quickly as though reading Mali's thoughts. 'Out with some flossy he was, not that it's any of my business.'

Mali pursed her lips, torn between snapping at Katie and curiosity about the woman Dad was with.

'Young piece was she?' she asked at last. 'Fur collar hanging round her neck and a hat that looks as if it's been dragged through a hedge backwards?'

Katie laughed. 'That's her all right. Flour all over her face, eyes as black as Hades, hanging on his arm so she was just as if she owned him.'

'Rosa,' Mali said angrily. 'I thought Dad had finished with her. She's only after one thing and that's the shillings out of his pocket, the scheming hussy.'

Katie looked at Mali with eyebrows raised. She was silent for so long that Mali looked in her direction.

'Well, don't you think I'm right then?' she demanded and her friend shrugged.

'I don't know do I? But your dad is a fine-looking man, sure he'd make a good catch for one like her that's been used to the streets even though he might be getting older.'

Mali felt anger run through her, and clenched her hands into fists as though to strike out. 'She won't set foot inside our house again,' she said fiercely. 'Not while I'm living there with Dad, she won't.'

Katie caught her arm. 'Never mind her,' she said. 'Sure an' doesn't your dad need a bit of fun like all men? I 'spect he's got his head screwed on the right way and he's just having his oats, as they say.'

Mali would not be appeased. 'It's not right, mind,' she said. 'Not so soon after my mam's funeral and to think he'd go to a woman of that sort, I could kill him for being so stupid.'

Katie shrugged. 'Sure an' isn't he just a man, they're all like little babes at heart, needin' a bit of lovin' and fussin', don't mean much to them so it don't, not always.'

'Well I'd better not see them together,' Mali said stiffly. 'If I do there'll be such a rumpus that Dad won't forget it in a month of Sundays.'

'I'm sorry I spoke, sure I am,' Katie said impatiently. 'Come on, we're nearly there, look as if it's hurryin' you are, make a good impression on Big Mary for if you don't you won't last long in the Canal Street Laundry.'

The large iron gates faced the canal and dripped rustily now with the rain that had fallen during the night. They were slightly open and Katie pushed Mali through into the yard. The smell of the laundry was like nothing Mali had ever experienced before, a mixture of cabbage water and stale urine and she wrinkled up her nose, pausing a moment to look at the rectangular buildings before her.

Small windows stared down like blank eyes and on one wall, a rickety staircase meandered upwards towards a small door.

'That's the packing room.' Katie followed the direction of Mali's gaze, pointing to the top floor. 'But I 'spect you will work the boilers first, need a bit of elbow grease for that so you do.'

'I'm not afraid of work,' Mali protested hotly. 'What are the boilers like?' she added uncertainly.

'You'll soon find out,' Katie whispered. 'For there's Big Mary standing in the doorway waitin' for us to go inside.' She gave Mali a push and clattered away up the wooden staircase.

'You Mali Llewelyn?' Big Mary asked briskly. She stood with huge arms akimbo over her white-aproned, ample bosom. 'Come on in then, won't get no work done skulking around out there will you?'

The interior of the boiler room was filled with steam and at first Mali could hardly see. She coughed a little and Big Mary propelled her forward over the slippery stone floor towards the end wall where monstrous boilers reared up, large and cylindrical, emitting ominous thunder-like noises.

'You can start by fetching coal and keeping the fires going.' Big Mary took a tongs and deftly opened a door at the front of one of the boilers. A rush of heat caught Mali's face and she backed away spitting acrid specks of dust from her mouth.

'There's soft you are girl,' Big Mary said, giving her a goodnatured push. 'You don't breathe in when you're stoking the fire, keep your mouth shut, that's if you can.'

Gingerly, Mali edged forward again, watching as Big Mary placed egg-shaped pieces of coke on the flames. The heat was intense but the woman did not seem to notice it.

'Here,' she pushed a wedge of cardboard forward, 'kneel on this, save your legs a bit.'

She stood back and watched Mali's inexpert attempts to place the coals within the boiler mouth.

'That's right, now close the door, watch it or you'll burn your fingers, there, that wasn't so bad, was it?' She folded her arms and waited for Mali to lift the copper scuttle and move on to the next boiler.

'Right then, you carry on by here, *merchi*,' she said approvingly. 'I've got to do my rounds, see if everything is shipshape, but I'll come back later, righto?'

Mali felt quite alone in spite of the women working all around her. Big Mary had at least noticed her existence, now she felt as if she had suddenly become invisible. Kneeling on her pad of cardboard, she glanced around. Through the steam she could distinguish the figures of the washerwomen who moved ghostlike amid the haze, enveloped in huge white aprons. Occasionally, one of them would climb up a short flight of steps and open the lid of the boiler, poking the washing with a long stick as though attacking it.

As her eyes became accustomed to the steam, Mali began to make out the shapes of long sinks almost like horse troughs, ranged along one wall. These were equipped with mangles fixed to one end, and resting in the soapy water were metal scrubbing boards over which the women laboured ceaselessly.

Soon Mali's back began to ache, her knees were sore and already she had a blister on her hand where she had inadvertently touched one of the boiler doors. She felt as though she was on a treadmill for no sooner had she finished stoking the row of fires than she had to replenish her scuttle with coke and begin again. She began to work mindlessly, too tired even to think. The hours dragged by and Mali was almost dizzy with fatigue when she heard a hooter wail through the buildings.

The women abruptly stopped work but still no one even so

much as glanced Mali's way. She sat back on her heels, brushing her hair from her hot face, staring round in bewilderment. At the far end of the room, near the doorway where the steam was thinnest, the women were crouching in a circle on the ground, opening packages of food, and the rise and fall of their voices drifted to where Mali knelt alone.

Big Mary swept into the room, her eyes searching for and coming to rest upon Mali. She sailed forward like a ship charging through the waves and though Big Mary's face was unsmiling, Mali no longer felt friendless.

'Come on, *merchi*, it's time for grub. There's soft you are, mind, sitting by there and you with only fifteen minutes to eat your fill. Wash, quick girl, and follow me.'

Mali ran the cold water over her hands, unable to remove anything except the surface dust, but she had no time to worry about the black caked in the creases of her palms, for Big Mary was already leaving the room, then leading the way up the rickety staircase.

Mali found that she was now entering a different world, serried rows of washing hung on lines to dry, with the smaller linen draped over wooden clothes horses. Big Mary marched onwards and Mali found herself in the packing room where the scent of hot, clean linen drifted pleasantly towards her. Stacks of clean, neatly folded sheets were piled upon wooden trestles and over all there was an air of peace and tranquillity which Mali drank in greedily.

'Is that you Mali Llewelyn?' Katie smiled at her from the table at the centre of the room where the more privileged girls were gathered at a small table. 'For sure you look like the divil himself you're so black.'

Mali sat beside Katie, aware that she was the object of scrutiny. Opposite her sat Big Mary and she was biting into a piece of brown bread.

'Get chewing, *merchi*,' she advised. 'You've only ten minutes now.'

Self-consciously, Mali drew the edges of her apron inward, attempting to hide the streaks of dirt, feeling foolish because she had not thought to bring food.

At her side, Katie nudged her. 'Here have a bite of my grub, you didn't think to bring any did you?'

Mali's stomach had begun to turn over with hunger; she took a thick slice of bread and began to chew it eagerly.

'Big Mary's taken a liking to you sure she has,' Katie whispered. 'She's only leavin' you down in the boiler room until the regular girl gets back to work. Bring you up here with us then she will.' Katie regarded Mali steadily. 'But you have to prove yourself willin', that's Big Mary's way, she helps those who helps themselves, like God.' Katie crossed herself quickly, frightened at her own blasphemy.

Mali ate in silence. She did not dare to hope that she might be relieved from the work of crawling round on her hands and knees feeding the coke ovens of the boilers and elevated to the job of packing clean linen. She was bone weary, almost ready to fall asleep, and the day was only half over. How could she bear to work until darkness fell when her whole body ached as though she had been kicked?

The break was over almost before it had begun and the loud wail of the hooter bellowed through the building. Big Mary rose to her feet and as though worked by clockwork, the girls rose too and moved back to the tables where the long sheets waited to be folded.

'Get off with you,' Big Mary said to Mali. 'You can find your own way back.'

Katie gave Mali a gentle push. 'Go on, don't stand there like a lemon, see you at home time.'

Mali carefully edged past the tables and returned through the drying room, eyes downcast as she faced the prospect of feeding the fires again. The stairs seemed to move beneath her feet as she descended them and then she was through the door and into the steam of the boiler room again.

She began the round of opening doors and pushing coke into the flames and her heart began to pound with fear as she saw that one of the boilers was nearly out.

'The washing's stopped bubbling up here.' A woman looked down at her from the top of the steps. 'Didn't you see to the fire before grub, girl?'

Dumbly Mali shook her head and the woman came to crouch down beside her, staring into the open doorway with dismay.

Amid the ashes was only a small flicker of life. The flame

lapped blue and green over the remaining nodules of coke, fading almost into extinction even as Mali watched.

'I'd better fetch more fuel,' she said desperately and the woman standing looking down at her sighed in exasperation.

'Well get on with it then for Gawd's sake, there's no good to be done by just staring at it like that.' She mounted the steps at the side of the boiler and lifted the heavy lid.

'See, there's hardly any steam, the water will be cold if you don't get a move on.'

Mali took the scuttle and carried it to the store where the huge mounds of coke were kept. She worked frantically, only half filling the bucket-shaped vessel before hurrying back to the boiler room. A tall rough-looking woman wearing a man's coat and cloth cap was standing near the boiler. She stared at Mali almost contemptuously, her chin poked forward.

'Better hurry, girl.' Her tone was menacing. 'Cos I'm not as patient as Sarah 'ere and if my boiler goes down, you'll feel the back of me hand.'

Mali opened her mouth to protest and then closed it again, there was no point in wasting time arguing. She drew open the door of the boiler, scarcely feeling the heat on her fingertips, and looked desperately at the feeble embers of the fire.

'That's past savin'.' The woman with the cap rummaged in her pocket and took out a small clay pipe, clamping it between her teeth before crossing her arms and settling herself down on her thin haunches to watch the spectacle.

'Who'll lay me a shillin' bet that the girl don't mend the fire?' she said with relish. 'That will teach Big Mary to put a silly young snippet in place of Doris.'

'Be quiet, Aggie. There'll be no giving or taking of bets, right? Why, Big Mary would have your guts for garters.' Sarah pushed at Mali's shoulder impatiently.

'Build it up again, there's a good girl,' she said almost desperately. 'I don't want to stay here late tonight just because you've neglected your work. See I've got to get these sheets out by tonight. Stupid I call it putting a green girl to do a job like this.' Her voice was rising, attracting the attention of the other women, and for a moment Mali felt panic sweep through her. She wanted to run from the laundry out into the street and follow the snaking line of the canal back to the safety of Copperman's Row. She took a deep breath, telling herself to be calm, a simple job like mending a fire even if it was one that kept the huge boiler going was not about to defeat her.

Mali looked around her, searching vainly for paper to thrust into the oven mouth; the only kindling she could find was the cardboard upon which she had been kneeling. Quickly, she tore it into small pieces and fed it into the dying flames. Smoke curled upwards in a thin spiral and Mali coughed a little. Behind her the woman was still complaining bitterly.

'I'll never get home to my husband tonight, have the broomhandle to me he will, he'll be that grieved if I keep him waiting for his bit o' supper.'

Carefully Mali placed some pieces of coke on the small blaze. Her heart was thumping loudly in fear and she closed her eyes, praying the coals would take. She flapped her hands, fanning the flames and to her delight, the smoke dwindled and a swift roar told her the fire was well and truly ablaze.

'Well we can thank our stars for small mercies I suppose.' The woman sighed as though disappointed that the small drama was over. Mali rubbed her hands across he face, unaware that she was streaking her cheeks with coal dust.

'What's been going on here then?' Big Mary was standing watching the little scene, her arms akimbo. 'God almighty, Sarah, I thought you were giving birth the way you were carrying on.' She moved forward, bending to peer into the furnace.

'Nearly died on you, did it *merchi*?' She brushed back a stray wisp of dark hair escaping from the tight bun at the back of her head. 'Well don't worry about it, it isn't the first time and it won't be the last. Now for heaven's sake let's have a bit of peace here is it? Come on, Sarah, get back to work.'

When the women had dispersed, Big Mary stared down at Mali.

'You'd best be more careful next time, or things might not go too well for you. Some of the women are a bit more wild than Sarah, she just moans and groans and plays merry hell with her tongue, others might lash out with a fist first and ask questions later, so remember what I've said, mind.'

'I'm sorry.' Mali stared down at her dusty hands. 'I won't let it happen again.' She moved to the adjoining boiler and Big Mary followed her, the glimmer of a smile warming her face.

'Well there's no need to feel as if you've stolen a baby's bottle from out of its mouth, come on, it's not such a bad job once you get used to it.'

Mali watched her go with a sinking feeling in the pit of her stomach. It was all very well for Big Mary, she didn't have to work with women who either ignored or berated her. With a sigh, Mali knelt on the cold damp ground, unaware that her hair had come loose from its restraining ribbon and was falling over her face. All that concerned her now was to keep the boilers going at whatever cost to herself.

The hours dragged wearily on and Mali's back and legs began to ache with the constant bending. Her knees were rubbed raw beneath the thick wool of her stockings but she would not complain, she wanted a job at the laundry and she'd got it and she was determined to stick it out. Her mouth became dry, her lips caked with coal dust, and her eyes felt as though they were full of cinders. She moved now from instinct, feeding fire after fire, too weary to think.

The sound of the hooter echoing through the building was such a relief that she fell back on her heels sighing softly, the coke dropping from her hands. Sarah looked down at her and there was a hint of compassion in her tired face.

'You're not done yet, lovie,' she said, her brisk tone belying her expression. 'My wash isn't finished, got to give it another fifteen minutes at least.'

Mali struggled to her feet, the coal bucket was empty. It seemed a great effort to lift it and walk to the door of the coke house where mountains of egg-shaped fuel rose to touch the ceiling. She picked up the small shovel and heard the clatter as the coke showered into the bucket. The pain in her arms was like toothache and tears of self pity burned her eyes. Angrily, she brushed them away and half dragging, half carrying the bucket, returned to the boiler house.

'Here, give me that and get off home, *merchi*.' Big Mary took the bucket easily and opened the door of the furnace, throwing the coke inside. Mali stood staring at her for a moment and then turned and made her way towards the door. 'Early tomorrow, mind,' Big Mary called after her. 'And tie some padding round your knees, you'll find the work less painful that way.'

Outside it had grown dark, and the pungent smell of bad eggs drifted from the copper works, penetrating closed doors and windows mercilessly. A sudden burst of shooting sparks illuminated the roadway where a group of girls from the laundry were gathered. Mali moved forward wearily and stood on the outskirts of the crowd, resting her hand on Katie Murphy's shoulder.

'Jesus, Mary and Joseph is that really you Mali Llewelyn?' The Irish girl backed away in mock horror. 'Or is it some demon from Hades that I'm seeing?'

Mali was in no mood for laughter; she rubbed tiredly at her burning eyes and shook her head without replying. At once, Katie put her arm around Mali, contrition on her face.

'The spirit has gone out of you so it has. Come on home with me and let me ma feed you, sure 'twill give you strength to go to cook some grub for your dad.'

Mali felt warmed; the prospect of returning to her kitchen and lighting yet another fire before she could eat had been a daunting one.

'All right,' she said and then wondered if her tone had been ungracious. 'It's good of you Katie,' she added quickly. She would have moved away then along the hard cobbles of the street but a big girl with hair braided tightly around her head barred her way.

'You're the one who's taken Doris's job away from her aren't you?' Her eyes glittered redly in the light from another gust of shooting sparks. Mali stepped back a pace, staring up in bewilderment.

'Hey, Sally Benson, there's no call to go picking on me friend,' Katie said swiftly. 'She don't know Doris from a pig's arse so how can you put any blame on her? We've seen that Doris is swelling up more with every week that passes and it's not dropsy she's got that's for sure.'

'What's the matter with you, blackface, got no tongue?'

Sally ignored Katie and poked a finger at Mali's shoulder. 'Come on there's a good girl, answer when you're spoken to is it?'

'I don't know what I'm supposed to say.' Mali's voice shook in spite of herself and she knew that Sally Benson sensed her reluctance to quarrel.

'No guts either, should have known it, a mewing little brat who's never done a day's work in her life before, spoiled by your daddy is it?'

'Come on now haven't you got a home to go to?' Big Mary pushed her way into the crowd. 'Oh you are the one causing trouble, Sally, I might have known it. Picking on new girls is your sport for the day isn't it? But you'll feel the back of my hand if you don't scarper, mind.'

Mali walked along Canal Street, almost too weary to put one foot in front of the other, all she really wanted to do was to fall into a soft bed and sleep. Suddenly she became aware of someone barring her path. She looked up and was dismayed to see Sterling Richardson staring down at her, running his eyes over her begrimed dishevelled figure as though he had never seen anything like it in his life.

'What in heaven's name have you been doing?' he asked, his eyebrows lifted in amusement.

Mali glared at him, her defiance concealing the chagrin she felt at being caught in such a state.

'Honest work, that's what I've been doing,' she said. 'Stoking boilers down at the laundry. Not that it's any business of yours.'

Sterling gave a wintry smile. 'Then good luck in your new job,' he said abruptly and walked quickly down the street as though he regretted having stopped at all.

Katie tugged her arm. 'Good of Mr toffee-nosed Richardson to pass the time of day with you,' she said lightly. 'Never mind,' her voice held a hint of laughter, 'there's nothing wrong with you that some hot water and good food won't cure. Come on, black face, sure and won't I race you to Copperman's Row?'

'Go race yourself, Katie Murphy,' she said ruefully. 'I'll come along in my own good time.'

Mali brushed aside her tangled hair and paused to look up at

71

the turgid clouds above her. In a sudden mood of optimism she made a silent vow that she would be the best boiler stoker the Canal Street Laundry had ever known.

Chapter Seven

Rickie Richardson sat in the humid, smoke-filled bar of the Cape Horner, staring out of the dusty window moodily. Across the road, in the grey waters of the dock, the towering masts of the *Eleanor May* bobbed to and fro with the wash of the tide. The sailing ship, paintwork peeling and shabby, had come in for repairs and she stood out now like an old scar in comparison to the shiny new steam packets that were hove to alongside her.

In spite of the coldness of the weather, fishermen sat on the quayside mending their nets, hands blue, faces gaunt with concentration. Rickie shivered, rather them than him be on the receiving end of the easterly wind that was blowing in off the water.

His thoughts turned inward and he saw again in his mind's eye the letter that had crystallised for him all the resentment and bitterness he had always felt for Sterling. It was as though he had sensed even from an early age that he was being usurped from his rightful place in the order of things. And the letter had been proof of that, God knows.

He glanced around him, suddenly aware of the crowded bar. It was about time Glanmor Travers turned up, he was late, Rickie thought – in irritation. He settled back into his seat and hunched his shoulders, blocking everything out so that he could concentrate on his thoughts.

It had been Letty who had brought it to him. He had been bedding the maid for some time and her gratitude knew no bounds. She was a plain little thing and at first he had taken her with very little enthusiasm, simply as a release for his natural

73

urges. But she had turned out to have a surprisingly fine body, her breasts when freed from her impeding undergarments were full and high, her waist small and her hips shapely. But better than that, she was convinced that she was in love with him and her adoration warmed him.

At first she had been afraid to show him the letter, her pebble-brown eyes looking at him doubtfully and he, not understanding the importance of the paper she held between her small fingers, had grown impatient.

He had told the maid in no uncertain terms what she could do with the letter. She had pressed it upon him then and once he had begun to read he was suddenly alert. The blood had been pounding within his head as he'd read the words penned in passion and love, words that had the power to change his entire life.

His mother, proud, upright Victoria Richardson, allowing another man to take her into his bed as if she was some little parlour maid, it was unthinkable! And yet the more he allowed his mind to dwell on it, the more it all fitted into place. He had known all along that Sterling was the apple of his mother's eye. He had often watched covertly as she brushed back the golden hair from the clear brow of her elder son, her affection plain for all to see.

Later Rickie had felt the biting pain of rejection when he alone had been sent away to receive what his parents had called a 'good education'. It was abundantly clear then that there was some vital difference between himself and his brother. As he had stared at the letter, his first instinct had been to rush from his room and arouse the household, to shout aloud the momentous discovery he had just made. In his impatience, he had pushed Letty aside, half out of his bed, and then sweet reason had asserted itself.

'Have you read this?' He had spoken harshly to the trembling chambermaid and dumbly she had nodded. He had taken her arm, dragging her back into the warmth of the blankets.

'And what did you make of it all, pretty little Letty?' He had smoothed her hair back from her hot face, soothing her fears. Tentatively, she had smiled at him.

'I know enough of writing to understand that you are Mr

Arthur's real son and that Master Sterling is not.' She had bitten her lip worriedly.

'You mustn't breathe a word of this to anyone, do you understand?' His tone had been silky and she had crouched against him, her hands running over his body in a way that sent shivers along his spine.

'I wouldn't do anything to harm you, Master Rickie.' Letty's eyes were limpid. 'I love you so much that I would die for you.'

He had bent his head and kissed her, after all if it had not been for her prying, he might never have known the truth. He had made it good for her then, knowing within himself it would be for the last time. She was a danger to him now, he wanted to be the only one with the knowledge that could split the Richardson family asunder.

She was sweet beneath him, moaning her surrender. He would miss little Letty, there was no doubt about that, but then maids were two a penny, he would soon find fresh fields to explore.

His first job the next day had been to contact Glanmor Travers with whom he'd shared rooms at college.

'There's this chambermaid.' He'd spoken lightly. 'Had my fill of her now but she's young and willing enough, any notions as to how I can be rid of her?'

Glanmor had laughed shortly. 'Me, ideas? I'm full of them,' he'd said with an air of supreme confidence. But that had been two days ago.

Rickie glanced at the round face of the clock ticking away the minutes on the barroom wall. Perhaps Glanmor Travers was not as clever as he pretended to be and had found no solution to the problem after all.

The doors swung open, allowing a flurry of cold air into the bar. Rickie leaned back in his chair, sighing with relief.

'About time you showed up,' he said dourly. 'I was just about to leave as a matter of fact.'

Glanmor shook his head. 'Oh ye of little faith,' he said reprovingly. 'Wait just a moment, while I order a hot toddy, I'm frozen.' He lifted his hand and the landlord nodded, familiar with his customers and their requirements.

'Now, why are you looking so worried?' Glanmor sat opposite Rickie, resting his arms on the stained wooden

75

surface of the table. 'All your problems are over, dealt with by the efforts of your reliable friend. Tomorrow, Letty will be nothing but a memory.'

Rickie looked at him expectantly. 'What are you going to do with her?' he asked, but to his disappointment, Glanmor shook his head.

'Best you don't know too many details, suffice it to say she will be placed in a position where she will be out of your way and where she can do little harm.'

'Harm?' Rickie echoed the word. 'She can do nothing to me, what makes you think otherwise?'

'There's usually a reason for getting a worn-out doxy put aside,' Glanmor said, tapping the side of his nose knowingly. 'But you know old Glanmor, the soul of discretion, that's me, so don't worry your head about it any longer.'

Rickie drank a little of the thick dark ale, staring over the rim of his glass. Glanmor was digging into his pocket, paying the landlord for the steaming toddy of whisky and hot water standing now on the table before him. Glanmor was not a handsome man, there was too much of the ferret in his narrow eyes and sharp features for that, but perhaps to women there was something compelling about the man's confidence and the air of toughness he exuded.

Rickie did not even like Glanmor. He had been a useful roommate at college, there was no denying that but his arrogance and his attitude of being hard done by irked more than somewhat when one was forced to spend a great deal of time with him.

'Well, do I proceed?' Glanmor said and Rickie became aware that he was staring.

'Yes, why not?' he said quickly. 'I'm sure you know what you are doing. Now, how much do I owe you?' Rickie had soon learned that Glanmor did no favours, not for anyone.

'Nothing, at least not now but perhaps later on there might be a return gesture of thanks?'

Rickie was uneasy. 'Come along, Glanmor,' he said with false heartiness, 'it's not like you to be so reticent, shall we make it a nice round sum, say ten guineas?'

Glanmor stared at him levelly, his narrowed eyes seeming to

gleam in the light from the fire burning alongside him. He shook his head.

'There's nothing at the moment. I shall not let you forget you owe me a favour, don't you worry.'

But Rickie was worried, he did not like being indebted to Glanmor; perhaps consulting him on the subject of Letty had been a mistake. He drank down his ale and rose to his feet.

'I'd best be off home, I've sat around this freezing bar for long enough.' His tone was surly and he saw a fleeting expression of anger cross Glanmor's face.

'When will it happen?' he asked abruptly. 'I don't want this business hanging on any longer than necessary.' Glanmor took a slow drink from his glass, deliberately keeping Rickie waiting. He was a sadistic bastard, Rickie mused.

'Consider it done,' Glanmor said at last. Rickie would have moved to the door but Glanmor's hand on his sleeve stopped him.

'Did you know that brother of yours has given me notice?' His tone revealed his bitterness. 'That's all the thanks we Travers get for working faithfully for the Richardson family all these years.'

Rickie felt bewildered. 'I had no idea,' he said. He wrapped his collar more tightly around his throat, doing up the top button, giving himself time to think. Why had Sterling suddenly dispensed with Glanmor's services? He did nothing without good reason, what did he have hidden up his sleeve now?

'Nothing I can do about it if that's what you're hoping for,' he said shortly. 'You know as well as I do that Sterling doesn't give a horse's fart what I say about anything. He won't reinstate you so perhaps you'd better take that ten guineas I offered you.'

Glanmor sneered. 'No thanks, and you must be a fool if you think I'd even consider working for your brother again, ever. He can go to hell his own way and he will from what I've heard.'

Richard sat down again, leaning forward, his arms on the table. 'And what might that be? Come on Glanmor, you know you mean to tell me sooner or later.'

Glanmor leaned back against the seat, his eyes shrewd. 'They really don't tell you anything, do they? Well it seems that your brother isn't content with the rich pickings he's getting from the copper, he wants to go into steel too. Work's about to start on changing the furnaces any day now.' He shrugged. 'Some people are never satisfied with what they've got, always looking for new ways to line their pockets. What a pity you won't inherit, Rickie.'

'You could just be wrong about that.' The moment he had spoken, he realised his mistake. Glanmor's eyes lit up and he sucked in his breath on a whistle.

'Holding out on me, boyo, well don't tell me, not if you don't want to, but I shall find out anyway, sooner or later.'

His laugh echoed behind Rickie as he left the public bar of the Cape Horner. It was sharp and cold on the quayside and Rickie stood for a moment staring down at the pewter water running high between the ships berthed in the dock. He was furious with himself for giving away too much back there. Glanmor was like a dog with a rat, he wouldn't give up once he'd sunk his teeth into something. Rickie did not feel like the walk back up the hill and so he took the tram, swinging himself aboard easily, seating himself near the doorway. A cold draught of air blew against his cheeks and he sank back, hands in his pockets, wishing himself home near the warmth of the fireside.

He turned his head to look out of the window. Down below he could see the shops of the town spread along a street shaped like a question mark. It seemed peopled by midgets, dark figures scurried to and fro, small shadows seen from a distance.

It was growing dusk, the sky fading to a dull indigo. There would be no sunset, not tonight, for the clouds were grouped thick and heavy, hanging low over the sea. To the east was the river, dull and dirty, lit occasionally to a glowing red by sparks from the forest of chimneys above the copper works. In pride of place was the Richardson Copper Company, the squat buildings lying near the banks of the Swan, standing like a monument rising up from the scarred land. This then was the inheritance that should have been his, and anger burned low in his gut as he thought of Sterling lording it over all, strutting about the sheds, issuing orders, hiring and firing, little better than a thief.

He alighted from the electric tram and watched it roll away

back down the hill. The gaudy advertisements for Rowntrees' Cocoa and Cherry Blossom Boot Polish slid away into the growing dusk. He began to walk briskly along the pathway towards the house that lay back from the road as though disdaining contact with anything other than itself. Plas Rhianfa was elegant and gracious and the pain within Rickie was burdensome as he realised it would never be his. Sterling would possess it as he possessed everything else; was there no justice?

The trees that edged the long wide driveway swayed and moaned above him, bare branches waving like skeleton fingers in the wind. Rickie glanced upwards and paused for a moment to stare at the lowering clouds. He would not let Sterling get away with it, damn it.

He entered the hallway, brilliantly lit by the chandelier overhead, and looked around as though seeing his home for the first time, the rich patterns of the carpet glowed up at him, the colours jewel bright, swamping his senses. All this should be his, and by God he meant to fight for it.

From the drawing room he could hear the sound of Victoria's voice and carefully he moved towards the wide staircase. He had no wish to be sociable to anyone at the moment, least of all his mother.

'Bitch!' His own vehemence startled him and he ran the rest of the way up the carpeted stairs and along the broad, spacious landing. Inside his room he closed the door and leaned against it for a moment, staring around him. A big fire roared in the grate – kept alight, no doubt, by the faithful Letty. The drapes over the bed were fresh and clean, the quilt thick and silky. The sheets were of finest linen, pristine white and folded just so. If he had taken his home for granted until now, it was because he had not realised that it was rightfully his.

He lay on the bed and put his hands behind his head, staring up at the ornate ceiling. Tomorrow, he mused, he would see Gregory Irons. If the man lived up to half the reputation he'd gained for being the shrewdest if not the most crooked lawyer in Sweyn's Eye then he should be able to help him sort out what the letter meant in terms of the inheritance.

There was a timid knocking on the door and before he could speak, Letty was in the room, her face pale and tear stained.

'Master Rickie, you've got to help me.' She came close to where he lay, staring at him wide eyed, her hands outstretched to him in supplication. His first reaction was to order her out of his sight but on reflection, this might be the last time he would see her. In any case, he was curious.

'Come and sit beside me, tell me what's troubling you.' He placed his arm around her shoulder, drawing her soft warm body close to him. Her eyes stared into his imploringly and he kissed her trembling mouth before she could burst into tears.

'What is it?' he urged and she leaned her head against his neck, sniffling in her misery.

'Cook has made me pack my bag,' she said in a small voice. 'She says I'm to leave here at first light.'

'Now why would Mrs Griffiths tell you that?' Rickie asked. His hand was searching in the bodice of her heavy gown and at last his fingers came in contact with her firm breast.

'You know I can't do without you,' he said softly. He pushed her back on the bed, ignoring her small protests.

'I must go downstairs, Master Rickie, cook will be going on at me again if I'm away too long.'

'Never mind cook.' Rickie's voice was hoarse. 'There are more important things to worry about than that old crusty virgin.'

'No, please, not now, Master Rickie, I just can't think of anything except having to leave here.'

'Don't be silly, I won't let any harm come to you.' He kissed her, silencing her words and at last, she relaxed beneath his searching hands.

'I love you, Master Rickie.' She breathed his name as though it was a prayer. 'I'd be that miserable if I was sent away.'

'Hush, it won't come to that.' The urge was strong within him and roughly he lifted her skirts, thrusting against her so that she cried out in pain. It gave added spice to the event that this was to be the last time, at least with Letty, soon there would be a new chambermaid to amuse him.

It was over quickly and Letty lay like a bundle of soiled washing in the softness of the bed. Rickie moved away from her, looking into the darkness of the sky through the window.

Suddenly he shivered. Out there somewhere was Glanmor Travers, scheming and plotting his way through life, a man who should not be trusted at any price.

'Master Rickie.' The small voice from the bed captured his attention. 'It will be all right won't it, you will speak to Mrs Griffiths?'

He turned to look at her, trying to hide his impatience.

'Go on now, back to the kitchen before she misses you and yes, I'll have a word with cook, don't worry about a thing.' He bundled her forward, taking a quick look along the corridor before thrusting her outside and closing the door in her startled face. It was a good thing she was leaving Plas Rhianfa, she was becoming far too clinging, demanding his attention as though it was her right.

He drew his chair nearer to the fire and stared into the flames, there was a great deal for him to think about and Letty was the least important of them all. He settled himself back and closed his eyes, his feet stretched out to the blaze. One day all this would be his, he would be master not only of Plas Rhianfa but of the Richardson empire.

Outside the wind was rising sharply and frost made patterns, complicated and beautiful, on the windowpanes but Rickie saw nothing, he was locked inside his own imaginings.

It was cold when he awoke, with a pale sun shining in through the open curtains. The fire was dead and grey and he sat up stiffly, aware that he had not gone to bed at all but had slept all night in the chair. His neck was stiff and the back of his legs ached and he cursed the servants for not showing their usual efficiency in attending to his fire at first light.

He rose and pulled savagely at the bell rope. He was cold and uncomfortable, his mouth was dry and he felt as if he had been awake all night. There was no hot water on the stand beside his bed and no morning tray waiting for him. He pulled again at the rope and shrugged himself out of his jacket.

'Excuse me, Master Rickie.' Gwen the kitchenmaid elbowed her way into the room, her apron damp and her hair escaping from under her mob cap. She was a singularly unattractive wench, Rickie thought distastefully as she moved into the room, her large hips swaying, her heavy breasts straining against the coarse material of her gown.

81

'Cook says I have to see you this morning, there's no one else you see, for Letty's been sent away in disgrace.'

She poured the tea and impatiently Rickie took the delicate bone china cup from the tray.

'What on earth are you babbling on about, girl?' he said as though her words were not filling him with triumph. She stood before him, hands raw and large, clasped together under the mound of her stomach.

'Donno what she did, pinched something as I heard it, but she's been sent packing anyways and I've got to do for you until there's another chambermaid.' She smiled at him coquettishly; it was clear she knew there was a deeper meaning to Letty's departure. Was there no hiding anything from the servants?

'Light the fire and bring up some hot water, as soon as you can,' he said abruptly. He drank his tea and threw himself across the bed, staring up at the ceiling. He would wash and dress and then go down to breakfast and later, he would seek out Gregory Irons, it was about time he made his first move in the fight to gain what was rightfully his.

Chapter Eight

Mali awoke to the sound of chapel bells ringing and she rubbed at her eyes sleepily, relishing the knowledge that today she did not have to go to the laundry and stoke fires all day long. She sat up in bed and stretched her arms above her head, conscious of the cold wintry air that permeated her bedroom. For a moment, she indulged herself in the luxury of snuggling down into the warmth of her blankets once more, even putting her head beneath the bedclothes, closing her eyes with a delicious sense of delaying the moment when she would have to arise and begin her chores for the day.

There was the salt fish to cook, resting now in its bowl of water where she had placed it, hard as a board, last night before she'd gone to bed. She would boil it slowly, just at a simmer, and top it with butter and a poached egg just the way Dad liked it.

Suddenly, Mali's sense of wellbeing vanished as she remembered Davie's return home from the Mexico Fountain smelling of cheap perfume, a hangdog expression in his eyes, and it had become clear in that moment that he was still seeing Rosa, spending his time and money upon a girl who cared nothing for him. What fools men could be.

She quickly threw back the blankets and stepped out onto the cold linoleum that covered the creaking wooden floorboards, padding towards the marble-topped table in her bare feet. Shivering, she splashed water from the tall jug into the large china bowl, washing her hands and face with her own home-made soap. It was a relief to draw on her long woollen stockings and a thick wool skirt topped by a flannel blouse, knowing that soon she would be warm enough for she would be busy in the kitchen all morning.

It seemed child's play lighting the fire after her week of working in the boiler house. She set the twists of paper in a neat pattern and then topped them with pieces of stick, lastly using up the cinders before covering the whole with gleaming coal richer and more fiercely burning than the coke used at the laundry.

Within half an hour the kitchen was snug and cosy and the kettle steaming on the newly blackleaded hob. Outside the bells rang with more urgency than ever as if to stir the consciences of the inhabitants of Sweyn's Eye.

Mali drank her tea hot and sweet, cradling the earthenware cup between her hands, absorbing the warmth through her fingertips. She moved towards the window and gasped as she saw the thin layer of pure snow that encompassed the landscape. Even the slag tip was a beautiful white mountain. Figures moved through the brightness, heads bent against the wind that still brought with it flurries of snow, a late last cry from winter, before giving way to the softness of spring.

Mali thought she could see Katie among a group of people labouring through the snow, at any rate, she glimpsed a bright splash of red-gold hair above the dark collar of a coat and guessed that the Murphy family were on their way to mass at St Joseph's Church down in the hollow of the valley.

She had gone once with Katie to a Catholic service and had liked the way Father O'Flynn had greeted his flock with an easy familiarity that was lacking in her own chapel.

Pentre Estyll was Welsh Baptist, narrow to the point of austerity, where even a ribbon set among a child's curls was frowned upon as being worldly and against the teachings of the Good Book.

Once, when she was very little, Mali had witnessed the gruelling sight of a young, white-faced girl taken to stand before the Set Fawr, the great bench occupied by a frightening array of deacons, there to be castigated for some sin of which Mali had no comprehension.

The young girl had begun to cry, her sobs echoing up into the glowering rafters. Distressed, Mali had tugged her mother's skirts, asking in a loud whisper what the lady had done wrong, but Mam had hushed her, a frown marring the clear line of her forehead.

Later it had been Davie who had tried to explain the matter to her. He had taken her upon his knee and brushed back her unruly hair and kissed her cheek with warm affection.

'She is carrying a child within her,' he explained. 'That would not be wrong except that she has no husband, a babba needs a father as well as a mammy so remember that, little one, and don't bring home trouble to your mother and me.'

Mali had been too afraid to protest that she still did not understand why the men in their high-buttoned coats and stiff moustaches over even stiffer collars had looked so disdainfully at the pitiful, beaten creature standing before them.

She moved back now to the warmth of the fire and finished the tea quickly, she must not stand around dreaming, there was a great deal to be done. She put the salt fish on to boil and then began to clean the turnips and carrots ready for dinner. Dad would no doubt complain that she was failing in her duty by not going to morning worship but she would make up for it by attending Sunday school and evening prayers. With a wry smile, she wondered how it was that Davie could ignore the chapel with impunity.

It was quiet now with the pealing of the bells hushed, and only faintly carried by the wind could she hear the sound of voices raised in hymn singing. She thrust a spoon into the huge black pot balancing on the flames and the fish moved in the simmering water as though coming to life.

Quite suddenly, with the familiar chores accomplished, she thought of her mother lying in the cold earth covered now by a blanket of snow, and her eyes grew moist with tears. Soon spring would come and then summer but Mam would see none of it.

The sound of movement from upstairs startled her. Davie was up and about and would be ready for his breakfast. She shifted the coals with the long-handled poker, causing the water in the pot to boil more vigorously. Rubbing her hands on her apron, she went to the larder with its cold stone slab and took out a loaf of bread, placing it on the wooden board so as to make the cutting easier.

'Morning, Mali.' Her father looked bright-eyed as though

85

he had not stumbled in through the door last night with a belly full of drink, wanting only to fall into his bed and sleep.

'Morning, Dad,' she said brightly. 'Breakfast is nearly ready.'

He smiled and settled himself before the fire, stretching out his long legs towards the warmth.

'That's all right, *cariad*, you've worked hard all the week and should have stayed abed this morning.'

'There was the fish to cook,' Mali explained. 'Wouldn't keep any longer, be throwing it out to the cats if I didn't boil it today.'

Davie grinned. 'That's a fine thing to tell a man just before he eats his grub isn't it? Well I suppose it's all right, smells good anyway. That's what woke me up, the smell I mean, starving I am, could eat a scabby horse between two pit props I could.'

'Well make do with salt fish will you?' Mali said smiling. 'There's a nice poached egg to go with it though.' While they ate breakfast, Mali watched her father covertly. Deep inside her was the need to talk to him about his association with Rosa, yet she feared his displeasure. When his belly was full, that was the moment to speak, she decided.

'Seen the snow?' Davie asked. He bit into a great slice of bread and ate with relish. Mali stared at him as though trying to see him through the eyes of another woman, one not related to him by blood. He was handsome and big and lusty, not all that old, she supposed and yet he was surely not so lacking in discrimination as to be fooled by a girl the like of Rosa?

'Why are you looking at me like that?' Davie asked, his green eyes alight with amusement. 'Have I grown two heads or something?'

This was the time then. Mali took a deep breath and her heart was suddenly beating rapidly.

'It's this woman you're seeing, Dad.' The words came out in a rush and Mali saw Davie frown, moving back in his chair as if attempting to put as much distance between them as possible.

'I'm sorry Dad but I must speak,' she continued desperately. 'Rosa is common, she's not even clean and tidy, what can you see in her? If you want someone to take Mam's place, you could surely do better than that?'

Davie moved uncomfortably in his chair.

'You don't understand, Mali,' he said. 'A man needs certain things, company and more.' He lifted his huge hands. 'I can't explain it to you.' His face was red and angry and he pushed his plate away from him, staring down at the remains of the fish as though it had reared up and suddenly bitten him.

Mali swallowed hard. 'But Dad, she's just a cheap flossy, a girl who will go with any man for a shilling, how could you bear to be near her and after Mam was so perfect?'

Davie hung his head. 'Your Mam was one on her own,' he said. 'She was the sun and moon to me Mali, but she's gone and I have to do something to remind myself I'm still alive.'

He rose abruptly from his chair. 'Enough, I'm going to chop sticks for the fire and shouldn't you be getting ready for Sunday school?' He moved away through the kitchen and out into the yard and Mali sank back in her chair, knowing herself defeated. It was as if Dad had become trapped by this Rosa, this woman of the streets who cared nothing for him except to relieve him of his money. Why didn't Dad look round for a respectable woman if he could not live without one?

In a fury, she mixed up fruit and flour to make Welsh cakes for tea, cracking an egg into the bowl with an excess of zeal as though it was Rosa she was attacking. It was an effort to lift the heavy griddle onto the fire but she wouldn't ask Dad for help, not after the way he had walked out, his face set and hard, his eyes the colour of the bottom of the ocean.

She dropped a little fat onto the griddle and it spat viciously, an indication that the heavy iron plate was hot enough to receive the rolled circles of pastry that would flatten out into small circles, browned both sides with delicious hot fruity centres. While the cakes were cooking, Mali flipped them over with the skill of long practice. She sighed heavily and from the larder fetched a tin in which to keep the cakes until they were needed for tea.

The morning seemed to drag by and Mali was happy when at last her chores were finished, the dinner over and done with and the dishes washed and put away. Sunday school was not very exciting but at least it would take her away from the sound of Dad chopping at the wood in the yard as if he was taking out his spleen on it.

It was cold in her room and she shivered as she dressed in her best black serge skirt and the dark striped calico blouse with its pin-tuck pleats down the front, one of the last garments Mam had made for her. On Sundays, Mali did not wear a shawl but a straight, heavy woollen coat that was nipped in at the waist and was meant to reveal an hourglass figure. It was a trifle too big and hung loosely over Mali's thin frame but it was warm and neat and that was all she required it to be.

It was about half an hour later when she let herself out of the house. Dad was still out back chopping wood, ignoring the snow that was falling heavier now. Mali felt her boots slip a little and her hat wobbled precariously on her head as she grasped the wall for support.

'Going to chapel, Mali?' Dai End House was smiling at her in approval even though he himself obviously had no intention of making his way down the hill to Pentre Estyll. He was coal black and his brushes were slung over his shoulder, it was quite apparent that he was working.

'Yes, taking Sunday school class as usual,' she replied. 'But who is having chimneys swept on the Sabbath then?' She was curious, most of the inhabitants of Copperman's Row were God-fearing people abiding by the laws set out in the Bible. Dai End House had the grace to look sheepish.

'It's Mrs Benson. She claims she's too busy midwifing most of the time and can't keep regular hours like other folks, has to have the work done in between delivering babbies. Right enough, mind.' He raised his grubby hat to Mali before passing her and continuing on his way, a ludicrously black blot against the whiteness of the snow.

On Sunday afternoons the chapel was not nearly as awe-inspiring as usual, Mali decided as she stood in the doorway staring round her. The long dark pews were the same as ever but children sat in groups placed according to age. There was not the usual reverent silence either, a babble of young voices filled the building, rising into the heavy oak rafters. It was only at the end of the hour that the groups merged into one congregation, heads bent before the altar as the deacon led them in prayer.

It was Mali's task to teach the older children, pupils of ten and upwards, for her aptitude for reading and for understanding the scriptures had been taken for granted. She was after all the daughter of Mrs Llewelyn, a woman of rare delicacy and learning, one whose father had himself been a lay preacher. At first, Mali had enjoyed being singled out and yet gradually, she found that she had become separated by her position from others of her own age.

That afternoon the pupils in her class seemed unusually trying and difficult and after a time Mali felt her head begin to pound. She was relieved when at last the bell rang and the children rose as if by one accord and moved to the pews nearer the dais upon which stood the pulpit with the open Bible resting upon it. Mali glanced round her stealthily, wondering if she could slip out without being noticed but she was too late, the organ was already swelling into life. Later, as she retraced her steps along the road towards Copperman's Row, she paused to stare at the docks spread out below. The sea, from a distance, was calm, fanning outwards towards the edge of the world – a grey, pewter flatness broken only by the darkness of a ship moving away on the tide.

'Mali, what are you doing standing there in the snow like a fool?' Katie caught her arm and clung, laughing, her red-gold hair escaping from under a woollen scarf, her cheeks flushed with cold.

'Come on, let's get back home, sure it's freezin' to death you'll be if you stand there much longer.'

Mali smiled warmly. 'Katie, you're just the one I want to talk to. I've had a word with Dad, told him off about seeing this Rosa.' Her words came hurriedly and Katie raised her eyebrows comically.

'Fools rush in where the angels fear to tread, right enough,' she said. 'And a lot of good it did you by the look on your face, you can't say I didn't warn you to keep your nose out of other people's affairs.'

She laughed apologetically. 'I'm sorry Mali, but you can't interfere in what your Dad wants to do.'

Mali shrugged. 'I suppose you're right, for Dad simply lost his rag and went out the back to take out his temper on the wood, chopping it as if it was his worst enemy. It's splinters I'll have not fire blocks by the time he's finished.'

The two girls walked slowly up the hill. Already darkness

was closing in, giving an eerie glow to the whiteness of the snow on the ground. Lights spilling from windows threw pools of brightness and warmth, illuminating Katie's red hair and Mali's earnest face.

'Can I speak now?' Katie asked. 'For I've something powerful important to tell you.' Her eyes shone like cats' eyes through the gloom and Mali looked at her, suddenly aware that there was a contained excitement about her friend.

'Yes of course you can speak,' she said quickly. 'What is it, Katie?'

'It's me and Will.' The Irish girl hung her head for a moment and stopped walking and the glow from the street lamp fell like a blessing on the brightness of her hair. When she looked up, her eyes were soft and dreamy, the contours of her face subtly altered. She looked the way Mali sometimes felt in chapel when the music rose to a crescendo, haunting and yet brave, stirring up inward feelings.

'We're man and wife now.' Katie's voice was little more than a whisper. 'At least in the sight of the Blessed Virgin.'

Mali felt suddenly cold. 'Katie, what have you done?' she asked in a small voice. 'Surely you haven't . . .' Her voice trailed away.

Katie became defiant, she tossed back the hair that had fallen over her forehead, her scarf slipped now to the back of her neck.

'Don't sound so prim and vinegary.' She spoke sharply and Mali sensed her hurt.

'I'm sorry, Katie.' She put her hand on her friend's arm. 'Come on, we'll walk towards home and you can tell me about it.' Mollified, Katie fell into step beside Mali.

'It was so wonderful,' she said almost wistfully. 'His mother had gone out visitin' her sister so we had the house to ourselves though the old besom didn't know that of course. Crept in we did after we watched her leave and then Will took me up to his bedroom.' She paused. 'It was so cold in there, Mali, and yet though I was shiverin' 'twere not from the chill. Took me in his arms so he did, held me so close I could hear the beating of his heart like thunder in my ears. The breath was gone from me, I couldn't think of anything but the crying of me inside, I wanted him so badly, you see.'

90

They had reached the end of Copperman's Row and Mali paused, staring along the roadway white and shimmering, the snow untrodden and pure. Katie what have you done? a silent voice inside her asked fearfully.

'Does he love you, Katie?' she asked quietly. 'You're too good to throw yourself away on just any man. Will he marry you, properly in your church?' She faced her friend and saw a fleeting shadow of doubt pass over the delicate features, then Katie lifted her head.

'Of course he will marry me, he loves me and soon we shall be together, I told you before, we won't wait any longer than the time it takes to get the dibbs to pay the priest.' She made a wry face. 'His mother will have a fit o' the vapours when we tell her though, Mrs Owens is chapel like you and she don't hold with Catholics.'

Mali felt uncertainty like a glimmer of pain inside her. Katie in spite of her pretence at being wise was too trusting by far and it would not be difficult for a slick-talking young man to charm away her fears, especially as she believed herself in love.

'Look I must go home now, give Dad his tea,' she said. 'But I'll miss chapel this evening and when Dad goes down to the Mexico, you can come in and talk some more, all right?'

Katie smiled. 'Tis a good friend you are, Mali Llewelyn,' she said softly. 'And talk I must or I'll be fit to bust with the joy that's in

As _____ lf into the warm kitchen, she became aware
th_____ upied by someone other than her father.
_____ fume hung in the air and when Mali
_____ w a pair of shabby boots discarded
_____ From upstairs came the sound of
_____ enly Mali froze. Dad had that
_____ She would not have believed

_____ battling with her feelings
_____ ember, it was only the
_____ brought her to her

_____ d there stood Rosa, red

cheeked, her bright hair dishevelled and behind her Davie, his mouth dropping open in dismay at the sight of his daughter.

'Get her out of here, Dad.' Mali did not recognise her own voice. 'Get her out before I kill her.'

'No *cariad*, don't lose your rag.' Davie held out a hand placatingly, pushing Rosa before him into the kitchen. 'Get your duds on, gel, I'll take you home.' He spoke sharply to Rosa but she stared up at him defiantly.

'Throwing me out it is Davie boyo, and after you jest bedded me, too!'

Mali could bear no more, she flung open the door and then she was running, careless in the snow, not hearing Davie's voice behind her calling anxiously. Her one thought was to get away from the sight of Rosa who thought she could take the place once occupied by Mam.

'Over my dead body!' Mali shouted the words to the sky and they seemed to echo upwards into the silent hills.

Mali did not afterwards remember how far she ran for inside her raged a fury that would not be quenched. She was forced at last to stop and rest for her breathing was ragged and her heart pounding as though it would burst. She leaned against the rough bark of a tree and stared around her and for the first time realised she was high up on the hill, and spread far below her was the town, lights just beginning to twinkle as dusk fell.

Mali was suddenly startled to hear the sound of a man whistling and it seemed he was coming towards her. She did not know exactly why she was afraid, perhaps it was because she was on unfamiliar territory. She made to run back the way she had come but in her panic, her foot slipped and then she was falling into the snow, her voice rising in a thin cry.

She was picked up in strong arms, held aloft and even as she began to struggle, relief flowed through her.

'Mr Richardson!' She relaxed against his shoulder and returned his smile reluctantly, wondering how it was he seemed always to catch her unawares and when she was looking less than her best.

'My name is Sterling,' he said reasonably as he set her down. 'I'm not exactly the Ancient Mariner you know, not so much older than you, really, believe it or not.'

She looked away from him shyly as he took her hand and drew it through his arm.

'I don't know why you're up here near my house,' he said lightly. 'Looking for me were you?'

'No, I was not!' She spoke with such ferocity that he laughed.

'All right you weren't looking for me but you shouldn't be roaming around alone, not when it's getting dark, should you?'

'I suppose you're right,' she said, 'but somehow I had to put as much distance between myself and Copperman's Row as possible.'

He thrust his hands into his pockets and stared up into the night sky and was silent for a long time.

'See how clear the stars are Mali?' he said at last. 'That constellation is the Great Bear, you can just make it out if you look carefully.'

He talked to her quietly, of anything and everything until gradually she became calmer. She smiled up at him sheepishly.

'I suppose I must have looked like a demon out of Hades, running about the hillside, my hair wild,' she said.

Their eyes met and held and Mali found herself entranced by the way the corners of his mouth turned upwards.

'Would you like to tell me what's wrong, now?' His voice was resonant, sounding beautiful to Mali's ears. She felt strength flow from him and suddenly she wanted to confide in him.

'It's my dad,' she said, 'he's taken up with a woman of the streets, a real no-good hussy, all cheap perfume and shabby clothes. How can he want her after my mother?'

Sterling was silent for a long time and Mali searched his face anxiously.

'Do you think I'm wrong too? My friend Katie says I shouldn't interfere.'

Sterling put his hands on her shoulders and Mali felt the tingling warmth of him soar through her blood. She drew away from him quickly, afraid of the new, strange sensations.

'You're bound to feel hurt,' he said gently. 'But perhaps it's best if you let things run their course. Some women have a way of getting into a man's blood against his better judgment.'

93

'You're on his side.' Mali's voice was muffled for deep within her she knew that she was no longer entirely wrapped up in the problem of her father and Rosa. She had become increasingly conscious of Sterling Richardson's tallness and masculinity and even more aware of the gulf that separated them.

'I'm not on anyone's side, Mali,' he said, 'but I can understand it when a man wants something so badly he'll go to any lengths to get it.'

Mali turned to look at him and his eyes were now gazing down into the valley. 'But you're not talking about a woman, are you?' she said.

He shook his head and moved forward, standing silhouetted against the sky, a godlike creature from a dream. Mali followed him and when he spoke again his voice was hard.

'It's my ambition to restore the works to its former glory. As it is we're going broke, Mali. If I don't pull us out of the mire the company is finished and the Richardson family along with it.' He sighed. 'I can't blame my father, he was getting old, past his prime. He would not accept change but I must make good his mistakes.'

Mali felt that she had been selfish, pouring out her worries upon Sterling when he had enough of his own. She slipped her hand within his shyly, wanting to comfort and he smiled down at her, understanding. Mali's heart contracted, she felt she had reached out to him and found a spirit akin to her own.

'I think I'd better take you home,' he said and his eyes were alight with something that touched Mali so that she could hardly bear the pain of it. It was as though the flickering of a candle flame lay between them, shimmering and lovely and so intangible that it might disappear at any moment.

Sterling began to lead her downward, guiding her over the rough, uneven ground. And as they walked, they spoke together lightly, saying nothing of great consequence, but Mali felt a bubbling happiness rise within her so that she wanted to lift her arms to the heavens and laugh out loud.

He took her as far as the corner of Market Street and when he said goodbye, the softness and beauty was still between them.

She ran then as though her feet had wings and joy flowed

through her like sweet wine. Copperman's Row appeared to be a fairyland of white snow lit by shooting sparks and Mali felt she wanted to stay awake all night so that she might not lose the memory of the hours she had spent with Sterling.

Chapter Nine

It was a brisk morning, the sun weak and wintry but none the less pleasant, slanting through the bare branches of the trees. Sterling stepped out of the arched doorway of the Mackworth Arms and stared across the cobbled street towards the harbour, breathing in the familiar scents of tar and salt. He listened for a moment to the small tugs issuing warning to the larger vessels, ships with billowing sails that creaked and groaned in the wind and the less beautiful steam packets that could cut the time of a journey by almost half.

The air was like wine with no sign of the pall of smoke that normally hung shroudlike over the valley. Sterling took a deep breath, staring down the snaking line of the main street as it meandered along the curve of the bay. The tall posts of the gas lamps stood like markers against grey stone houses and he reflected that it was an ugly, shapeless town and yet the rising folds of the hills that flanked it and the soft swell of the sea somehow beautified it.

He strode round the back of the hotel and stared in satisfaction at the gleaming Austin Ascot he had just acquired. It had cost him four hundred pounds, the windsheets and headlights coming as extras, but it was worth it. It seemed to stamp his own individuality, mark the change in ownership of the copper company, a flag to wave at the world as a warning that Sterling Richardson intended to do things his own way.

It was pleasant if cold driving the Ascot along the road towards the works; he found the car amazingly easy to steer and far less temperamental than Foxy, though nothing would ever replace the feeling of a good horse beneath him.

His thoughts turned to the ticketing that was to take place later on that morning; with him Ben would attend the auctioning of the ore as he had always done even though now the old man's eyes were not as sharp as they used to be. He turned the Ascot into Stryd Fawr, the high street which was crowded even at such an early hour. Among the crowd he saw cockle women wrapped in heavy Welsh shawls, distinctive tall hats upon their heads, baskets of shellfish on their arms. None of the people thronging the pavements seemed aware of the cold breeze coming in off the sea.

Sterling slowed the Ascot, breathing in the smell of hot fresh bread that emanated from a van pulled up before the baker's shop. The horse was moving impatiently between the shafts, drawing the van almost onto the pavement. A stream of urine came from the animal in sudden gushes, running in yellow rivulets between the cobbles. Sterling pressed the horn, impatient to pass, and after a moment the driver came out of the shop and climbed aboard the van, calling raucously to the horse to get a move on along the crowded road.

The main street was soon left behind him as Sterling drove up the hill towards the works. Green Hill was the Catholic area of the town and could not have been given a more blatant misnomer. Dingy courts were entwined together in a maze of dark alleyways leading to cottages that defied all efforts by the occupants to preserve a state of cleanliness.

A great deal of the dust and grime came from the works spread along the river and there seemed no cure for it except perhaps closure of the very works that gave the inhabitants of Green Hill their livelihood.

'Morning Ben.' Sterling strode into the office a few minutes later after parking his Ascot in the end stable cleaned out and modified for the purpose. 'Good day for the ticketing wouldn't you say?'

'Aye, not bad sir.' Ben took his handkerchief from his pocket and dabbed at his whiskers. 'Good load in from Chile for the auction, so I've heard,' he continued, his voice slightly muffled by the folds of linen. 'Course you can't beat the Cornish ore but nowadays we must take what we can get.'

Sterling took off his coat and rolled up the sleeves of his

shirt. 'Let's go and have a look at the sheds, then, see how the new furnaces are shaping up.'

'The workmen have not finished installing them yet sir.' Ben spoke almost reprovingly as though Sterling was expecting miracles.

'Let's get over there anyway,' Sterling said a trife impatiently. 'You know I like to check everything over at least once a day.'

As always the sheds were a steaming cauldron, the remaining calcinating furnaces roaring full blast. Each one of them was capable of devouring over three tons of ore, reducing the rock-like substance to a shimmering, molten mass, glazing over with dross that must continually be skimmed away, 'fishing' as the workers called it. This was the first stage of refining and would take anything up to twenty-four hours to complete.

Sterling nodded in satisfaction, the ore was not clotting but flowing freely. He folded his arms over his chest, watching as the copper was granulated with water after the first roasting; he found it curiously satisfying to see the product begin to take shape.

Ben was mopping his face, rubbing the steam from his glasses, coughing to draw Sterling's attention to himself, it was clear he did not find it fascinating to stand and stare as Sterling did.

'How's the tough pitch coming along?' Sterling had to raise his voice to be heard over the roar of the bubbling metal. Ben nodded his head.

'It's good, sir.' His dour face almost broke into a smile. 'You know I have a knack of picking out the best ore even though I'm not a chemist.'

'Right enough,' Sterling conceded, 'let's go look at the 'finery work and then we'll return to the office.' He supposed it wasn't fair to drag Ben around the works and yet shaking him off was like trying to free himself from a limpet, he thought ruefully.

Ben followed close in his footsteps, still mopping his brow. He was game enough, Sterling had to admit; perhaps it was time he reassured the old man that he would not be pensioned off – at least not yet a while.

'I don't know what I'd do without you, Ben,' he said. 'I hope you're not thinking of retiring?'

Ben removed his spectacles and polished them vigorously, trying hard to conceal his pleasure.

'Don't worry sir,' he said, almost puffing up his chest with pride, 'I'll be here for some time yet, I know you need me.'

The refinery where the last part of the smelting process was carried out was no less hot than the calcinating sheds and Sterling felt the sweat trickling down his back, running like water along his shoulders. How the 'finery workers survived in such conditions he did not know. Indeed, they were forced to take a rest and step away from the furnace mouth every ten minutes or so. Also the men drank huge draughts of water or even thick brown ale when they could afford it, for they sweated profusely and needed to replace lost moisture. He saw one furnace man take off his boot and pour a stream of liquid from it as though he had been walking in a river. But these coppermen were the topnotchers, the highest paid workers in the company, young strong men with muscles like steel and nerves that were even keener.

Sterling watched as a green oak sapling was fed into the steaming liquid that by now was gleaming like gold. Bubbles appeared on the surface of the molten metal and huge bursts of steam gushed forth, eliminating the remaining oxygen from the copper.

Sterling became aware that he was being watched. He turned sharply and saw a youth, ladle in hand, standing with feet apart, head back in an air of defiance. He could not have put into words more clearly his obvious disregard for the presence of the company owner.

'Who's that?' Sterling jerked his head in the youth's direction and Ben, following his glance, coughed into his handkerchief.

'That's young William Owens, sir,' he said. 'His father worked here once, rest his soul. Good family they are, the Owens.' He paused. 'Haven't had much to do with that one though, looks a bit uppity if you ask me.'

Sterling watched as the boy turned his back and ladled a scoop of molten copper from the furnace, tipping it swiftly into the waiting mould. His actions were careless and some of the gleaming liquid spilled onto the dampness of the floor. Immediately, the metal spat in all directions, cooling fast, becoming lethal weapons. Once touching flesh the metal would harden and set and would need to be prised out with a knife.

'That was not very clever.' Sterling approached Will Owens and spoke mildly. 'If you can't do the job then I suggest you get out of the sheds, there's a place for boys in the washroom.'

Will Owens smiled, he was a goodlooking youth with deep dimples in his swarthy skin. His hair was dark and his eyes implacably cold. He rubbed his sweating hands on the front of his red flannel shirt.

'Sorry, sir,' he said amiably. 'It won't happen again.'

'Make sure it doesn't.' Sterling was aware of the aggressive note in his voice and tried to moderate his tone a little. 'It's not only your safety that concerns me but that of the men working around you.' He turned to the manager hovering anxiously in the background. 'Come on, Ben, let's get out of here.'

It was cold in the yard yet even the biting wind seemed welcome after the searing heat of the sheds. 'He's a cocky young sod, that Will Owen,' Sterling said. 'I must keep my eye on him.' He wondered if he had ever been as young and immature as Owens or had he always known that the responsibility for the company would one day be his? Perhaps he envied the boy his freedom? Ludicrous, he thought wryly. Doubtless Owens would have given his right arm to change places with Sterling Richardson.

' 'Scuse me, sir but it's high time we were leaving for the ticketing.' Ben was consulting the heavy fob watch hanging on his waistcoat with a studious expression on his cold-reddened face. 'If we don't get a move on they'll start the bidding without us.'

'I'll get my coat.' Sterling glanced at Ben. 'I hope you'll enjoy riding in my Ascot.' He spoke dryly. 'I'm not bothering to take the horse and trap today.' Ben's expression was one of comic dismay.

'Me ride in that contraption, sir, you're not serious are you?'

Sterling laughed. 'Come along, get your overcoat from the office and button it up well; oh, and you'll have to hold onto your hat. Don't worry, you'll enjoy the experience once you get used to it.'

Ben was funny in his mistrust of the automobile; he stood staring at the Ascot as though it was the instrument of the devil.

'Get in, it won't bite.' Sterling concealed his amusement. 'I'll drive slowly, I promise, you'll be quite safe.'

'Yes, sir, right away.' Ben moved with more alacrity than usual, anxious to dispel the impression that he was afraid of the motor car. He sat awkwardly in the high seat, staring down at the cobbles as though wishing himself anywhere but in this newfangled invention that aspired to replace the horse.

'Quite a nice-looking machine, sir.' He spoke heartily as though not at all awed by the gleaming metal body and the powerful engine that sprang alarmingly into life as Sterling swung the starting handle.

'Not bad, is it?' Sterling smiled as he jumped into the seat beside Ben.

Once out onto the road, Sterling gave the car a little more thrust, increasing the speed, overtaking the flow of horse-drawn vehicles on the busy roadway leading to the centre of town. Ben clung fiercely to the seat, his face growing even redder than usual and regretfully, Sterling slowed the Ascot to a more moderate pace.

The cobbled street followed the curving line of the River Swan upon which was a ship, sails unfurled, gliding gracefully along high in the water. At her stern was a flotilla of flat-faced barges, piled high with green ore that glinted in the sunlight and Ben, forgetting his fear of motoring, pointed eagerly.

'The ore is going to auction now by the looks of it,' he said. 'I 'spects they'll take only the best samples to the Mackworth Arms as usual. Cunning devils these middle men, paying the foreigners a pittance and charging the smelters top rates.'

Sterling glanced at the manager quickly. 'This is the main reason for the decline of the copper trade, you know, Ben,' he said mildly. 'Perhaps now you'll understand my wish to make changes in the works.'

Sterling drew the Ascot into a small side road leading to the back of the hotel. 'Home sweet home.' He pulled up the handbrake and the car shuddered to a halt.

Ben climbed down from his seat stiffly, lifting his legs one by one as if to reassure himself he had sustained no injuries during the drive.

'Are you staying here then?' He jerked his head towards the rather dingy back of the Mackworth Arms. 'Quite handy, I suppose, after the ticketings you'll be able to go straight to your room.'

'It's all right as a temporary measure but I'll be glad when my own house is refurbished all the same.'

The bar of the hotel was crowded with buyers, smelters from all over South Wales. Most were well-clad businessmen wearing expensive overcoats and neat starched collars above well-filled waistcoats, but some were the small men, those who ran one or at the most two furnaces with the help of a handful of workers.

Glancing round, Sterling saw James Cardigan among the throng of people but before he could look away, James was raising his hand in acknowledgement.

'Morning Sterling, my boy.' He spoke cordially. 'Good turnout for the auction, we shall have to be on our toes today.'

Sterling concealed his irritation. 'Indeed we shall,' he agreed. 'But really James, there was no need for you to come along.' Although aware of the brusqueness in his voice, Sterling was powerless to alter his tone. James half turned away, exasperation and something else that Sterling could not read in the darkening of his eyes.

'It simply occurred to me that you might need a little support, seeing as this is your first time alone at the ticketings,' he said.

'You are mistaken.' Sterling spoke a little more smoothly. 'While my father was ill it naturally fell upon me to arrange the purchase of the ore, didn't you realise that?' If his tone implied criticism, Sterling thought, then so be it.

'I suppose I didn't think,' James conceded and Sterling felt almost sorry for him.

'As a partner, you are fully entitled to attend,' Sterling said. 'But you mustn't feel duty bound. I have Ben to fall back on and I think even you must bow to his judgment.'

'In that case, I shall leave everything to you.' James stepped back a pace. 'I'm sorry you are rejecting my support, Sterling, for I believe there is more between our two families than mere business ties, but I will not presume to push myself where I'm clearly not wanted.'

As James left the room, Sterling felt only relief. He resented the implication that he could not be astute at buying simply because of his youth. Where was James Cardigan, or Dean Sutton come to that, all the long months of Father's illness when a little help would have been appreciated?

Ben appeared at Sterling's side with a list in his hand. 'Look, sir, these are the asking prices, not much to choose between ores from Chile and those from South Africa.' He pursed his lips thoughtfully. 'I'd plump for the Chile load if I were you.'

Sterling nodded. 'I agree. Come on Ben, let's take our place. There are seats near the back – that way we can see who's buying what.'

The bidding was keen and Sterling found himself in the position of having to pay twenty guineas a ton for the crude ore.

'At this rate we'll need to sell twice as many brewing vessels just to break even,' he said in a whisper to Ben. The old man nodded his head slowly.

'I'm beginning to think you're right about the changes, sir,' he replied. 'We'll need to look at byproducts of the copper such as zinc and spelter, no doubt about it.'

Sterling kept his own council. It was steel he was more interested in, the hard sheet metal that was far stronger than copper and for which there seemed to be an ever growing demand. Well he had taken a step in the right direction with the introduction of new furnaces, he mused, but that was not enough, he would need to expand in a big way, even if it meant mortgaging Plas Rhianfa to the hilt. It was nothing but a great white elephant anyway, a symbol of the once great Richardson empire. His new house was much more practical with its modest four bedrooms and a manageable acreage of land. If matters came to the worst, Mother and Rickie could always move in with him, though the prospect of such an eventuality was enough incentive to spur anyone on to success, he told himself ruefully.

By the time the auction was over, he felt cloistered and in need of liquid refreshment.

'Take the rest of the day off, Ben,' he said evenly. 'The works can do without us both for an afternoon.'

Ben looked disapprovingly at him, taking out his handkerchief as he always did when perplexed and dabbing at his waxed moustache with it.

'If it's all the same to you, sir, I'll take the tram back up to Green Hill.' There was the merest trace of a smile in his pale eyes behind the glasses. 'A much more enjoyable means of transport than the car if you don't mind me saying so.'

'All right, Ben, please yourself.' Sterling left the crowded room which was still filled with the sound of many voices arguing loudly over the day's prices, and made his way through the heavily curtained and carpeted foyer with its plethora of potted plants. As he hurried up the stairs towards his room, the long corridor was empty and silent after the clamour below. He breathed a sigh of relief, taking his key out of his pocket, but to his surprise the door to his room stood open.

'Bea.' Sterling could not keep the surprise from his voice. 'What on earth are you doing here?' He moved into the room and closed the door, staring at her as though he'd never seen her before. She was seated in a chair near the window and had been presumably passing the time by watching the people on the pavement far below.

'I've brought you some patterns.' She smiled shyly. 'Look, isn't this material simply lovely? Just what you'll need for the curtains in the drawing room.'

'Bea, do you know that your father is downstairs and half the town with him?' He shook his head in exasperation. 'You were foolish to come here alone.'

Bea smiled up at him. 'Don't be angry, I didn't come alone, Bertha is with me. But even a maid likes a little time off now and again, she's having tea with her sister who lives in one of the cottages on the dock, she's not a stone's throw away. In any event, who will know except us? And don't worry about Daddy, he left some time ago. I saw him striding along the street at a great pace.' She bent down and brought a bottle out of her bag.

'This is for you.' She held it out to him smilingly, engagingly. 'It's to celebrate your inheritance. I don't expect anyone else has thought of making a toast to your future success. I wish I'd thought of it last week when I came to measure the windows at your house but in any case the builders were much in evidence making a dreadful fuss and noise.' She looked round her. 'This is much better.'

'All right, Bea,' Sterling sighed, 'it's a nice thought, but just one glassful and then you must be going. I don't want anyone gossiping about you.'

Bea's eyes were shining as she looked up at him. 'It's very kind of you to worry about my reputation Sterling, but I'm a woman now, or haven't you noticed?'

She was wearing a soft silk blouse through which the swell of her breasts could clearly be seen. Sterling looked away sharply.

'You certainly seem to have made yourself at home,' he said wryly, looking at her discarded coat and the large hat with numerous velvet bows decorating the crown. 'I'll ring for some glasses and then we'll have that drink before I take you home.'

'No need for glasses, I've brought my own.' Bea delved into her bag once more and busily unwrapped the glittering crystal goblets.

'Here's to you and me, Sterling, may we both prosper.'

The wine was heady and potent and Bea seemed determined to keep refilling his glass. Sterling sat on the bed; he had eaten very little that morning and he began to feel lightheaded. Bea settled herself beside him, pouring yet more wine, her eyes dark and lustrous.

'Hold on,' he protested, 'or you'll have me falling asleep and then you'll have to go home alone and serve you right.' He smiled, softening his words.

'Good isn't it?' Bea held her glass aloft, her cheeks flushed and her hair escaping from the confining pins. She looked desirable and slightly drunk and he found himself leaning forward to kiss her cheek. But she turned her face and his lips were upon hers and then he was holding her close, enjoying the resilience of her body against his own.

She seemed to be drawing him downwards upon the bed, her eyes wide, offering an invitation he could not resist. As he kissed her neck his hands were busy undoing the buttons of her blouse. Her skin was warm to the touch soft and fragrant, swamping his senses.

'Bea,' his voice was thick and as if she knew he was about to say something she didn't wish to hear, she raised herself up and pressed her moist mouth against his. Her arms were clinging around his neck, her body arched and her eyes were closed. It was clear she wanted him and deftly he opened the hooks that held her skirts in place. Eagerly now, he undressed her and stood back staring down at her nakedness.

She was so beautiful that it took his breath away. Her breasts were full and firm, her waist small. Her hips rose invitingly and Sterling moved down upon her, though even with his senses reeling he was careful not to bruise her sweet white flesh. She moaned a little, whether in pleasure or pain he could not tell.

He held her close, thrusting with more vigour now while she clung to him, head flung back, mouth open and small gasps escaping her full lips. She was a woman ripe for love, he thought ruefully, and if he had not harvested her then another man would soon have done so.

They moved together in a sweet age-old rhythm, she was past pain now, he realised, and was fully aroused, a mature woman needing release from her frustrations just as he did. Gently he turned on his back, holding her above him and her hair cascaded over her face so that she looked like a wanton.

At last she cried out in ecstasy, her face contorted by passion. She slumped sweetly against him, her hands cupping his face, her eyes staring down into his.

'I love you for that, Sterling,' she said, 'for giving me the greatest gift I could have asked of you.'

Carefully he moved away from her, stunned that he'd taken her as though she were some little hoyden from the whore-house on the Strand.

'Bea,' he began but then she was behind him, her arms around his waist, her face pressed against his back.

'Hush, please don't say anything and don't look round for I'm going to get dressed now.'

By the time Bertha came knocking at the door of the hotel room Bea was seated demurely in a chair near the window. Her hair was the perfection of tidiness but in her eyes there was a light that no one, least of all the perceptive Bertha, could miss.

Bea kissed Sterling's cheek with mock innocence. 'I may be allowed that much, mightn't I?' she asked archly. 'After all, we are almost like brother and sister. Please don't come downstairs, Bertha and I will take the tram home.'

When he was alone, Sterling sat staring at the empty wine bottle and wondered why the events of the last hour had left him feeling vaguely dissatisfied. He was almost inclined to call off the arrangement they had made to meet again and yet he needed a woman as did any fullblooded man and Bea was beautiful as well as passionate.

He moved to the window and stared out into the waning afternoon sun lying in great pools on the yard below. It was about time he was moving for there was still a great deal of work for him to do before nightfall.

Chapter Ten

March came into Sweyn's Eye with scarcely any lessening of the bitter cold weather and Mali shivered as she looked up at the greyness of the early morning sky which seemed to hang low over the Canal Street Laundry. At her side, Katie was sleepy and uncommunicative, holding her shawl around her head and shoulders with hands that were blue with the cold.

'How's William?' Mali asked and the words came out on small puffs of freezing air. Katie showed some animation for the first time since they'd left Copperman's Row.

'He's hale and hearty, so he is, fine buck of a man as I'm always tellin' you.'

Mali thrust her hands deep into her pockets and stared down at her black shiny boots, wondering if she would ever have a young buck come courting her. Katie coughed a little.

'Jesus, Mary and Joseph but it's cold, I'll be that glad when the spring weather comes in. And how's your dad doin' at the copper? Will tells me they all have ter work so much harder now that young Mr Richardson is the boss, a real slave driver he is, so it seems.'

'I'm sure that's not true,' Mali said quickly and at her side Katie gave a sniff that sounded more than a little derisory.

'I was forgettin' he's your idol Mali Llewelyn, and him so far above you as God himself.'

'Hush,' Mali said quickly; she did not like to hear Katie uttering blasphemy, somehow it unsettled her. In any event Sterling Richardson did not think himself far above her, he had given her his friendship, talked to her as though she was his equal, and she would not listen to a word against him.

'Dad's still meeting that woman,' she said, deliberately changing the subject. 'I keep smelling her scent on his clothes. There's dull men can be some times.'

'Seen him with her the other night so I did,' Katie replied. 'She clings to his arm as if she's in danger of falling down drunk in the roadway and that tatty fur thing around her neck makes me go cold all over so it does. Taken off some poor creature who never did any harm to no one and those dead eyes looking up at ye so forlorn.'

Mali laughed. 'Those are not real eyes, Katie, don't be silly. They're only glass.'

'I don't care a fig leaf about that, all I know is that once that was a fox and now it's dead and hung round her neck. No wonder she 'as to wear scent.'

They quickened their pace as the gates of the Canal Street Laundry came into sight.

'Look sharp, Mali.' Aggie stood alongside the entrance, her cap squashed firmly onto her thinning grey hair. 'Get boilers lit and no letting them go out today, is it?'

It irked Mali that she had never been allowed to forget her one mistake. Without replying to the old woman, she turned to Katie. 'I'll see you at grub time.'

'Sure and so you will.' Katie ran lightly up the narrow staircase and Mali moved towards the doors of the boiler house only to find Big Mary barring her way.

'Not in there *merchi*, not this morning. Doris dropped her babba some weeks back and is fit as a flea again and now she wants her old job back, which is only right and proper, mind.'

Mali looked at her in consternation. 'But what about me?' she asked, fearful of being dismissed.

Big Mary smiled. 'The way I look at it is this, you've proved you've got guts and that you're not afeared of hard work. You've got a bit up here, too.' She tapped her head. 'I'm bringing you up to the packing room – which is a privilege mind, so take care you earn it.'

Mali felt relief and a mingling of pride and triumph. She had done her job as stoker on the fires and done it so well that she was to be rewarded.

'Thank you, Mary,' she said and she was unable to keep the joy from her voice.

'Right, don't stand round all day, get up the stairs and begin work and tomorrow wear some decent clothes, you're a packer now.'

Katie's eyes lit up when she saw Mali making her way down the long room towards her.

'In the name of the Blessed Virgin what are you doing here?' she asked, but by the smile turning up the corners of her lips Katie already knew the answer.

'I'm a packer now, like you,' Mali said proudly. She settled herself next to Katie on the long wooden bench and stared at the neatly folded sheets before her.

'Don't you be worried,' Katie said. 'I'll show you how to pack properly and how to tie the safest knots and how to snap the string, you'll be the best packer here, next to Katie Murphy, that is.'

'In a pig's arse.' Sally Benson stood before the table, hands on hips, her hair tied severely away from her face giving her a somewhat bovine appearance. 'She can't even keep a boiler alight so my aunt Aggie tells me, and what good will she be as a packer? I'm not carrying her for one and if you do her work Katie Murphy you're a bigger fool than I took you for.'

Katie rose to her feet, her eyes fiery. 'Shut your gob Sally or be Jesus I'll shut it for you.'

Mali caught Katie's arm. 'Take no notice,' she said quickly, 'It's only talk. Sticks and stones may break my bones but words will never hurt me.' She smiled as she repeated their childhood chant, trying to ease the tension.

'Fool.' With a look of disgust, Sally Benson turned away, her departure hastened by the sight of Big Mary entering the room.

'I hate that bitch,' Katie said through clenched teeth. 'She's always trying to poke fun at me and so far I've put up with her jibes because I'm afeared to start brawling and perhaps lose my job. But if she's goin' to pick on you then something must be done about her.'

'Leave it be and just show me the packing, there's a good girl,' Mali said, but she was grateful and touched by Katie's loyalty.

The morning passed swiftly and pleasantly for Mali, it was good to be in clean surroundings with the scent of hot fresh linen permeating the long room. It was a far cry from hauling scuttles of coal to and fro and crouching in the dust feeding the fires, breathing in the acrid taste of smoke and cinders. She soon became nimble at folding the huge linen sheets that belonged to the big houses of the area and placing them on shiny brown paper, packing them as though they were sandwiches. Unwary of the sharp edges of the paper, she cut herself once and instantly sucked at her finger, fearful of spilling blood onto the crisp linen.

'I see you're taking to the job like a duck to water.' Big Mary paused at the table, staring down from her great height at Mali. She was dark haired, with large features and piercing black eyes and there were those who said there was a bit of the gypsy in Big Mary. And yet there was a noble, determined cut to her brow and chin that commanded respect far more than did her immense stature.

'Find it a bit different to the boiler room, don't you?' Big Mary leaned over and neatly folded a corner of a sheet into place, flicking it with her fingers and deftly eliminating the creases.

'It's lovely here,' Mali agreed. She was a little in awe of Big Mary and fumbled a little over the packing. 'Katie's been a good help to me,' she said. 'Teaching me knots and things, I expect I'll improve, get much faster once I'm used to it.'

Big Mary nodded and continued along the workroom, her eagle eyes missing nothing. Mali sighed with relief, she had been nervous with the overseer watching her.

'What's wrong with you, are the fleas bitin' again?' Katie's laughing eyes met Mali's. 'I see you're a little bit afeared of Big Mary and 'tis only natural, so I was myself until I came to know her better. Don't do to take no liberties but for all that she's a good boss to work for.'

Mali stared down at the string in her fingers. 'I suppose I am a bit frightened but it's of getting the boot, Katie. I don't know what I'd do now if I had to stay at home, especially with that Rosa coming and going at all times of the day and night. Thinks she owns the house, she does. Aye, and Dad along with it.'

'Don't take on so.' Katie rested her hand on Mali's arm. 'Your dad is a grown man and can't get what he wants from you. Though I've heard tell of men who abuse their own daughters, so be grateful for Rosa and don't take it all so seriously.'

Mali stared at her friend soberly. 'But he's talking of marriage, Katie, how could I bear to have that woman living under the same roof?'

'And who says he's talking of marriage? She does, not him I'll be bound, for your dad's got more sense than that. Jesus, Mary and Joseph, do you tink he'd walk up the aisle with the likes of her? Ashamed he'd be and that's the God's truth.'

'I suppose you're right.' But even as Mali settled earnestly to work she could not help thinking that perhaps Rosa was even now sitting before the fire in the small house in Copperman's Row.

A short time after the girls had finished their grub break, a ripple of excited chatter passed between the packers. Big Mary moved at a swift pace along the room, her eyes more keen than usual and with a manner that could almost be described as flustered.

'Mr Waddington is coming on a tour of inspection, girls.' Big Mary's voice rang commandingly down the length of the packing room. 'He has already been around the boilerhouse and will be by here with us in just a few minutes so look sharp all of you and on your best behaviour, mind, or it's me you'll have to answer to.'

'Blessed Mother save us.' Katie crossed herself quickly and jogged Mali's arm. 'Don't just sit there gawping, look as if you're busy even if there's nothing to do but tie the same knot twice.'

Mali felt her heart begin to beat swiftly as she wondered why everyone was so nervous.

'Is something wrong?' she asked and Katie rolled her eyes towards heaven in exasperation.

'Mr Waddington is the owner of the Canal Street Laundry, sure an' you must have heard of him.' She began folding her parcel of sheets rapidly as though in fear of her very life.

The door opened and a tall man with greying hair came into the long room. He wore an overcoat that reached almost to his ankles and around his neck was a bright silk scarf. As he drew nearer, Mali could see that his moustache was neatly waxed and his eyes were twinkling, he did not seem at all like the ogre she had been expecting.

He moved around the tables, speaking to one girl and then another and each of them bobbed him a curtsey. Mali bit her lip as Big Mary led him across the room, hoping that she would not be all fingers and thumbs.

'This is our new girl, Mali Llewelyn, Mr Waddington.' Big Mary spoke deferentially. 'I think she is going to be very good once she gets the hang of things.'

'Fine, just fine.' Mr Waddington scarcely looked at her and Mali felt a sense of disappointment as he passed her by and moved on to the next circle of waiting girls.

'I don't know what the fuss is all about,' she whispered to Katie. 'He's just an old man, that's all.'

'Maybe so,' Katie replied, 'but he could buy and sell half the town if he so wished, he's so rich that his cellar is filled with gold so I've heard.'

Mali heaved a sigh of relief when Mr Waddington at last disappeared down the stairs. 'How often does he come round inspecting the laundry?' she asked and Katie bit her finger thoughtfully.

'About once a month, I suppose, to be sure I'm not that certain but he's always very nice to us, gives us a gift at Christmas an' all. Last time I got a silk scarf and a blue ribbon but then I think Mr Waddington tells Big Mary to buy for us and she picks out what she thinks we'd like.'

It seemed as though the entire laundry was upset by the visit of the owner, for several minutes after he'd gone there was a babble of voices as the girls vyed with each other, each claiming that Mr Waddington had given them more attention than anyone else. Mali wrapped her linen carefully, quicker now at the tricky knots, feeling only an impatience to get home and fall into a chair and rest. Not that there was much chance of that, she thought ruefully, there was a great deal of ironing to be done as well as some mending.

Aggie from the boilerhouse came to the door of the long room, her sleeves rolled above her elbows and her arms and hands red from the steam. She looked round truculently, her clay pipe clamped between her lips. After a moment, she removed the pipe, gesturing with it towards Mali.

'Hey you, new girl, you've to make tea for the boss, and quick about it.'

Mali looked at her in bewilderment. 'Me?' she asked pointing to herself, and the woman nodded vigorously.

'Yes, you who let the boiler go out, come on, there's no good to be gained by keeping the boss waiting.'

Katie gave her a gentle push 'Go on, you'll see a small building out in the yard, that's the office. It's there you'll be making the tea, you'll do just fine so don't go worrying.'

Mali hurried down the stairs and out into the coldness of the early afternoon sunshine that was still pale but offering, in its slanting rays of brightness, a promise that spring was on the way.

At the same time that Mali was crossing the yard of the Canal Street Laundry, Will Owens was leaving the gates of the Richardson Copper Company, his shift over for the day. His arms ached as though a fire burned in his muscles, his face was caked with particles of copper dust and his throat was dry. The jug of brown ale he'd drunk while on shift had only whetted his appetite for more and so he turned his footsteps towards the harbour and the welcoming open doors of the Cape Horner.

He was not in a very good frame of mind for Sterling Richardson had been round spying again, watching his every move, treating him as though he were some ignorant child with a snotty nose. Will prided himself on his physical strength, he knew he could whip young Mr Richardson to a pulp if it came to a fist fight. But that was not the style of the gentry, they preferred to wound with words and looks, giving out disdain and expecting gratitude in return.

The public was crowded and Will made his way to the bar, shouldering men aside, eager to slake the thirst that was clawing at him like a tiger. He had worked long and hard, on shift at first light, ladling molten copper until the veins stood out proud on his arms and neck and for what? For the benefit of the uppity Richardson family who weren't even Welsh, damn them.

He took his mug of ale and sat near the open fire that roared in the huge grate, oblivious to the man slumped on the oak settle beside him. He took a huge draught of beer and enjoyed the feeling of it trickling down the back of his throat.

'Been working the copper?' The man at his side leaned forward, lean face and narrow eyes in a ferrety face, turned towards him. Will nodded.

'Aye but what's it got to do with you?' He did not feel in the mood for friendly conversation but the man at his side was persistent.

'Used to work for the copper company myself until that bastard Richardson saw fit to dismiss me.'

Will was suddenly interested. 'Is that so, what work did you do?' He eyed the man who was perhaps a year or two older than himself, a dandy in a striped waistcoat and trousers to match and a topcoat of finest worsted. 'Not at the furnace mouth, I'll be bound.'

'I was a chemist, Travers is the name, Glanmor Travers. What do you think of your new young boss then?'

Will spat in the sawdust on the floor. 'Don't give a cuss for him,' he said flatly.

Travers smiled slowly. 'Then we've something in common.' He lit a cigar and puffed out the fragrant smoke, watching as it spiralled up towards the grimy ceiling. 'I've seen you here before,' he remarked. 'Thought you looked like a well set up chap and one with a bit of sense in your head, how's about we get together, see if we can't do Mr Sterling Richardson a disfavour?'

'What would you have in mind?' Will concealed his eagerness.

Travers shrugged. 'As yet, nothing very concrete.' His slow, somewhat unpleasant smile appeared again. 'But just give it time, I'm sure I can come up with something.'

'Right you are.' Will slammed his mug on the table top in front of him, staring meaningfully at its emptiness.

'Like another?' Travers asked obligingly, and holding up his hand snapped his fingers in the air.

The landlord appeared at his side as if by magic, leaning over Travers and rubbing his hands against his apron. 'What can I get for you sir?' he asked and Travers pointed to the mug.

'More ale for my friend here and a hot toddy for me. Have something yourself, Landlord.'

It was easy to see why Travers was fawned upon, Will mused, if a man had money to throw around it was no wonder he had people like the landlord of the Cape Horner at his beck and call. But Travers would find he could not buy Will, not for a king's ransom. Yet though he did not trust the ferret-faced chemist, he was instinctively drawn to him for here was another who shared his resentment of Sterling Richardson. He decided that for the moment, he would play a waiting game, see what transpired. In the meantime it would do no harm to keep in the man's good books.

'The next round is on me,' he said picking up his full mug of ale and drinking thirstily. 'There seems to be quite a lot for us to talk about.'

Travers was looking at him as though he could see right through him and that disconcerted Will. He shifted uncomfortably in his seat.

'Anything wrong?' he asked a little more aggressively than he'd intended and Travers leaned back, smiling to himself. After a moment, he shook his head, dragging on the end of his cigar, his heavy-lidded eyes half closed.

'I was just thinking how fortunate it was meeting like this, I'm sure it will be to our mutual benefit.'

'Aye, you could be right.' Will was feeling lightheaded, he had eaten nothing all day and his belly growled with hunger. Shortly he would have to leave for home and eat the food his mother would have put on the table for him and after that he was to meet Katie.

There was a sudden stirring in his loins. Perhaps he would take her up onto the Town Hill, to the old, disused hut they had found that hid them from prying eyes. Katie was a lovely girl and liked what he did to her right enough but the trouble was she imagined that he was serious about her. It was easy to tell that she was hoping for a ring on her finger but girls like Katie Murphy from a family of poor Irish were for pleasuring, not marrying. He placed his empty mug on the table and leaned forward.

'Landlord, another round of drinks over here,' he called and when the man scuttled to do his bidding, he flushed with pride.

It might be a good idea, he decided, to keep in with this man Travers, perhaps there were a few other little tricks he might learn from him.

Chapter Eleven

The moon lay low over the horizon, incandescent and magnificent, cutting a pathway of light through the inky seas. The wind drifted inshore, bringing with it the tang of salt as it ruffled the grass on the western slope of the hill above Sweyn's Eye. Below in the valley, even the sprawling ugly copper works were beautified by the silver glow.

Katie sat beside William, her breathing ragged and uneven, for a few minutes ago she had been cocooned with him in the privacy of the old hut. He had held her so fiercely and so close to him that his heartbeat had mingled with her own. She had been one with him, lifted high on the wings of passion, her self doubts lost in the joy of the moment.

He had left her arms abruptly then, swinging open the creaking door of the shed and striding half clothed outside. Seating himself on a small tump of grass, he stared out to sea, a brooding dark look on his face.

Katie knew the bite of his rejection and it cut deep. She buttoned up her bodice, feeling like a street girl, for William had torn himself from her embrace as soon as his crisis had come, showing no consideration for her feelings. He had left her unsatisfied and strangely empty and tears she feared to shed trembled on her lashes.

It seemed unbelievable now that she had once boasted to Mali about her cleverness. She had flaunted her knowledge of how to avoid conceiving a child and now, like a punishment upon her, it was the thing she most wanted in all the world.

She gazed up into the sky and the stars were blurred by her tears.

'Blessed Virgin if you can hear, please help me,' she whispered.

Suddenly her thoughts crystallised and with startling clarity, she realised that all that she had valued so little – a home, children and a man to come back to her each night – were the very things she longed for. A son just like William to hold close in her arms. Jesus, Mary and Joseph, she wanted the babby so much that she could almost feel him suckling from her breast.

A strange rebellious longing had come upon her when she knew William was coming to his moment, she had briefly held him fast, defying him to withdraw from her, but then she had been afraid, feared of his anger and scorn and more deeply of the fact that he might leave her should she demand too much of him. And so her arms had released him and had felt cold and empty.

She raised her head and looked up at him, he was buttoning his trousers, tucking in his striped flannel shirt, and he seemed oblivious to her presence. How wonderful it would be to lie beside him in a real bed, she thought wistfully.

He crouched down, tying the laces on his boots, and she reached out a tentative hand to touch his fingers. He smiled but his eyes were pools of darkness and she could see no expression in them.

She bit her lips, feeling the sting of tears on her lashes, for it seemed to her that once William had tasted of her flesh he almost despised her for what she had given him so willingly.

She wondered what he must be like when he was working in the copper, for sure his mind never strayed to her and yet she thought of him constantly as she packed sheets and wrapped them in brown paper and tied knot after knot. Even as she laughed and joked with Mali, William was there like part of her, influencing everything she did.

When she thought of him working in the heat and stink of the sheds, she died a hundred deaths. Her vivid imagination saw him labouring before the terrible, gaping mouth of the furnace and sometimes in the night she could awake in terror having dreamed that the copper, molten and cruel, had spewed forth to smother him.

The grass beneath her felt soft now, like a bed, and she wished that she could lie here in William's arms all night. In spite of the darkness, the hour was not late and in the public bars the men would still be drinking ale, singing out their misery and pain and then groping beneath the skirts of fancy women who opened their legs for a few pennies.

She wondered if she was as sinful as they, letting William have his fill of her before she was properly betrothed to him. Did he think of her as a side piece or did he love her, just a little? These were questions she could never ask for William was a man who kept his own counsel.

Katie pushed back her long flowing hair that shone like red silk in the moonlight. She had no idea that her beauty was rare and fragile and it was a source of wonder to her that a man like William should desire her.

He leaned towards her now, his mouth warm against the column of her throat and she clung to him, grateful that he had come back to her from the lost world of his own thoughts. She took his face in her hands wanting to kiss his mouth, but he was unresponsive and after a moment, he drew away.

'We'd better go.' He rose to his feet in one swift movement and stood tall against the backdrop of the sea and sky. Below them, the waves washed softly against the silvered beach and in the silence of the night, Katie could almost imagine that the two of them were alone in the world.

'I don't want to go home, not yet.' She spoke softly, pleadingly, but William reached out his hand, drawing her to his side. She brushed down her skirts and pulled her shawl around her shoulders, head bent to hide her tears. It was difficult to push her feet into her boots and William, impatient with her, strode away down the hill, hands thrust deep into his pockets, head back, whistling a thin tuneless melody that fell coldly on the night air, and Katie was bereft.

Hurriedly, she caught him up and in silence they continued the trek down the grassy slopes of the Town Hill which, being high above the town, had escaped the virulent copper smoke and was not barren of verdure as was the Kilvey Hill on the opposite side of the valley. Katie skirted a prickly gorse bush and followed William as swiftly as she could for he was taking long strides and was outpacing her.

She stared at his back and knew deep within her that theirs was no love union for William despised the background from which she'd come. He had been unable to conceal his disdain when he'd first taken her home, standing outside the small cottage in Market Street over which hung the continual smell of fish.

He himself had been given a good chapel upbringing and his mother was the widow of a copperman, a 'finery worker who was paid top money and this was something that Katie was not allowed to forget. William did not put his feelings into words, he did not need to, but his intolerant attitude to the Irish Catholics in the Green Hill district bruised and hurt so much that she sometimes retreated into a well of silence.

'You'll be all right if I leave you here, won't you?' They had reached the corner of Market Street and Copperman's Row now and he was moving from one foot to the other as though impatient to be gone. Looking at him, Katie found it hard to believe that on occasions he held her close and whispered words of love into her ear. He was like two people, so changeable that she felt she did not know him at all.

'Of course I'll be all right,' she replied but her heart was heavy as she watched him stride away. He had made no mention of when they would meet again. His manner towards her was becoming more and more casual and it troubled Katie, for she liked to know where she stood. But she had learned a sharp lesson right at the beginning of her relationship with William, he was a man who did not like to be pinned down.

'And where do you tink you've been until this hour?' Katie's father stood in the doorway under the slanting light from the gas lamp on the pavement. He was bare to the waist and his red hair gleamed with droplets of water and she knew he had been trying to wash away the interminable smell of fish.

Katie slid past him into the warmth of the kitchen and moved towards the fire that burned low in the grate. Alongside the hearth, in his pram with no wheels, baby Sean lay grizzling, his face red, his small fists waving in the air as though in protest.

'I'm talking to you, girl, where have you been?' Tom repeated his question and Katie took a deep breath before answering him.

'I've been walking up in the hills.' She put her shawl carefully over the back of a chair, hoping that no telltale pieces of grass would shake loose from its folds. 'And I've been down near Mount Pleasant where the houses are tall and posh, and thinking I was how much I'd like to live in one of them. Blessed Mother, is that wrong of me now?'

Her father gave her a sharp cuff across the head. 'Don't you go taking the name of the Virgin in vain for I'll not have it. Now will you stop that babby's noise, for his crying fair destroys me?'

'Where's me mother?' Katie lifted Sean in her arms and he lay against her sweet and heavy. Tom jerked his head in the direction of the stairs.

'Gone up to bed, she's settled the other childer down for the night and was waiting for you to come home to see to Sean.'

'Well I'm here now.' Katie felt guilty at the reproach in her father's voice for he was useless with the little ones. 'And all the boy needs is washing and changing.' She rested Sean on her knees. 'Then he'll go off to sleep for he's a peaceful enough child.'

The baby gulped into silence, his chin quivering with the prolonged effort of his crying. His small plump arms with bracelets of flesh around the wrists were still now as he lay quiescent, seeming to know instinctively that he was being cared for by loving hands.

Katie smelled the acrid tang of the boy's urine as she dropped the sodden cloth from his loins onto the floor. 'Poor babby, you only want to be clean and dry don't you and sure that's not much to be asking from life.' She kissed his round cheek and his searching mouth turned as though seeking succour.

'There, I'll put some egg white on your little sore backside and soon you'll feel much better, my babby.'

When she had dressed Sean in his nightclothes with the long overgown, the end of which was pinned up over his feet, she rose reluctantly from her chair. There was nothing more she could do for the little one now except give him to her ma to suckle.

'I'll take him up then Dad,' she said. 'Are you going to kiss him good night?'

'I'll kiss him sure enough, glad to have some peace from the boy so I am.' Tom's arm rested on his daughter's shoulder for a moment. 'Such a fine little mother you'd make yourself, Katie girl, when are you going to bring a fine young buck home to meet your ma and me?'

'Oh go away with you, Dad.' Katie brushed his arm aside. 'Sure there's plenty of time for that.'

When Katie entered the bedroom, her mother was fast asleep. Jess's cheeks were sunken for she had lost most of her back teeth and yet there was still an air of prettiness about her as, with her dark hair loose about her face, she relaxed against the pillows.

'Mammy, wake up,' Katie said gently. 'Sean wants feedin' so he does.' She sat at the side of the bed waiting as her mother rubbed her eyes sleepily.

'Oh give the boy here, 'tis only a moment since I closed my eyes.' Jess put the baby onto her thin breast and waved her daughter away.

'Go and make me a cup o' tea, there's a good girl,' she said, her hand resting on her throat. 'I'm that parched I could drink the sea dry so I could.'

Katie left her mother and looked into the small box-like bedroom next door and saw that her brothers were asleep. Kevin and Michael were like two peas in the same pod and with scarcely a year between them they were almost like twins. She sighed, it might have been good to have one other girl in the family, a sister in whom she could confide her feelings and doubts about William.

She paused in the darkness of the landing, looking down into the well of the stairs. She could feel again the way William's strong body had taken possession of her own and love flowed through her like fire. She felt sure that the Holy Mother would forgive her the sins of her flesh even if Father O'Flynn would not.

When Katie returned to the kitchen, her father was sitting before the fire, his long legs stretched out towards the dying embers. He looked tired and Katie noticed that there was a hole in the toe of his sock. She rested her head against his shoulder.

'Sure an I'll have to do some darnin' round here,' she said. 'Just look at you with your big feet showin' for all to see, it's ashamed I am.'

Tom smoothed the hair back from her face. 'You're right girl, but you won't do any darnin' on these socks – not tonight at least, for I'm off down the Mex' for a pint before the public closes.' He drew on his boots and Katie watched him in silence for a moment.

'Do you have to go out, Dad?' she asked at last. 'It's gettin' that late, you should be in your bed by rights, you look tired.'

'Ah but a few pints of ale will liven me up,' he smiled. 'An' since when do I have to answer for my doing to me own daughter?' He opened the door and a rush of cold air swept into the kitchen.

'Look tired yourself, so you do, there are shadows beneath those eyes of yours that I don't like to see so get off to your room now, do you hear?' He left, closing the door with a loud bang and Katie sank into a chair, staring into the almost dead fire.

Soft footfalls sounded on the stairs and Jess poked her head into the room, staring round her with wide eyes.

'Has himself gone out then at this time o' night?' she asked. Without waiting for a reply, she came into the kitchen, hugging a thick knitted shawl around her thin frame. The night-gown that trailed over her bare feet had been patched so many times that it had the appearance of a quilt.

'Dad's only gone for a pint or two,' Katie said in her father's defence. She watched as her mother rubbed her eyes sleepily and a great sadness filled her. She wondered if her mammy had ever loved Tom or he her, at any rate they were almost indifferent to each other now, like strangers sharing the same house.

'I think Dad only drinks so that he can sleep soundly in his bed at night.' She didn't know why she felt it necessary to defend Tom and she wasn't surprised when Jess sniffed derisively.

'There's more on your dad's mind than sleep when he's in his cups, girl,' she said softly. She sighed long and hard. 'And I'm far too tired to put up with his pesterin' tonight.'

Katie was embarrassed to hear her mother talk that way and she rose, placing a few sticks on the fire, bending over the embers to blow on them and bring them into life.

'Do you want that cup of tea now, Mammy?' she asked and

her mother's chair creaked as she rocked herself to and fro, hugging her shawl around her shoulders.

'I do that.' Her mother pulled at the back of Katie's skirt. 'Look at me girl, you've been out with that young pup William Owens haven't you? Tell me the truth now, 'cos I know it sure enough when you lie to me.'

'Yes, I've been out with William, so what about it? I haven't been doing any wrong.' The words almost burnt her lips but she had to say them. Her mother wasn't convinced.

'Look, girl, don't go bringing trouble home here now will you? Your father thinks the sun shines out of your ass, he'd kill you for sure if he thought you was playin' around.'

Katie's mouth was dry, she didn't know what her mother expected her to say and so she remained silent, edging the kettle over the small flame, hearing the welcome sound of the water singing to the boil.

'Take a lesson from your own mother,' Jess continued remorselessly. Her hand gestured to the drabness of the room with its meagre furnishings. 'I don't want you to end up like this, you can have better, believe me, but you must hold out on a man, don't give him nothin' until he puts a ring on your finger. Please Katie, listen to your mammy, I only wants what's good for you.'

The urgency of Jess's voice surprised Katie. She watched her mother lean forward, the shawl slipping from her thin shoulders. 'Be good, Katie, that's all I'm asking you, for the joys of the body don't last.'

Katie hung her head and her glowing hair fell like a curtain of silk over her face, a shield between herself and her mother's probing eyes. Surely her mother's words were not true, life could not turn sour, not while she had William to love.

Jess sighed again, heavily. 'From what I know of this William Owens, he's not the sort for marryin'. Seen his kind before, burnin' with a fever he is, wishin' only to leave this place behind him and look for better things, he's not for you, my little Katie.'

Pain raged low in Katie's belly, she felt that she would explode with the anguish rising inside her. 'What are you trying to do, Mammy, destroy me?' she asked and the tears slipped soundlessly down her cheeks. In a moment, Jess had gathered her into her arms, holding Katie to her thin breast.

''Tis to save you hurt I'm speakin' so,' she said, her voice harsh. 'And lettin' a man take his pleasure o' you does not bind him, beast gives as much to beast.'

For a long moment, Katie clung to Jess knowing instinctively the truth of her words. At last, uneasily, she drew away from her mother.

'Things have changed now, Mammy,' she said. 'It's different to when you were a girl back in Ireland.' And yet within her was the unwanted thought that the only time she actually possessed William was when he lay in her arms, wanting her.

Jess smiled thinly. 'Men do not change their nature, Katie.' She returned to her seat and resumed rocking to and fro, her eyes more heavily shadowed than ever. 'You must learn that for yourself no doubt, but just believe this, what a man gets easily, he does not value highly and that's the truth an' I'll swear it by all the saints in heaven, so I will.'

Katie made the tea and as she stared down into the fragrant liquid, her spirits had never been lower and she wanted only to crawl into her bed and hide, hide from the truth that was clamouring inside her heart, body and soul that William only wanted one thing from her and that he could buy from any flossy in the street.

Chapter Twelve

Sterling sat in the office staring out, into the soft spring sunshine. He had just received an order from Smithson's, a large manufactory just outside the town, for two tons of zinc wire and at the competitive price of a hundred pounds a ton it was a very gratifying start to his new enterprise.

Once he'd had the idea, it had taken only a matter of weeks to convert the old outhouse into a small foundry, equipping it with moulding boxes, cores and sand at very little expense. It was more difficult finding a skilled pattern maker and a fettler but in that too he had been successful.

He had struck lucky because the production of zinc wire, which had such tenacity and strength that a cable one tenth of an inch in diameter was capable of supporting a weight of around twenty-six pounds, was not being produced at all in the vicinity of Sweyn's Eye.

'Morning, Mr Richardson, you're in early today.' Ben entered the office and ambled towards his desk, shrugging off his topcoat. In spite of the sunshine the day was sharp and cold.

'Look at this, Ben.' Sterling waved the order sheet at him. 'We're in business, the demand for zinc wire is increasing. I feel more than justified in turning that old building into a foundry.'

Ben stared down at the paper, reading it with agonising slowness. He plucked at the ends of his moustache, his lips pursed thoughtfully, his bushy eyebrows drawn together in a frown.

'Very good,' he said at last. 'But this order won't cover the cost of the main alterations you plan for the sheds. If you mean to go over to zinc processing in a big way then you'll need a lot more orders like this.'

'Let's walk before we can run, Ben,' Sterling said reasonably.

Ben dropped the sheet on the desk before him. 'The workmen don't like it you know, don't like it at all,' he said. 'They feel that their own jobs in the copper are threatened and you can't blame them.'

Sterling leaned forward in his chair. 'I've heard nothing,' he said. 'But then I don't suppose I would. You should have told me about this sooner. I expected some resistance of course but there's no need for any man to fear dismissal.'

Ben tapped the red ledgers on the desk before him. 'This is my responsibility, Mr Richardson,' he said stiffly. 'If you want someone to play the part of a spy then get someone more suited to the job.'

Sterling held up his hand. 'You're right Ben, of course, and I take it all back.' He chewed thoughtfully at the end of his pen. 'Still, it's just as well to be informed of what happens in my own works and your suggestion might be a good one. Who would prove the most useful of the men in that direction?' Ben shook his head, his mind almost visibly ticking over.

'If you're serious then I think that young pup Will Owens might be the one,' he said at last. 'Most of the workers are too proud to spy on their fellows, not a respectable job to give to anyone, if you'll excuse me saying so, but a keen, ambitious chap like Owens, he might just take it on.'

Sterling's first reaction was to discard out of hand the idea of asking anything of Will Owens but when he paused to think about it, Ben was right, no decent hardworking copper man would go cap in hand to the boss in order to tell tales on his fellows. It needed someone unscrupulous for that.

'It looks as if you have visitors, Mr Richardson.' Ben's voice brought Sterling back from his reverie and he looked up in time to see James Cardigan and Dean Sutton striding along the yard towards the office.

'I'd forgotton they were coming,' Sterling said. 'I suggest, Ben, that you go and check on the new furnaces, anything that will keep you out of the office for half an hour.'

Ben rose with as much alacrity as he could muster, and

swung open the door, allowing the two men to enter before beating a hasty retreat. Sterling rose slowly to his feet.

'Gentlemen, this is indeed a pleasure.' His irony was not lost on his partners, Dean's face flushed even redder than the cold had made it and James shook his head, seating himself on the chair Ben had just vacated.

'We haven't come here to quarrel with you, Sterling,' he said reasonably. 'It's just that we would like to know more about your proposed innovations, you've told us very little so far.' He coughed uncomfortably and looked at Dean who was pacing to and fro before the tall stove, holding his hands out to the flames in an absentminded gesture.

'All I can do is to apologise,' Sterling said affably. 'It's just that I didn't think you would be overly interested in my small plans.'

Dean swung around and stared directly at him and Sterling was surprised at the dislike in the American's eyes. Surely the changes he'd so far made could not have upset Dean that much?

'We are partners in the firm.' Dean sounded aggressive. 'Of course we are interested. You seem to think it enough to feed us titbits of information but it's not. My money isn't yielding very much profit at the moment and I'd very much like to know why.'

'Sit down,' Sterling said smoothly, 'and then I'll try to explain the situation to you.'

'Don't patronise me, boy,' Dean said, frowning heavily.

Sterling shrugged, where Dean Sutton was concerned it seemed he could do nothing right.

'It's just that over the past years the company has steadily gone downhill,' he said. 'My father was doing his best, I'm sure of it, but it wasn't enough. Countries like Chile and Australia have caught us up and passed us in the art of smelting. We have been too insular, keeping our process a secret, forcing other countries all over the world to find their own methods of production. Unfortunately they have proved quicker than our own.'

'I understand that, Sterling.' James's tone was pleasant. 'I'm sure you mean well but can we afford to make big changes here at the present moment? That's the question.'

129

Sterling turned to him quickly. 'I've made no big changes yet, all I've actually done is to convert an old building into a foundry at little cost.' He tapped the paper on the desk before him. 'This order for wire more than justifies those modest changes.'

Dean was not to be mollified. 'Well I don't think you are experienced enough to go ahead with any big plans for converting to zinc,' he said. 'Keep your little foundry by all means but forget any major developments.'

Sterling forced down the anger that was growing within him. Dean was being deliberately awkward and unpleasant.

He rose from his chair and moved over to the window. 'Don't worry,' he said at last, 'if I risk anything it will be my own capital.' What he didn't say was that the money was raised by mortgaging Plas Rhianfa.

'Well in that case, I think we must let you go ahead with your plans, Sterling,' James said encouragingly.

Reluctantly Sterling turned to face him. It was clear he had James's sympathy but Sterling needed to say what was on his mind.

'I must point out that if you take no risks, you gain nothing of the profits, either.'

James shrugged. 'That sounds fair enough to me.' He put on his hat and made for the door. 'Come along Dean, we've taken up quite enough of Sterling's time, let's go and have a hot toddy at the Mackworth Arms.'

Sterling watched them go then returned to his desk, and nothing could change the small glow of triumph he felt as he looked down at the order in front of him.

Bea entered Sterling's room in the Mackworth Arms and took her customary seat near the window, the same one she'd occupied when she had first ventured into the hotel six weeks ago. Since then she had come to love Sterling more fiercely than ever before and she shivered now as she remembered the hours of happiness they had shared, lying together in the large bed, stealing whatever moments they could without arousing suspicion. It was not altogether satisfactory but it was the best arrangement they could make, for the present at least.

They had spent one glorious afternoon last week, making love until dusk had touched the room with shadows. Sterling had raised her to heights that she could never even have begun to dream of.

She had enjoyed a blissful few days after the event, telling herself that it could not be wrong to give herself to the man she loved and hoped one day to marry, but then her euphoria had worn thin as the days passed and there was no sign from Sterling that he wanted to see her again. Indeed when they did meet at her instigation, it was amongst a crowd of workmen at his new house where she had been hard put to speak to him at all let alone have a private conversation. And the longing to ask him if he cared for her, even a little, had gone unappeased.

The room was growing dim and with a sigh, Bea rose and lit the gas lamp that jutted from the wall. She had bribed one of the chambermaids to let her into the room just as she'd done before and she had not been insensitive to the way the girl had looked at her. But by now it had become imperative to speak to Sterling alone.

Her heart seemed to turn over with fear and her hands shook as she arranged the folds of her skirts around her knees, sitting near the window once more, watching for his return.

It had not been difficult to send Bertha on another visit to her sister's house on the docks. Indeed her maid had been all too anxious to accept the unexpected break in routine but now, sitting alone, Bea hoped and prayed that Sterling would not be long for she could scarcely endure the fears and uncertainties that had raged within her ever since the morning she had spoken with Dr Thomas. She must confide in someone and soon.

She closed her eyes for a moment in pain and shame and yet beneath all the tension there was a small glimmer of happiness and hope. If only Sterling would marry her then all would be well. But what if he despised her once he knew the truth?

'Oh, God.' She covered her face with her hands, she had no one to blame for what had happened but herself, after all it had been none of Sterling's doing, she had seduced him, a woman desperate for affection. And her own description was much kinder than any that other people would apply to her if the truth should come out. She rose to her feet once more and stared through the window. She could see the tall pointing masts of a sailing ship and the lights from the harbour flashing over the water like jewels cast aside.

Sterling was late, what if he did not intend coming back to the hotel tonight? Fear held her in its dark grip and she rested her head against the window, fighting back the tears that threatened to course down her cheeks. What a sorry sight she must be, an unmarried lady bearing within her an illegitimate child. It was so ridiculous as to be absurd; people like her were the subject of music-hall jokes. At last, in resignation, she picked up her gloves and drew them on. She could wait no longer, Bertha would be returning from her sister's house and might even now be pacing the pavement outside the hotel.

Once in the street, she looked along the empty roadway and felt bereft. If only she could see Sterling, tell him of her dilemma, he would surely not allow her to suffer alone? He was young it was true but he had at least some regard for her, if not love, and he was possessed of a man's strength and confidence. God, how she needed that now.

'Miss Bea, I'm sorry if I've kept you waiting.' Bertha was staring at her anxiously and Bea forced a smile to her stiff lips.

'You haven't kept me waiting at all, so don't look so worried.'

'Is the carriage coming to fetch us, Miss?' The young maid was peering at her in concern. 'You're not looking at all well, there's pale you are.'

'I'm all right and we'll take the tram home.' Bea realised her tone was abrupt but how could she explain to the maid that she didn't want her father knowing she'd even been in the vicinity of Sterling's hotel? James was not a stupid man and it would not take him long to put two and two together.

She scarcely remembered the journey home, she was numb, lost in her own world of despair where she saw herself cast aside, perhaps sent away to the country in disgrace. She clenched her hands together in her lap but that must not happen, would not, for Sterling would take care of her once he knew about the baby.

It was good to be inside the brightly lit house feeling the warmth and familiarity of her childhood home settling around her. She felt secure here but she knew her feelings were false;

once her condition began to show then all her security would vanish.

She became aware of raised voices coming from the direction of her father's study. She could tell that her father was more angry than she had ever known him to be but his words were indistinguishable.

'Go on back to the kitchen, Bertha.' She drew off her gloves calmly, knowing that the maid wanted nothing more than to stand in the hallway listening. 'Off with you now, you must be ready for your supper. Tell Mrs Bevan I'd like a coddled egg and perhaps some pears and cream to follow. Hurry along Bertha, don't just stand there staring.'

The maid bobbed a curtsey and reluctantly moved towards the doorway leading down into the kitchen. Bea glanced round her quickly, almost guiltily, before moving towards the study. Her heart was beating absurdly fast, there was a fear low in the pit of her stomach that somehow her father had found out about her condition – was Dr Thomas with him now, perhaps?

But the other voice was young, not ponderous and heavy like that of the old doctor. It was difficult to identify the speaker for the words were spoken low but at last, Bea, hearing a sudden familiar inflection, recognised Rickie's voice.

Her fears subsided. He could know nothing about her and Sterling for the two brothers scarcely spoke to each other. No, he was here on business and even though it was something that was not at all to her father's liking it need not concern her.

She moved away towards the drawing room and stood for a moment staring into the flames of the fire. She had still not accomplished her task of seeing Sterling and yet in some strange way she was relieved for she could still hug her secret to herself for just a little while longer.

Some would no doubt say that she was unfortunate to have conceived a child so early in her love affair. She put her hands up to her cheeks, she still could scarcely believe that it was all happening and yet here she was thinking about making another assignation with Sterling. Was she past shame?

And yet a soft smile upturned the corners of her mouth, her hands slid along the flat planes of her stomach and her features softened; she was carrying a child, hers and Sterling's child, and she could not be altogether unhappy in spite of the circumstances in which she found herself.

The sound of the study door springing open startled her and she moved swiftly towards the hallway. Her father was hurrying up the stairs and once at the top, he turned and looked down at Rickie with as much hate in his face as though he was seeing the devil incarnate.

'Get out of my house and don't ever let me set eyes on you again or you will be facing the business end of my gun, do you understand?'

That he had failed to notice Bea was patently obvious. He strode along the gallery and went into his bedroom, closing the door with a bang.

'What on earth has happened?' Bea followed as Rickie made his way outside into the great porch of the building. He turned to look at her and there was such bitterness in his eyes that she drew back in fear.

'Do you want to hear something funny?' His words fell from his lips like chips of ice. 'I have learned something that I imagined to be of great importance and yet no one, God damn it no one, takes any notice of me.' He rubbed his hair back from his face and he seemed distraught.

'Rickie, what is it, you look so strange?' Bea reached out a tentative hand but he seemed not to see her.

'I showed this letter to my solicitor,' Rickie waved a paper under her nose, 'and he said it proved nothing, nothing at all, because my brother was born in wedlock. And your father, that bastard ram who had been fishing in another man's pond, he tells me to do my worst. Here take it, see what sort of parents we've got for ourselves.'

He thrust a paper into her hands and moved off into the darkness before she could stop him. Slowly Bea returned indoors and seated herself before the fire in the drawing room. Carefully she smoothed out the creased sheet and began to read the words written in her father's hand, scarcely understanding what they meant. And then pain like she had never known exploded within her, she fell to her knees clutching her stomach while soundless retching sobs shook her. Horror hung over her like the touch of death itself.

'Sweet Jesus it can't be true.' Although the words seemed to rage within her they came out as nothing more than a hoarse whisper. She wished that she could swoon, faint away into an overwhelming darkness, but her mind was crystal clear. This then was her punishment, she was carrying within her the blood of her blood, for Sterling Richardson was her father's son, her own half brother.

Chapter Thirteen

It was late spring and the blossoms had come to the trees so swiftly that one day the branches stood out stark against the sky and the next were heavy with flower.

Mali stood staring through the kitchen window, willing the morning to come up fine and sunny for this was the day of the fair. Mali, along with the other women from the laundry, had been given a holiday and an extra shilling to put in her pocket and she felt like a child about to go to a birthday party.

She had made Dad an early breakfast and then had packed up his grub putting with it the usual twist of paper containing tealeaves and sugar for his brew. She had watched him walk into the dimness of early morning with a sense of sadness that he would not be able to have time off from the copper sheds, but the furnaces needed constant attention and someone had to see to them.

There were those who said the Richardsons were too mean to give holidays to the workers but Mali knew that Sterling was not like that. He was most certainly a stern man, some might even say hard, but she had seen something in Sterling that perhaps other people had missed.

She tweaked the ribbon of her hat into place impatiently; this was no time to be thinking of anything but the coming fair. Staring down at the new sprigged muslin skirt, bought with her very own money, she sighed in satisfaction.

Most of her wages she had kept in a stone jar under the sink, so that she simply had to delve into her savings to ensure she looked her best. All the young men of the area would be at the fair, sporting good, clean shirts with starched collars, eyes open wide for any girl who might take their fancy.

Mali felt a sudden tremor of nervousness at the prospect of parading before all and sundry in her fine new clothes. She could not help but feel glad that Katie had come to her last night, practically begging for her company.

'I don't know if William is going or not.' Katie's tone had been casual but the tightness of her grip on Mali's arm told its own story.

'You are going to come, now aren't you Mali, I can't go along to the recreation ground by myself an' for sure you'll enjoy it.'

Mali had smiled reassuringly. 'Of course I'm coming, I wouldn't miss it for the world.' And now here she was, ready before the sun had warmed the streets into life, waiting like a child at a party for some special treat even though she did not know what it might be.

There was a knock on the door and Katie came into the kitchen, her face wearing a freshly washed look, her hair gleaming like silk.

'Am I too early for you, Mali?' she asked breathlessly. 'For sure I had to get out of the house before me mammy makes me take the boys along to the fair.'

Mali laughed at Katie's rueful expression. 'I'm ready, I have been for ages, I'm that excited, you'd think I was Queen of the May or something.'

'Right then, it's off down the road for us, quick now before I hear the kids bawlin' and change me mind.' Katie dragged on Mali's arm anxiously and the two girls stepped out into the early light that spilled along Copperman's Row.

'I wonder if I'll meet a fine buck,' Mali said brightly. 'Someone nice and kind who will take me on the swingboats, a boy so strong that we'll soar above the rooftops, me sitting prim like in my seat and him pulling hard on the ropes. That would be so exciting.'

'There's only one buck I want to see,' Katie said softly. 'Oh Mali, love's such a strange thing. It makes for so much hurtin' it's more of a pain than a joy and yet I would not be without it for all that.'

Mali glanced at her friend. Katie had become noticeably thinner in the last few weeks and she had developed a short, harsh cough that seemed to trouble her day and night and yet it was the sadness in her eyes that worried Mali the most, for Katie had always been a girl who enjoyed fun and laughter.

The walk over the hill took the girls little more than half an hour and though Mali had suggested they catch the tram at Green Hill corner, Katie laughingly protested that the money could be better spent on the coconut shies or on buying new silk ribbons for their hair. Mali did not mind, for the sun was beginning to shine brightly. The air was fresh coming in from the sea for the recreation ground was alongside the curving golden stretch of beach.

Even at such an early hour, the fair was already in full swing. The raucous sound of the barrel-organ at the edge of the field drifted towards the girls and Mali felt a sudden surge of excitement. This seemed a day when anything could happen, perhaps even the fulfilment of some of her dreams. At any rate she meant to enjoy the holiday.

Yet even as the thoughts whirled through her mind, she knew that work had become much more than a means of earning money. She had over the weeks gained great satisfaction from the routine of folding sheets and wrapping them and now she had been promoted to the position of writing out the labels for the packages, itemising the linen and checking the list against the customer's own record of what had been sent to the laundry; she felt she was an important part of the business. It was still a regular part of her duties to take Mr Waddington his tea. He seemed to like her even though he scarcely spoke more than a few words of polite thanks as she put his tray on the desk before him, but he always smiled at her as she bobbed him a curtsey.

'Hey, you're far away. Dreamin' are you?' Katie jogged her arm. 'Look, there's ice cream, shall we buy some?'

Mali made a rueful face. 'Not at this time of the morning thank you, I'm going over to look at the sheepdogs. See, they're getting ready for the trials down the far end of the field.'

'Watch the silly sheeps if that's what yo' want,' Katie said. 'I'm going to look at the penny stall, see what I can win for myself.'

Mali stared down at the dusty ground beneath her feet. Her boots, shining when she'd left home, were dull and dowdy, looking as though she had been walking for hours in them. The hem of her skirt seemed to have become entwined in a bramble branch.

'Can I help?' The voice that spoke close to her ear as she bent to pull at the brambles was resonant with suppressed laughter. Mali felt the colour sweep into her face as she looked up to see Sterling Richardson leaning over her.

His fingers were deft and strong and soon she was free and he was smiling down at her, his hair gleaming in the sunlight.

He seemed god-like to Mali in that instant, so tall and so strong and masculine that she felt amost in awe of him.

He began to walk along the field towards the avenue of trees that bordered the recreation ground and paused for a moment to look back at her. 'Coming?' he asked lightly, as though he did not mind whether she did or not, and Mali found herself hurrying to catch up with him.

She was aware of her new skirt whispering around her feet and of the warm breeze fanning her hot cheeks. The sky overhead seemed a more brilliant blue than she'd ever known it to be and the few clouds were so white and fluffy that they might have been made from cotton wool.

They walked in silence and Mali could not help feeling tonguetied and gauche. She glanced up at Sterling's tallness and her heart missed a beat as she noticed the way his hair curled golden and crisp on the whiteness of his collar.

Turning, he met her eyes, and she felt as though she was drowning in deep violet seas. She looked away quickly, hoping he could not hear the way her heart was thudding in her breast. Why could she think of nothing to say to him? She should be laughing and happy, able to enchant him with stories of the laundry. But then, she imagined he was used to the ways of ladies of quality who spoke finely and confidently, as he did, and would find such conversation dull.

'You are very silent,' he said glancing down at her. 'And why are you here at the fair dressed in all your glory instead of working at the laundry?'

'Mr Waddington has given us the day off,' Mali said, not looking at Sterling. She felt he was amusing himself at her expense and pride rose thick and hard in her throat.

'Very good of Mr Waddington,' he said at last, 'but then he

doesn't have to worry about furnaces going out. They are a little different to wash-house boilers, you know, Mali.'

As before, the sound of her name on his lips had the power to thrill her. She tried to recall the times when they had spoken lightly together, confided in each other. There seemed to be a barrier between them now and she knew it was only her own awareness of him as a man that held her tonguetied.

He seemed to sense her shyness for he began to talk and as always she listened breathless with enchantment. He had the power to invest even the most casual conversation with magic and beauty and Mali was content to be at his side.

After a time, she managed to look up at him and at the same moment he turned his head. His eyes, in the sunlight, seemed clear and blue and the liking in them was unmistakable. She took a deep shuddering breath as he moved nearer to her.

For a moment the world seemed to spin in a haze of blue sky and tall trees full of blossoms and then everything was normal again as he looked away from her.

'Let's leave the fair,' he said decisively. He took her hand and she sighed softly, almost holding her breath with happiness. She thought briefly of Katie but being with Sterling seemed to be the most important thing in the world.

It was calm on the long stretch of the beach and the golden dunes hid the recreation ground from view. Before them the sea lapped the shore and the small, white-capped waves sucked at the many pebbles as the waters retreated.

Mali threw her hat on the sand, trying vainly to tie back her unruly hair. At last, Sterling took the ribbon from her hand.

'Come here,' he said with gentle impatience, 'let me do it.'

The feel of him lifting the soft dark hair away from her neck was something Mali would always remember. His fingers brushing her skin were warm like a caress and she remained quite still, fearful of breaking some magical spell that must have weaved itself around them.

Taking her hand, Sterling drew her to her feet and with her fingers curled in his, she moved along the water line watching the small, gentle waves run up the beach to retreat with the sound of many pebbles being dragged along the wet sand.

Without speaking, Sterling kicked off his shoes and walked into the water and after a moment, Mali knelt and undid her

140

boots with clumsy fingers. She stepped into the sea behind him and when he looked at her his gaze seemed to reflect sun and the deep blue of the shimmering water.

'You really are very lovely, Mali Llewelyn,' he said and she could not tell from the look on his face if he was teasing her or not. But he must have been speaking in fun for the next moment, he had reached down into the water and was throwing a glittering cascade over her.

After a time, they sat together on the firm golden sand near the sea wall and Sterling leaned back, eyes closed, his bright hair falling over his forehead so that he seemed less stern than usual.

Mali studied him covertly, learning by heart every inch of his face from the straight level brows to the curve of his mouth beneath the moustache. His chin was firm, his jaw square, determined. He was a fine man, Mali thought to herself, the woman who won his heart would be fortunate indeed. And then she wondered why she felt a sudden sadness.

As Mali stared at him in silence, her body felt as though it was soaked in an ocean of joy. She knew that the sun and the sea and the fairground atmosphere would be hers again but it needed Sterling's presence to make it all magical.

He opened his eyes and then he was looking directly at her. Suddenly Mali was up and running barefoot along the beach, panic driving at her heels and excitement turning her stomach over. She could hear Sterling behind her and then he had caught her in his arms. She felt the soft breeze blow her hair across her face as the ribbon slipped from its place.

So slowly that he seemed scarcely to move, Sterling bent his head. For an endless stretch of time his mouth was poised over her own. She waited, still and breathless, blinded to everything but him.

The moment his lips touched hers, the world seemed to spin away into circles of golden light. His arms tightened around her and above them the seagulls screeched and fought, crying into the still air with harsh sounds.

The magic seemed to go on and on, she was aware that her arms had wound around him and that she was arching her neck so that her face was upturned to his. She wanted to laugh and cry at the same time, to shout her joy into the soft breeze.

141

Then he released her so suddenly that she almost fell.

'I think we should be getting back to the recreation ground.' He seemed distant, his eyes which seemed to change from light blue to violet according to his mood stared now away across the water. He was aloof from her and it was almost as though she had ceased to exist.

Then he seemed to sense her bewilderment. He smiled but it was impersonal, as though she might be a stray dog that he wished to show some kindness to.

'You shall come and sit with me on the platform,' he said decisively. 'I need a friendly face beside me if I'm to get through the prizegiving without falling asleep.'

She tried to protest but he hurried her away from the beach, scarcely giving her time to do up her boots. The sounds of the fair were swamping her thoughts, the bright wooden horses came into view plunging and rising on a nonstop merry go round.

As Mali went with him across the ground littered now with papers and half-eaten toffee apples, she was aware of the curious glances that followed her. She felt treumulous misgivings about sitting on the platform with him, what would people say? But Sterling did not hesitate, he led her quickly towards the far end of the field where the races were to take place.

It was the custom on the first day of the fair for the Sunday school superintendents and the more senior teachers to bring the pupils out for their annual treat. It was for this purpose the races were organised, and as a child Mali had taken part in them herself. She had stared up at the dignified ladies and gentlemen on the raised platform draped with flags from the various chapels, never imagining that she would one day sit among them.

The dais loomed large and imposing, the bright flags fluttering in the breeze. Several local dignitaries were already seated in high, hard-backed chairs and Mali's heart began to beat so swiftly that she could scarcely breathe. She stood quite still, hands clenched to her sides, overcome with fear and it was only Sterling's hand on her arm that propelled her forward.

Mali sank into the nearest vacant seat, staring straight ahead of her. Her colour was high and she had never felt so conspicuous and embarrassed in all her life.

'Good day to you, Mali, I must say I didn't expect to meet one of my workers up here on the platform today, but the surprise is a pleasant one for all that.'

Mali turned slowly and her eyes widened as she saw Mr Waddington smiling at her affably, his silk scarf hanging around his thin neck in spite of the warmth of the sunshine. She did not know what to do, she could hardly bob him a curtsey in the circumstances. She tried to return his smile but her face felt frozen, her lips stiff.

Sterling had seated himself beside her and now he leaned forward. 'Good day Ronnie. This young lady gave me the impression earlier that I'm not such a generous boss as you apparently are. Made of stern stuff is this Mali Llewelyn, solid gold, I should take good care of her if I were you.'

Mr Waddington nodded, not realising that Sterling was jesting.

'As you say dear boy, she's worth her weight in gold and I do appreciate her, you may be assured.'

Mali leaned back in her seat, mortified that the two men knew each other and were talking about her as though she did not exist. She glanced around, wondering if she might make her escape, but the mayor was on his feet and had begun to speak to the crowd of people gathered around the platform.

Mali resigned herself to remaining where she was at least for the moment. She glanced sideways at Sterling and he was seated easily, his long legs stretched out before him, not at all discomfited. But she was among folks that her father would call her 'betters' while he was with his own kind. It opened the divide between them wider than Mali could ever have imagined. What did she think she was about, romping over the sands with a man like Sterling Richardson? Tongues would soon start to wag about her if she wasn't careful.

Miserably she watched as the small girls from the Sunday schools, wearing their best dresses under frilled starched aprons, balanced hardboiled eggs on wooden spoons. She tried to join in the laughter but her hands trembled and her stomach felt as though it was inhabited by a hundred butterflies.

It was when Sterling rose to make the presentations that she realised the enormity of what she had done by sitting on the platform with him in full public view. Mrs Jones from Pentre Estyll Chapel led the winners from her class forward and her eyes rested frostily on Mali as though she had suddenly become untouchable.

The woman drew her skirts aside, turning her back on Mali, stiffly ordering the children forward one at a time. Mali huddled lower in her seat, her eyes downcast, and it occurred to her for the first time that she could easily be taken for Sterling Richardson's flossy.

Her cheeks flamed, she glanced neither to right nor left but sat in burning, shamed silence. The prizegiving seemed to drag on endlessly as child after child was handed a hymn book or a small testament and allowed to shake hands with the owner of the copper company. Mali closed her eyes, wishing that she was home again in the silence of her own kitchen.

At last, the ceremony was over and as a loud cheer rose from the crowd the sound seemed to echo in Mali's mind. As the clapping rose to a crescendo, she slipped from her place and hurried down the steps and then she was running the length of the recreation ground, wanting only to hide herself away where no one could see her.

Chapter Fourteen

Sterling sat in the office staring out into the rain-washed yard. Men were leaving after the night shifts, collars high around their necks, some with flannel scarves over the lower part of their faces. It was a cold wet morning, as far removed from the weather at the fair as winter was from summer.

Sterling tapped his pen against the sheet of paper before him and his mind was not on the columns of figures but on Mali Llewelyn and her sun-drenched face upturned to his, her small nose sunburnt, her eyes full of life and laughter. He had not enjoyed himself so much for a very long time, he had been stimulated by her company and she somehow managed, without flattery, to make him feel ten feet tall. When she had disappeared without a word, it did not take a great deal of intelligence to work out the reason behind her sudden, hasty departure for he had seen the derision in the eyes of the prissy Sunday school teacher as she had walked past the chair where Mali was seated.

'Vinegary old witch,' he said out loud. He moved restlessly to the window, the rain was beating up from the cobbles hard and cold. A cat slid wetly around the corner and stood mewling at the door. Sterling opened it and the small animal ran gratefully to the stove and began to lick its fur.

Mali had been just like a kitten, he mused, innocent and unselfconscious, her happiness reflected in her face. It had not seemed wrong to take her onto the platform with him but he might have guessed that others would put their own interpretation on the situation. Since then, she had scarcely been out of his thoughts. He wanted very much to see her again and yet perhaps it was not wise to awake in her hopes that could never be fulfilled. He had seen the way she had looked at him, the admiration that could so easily become something more shining through her expressive face. She was not a flossy and could hardly be his wife so what was the use in pursuing the friendship they had built up between them?

He would be better off turning his attentions to Bea, she would be so well suited for him that it was surprising that their respective parents had not been pushing them together long before this. He thought of the last time they had met, when he had taken her to bed and made love to her. He really should have made an effort to talk to her before this, he thought guiltily, his attitude must seem casual to say the least.

She might be feeling slighted by his lack of attention, after all it was not very gallant to form a relationship with a lady and pursue it avidly for some weeks and then act as though she did not exist.

Bea had been busily engaged at his house too, walking about the rooms with samples of cloth, trying to decide on the best colour schemes for his home. The last time she had been there the place had been filled with workmen and Bea had looked a trifle anxious as though she had something she particularly wanted to say to him. He would go to see her one day soon, he told himself, but in the meantime there was plenty to be done.

He looked down at the figures before him and for once he was not studying copper or even zinc, what interested him now was the price of coal.

The output of anthracite had risen to over four million tons a year, over half of that being exported to Canada. Interestingly, most of it was being shipped through the docks at Sweyn's Eye.

It was the special properties of anthracite, slow burning and yet producing great heat, that made it so successful a commodity. It had been found suitable for fuelling space and central heating boilers and so anthracite had become very much in demand both on the continent and in Canada.

He turned over the page and bit on the end of his pen thoughtfully; patent fuel works would be a good outlet for the vast amount of small coal any pit amassed. The coal dust, compressed into briquettes, was being shipped from the new

King's Dock in the town at the rate of one million tons a year.

On an impulse, he opened the files, searching for a time among the dusty papers before locating the deeds to the pit owned by Alwyn Travers. His pulse quickened with excitement, it was as he thought, the Kilvey Deep was an anthracite mine. It should by rights be making a fortune yet Travers had not paid his dues in the last three months. Well, the man would be given a little more time to make good his debt and if he failed to do so, the mine would be forfeit. Coal would make a good side line, Sterling thought in satisfaction.

The door swung open and Ben shuffled into his office, his moustache dripping with rain, his sharp eyes missing nothing. After taking off his coat and hanging it near the boiler, he fingered the file that Sterling had just been reading.

'Here early today, Mr Richardson.' Ben glanced meaningfully at the file. 'Going to do something about Alwyn Travers at last are you?' Without waiting for a reply he moved towards his own desk and seated himself stiffly in his chair. ''Bout time too, that's what I say. Give folks like him enough rope and they always hang themselves.'

Sterling regarded Ben steadily. The old man was loyal to the Richardsons for he had been with the firm for many years, long before any of the partners had been brought in as a desperate measure designed to inject new finance into the company. Perhaps it would be a good idea to try out Ben's reactions to the idea that had been buzzing through Sterling's mind for some weeks now.

'I'm thinking of going into coal.' He leaned back in his chair, studying the changing expressions on Ben's face. 'You know as well as I do that there is great demand for anthracite, a trend that should continue for some time yet. And too there are the patent fuel markets. What do you think, Ben?'

The old man went through his usual pantomime of bringing out his great handkerchief and rubbing at his nose with it, careful not to spoil the stiffened line of his moustache.

'If it means taking the pit from Alwyn Travers then I'm all for it,' Ben said at last. 'Not a man to put his back into anything that one, does as little as possible with the result that anyone working for him adopts the same lazy attitude.'

'My sentiments exactly,' Sterling said. 'But I mean to branch out further than that, Ben. Yes, take over the Kilvey Deep but also acquire other pits, perhaps the string of them that run from Mynydd Newydd down into the Pentre. The Kilvey Deep is the key to it all for it has the Cornish beam engine which pumps the water from all the other pits.'

'Aye, you're right.' Ben's eyes glowed behind his spectacles. 'Those mines, properly run, should bring in a steady income right enough and should finance any improvements you wish to make in the copper company.'

Sterling closed the book with a snap of finality. 'Not a word about this to anyone, Ben.' He smiled at the old man. 'Not that any words of caution are needed as far as you are concerned, like the proverbial clam when it comes to business aren't you? I don't tell you often enough how grateful I am for your support, Ben.'

The old man coughed into his handkerchief, removing his spectacles and rubbing at them furiously. He said nothing but it was quite apparent that he was pleased with Sterling's praise.

'Right, I think it's time I went down to the sheds, the morning shift should be well in progress and I'd like a word with William Owens.' As Sterling rose to his feet, he saw a shadow of disapproval cross Ben's face. 'We all must do things we don't like on times, Ben,' he said ruefully, 'it's what is called a matter of survival.'

He left the office and hurried through the cold, pelting rain towards the sheds. The works were built on the side of the river Swan, downhill from the office block. Forests of tall chimneys pointed to the overcast sky, shooting bursts of steam and flurries of sparks that reflected redly in the turgid waters of the river. A fleet of barges moved slowly upstream, the cargo of ore dulled by the rain.

Sterling turned indoors, droplets of rain running inside his collar. In direct contrast to the chill damp weather outdoors, the interior of the works was heavy with oppressive heat from the roaring furnaces and Sterling knew he would never become accustomed to the overpowering stench generated by the sulphur expelled from the molten metal.

He watched for a moment as the men in the tew gang took it in turns to fill a ladle and, moving in a circle, keeping a safe distance from each other, tip their liquid burden into the moulds. He waited until Will Owens stopped for a drink and then moved towards him. The smell of ale was strong and with a quick glance into the jug at the youth's side, Sterling saw that it certainly was not water he was drinking.

'I'd like a word with you,' he said abruptly. 'I've a proposition to make, all you have to do is keep me informed as to the mood of the men, what they feel about the new furnaces, that sort of thing.'

'And what do I get in return?' Dark eyes hostile in the red glow of the furnace regarded him steadily.

'What would you say to an extra five shillings?' Sterling's tone was clipped. 'When you think about it, it's a fair amount of pay for very little work and we can be useful to each other.'

Will took a long swig from the jug, holding it over the back of his arm as he raised it to his lips, his dark eyes never wavering even as he took great gulps of the dark beer. At last he placed the jug back on the ground and rubbed the back of his hand across his lips.

'All right, I'm willing to be a *bradwr*, a traitor to my class for a bit of extra gelt.' He did not smile, indeed there was no expression at all on his face and Sterling realised that he had underestimated the youth. Will Owens; he was cold and calculating and meant to get what he wanted at all costs. He was not to be trusted and perhaps it was just as well that they were open enemies.

'Good.' He began to move away. 'Start right away and when you have anything to report, slip a note into the office.'

'No fear.' Owens spoke quickly. 'Nothing in writing, is it? Could hang myself that way. No, you come in and talk to me when I stop for a break and I'll be sure to make it short and to the point so that no one notices anything.'

Sterling moved around the ring of men and nodded to Davie Llewelyn who was working swiftly and with the expertise born of long practice. 'Morning, Davie,' he said and was startled to see the big man rest his empty ladle on the ground where a small trickle of copper spat and hissed in the dampness.

'Mind if I speak to you, sir?' His tone was respectful but there was a wary look in the man's eyes that put Sterling on his guard. 'Made a show of my girl you did, Mr Richardson,' he said bluntly. 'Don't want people talking about her you understand, a good girl is Mali and no one dare say different, not in my hearing.'

He paused to wipe the sweat from his eyes. 'Meant to be kind you did, so she told me, but can't go on, things like that, not in Sweyn's Eye, mind. They'll be calling my girl a flossy next and then what chance would she have of meeting a fine young boyo and settling down?'

Sterling was slightly taken aback, he stared at Davie for a long moment before speaking. 'I see your point,' he said at last.

Davie sighed with relief and Sterling realised that it must have taken a great deal of moral courage for the man to confront him. Sterling could not help but admire him for it.

'Thank Christ you did not take offence, sir,' Davie was saying. 'But a girl soon loses her good name which is all she has to offer a man, isn't it?'

Without waiting for a reply, he returned to his job, falling into place among the circle of men who moved around the furnace mouth filling the great ladles with molten copper and unloading them expertly into the moulds in a never-ending round of activity.

Sterling left the sheds and walked quickly up the slope towards the office block. The rain had abated now but low grey clouds mingled with the yellow smoke from the chimneys. Sterling paused, staring up at the sky lost in thought.

He had enjoyed being with Mali that day on the beach, he could see again her dewy skin and the brightness of her eyes that were green as the ocean. He felt again the soft silkiness of her abundant hair as he'd tied it up in a ribbon. And the innocent sweetness of her mouth had touched a chord within him that he did not care to examine too closely.

On an impulse, he left the yard and walked through the gates of the works and out into the road. A milk cart was bumping its way along the cobbles, the churns clanking noisily in the early-morning silence.

He felt restless, not at all in the mood for work, it might be as well to have a long drink of ale. He took his watch from his waistcoat pocket and consulted the ornate face. The Mexico Fountain had been open since six o'clock and it was now almost seven. He would more than likely be drinking alone but then when had that ever bothered him?

'Mr Richardson!' Mali was standing before him, her face pale and her eyes shadowed as though she had not long been awake. She moved uncomfortably from one foot to the other.

'Good morning,' he said formally. 'I have just been speaking with your father.'

Mali blushed fiercely and looked away from him. 'I'll have to go,' she said, 'I'm late for work already.'

'As you are in such a hurry to run away, may I see you this evening?' Sterling asked. 'I shall be down at the cemetery later on, I hope you will be there too.' Sterling did not wait for Mali's reply but turned quickly away, striding purposefully towards the open doors of the Mexico Fountain.

Mali stared after him, her cheeks aflame, her hands trembling. He had practically ordered her to meet him that night, he was so high handed that she felt she should have rebuffed him at once. And yet when she had looked up into his face, she had once again been on the golden sands with the soft breeze lifting her hair and the seagulls crying overhead. She had felt his mouth take possession of hers, experienced the exhilaration of the kiss and had become weak and trembling.

She was foolish to herself and she knew it. She would only find heartbreak in continuing an association with Sterling Richardson. Even if the words Katie had said to her about men like him wanting only to tumble a working girl weren't true, what good could come out of such an arrangement?

She realised that she was still standing in the street and that the time was going by and if she did not want to spoil her good record at the laundry she had better hurry.

She moved away down the street, past the Mexico Fountain, and could not help peering through the high window to catch a glimpse of Sterling.

'You are a silly little idiot, Mali Llewlyn,' she said to herself in a whisper. 'Open your eyes girl, it's high time you started to act like a woman. You'll not go to meet Mr toffeenose Richardson tonight and if he wants to wait around in graveyards then more fool him.'

Late in the afternoon, when the rainy weather had given way to a chilly dryness, Rickie Richardson was making his way down through the town towards the dock area and the warm lounge of the Cape Horner. He was feeling dispirited and restless and a dull anger burned within him. He had cursed himself for a fool a hundred times over for handing Bea Cardigan the proof of Sterling's birth and God only knew what she would do with the information. She would not confide the truth in Sterling, of that at least he felt certain, for Bea had imagined herself in love with Sterling, he had seen it in her eyes many times. It must have been a rude shock for her when she had read the letter written in her father's own hand.

A swiftly ridden horse and buggy splashed through the puddles in the gutter sending up a muddy spray, some of which caught the bottoms of his striped trousers. 'Damn and blast,' he muttered and directed a dark look towards the driver who appeared not to notice him. And yet if he had been the owner of the copper company, everyone would be touching their forelocks to him, he thought mutinously. There must be some way of shifting Sterling whatever the solicitor chap Irons had said.

He crossed the road, not seeing the gulls that wheeled and called overhead, a sure sign so the fishermen said of an approaching storm. He made his way quickly into the public bar of the Cape Horner and saw at once that Glanmor Travers was in his usual position with his feet stretched out before the roaring fire.

'Come and sit here, Rickie, I've kept a place for you,' Glanmor said glibly, though the fact that there was an empty seat beside him was due more to luck than judgment, Rickie thought sourly.

'Glad to.' He spoke affably for Glanmor was inclined to turn nasty after a drink or two of porter. 'Cold enough to freeze a brass monkey.' He sat near the fire and stared at the other man, wondering how much it was safe to confide in him. Should he tell Glanmor the truth about Sterling? Perhaps not, maybe for the moment he would keep that piece of information as his ace in the hole.

The door was pushed open and a group of smelters came into the bar, bringing with them a flurry of cold air. Rickie sniffed and made a wry face at the awful stench that emanated from the men's clothing, hoping none of them would come too close; but to his surprise Glanmor was gesturing to a dark-haired youth, inviting him to join them.

'Will Owens, come and sit here, have a drink on me,' Glanmor said heartily.

'What you up to mixing with the workers?' Rickie asked in a low voice and Travers shook his head knowingly.

'Rickie, this is Will Owens, a man who shares our mutual dislike of Sterling Richardson.' He turned to the youth who was straddling a chair as though he owned the bar. 'Anything been happening that I should know about?'

The youth gave a short laugh. 'There's something that will make your mouth water, now,' he said triumphantly. 'The boss man has only asked me to be his spy, hasn't he? Go round with my ears flapping listening to the men's grumbles and then tell them all to him so that he knows what's going on.'

Rickie looked at Will Owens and found it difficult to hide his disdain, this copper worker was above himself and might need a sharp short lesson one of these days, but in the meantime, it would be interesting to listen to what he had to say.

Travers was all but rubbing his hands. 'If you pass on only the information I want you to give him then we should be in a very good position to throw a spanner in the works.'

'What's going on then, Glanmor?' Rickie asked and Travers winked hugely.

'We all know you and your brother are not the best of pals,' he said. 'And there's a few more of us waiting in line to bring him to his knees.'

Will Owens looked sharply at Rickie. 'Brother? Are you Mr Richardson's brother then?' he asked in disbelief. Rickie nodded.

'Yes, but that need not bother you, I have my own scores to settle.' He pushed down his dislike of the cocky copperman and tried to appear friendly. 'What do you think is going on then?'

'Nothing as yet.' Will sounded reluctant to speak and yet Rickie sensed that the minute his back was turned the youth would spill his guts to Travers. Well, he must just bide his time, keep his eyes and ears open and trust to no one.

He listened for a time, gaining a certain satisfaction from the young copperman's grumblings, but soon the effects of the porter began to tell on him and he felt decidedly sleepy. He stretched his arms above his head before resting a hand on Travers' shoulder.

'We must do this again and soon,' he said with a friendliness he was far from feeling. Smoothly, he rose to his feet managing to ignore Will Owens as he made his departure.

Outside in the street, the light was fading fast. Clouds floated overhead but the cobbled streets were dry. Rickie made for the tramway depot and was just in time to see the tail end of the vehicle, brightly lit in the darkness, vanishing from sight.

'Blast it!' he said aloud while inwardly he seethed over the injustice that allowed Sterling to have everything including a brand new Ascot while he was forced to stand around street corners waiting for a tram. Well, he knew something that his brother – his half brother, he corrected himself – did not, and it hung around him like a talisman.

One day he would find a way to use the knowledge against Sterling, he thought angrily. This copperworker Will Owens might prove useful in that respect, there was no knowing what titbits of information he might come up with. In any case, Owens was another nail in Sterling's coffin and that in itself was enough to give Rickie a feeling of satisfaction.

Chapter Fifteen

As Mali made the tea for Mr Waddington she wondered how it was she could feel so miserable one moment and the next be gloriously excited because she had met Sterling in the street and he had asked – or rather told – her to meet him later that night. She swirled the tea round in the pot, allowing it to steep before pouring it hot and fragrant into the bone china cup.

Everything in her life seemed to have changed since that day at the fair and Mali's feelings had plunged between hope and despair. Even Katie had managed to make matters worse by being offhand because she'd been left alone at the recreation ground.

'It was all right for you.' Her tone had revealed hurt feelings rather than anger. 'You were gadding about the beach in the company of the great copper boss but I was on my own wanting to see Will and yet afraid lest if I did see him he'd ignore me.'

Mali had tried to explain. 'It was so lovely, Katie, I was so happy, running on the beach as free as a bird. It was only when that old chapel woman froze me with her eyes that I realised how it must look to other people.'

'Well, serves you right.' Katie's tone had been softly reproving. 'You're falling in love, you poor soft babby.'

'Of course I'm not!' Mali had denied it hotly. 'It was only a bit of fun, that's all it was.' But Katie had only shaken her head sadly.

If that was not enough, she had Davie onto her about it, too. His green eyes had been fiery.

'A daughter of mine making a public spectacle of herself,' he said hotly. 'Like a flossy you was, girl, sitting up there with all them toffs. I'll tell Mr Richardson a thing or two when I see him, you may be sure of that.'

He had too, from the little Sterling had said that morning, and Mali burned with shame, wondering what had passed between the two men. She still warred within herself over whether she should meet Sterling or not and yet, deep down inside she knew she would go to the cemetery, she could not help herself.

Mr Waddington was rummaging among an assortment of papers on his desk, his grey hair tangled as though he had been running his hand through it, and he smiled in relief when he saw Mali.

'Ah, a cup of tea, and never was it more welcome. Just have a look by there and see if you can find me a bill for fuel will you? My eyes aren't what they were nor my old brain either for I feel sure I'm being cheated by the coal merchants.'

He moved away from the desk and drank his tea gratefully and Mali, hesitant at first, began searching through the muddle of papers. She quickly found the missing bill and began to make calculations on the corner of the page, unaware that Mr Waddington was watching her carefully. She looked up at him at last.

'Have you any other bills from Lewis Lewis & Sons?' she asked, forgetting her diffidence in her absorption in her task. 'This one is added up wrongly and you are being asked to pay fifty shillings more than you owe.'

Mr Waddington put down his cup. 'Just a minute, dear, I shall get them all out and you can go through them, that is if you're willing, of course.'

Mali's eyes were shining. 'This is just the sort of work I enjoy, Mr Waddington,' she said. 'My mam was the one for figures, though, she could run rings around me, jump over my head she would but for all that I love to add and subtract and write numbers down on the page.'

'Well, there's a great deal of that for you to do here,' he said ruefully. 'Since my daughter was taken by the lung fever there's been no one to help me and I would not bring in some clever miss from outside.' He shrugged. 'But I see I've allowed it all to get into a muddle and I'd be most grateful to you if you could sort it out for me.'

It was only when Big Mary came searching for Mali that she realised how long she had been missing from the packing room.

'*Duw*.' Big Mary's face was a picture of surprise as she saw Mali seated at the desk alongside Mr Waddington. 'What's happening then, I thought you'd run off home Mali Llewelyn.'

Mr Waddington rose to his feet. 'Blame me, my dear,' he said affably. 'And you must find yourself another checker for Miss Llewelyn is now my own little helper. She is a find in a million, she can actually count and figure far more quickly than I ever could.'

Big Mary's mouth dropped open. 'Mali Llewelyn, office helper is it?' she said and a slow, pleased smile spread over her face. 'I always knew there was more in her than met the eye. Good for you Mali but you ask Mr Waddington for a bit more money, mind, office helpers get more than checkers.'

Mr Waddington laughed. 'Done, it's a bargain and very pleased I am with it too. Now back to work, Mali, I know it's going to take you some time to sort out the mess I've got myself into but you can do it, I have every confidence in you.'

The time seemed to pass on wings and Mali felt by the end of the afternoon that she had made good progress and was well on the way to sorting out some at least of the paperwork. Her back was stiff from bending and her eyes ached and all she could see before her was pages full of figures. But already she had found at least ten discrepancies. It seemed that some of the local merchants had not been above taking advantage of Mr Waddington.

'Well, Mali, I see you are going to save me money,' he said, 'and, contrary to what the good folk of the town believe, I'm not a rich man.' He drew on his coat and his bright silk scarf. 'Now off home with you and don't bother to come in until nine tomorrow, that's one advantage of promotion and well deserved it is too.' He looked down at her. 'No aprons tomorrow but a neat dark skirt and coat will suffice.'

Outside in the yard, Mali waited for Katie and shivered as she looked up at the grey cloudy sky. It was going to be freezing down at the cemetery, such a difference to the wonderful sunny happy day she had spent with Sterling at the fair and yet there was a great bubbling joy inside her when she remembered the way he had approached her in the street and asked her to meet him.

She would tell him of her promotion, she mused, and he would understand, more than anyone, the satisfaction she had gained from working on the books for Mr Waddington.

'Oh, so there's my hoity toity friend waiting for me.' Katie grinned from ear to ear. 'Risen up to office girl sure enough and not long ago the same friend was a blackfaced boiler stoker.'

Katie caught Mali's arm and hugged it to her. 'It's fine so it is and I'm that happy for you though there are others not so pleased.'

'Hey, stuck up pig, not speaking to us now, is it?' Sally Benson came running along the yard, her face screwed up with anger, and Mali wondered what she had ever done to the girl to warrant such enmity.

'How come you get to work in the office, hey?' she pushed at Mali's shoulder, her finger sharp and jabbing, and Mali felt anger begin to uncoil inside her.

'Because I'm smarter than you for a start,' she said, keeping her voice level. 'And perhaps I haven't got such a loud voice either, sound like a cockle woman you do not a laundry worker.'

Sally Benson fell back in surprise, her mouth dropping open. In the sudden silence, Katie dragged at Mali's arm, drawing her away from the laundry gates.

'Jesus, Mary and Joseph I thought she was going to swipe you one then.' Katie's harsh whisper dispelled the mists of anger that were clouding Mali's mind.

'Yes,' she said in surprise, 'I thought it would come to blows myself, not very dignified for an office girl's first day, is it?' she laughed a little nervously and Katie looked at her with a pained expression on her face.

'Dignified is the least of your worries, my girl,' she said. 'For sure Sally Benson is the strongest girl in the Canal Street Laundry, 'cept for Big Mary of course. If Sally got a hold on you, sure you'd be singing and playin' the harp up in heaven.'

'I know it,' Mali said. 'I wouldn't like to have a fist fight with

158

Sally but there's nothing stopping me giving her a bit of lip back is there? She can't get away with everything after all.'

'Well you just keep your nose out of that Sally's way or you'll be getting it busted for sure and no man is going to look at you then, never mind Mr Richardson.' She looked slyly at Mali. 'Sure an' can't I tell you're plannin' on seein' him again, it's in your eyes plain to see.'

'Am I a fool, Katie?' Mali asked slowly. 'It's just that I want to be with him so much that it hurts.'

'Sure an' don't I know the feeling only too well?' Katie said softly. 'William took me home on the day of the fair, kissed me as if he loved me so he did an' yet there's been no word at all from him since, he's a puzzle is that one, sure I don't know what to expect next.'

Mali sighed heavily. 'I don't know anything about men, Katie, but I do want to be with Sterling Richardson more than I've ever wanted anything.' She looked away across the dull waters of the canal. 'I know I can't be his wife, I'm not his sort, he will marry some fine lady. But I think I would take anything he offered me.'

Katie shook her arm. 'Don't talk like that and don't look at me with those accusing eyes either,' she said hotly. 'It's not the same thing with me and Will, he's my own sort but Mr Richardson, why he would set you up fine, give you everything you wanted until he grew tired of you, then you would be out on the streets an old worn out flossy, selling yourself for a few pennies. That's not the life for you, Mali.'

'I expect you're right,' Mali said miserably, 'but I've got to see him, just this once more.' She stared along Copperman's Row and wondered if Dad would be home. He had been on early shift and should have been finished an hour since but there was no smoke rising from the chimney.

'Will I see you later, Katie?' Mali asked. 'I'd like to talk to you after I've seen him.'

Katie squeezed her arm. 'Sure an' I'll be there, just knock my door and we'll get together any time you say.'

The house was cold and empty and there was no sign of Davie. Mali went to the dead fire and set a light to it and soon the flames were curling upwards, sending a warm glow throughout the kitchen, but somehow she felt very alone.

She pulled the curtains across the windows and lit the gas lamp, and shivered as she stared round her at the emptiness. If only her Mam was here to confide in, Mali thought as she moved towards the yard with the huge black kettle ready for filling in her hand.

The water drummed against the bottom of the kettle, splashing up against Mali's blouse, but she didn't notice. What would her mother have said about Sterling Richardson? She would speak to her just as Katie had done, Mali decided, warn her no doubt of the dangers of such an association. No good could come of it, for men like Sterling Richardson did not marry the Mali Llewelyns of this world, they simply used them and then discarded them. But he was not like that, her mind cried out desperately.

She made herself a meal of fried bacon and eggs and had just sat down at the table when the door opened.

'There's a smell to warm a man's guts.' Davie came into the room and Mali's smile of welcome faded as she saw that behind him was Rosa, her dingy hat falling over one eye, and it was clear that the pair of them had been drinking. Suddenly Mali's appetite vanished. She rose to her feet and faced her father but he held up his hands, a stern look on his face.

'No quarrels, now,' he said flatly. 'Rosa is coming to supper and that's that and I won't hear nothing said against her.' He moved to the back door and stood for a moment, his hand on the knob.

'I'm going to wash up, get some of this grime off me, the copper stings like a hundred wasps. Boil up the kettle, Mali, and Rosa will bring the hot water out the back for me, won't you lovie?' He smiled fatuously and Rosa blew him a kiss.

''Course I will, Davie my fine boyo, an' I'll scrub yer back for you.' She laughed uproariously. 'And yer front too if you lets me.'

Mali pushed her plate away, her stomach churning with anger as her father went outside. Rosa stood swaying slightly, a silly grin on her face.

'And don't you look down your nose at me, my girl,' she said, her words slurring into each other. ''Cos we all knows what you gets up to when you goes to the recreation ground with your betters. I seed you down on the beach, lying in the sand with 'im, that Mr Richardson, up to no good you was but I haven't told on you to your dad, he thinks you were at the fairground all the time.'

Mali opened her mouth to protest but closed it again. What was the use? Whatever she said now, Rosa would be determined to believe the worst.

'Here, the kettle's boiling, you'd better take Dad the water.' She lifted the huge kettle from the flames. 'I'm going out.' She drew on her coat and Rosa stood staring at her curiously.

'Going to meet your man, is it? Have a bit of lovin' on the side, well who can blame you? Have fun then and give him a big smacker for me.' Her laughter followed Mali as she hurried away from Copperman's Row.

The cemetery looked eerie and unfamiliar in the darkness and Mali stood on the path beneath the gas lamp staring round her fearfully. To her left, high up against the wall that guarded the grounds from the loose boulders running down the hillside, was her mother's grave. Below her in the well-kept lawns with marble headstones rising like jagged teeth was buried Arthur Richardson, Sterling's father.

'Mali.' His voice came soft from the darkness and she turned quickly, her heart beating so swiftly she could hardly draw breath. He was standing before her then, the shadows falling across his face and his hair glinting like a halo.

She was tonguetied, not knowing what to say, but speak she must or she would throw herself into his arms like a wanton. 'I'm going to my mother's grave.' There was a hint of defiance in her tone, as though warning him that she was not here for his sake alone.

She turned and moved slowly up the hill, aware that he was following her in silence.

'I've been promoted.' She said brightly and yet the triumph she expected to feel was absent. 'Office girl to Mr Waddington, that's my job now.'

'I'm sure you deserve it, Mali,' Sterling said softly.

'Not bad is it?' Mali attempted to smile. 'From blackfaced boiler stoker to office worker in a few short weeks.'

'You are a remarkable girl, in many ways,' he said and his

tone sounded abrupt. Hurt, Mali turned from him, tossing back her long hair.

'Sorry if my talking upsets you,' she said huffily.

'Sweet foolish Mali.' He caught her arm and turned her to face him. 'I shouldn't have asked you to come here tonight.' His hand dropped away from her slowly.

He turned and walked on ahead, coming to a stop under the trees that shimmered and swayed, making a soft sound like many people whispering.

Mali stared down at the soft grassy earth, wondering what Mam would say to her if she were alive now. Sterling seemed to sense something of her thoughts.

He drew her even closer. 'You're shivering.' He almost whispered the words. Slowly, his mouth claimed hers and she was drowning in sensations that threatened to overwhelm her.

It was she who drew away. Her entire being felt alive, awakened to responses that were unfamiliar and yet achingly desirable. Her nerve ends tingled and her heart beats sounded loudly in her ears. Her breathing was ragged and her body cried out for fulfilment.

This then was what love was like, this torment, this clamouring between what was desired and what was right.

His hand touched her breast and Mali closed her eyes against the exquisite pain of knowing she must end the sweetness of their passion before it was too late.

'No!' She moved right away from him, clasping her hands together to stop them from trembling.

He spoke distantly as though he had gone far away from her. 'I'll take you home.'

Mali felt tears burn her eyes; she wished for a moment that she could return to the girl she had been but that was impossible. She was a woman now, with a woman's needs.

Without touching him she spoke. 'I love you, Sterling.' The words had to be said and what response she had expected she did not know but it hurt her deeply when he merely stepped away from her and looked up into the hills as though she did not exist.

'Come along, we'd better go,' he said and he might have been talking to a stranger for all the emotion that was in his voice. Mali stared at him, trying to gain some crumb of comfort, but they were walking beneath the trees now and it was too dark to see his face.

'Just as far as the Mexico Fountain will do,' she said stiffly and he remained silent as he strode along a little in front of her now.

They crossed the bridge over the river and a shadowy moon threw patterns onto the water. Mali looked down into its depths and wondered how she was going to live the rest of her life knowing she could never be with the man she loved.

When Sterling left Mali, he walked rapidly towards the Mackworth Arms. As bitter rain had begun to fall and he cursed himself for his foolishness in not bringing the Ascot. And yet he knew it was not the inclement weather that made him restless and moody, it was the feeling deep within himself that he had somehow betrayed Mali.

'Don't be absurd,' he told himself harshly. Even Mali herself recognised there was no future for them together.

He cared not a fig for convention nor even for the fact that Davie Llewelyn had warned him against pursuing Mali, but common sense told him it would not be fair to take her from her natural surroundings. She was not the sort of girl who could indulge in an illicit affair and he had no intention of forcing her against her better judgment.

As he entered the foyer of the hotel, the night porter touched his cap in salute.

'Nasty night, Mr Richardson. You look wet through, shall I bring you something hot, sir?'

Sterling shook his head. 'No, but you can bring me a bottle of whisky.'

In his room, he threw his coat savagely over a chair, listening to the rain tapping miserably against the window. He supposed he should be grateful that matters had not got out of hand, at least there had been no lasting harm done and the sooner he forgot Mali Llewelyn the better.

He undressed and drew on a warm robe and, returning to the window, peered out into the darkness of the night. For the first time in his life he knew what loneliness meant and it wasn't a feeling he liked.

Perhaps he had better settle down as soon as possible with a good and suitable wife. He immediately thought of Bea; she was a warm and passionate woman, they had always been friends and lately they had become so much more. And yet there was no joy in the thought of asking Bea to marry him. His blood cried out for Mali Llewelyn and in his mind's eye he could see her features warmed by the happiness they had shared that day on the beach. He heard the gentle lilt of her voice like a song, and the touch of her lips beneath his own had stirred his blood.

But desire was something that soon faded, he told himself, and Mali Llewelyn had been an experience that would soon be nothing more than a memory.

Chapter Sixteen

Bea Cardigan sat often in the privacy of her own room. She refused invitations to afternoon teas and even the occasional grand ball in favour of quiet evenings spent at home. She allowed no one to share with her the terrible grief that had clouded her entire life, changing her from a sociable woman into a recluse.

But she had come at last to the only possible solution to her problem and now, in her room, she dressed slowly, trying to prepare herself to face the coming ordeal with courage.

Her hands fumbled over the buttons of the richly embroidered voile dress as though reluctant to see the task finished. She sighed softly and at last she placed a large, heavily decorated hat upon her glossy hair and stood staring at her reflection for a moment, hardly recognising the pale drawn face that looked back at her.

She left the house silently as a shadow for she did not wish to see or speak with anyone, not even Bertha. The young maid had been the only person in the world in whom Bea could confide her trouble and it had been Bertha who had found a clean and trustworthy midwife.

Out in the lane leading from the house to the roadway, the sun fell in patches through the trees. Bea felt disembodied, not quite real, and she was glad when she reached the hubbub of the busy main street.

Why did this have to happen to me? Bea asked herself for the hundredth time. It was like a nightmare to know that she carried within her the child of her half brother. Her being revolted against the idea and yet, God help her, the love for Sterling remained.

She had avoided him of late and she was quite certain that he had not even noticed that she no longer swept joyously into his new house to help with the decoration. But how could she be near him and not fling herself desperately into his arms?

She walked slowly down the hill and away from the elegant buildings of the western slope of the town and gradually she left the main streets behind her. She was on unfamiliar territory now, walking alongside the canal, turgid and slow with brown fronds of grass waving like dead fingers just below the surface of the water.

She shivered, she must not be fanciful and yet her stomach turned over as she thought of the ordeal to come. She told herself that she must imagine going back home to tea, sitting in the familiar warmth of the drawing room, looking out of the long windows at the bay far below. And yet the hands clasping her bag were trembling.

The exterior of the house in Canal Street was respectable enough, lace curtains hung in the windows and the doorknob was brightly polished but the stone walls were begrimed by the copper smoke that hung like a pall all over this part of the town. Bea tapped on the door and waited in trepidation, half hoping Mrs Benson would not answer her knock. She glanced around her, fearful of being observed, realising that it had been a mistake to put on her new hat, for the women who passed her in the street either wore shawls over their heads or the tall Welsh hats that were falling from fashion now.

'Ah, come inside there's a good girl.' Mrs Benson was a large reassuring woman with a greying bun fastened up at the back of her head. She was, Bea noticed, immaculately dressed with a spotless apron covering her skirt and blouse. She was nothing like the dragon Bea had expected, her cheeks were pink and fresh and her eyes clear and direct.

'Come inside,' Mrs Benson repeated, 'don't give the neighbours a free show, is it?'

Bea hovered uncertainly in the sudden dimness of the small kitchen. A good coal fire glowed behind gleaming brass fenders and a large chest of drawers, smelling of polish, stood alongside her.

'Come on through to the other room girlie, and don't be afraid, there's nothing to worry about, I've done this job so many times, it's second nature to me now. Don't like it, mind,' she said honestly, 'but I feel there's always a good reason for a girl to come to me and I don't ask no questions.'

Bea followed Mrs Benson into the small room which probably served as a parlour, for a white sheet covered what appeared to be an upright piano and on the wall hung pictures, presumably of Mrs Benson's family.

'That's my daughter there, Sally,' she smiled. 'Working down at the Canal Street Laundry, she is, good job too, mind.'

'Yes, she's very pretty.' Even to her own ears, her voice sounded strange and Bea put a trembling hand up to her mouth. 'I'm sorry,' she said, 'it's just that I feel so . . .' The words trailed away as Mrs Benson began to set instruments out on a tray.

'There's a silly girl, don't I know how bad you must be feeling? Come on, chin up, you'll be all right so don't worry about a thing.'

She pointed to a screen in the corner of the room. 'Go behind there and take your underdrawers and your stockings off if you please. No need to be shy, I've seen so many tuppences in my life that I've lost count.'

Her motherly cheerfulness was reassuring and Bea quickly did as she was bid, telling herself it would soon be over and then she could start to pick up the pieces of her life again.

When she was ready, Bea stood uncertainly waiting for the midwife to call her to the table that was covered in a white pristine cloth. Suddenly the enormity of the situation overwhelmed her and she wrapped her arms around her stomach as though to protect her unborn child. A pointless and stupid act if ever there was one.

'Come on, over here if you please, that's right, let me help you up. Good, now lay back and try to be easy, let yourself go loose, that's a good girl, don't fight me now.'

Bea lay back and stared up at the cracks in the whitewashed ceiling, trying to detach herself from what was happening, but her heart was beating so furiously that she felt she would choke.

Mrs Benson sighed. 'Quite a few months gone, aren't you dear? You really should have come to me sooner but don't worry, we'll cure everything, you'll see.'

Bea closed her eyes, in a sudden and terrifying panic. She heard the scrape of instruments against the metal tray and did not even want to imagine what might be happening.

She longed to scream out for Mrs Benson to cease her ministrations, she did not want to continue this terrible nightmare. But she remained tight-lipped and silent, for what was the alternative, and had she not gone over and over it all in her mind on countless sleepless nights?

'This may hurt a little but it will soon be finished, there's a good brave girl, aren't you? That's right, keep quite still.'

From outside the window Bea heard the sweet sharp note of a bird in song; her heart contracted in pain and she wondered if she would ever get over the experience she was forcing herself to endure now.

Mrs Benson had moved away and was washing her hands in a basin nearby. Bea looked up at her questioningly. 'Is it all over?' she asked.

'Bless your innocence! No, it's not quite over girl, there'll be some bleeding but it's nature's way, nothing to worry about. Keep this bowl at your side and call me if you need me.'

Left alone, Bea lay on the hardness of the table and tried to keep calm. There was nothing to worry about, hadn't Mrs Benson said so? And she did this sort of thing all the time. Yet in spite of herself, tears welled in her eyes, she had never been so alone and unhappy in all her life.

The midwife returned after a time with a cup of steaming tea. Bea gulped it gratefully for her throat still ached with the effort not to cry. The liquid was hot and sweet and soothing and Bea began to feel a little better.

'That's right, drink it all down. It won't be long now, girl, just you be brave and we'll soon have you on your feet again.'

Bea looked at her imploringly. 'What is going to happen now?' she asked.

'It will all come away from you, of course,' Mrs Benson said gently. 'Just keep the bowl near you and use it when the time comes. I won't be far away, so don't worry your little head about anything.'

Then Bea was alone once more, staring at the whitewashed walls. The only window was covered by a heavy curtain that gaped a little. Through the aperture Bea could see a tiny sliver of back garden and to her surprise the sun was still shining. Yet she felt as though she had been in the small house in Canal Street for hours.

She turned her head restlessly and began to sit up. Suddenly, she could scarcely breathe for the pain that was beginning low in her stomach. Sweat broke out on her forehead and she remained motionless, afraid to move lest she would do herself some damage.

The pain was growing larger and soon it seemed to become the centre of her universe. She moaned softly in her fear as a strange sensation caught her and she was forced to bear down.

She placed the bowl in position, her hands trembling. She took a deep ragged breath trying to summon the strength to call Mrs Benson. She groaned low in her throat and looked downwards and to her horror, the bowl was no longer empty.

The foetus was perfect, no bigger than the palm of Bea's hand. Minute arms and legs were splayed as though in distress. Bea's heart constricted and she felt violently sick. She closed her eyes but the image remained to haunt her. She felt faint and must have called out in her pain for the door opened and the midwife bustled into the room.

'That's all right dear, come on, give it to me now.' Bea became aware that her hand still grasped the bowl and it took all the older woman's strength to prise it away from her.

A red haze was floating behind Bea's closed lids. Nothing was real, the horror was only a nightmare from which she would awake. But now she was tired, she must sleep and what did it matter if the world was slipping away from her?

How Bea had got home she did not afterwards clearly remember. There had been a vague awareness of Mrs Benson and a girl whom she called Sally, helping her into a small cart that smelled sickeningly of fish even though a rough blanket had been laid against the planking. The ride seemed to go on interminably and she – half fainting, half waking – felt every rut and bump on the roadway. She heard Mrs Benson speaking and had to strain to catch her words.

'Never seen one like this before, nothing gone wrong with her, not lost a lot of blood, only what's normal like but she's having such a bad attack of the vapours, must be her delicate upbringing I spects, not hardly like the usual girls who come to me.'

'Well you've done all you can, Mam.' The voice was rough and harsh and Bea withdrew into herself, instinctively disliking the girl whose face swam before her eyes.

At least the midwife had the sense to take the carriage round the back of the house and as fortune had it, Bertha came to the door.

'Oh my dear God, Miss Bea.' The maid supported her while Mrs Benson made hurried explanations.

'Taken poorly she was, right afterwards, nothing gone wrong, it's just the shock of it all I suppose.'

'Right,' Bertha spoke firmly. 'I'll get her to her bed and look after her, never fear.'

It was a relief to be in her room with the fire roaring in the grate for by now Bea was shivering uncontrollably. She felt Bertha lower her onto the bed and begin to take off her clothes, murmuring sympathetically all the while.

'You'll be just fine after a good sleep Miss Bea. I'll see to you, don't you worry. You need good red wine and plenty of beetroot to build up your blood again and before you know it, you'll be the same as you was before.'

Bea sighed heavily, leaning her cheek against the pillow, feeling herself sinking into the softness of her own bed. She might grow well and strong again but she would never be the same again, ever.

Bertha proved to be an invaluable friend and a dedicated nurse in the days that followed Bea's visit to Mrs Benson. Neither of them spoke of the matter and it was almost as though her ordeal had never happened, Bea thought sadly, except that the sight of the tiny perfect child haunted her mind, waking and sleeping, and she knew she would never be free of the memory.

James came to see her every day, readily accepting the story that she had been struck down with a summer chill. One morning he sat beside her, his eyes anxious as he held her cold fingers in his strong hands.

'My dear girl,' he said softly, 'I don't think I have ever told you just how much I need you and appreciate you. Since your mother died there's been no one close to me; perhaps that's my own fault. But seeing you sickly like this makes me realise how very fortunate I am to have such a devoted daughter.'

Bea smiled up at him, trying for his sake to be cheerful. 'You're a young man yet, Daddy,' she said, 'you should go out and about more, meet people, you might well marry again, you'd be a catch for any woman.'

James was gruff in his pleased embarrassment. 'Maybe you're right, Bea, I suppose I have allowed myself to become a bit of a hermit over the years and one day you'll be finding a fine young man to marry, which is only right and proper. Perhaps I shall begin to invite people here again, perhaps hold a ball at Christmas time, we shall see.'

As the days passed into weeks, Bea's strength gradually returned, she still kept to the house, even though the summer sun was pouring hot and strong through the long windows. She did not feel that she could face people, not yet, and so she remained at home, sitting in her chair, staring out into the softly scented gardens.

It was Bertha who coaxed her into going for a walk in the grounds. 'Please, Miss Bea, I'll come with you.' Her young face was eager, her eyes alight with affection and Bea's throat constricted.

'Just a moment,' she went to her jewel box and took out a small cameo that had been one of her mother's gifts to her. 'Have this, Bertha, it's my way of saying thank you, so don't refuse.'

It was so fresh and so balmy in the gardens with the bees droning between the roses and birds swooping overhead that Bea suddenly knew how good it was to be alive. She sat on the small wooden seat under the arbour of roses and breathed in the scents of summer as eagerly as a thirsty man drinks water.

'Miss Bea,' Bertha's voice sounded low in her ear, 'you've got visitors.' The maid stepped back a pace or two and Bea, glancing up, was startled to see her father leading someone across the soft green lawns towards her. Her heart plummeted in her breast and her hands began to shake as she recognised the tall figure walking alongside James.

'Sterling.' She breathed his name and somehow found the

courage to smile in welcome. Then he was seating himself beside her, capturing her hands within his, and unbidden came the ironic memory of him saying that he and she were as close as brother and sister.

'Bea, I'm sorry you've been laid up with a chill, I hope you're feeling better now, though I must say you're still looking very pale.'

James stood over them, his face closed and set and Bea understood him for the first time. She could even pity her father for carrying the knowledge within him that he could never claim his only son.

'I'm going back into the house,' James said, speaking carefully. 'Sterling has brought his mother on a visit and I'd better not leave her alone for too long, I don't wish to seem unwelcoming. Will you be all right dear, there's no point in tiring yourself out?'

Bea looked up at him. 'Of course I'll be all right father,' she said reprovingly. 'You know that Sterling and I have always been good friends, he's just like part of the family. You go and keep Aunt Victoria company by all means, I'm sure you two must have a great deal to talk about.' She could not keep the edge of bitterness from her voice and yet how could she blame her father for what had happened many years ago. How could he possibly have known the terrible repercussions his actions would cause?

Bertha hovered protectively behind the seat, out of earshot but within calling distance should her mistress require her services. Bertha knew nearly everything about Bea's association with Sterling for she was a bright girl and had missed nothing on the trips she had made with Miss Bea into town. She was an accomplice, and yet without possession of the truth, she could only assume that Mr Sterling had let her mistress down badly.

Bea untwined her fingers from Sterling's grip. 'It's very nice of you to come.' She knew she was speaking stiffly as though he was a stranger but the urge to fall into his arms and cry out her anguish was almost overwhelming. She looked away from him and across the sloping gardens that led down to the sea, trying to steel herself. She must be strong for she would inevitably meet with Sterling almost every day of her life unless one or the other of them moved away from the closed society of Sweyn's Eye.

'I've come to apologise for what happened at the hotel and to make amends.' Sterling's voice was vibrant as he leaned closer to her. 'Bea, I'm very fond of you. What I'm trying to say is, I'd like you to be my wife.'

Bea fought the hysterical laughter that rose up within her, the very words she had longed to hear from Sterling's lips had come too late. She turned to him, trying to keep her expression bright but unreadable.

'Sterling,' she spoke his name chidingly, 'you know as well as I do that we're not meant for each other, I'm very fond of you too but fondness is not passion, is it?'

He leaned towards her and kissed her cheek lightly before she could turn away. Her heart began to beat uncomfortably fast, for his nearness was affecting her, arousing the very passions that she denied feeling for him.

'I thought we suited each other very well in that direction, Bea,' he said softly. 'Don't turn me down without thinking about what I've said very carefully.'

'Have you spoken to my father about this?' she asked him abruptly and relief poured through her as she saw him shake his head.

'No, I think you're old enough to make up your own mind about something as important as marriage.' Sterling took her hand in his once more and she allowed her fingers to rest impassively in his.

'Yes, I am,' she looked away from his golden beauty for she longed to put her hands on his cheeks and draw his sensuous mouth down upon her own. 'And I don't want to marry you Sterling, I'm sorry.' She rose and moved away from him and her legs were trembling.

'You see I have given it all a great deal of thought ever since that first time we made love at the hotel. Incidentally, you shouldn't blame yourself for our affair or for the fact that I don't love you in the way a wife should love her husband.'

'That's a very harsh and abrupt conclusion, Bea.' Sterling rose from the seat and Bea saw him glancing towards the house. 'Damn, there's Mother. Bea, is that your final answer?'

He was close behind her and Bea fought for control as she moved away from him.

'I'm afraid it is, Sterling,' she said softly, keeping her back turned lest he see the torment in her face. She knew she was hurting him but a clean break and a final one was the only course she could take.

'Aunt Victoria, how lovely to see you.' She greeted Victoria Richardson as she had always done with a kiss on the round smooth cheek, and yet within her was a raging tide of emotion and bitterness. Why oh why had Victoria chosen James Cardigan as her lover?

'Bea, my dear, your father should have let me know you were unwell.' Victoria smiled, her unlined face revealing nothing of her passionate past. Bea was surprised at her own control as she was held at arm's length and studied from head to foot.

'You are not eating properly, my dear,' Victoria said reprovingly. 'You are far too thin and there is no colour in your cheeks.' She turned to James. 'You must take this daugther of yours away for a rest, can't you see for yourself that she is far from well?'

The thought lodged in Bea's mind, to get away from Sweyn's Eye and from Sterling and the turmoil of emotion the sight of him evoked in her.

'That's a very good idea,' she said decisively. Arms linked, she walked with Victoria back through the grasslands towards the house and her mind teased the prospect of leaving Sweyn's Eye. A rest taken somewhere far away might be exactly what was needed to erase from her mind her affair with Sterling and the nightmare of events that had followed.

'I think, Aunt Victoria, you have found just the right cure for me,' she said, and yet deep within her was a well of unhappiness that nothing would ever alleviate.

Chapter Seventeen

Davie moved from furnace mouth to mould with the unerring accuracy born of long practice. His huge muscles bulged and his great shoulders ached from the strain but he prided himself on doing the job he was paid for and in doing it well.

Behind him, Will Owens was falling out of step again, the boyo was a damned nuisance, not cut from the same pattern as his father had been. What's more, Davie strongly suspected that Will Owens was working as a songbird, pouring tales into the boss's ear, sneaking behind the backs of his fellows and doubtless all for the price of a pint or two of ale.

Davie had watched Mr Richardson go up to the boyo on several occasions, talking to him on the quiet, and though he liked Mr Richardson well enough and didn't blame him for keeping his ears to the ground, Davie didn't approve of songbirds and neither did the rest of the men.

Will Owens had already felt the chill of disapproval but none of the other coppermen had come out with what was on their minds and confronted the young toerag with it, none except Davie himself. Will Owens had flatly denied it of course and as there was never any proof of that sort of backstabbing, the subject had been dropped. But Davie had left the boyo in no doubt that he would be closely watched.

'Keep in step,' Davie growled as Owens came too near his back for comfort. 'I can feel the damned heat from your ladle near my arse.' Owens fell back a pace or two and Davie concentrated on tipping his burden of copper into the mould.

'Your turn for a break, Davie,' Sam Herbert shouted across to him, holding aloft the jug of ale that he'd been drinking from. Davie lowered his ladle to the ground carefully and left the ranks of men with a sigh of relief. He picked up his tea can and went to the stove in the corner of the room, lifting the big pot and making himself a brew. It was very rarely that Davie drank ale while at work; he preferred his tea, for alcohol clouded the mind and weakened the body – at any rate that's what he himself thought, what others did was their business.

'Saw that bastard Owens outside the office earlier.' Sam Herbert swigged his ale and wiped his mouth with the back of his hand. 'Can't stand the boyo, too upitty and cocky for my liking, though his dad was a good friend of mine and speak as you find, he was one of the best. Just as well he's not alive to see what sort of scum his son turned out to be.'

Davie drank his tea, swallowing deeply, and rubbed at his face with his sweat cloth. Sam was one of the older men in the sheds, past his prime and not able to ladle like he used to, but fit enough for bringing in the green trees for feeding into the furnaces.

'You keep your mouth buttoned, Sam,' Davie cautioned. 'Don't go getting yourself into something you can't handle. Toerag Will Owens may be but he'd not be above fisting you one if you offended him and you're too old and wise a ram for that sort of caper.'

Sam spat on the ground. 'It's hard to keep your mouth shut when a boyo makes you sick to your guts,' he said, his eyes dark as they followed Will Owens' quick movements. 'See how he tips copper as if it was soup, no care does he take with the stuff and it strong enough to burn off a man's both legs as quick as a wink. No respect for the copper and no fear and that is always dangerous.'

Davie swirled the last of the tea around the can and drank it down. Some of the tealeaves caught in his throat and he spat them out.

'It's back to work for me then, Sam.' He rubbed his hands carefully against his trousers, damp fingers were slippery and a firm grip on the handle was the difference between work well done and disaster.

'Saw your girl the other day,' Sam said conversationally. 'If I'm not mistaken she was with the boss.' Sam took a deep gulp of his ale and his eyes were turned away from Davie who had stopped suddenly in his tracks.

'Saw Mali? Where did you see her, at the fair was it?' Davie felt anger begin to burn in his gut, was he never going to be allowed to forget that his daughter had sat up there amongst the toffs like a common doxy?

'No boyo, not at the fair, down at the cemetery it was. Gone to see to my little babba's grave, the youngest, the one that passed on ten years ago or more, always go down once a week I do, my only boy, see, talks to him I do, soft in the head I may be but it brings me ease and so why shouldn't I do what I feel is right?'

Davie shook his head in bewilderment, trying to sort through the muddle of words. 'You saw my Mali with Mr Richardson down at Dan-y-Graig Cemetery, is that right?' He dabbed at his neck where the sweat was running in small rivulets down into the hair of his chest, waiting in growing impatience for Sam to reply.

'That's right, saw them myself I did, mighty fond he seems of your girl, Davie and I don't mean any harm by telling you but for all that watch young Mali, you know as well as I do what rams these bosses are, don't want but one thing from our women and then leaves them in the lurch as soon as there's any trouble.'

Davie rubbed the sweat rag over his face, concealing his fury. Mali was still seeing the boss after all he'd said, well she would just have to learn to heed him, even if it meant him taking his belt to her.

He found it difficult to find his rhythm again and he was slower than usual filling his ladle and tipping the molten steaming copper into the top hats. He knew that when the moulds were emptied after the copper had cooled, the round slices of metal would be uneven and that irritated him, he liked his work to be perfect and though it would be impossible to tell which ladler had tipped which wheel of copper it was enough that he himself knew his ladling was not up to its usual standard.

He had lost his place in line and was now working behind Will Owens. Davie watched the youth's back and felt like hitting out at him as if by an act of violence he might cleanse

177

away his anger and distress over Mali. He held his brimming ladle forward and deliberately sketted the boyo's leg and the next moment all hell broke loose as Will Owens hopped like a frog, tearing at his trousers, drawing the burning cloth away from his flesh.

'You bastard.' He looked up at Davie from where he was crouched on the ground. 'You did that on purpose and don't deny it.' He rubbed at the small livid mark at the back of his calf and from experience, Davie knew that though not serious, the burn would be stinging like a nettle patch.

'There's sorry I am boyo,' Davie said evenly. 'Careless of me that was but not done on purpose, mind.' He reached out to help Will Owens to his feet but his hand was brushed aside angrily.

'*Duw*, don't take it so badly, there's bound to be accidents some times, look how you were nearly tripping over my heels earlier on. Anyway, that's not much of a burn and a dock leaf will take the stinging away.'

Will Owens rose to his feet and hopped over to the bench near the wall. The furnaceman looked over his shoulder at Davie.

'Warming the songbird up a bit? That's something we'd all have liked to do.'

'Aye, it clipped his wings a bit but he'll not stop his tune for there's money to line his pockets whenever he sings.'

The furnaceman pushed a sapling into the molten metal and it hissed and roared like a wounded beast.

'God, it's like hell in this stinking shed.' Davie mopped his face. 'I'll be glad to have my shift over and done with.'

Will Owens rejoined the crew, his face sullen, his eyes murderous as they studied Davie.

'Go in front of me, David Llewelyn,' he said flatly. 'I don't trust you at the back.' He fell into line and the endless round of dipping and pouring began once more. Davie worked easily now, having found his second wind. Soon the day's shift would be done and then he could go home and eat his grub, wash himself down ready to meet Rosa. His pulse quickened at the thought and somehow as he moved from furnace to mould, his step was lighter.

It was raining again when Davie finished work and he drew

his coat around him, feeling cold after the heat of the sheds. As he passed the gatehouse, he glanced inside the office and saw Sterling Richardson bent over his desk. If there was any more talk about the boss and Mali then Davie would have to deal with the matter in his own way, Mr Richardson might take more notice of fists than he did of words.

Later that evening, Davie entered the smoky public bar of Maggie Dicks and stood for a moment looking around him. The piano in the corner was being played loudly and triumphantly by Dai End House, whose fingers, small for a man, roved over the yellowed keys with loving skill.

The stone floor of the bar was covered in sawdust and the cast iron tables, set about the room in haphazard fashion, were ornately decorated with images of Britannia, the oak table tops scarred by marks from beer mugs and pipe tobacco.

The small window looked outward upon a hill, long and steep, which during the heavy rains sent water pouring down to flood the small house. Even now, the landlord had taken the precaution of putting old worn-out matting against the front step.

There was no sign of Rosa and so Davie ordered himself a pint of ale and leaned against the bar, staring into the mirror behind the rows of bottles on the shelves. He looked young for his years, he thought with pride, his hair was still dark with no hint of grey and his face was comparatively unlined.

He felt that his association with Rosa had warmed him into life, for when his wife had died he had been empty and lost without her. He was not an articulate man but his emotions went deep and he had believed he would spend the rest of his days alone. Once Mali met with a fine young boyo, someone of her own sort, he had reasoned, a man who would offer her marriage and a home with fine children around the hearth, he would live out his life as a priest did with no women to give him comfort. But then he had reckoned without Rosa.

He had taken a fancy to her the first time they'd met; she had made up to him flattered him and though he'd seen through her wiles, it did not matter. He had taken her first in the lane behind the doors of the Mexico Fountain for she was offering a shilling stand-up and he had paid willingly. Soon, however, they began to meet more and more often and he found he was becoming increasingly jealous of her other clients.

'I've got a proposition for you girl,' he'd said, taking the bull by the horns. 'I'll court you proper like, you'll be my woman and no other man's, does that suit you? It's either that or we finish right here and now.' Rosa had melted against him, her eyes soft with tears, and for a moment she could not speak, she simply clung to his hand, trembling as though she was a young virgin.

'Oh, Davie, I can't believe it, a decent man like you offering for me. I don't have to tell you surely that the answer is yes.'

And so from then on, Rosa had become respectable though occasionally a customer who had been away from the area for a time would approach her and offer her a few shillings and Rosa would be highly delighted to decline the money and be proud to say that she was no longer a girl of the streets.

Old Sam Herbert came up to Davie and leaned on the bar next to him. 'That was a fine trick you played on our songbird.' He winked hugely. 'Though I doubt if it will be enough to teach the boyo a lesson. Still, shifts over for today so I shouldn't be talking about work, how about a hand of cards?'

'Sorry, Sam, meeting Rosa in a minute, she's late, busy dolling herself up I suppose.'

Sam looked at him gravely. 'Now Davie, I'm always being accused of putting my oar in where it shouldn't be but speak my mind I must. That Rosa is a flossy and has been since she was about twelve years old. Not her fault mind, her mam dying when she was little more than a babba, but for all that she's had more pokes than a worn-out archery target. Leopards don't change their spots, Davie, so for Gawd's sake look round, find a respectable woman, someone from the chapel so that you'll be well looked after in your old age.'

Davie had not moved a muscle all the while Sam had been speaking but when he looked up his eyes were cold. 'About one thing, you're right, Sam, you shouldn't put your oar in where it's not wanted. Now leave me alone for there's my girl now and I don't want her upset, right?'

He put his arm around Rosa and she looked fine and pretty in her soft cotton blouse and dark skirt. She had done her hair up and if you didn't know of her past, Davie thought, you wouldn't pick her out from any other woman in a crowd. Except of course that chapel women did not go into public bars.

As Davie looked down into her eyes, he wondered if he would ever actually get around to marrying her, that he wanted her in his bed was positive enough and he was tired of her going on at him, wanting to be installed in the little cottage in Copperman's Row.

It was for Mali's sake that he hesitated, he did not wish to hurt his daughter for he knew that her memories of her Mam must be very precious and it was too soon to be asking for her approval of Rosa.

'You're looking very handsome tonight, Davie.' As she snuggled up against him, Rosa smiled enticingly and he felt her hand touch his crotch for a brief instant. Even though such actions excited him, inwardly he disapproved of them for they were not ladylike and gave him pause to remember what her life had been like before he had come into it.

'Behave yourself, there's a good girl,' he said sternly. He moved away from her a little and she pouted up at him.

'You're in a bad mood with Little Rosa, what have I done now? You're always picking fault lately Davie, not growing tired of me are you?'

His face softened. 'No girl, I'm not tired of you and if I was you'd be out on your ear right this minute, back to walking the streets. No, worried about Mali I am, she's been seen with the boss again, down at the cemetery, and I'm wondering what game they are playing.'

Rosa laughed low. 'It's the oldest game in the world, Davie my fine boyo and don't you play it yourself often enough? It seems your girl is not much different to me for all that she turns her nose up whenever she sees me.'

'Don't talk so daft.' Davie was stung by Rosa's words. Mali was a good girl, and though he was angry with her for being silly and giving folks room to talk, he did not believe for one moment that she would do anything bad.

'You must learn to button that loose mouth of yours woman,' he said harshly. 'It's no wonder some husbands used to bridle the tongues of their womenfolk.' He took her arm roughly.

'Come on, we're getting out of here, I'm bone weary. I want to get home.' He led her through the doors of Maggie Dicks and out into the darkness, and a brooding sullenness had suddenly taken possession of him.

'I'm sorry Davie,' Rosa whimpered as his grip on her arm tightened. 'I didn't want to make you mad. Come on, give Rosa a kiss, a bit of lovin' always makes you feel better.' She pressed herself against him and in spite of himself Davie responded.

'Come on then girl,' he said in a sudden mood of defiance. 'Take you home I will and to hell with what other people say.'

Sterling closed the book with a snap of finality. It had been a long day and he had been in the office since early morning. He stretched his arms above his head and yawned, feeling that in spite of his weariness his energy had been well spent.

It had become clear to him as the spring had turned slowly into summer that Alwyn Travers had no intention of repaying the loan made by Sterling's father. Perhaps the man did not realise that records would be kept, he might even think that with the death of Arthur Richardson he was freed from any obligations, but he was soon to learn different.

Sterling had consulted with the firm's solicitors and they agreed that Alwyn Travers must be given one opportunity to make good his arrears on the mine and if he would not or could not meet the demand then he would be forced to vacate the property forthwith.

It was silent in the office, for Ben had long since left for home. His eyes had held an almost grudging glow of respect as he'd paused at the door to say good night.

'I think you will do very well in this business, Mr Richardson.' He had been polishing his glasses in the way he always did when he was embarrassed. 'You have a hard core of steel that was regrettably missing in your father, God rest his soul.'

Sterling had smiled ruefully. 'It looks as though I must be hard, Ben,' he'd replied, 'for everyone is depending on me for a living, from my mother to my young brother, not to mention my two partners.'

And it was true, Sterling thought ruefully, everyone seemed

ready to criticise him but not one came up with any constructive alternatives.

He rose to his feet now and shrugged himself into his coat, it had been a warm day, hazy with heat, and even among the slag heaps flowers flourished, bleached white by the metal deposits in the ground, with bees droning through the petals looking for nectar.

It had been a day to make Sterling restless and even though his mind had been occupied with matters of business, there had been moments when he had thought deeply about Mali Llewelyn. He admitted to himself that she had almost become an obsession for he had tried to forget her sweetness and the softness of her lips and the scent of her long dark hair and yet her image had continued to haunt him. He knew that he would seek her out again for his feelings were more compelling than any common-sense arguments that he put forward for his own inspection.

He locked up the office and moved into the softness of the evening, pausing for a moment, not wishing to return to the loneliness of his hotel room. Impatiently, he started up the Ascot, feeling it throbbing into life as he sat in the driving seat. He nodded abruptly to the man on the gate and drove out into the mean streets that surrounded the works.

On an impulse, he parked the automobile at the corner near the Mexico Fountain and walked slowly along Copperman's Row. It was twilight now and so no one noticed him pausing outside the door of Mali's home.

He glanced through the lace-curtained window and saw a slender figure moving about within the soft glow of the gas light. He tapped the glass and a startled face turned towards him.

'Sterling, what are you doing here?' Mali was at the door in an instant. She seemed distracted as she brushed back the hair that was hanging loose around her waist with trembling fingers. He touched it almost wonderingly and with a quick look along the row, Mali stepped outside and caught his arm, hurrying him away along Market Street and towards the canal.

'My father is angry with me for making a show of myself,' she said breathlessly, 'he musn't see us together or there'll be a hiding for me instead of words.' She seemed to realise then that she was clinging to his arm and she drew away self-consciously.

'Sterling, there's nothing for us to say to each other.' She leaned against the wall that ran along the roadway and stared down into the dark waters of the canal. Sterling reached for her and drew her close and she rested her head on his shoulder as though she was very tired.

'I thought you said you loved me,' he whispered softly, his mouth against the warmth of her neck. She moved away and her eyes were unreadable in the darkness but he could imagine them, vivid green and luminous, eyes that looked right through a man. A feeling of power was rising within him, there were no barriers he could not overcome, he wanted Mali Llewelyn, he might even be falling a little in love with her. He would possess her, he must rid himself of the fever that plagued him.

'Mali,' he spoke urgently, 'I need you, you must surely know that?' She moved like a startled faun within the circle of his arms, as though preparing for flight. He held her close, kissing her soft mouth passionately, oblivious to everything but his own desires.

Chapter Eighteen

Sterling sat at the dining table, holding a glass of wine and watching his mother, who seemed to be almost coquettish the way she fluttered her fan and giggled every now and then as though his remarks were the cleverest thing she'd heard in a long while. They had eaten their meal slowly and all the while, Sterling watched his mother carefully, wondering what was on her mind. Suddenly, Victoria leaned forward and rested her elbows on the table.

'Now, Sterling, I think I'd better tell you why I've invited you here this evening, I'm sure you must be wondering about the way I've been gossiping nonstop. Well, it's sheer nerves. You may not know it but you are a very disconcerting person on times, even though you are my son.'

Sterling smiled at her indulgently. His mother was making a big issue of something that was doubtless quite unimportant; she had probably overspent and her allowance was running out.

'All right, let's hear what you have to say and I promise to listen patiently whatever it is.'

Victoria was suddenly serious. She closed her fan with a snap and sat up straight in her chair and all at once she seemed young and vulnerable.

'James wishes to come courting me.' Her cheeks were flushed and her eyelids half closed and there was an air of waiting as though she expected an outburst from Sterling.

'I know it's rather soon after your dear father, after Arthur passed away but for the present the relationship between James and me will remain secret. I don't know if you'll approve or not, Sterling, I hope you will, but even if you don't it makes no difference. I am lonely and I feel I need some happiness from life.'

Sterling was stunned by her words. He remained silent, trying to combat his rising anger. 'When has all this been going on?' He could hear the edge to his voice and saw Victoria look up at him defiantly. He watched as she opened and closed her fan and knew that she was more nervous than she appeared.

'Nothing has been "going on",' she said angrily. 'James has come to call as a friend of the family, a good friend as he's been for years as well you know. It's simply that we both feel we have much to give each other, is that wrong?'

Sterling rose from his chair and moved across to the window, staring out into the grounds.

'I don't like James Cardigan, Mother, I never have,' he said abruptly. 'But it's your life and I can't very well tell you how to lead it.'

'No you can not.' Victoria rose and threw down a napkin, 'and as for not liking James, you have never given him a chance, how can you possibly claim to know what he's like?'

'And where do you intend to make your home, Mother?' He ignored her question and put one of his own. 'Not at Plas Rhianfa, I hope.' He turned to face her and he could see that she was very angry indeed, her face was flushed and her eyes sparkled with tears.

'If I wish to live here when I'm married, then I will.' She spoke stormily. 'This house may be part of your inheritance, Sterling, but I'm your mother and am entitled to live out my life here.'

He gave a short laugh. 'You may not have the opportunity because the place is mortgaged to the hilt. It's a great barn of a house in any case and I may sell it even if the business improves.'

'Oh, do what you like,' Victoria snapped back, 'I'm just not going to speak to you any further. Good night.'

She strode across the room, her head high, her elegant silk skirt swirling round her feet.

As the door slammed behind his mother, Sterling rubbed his face tiredly. Why had he not handled the situation with more tact? Who was he to condemn his mother for her choice of marriage partner?

'Good God, what was all that shouting about?' Rickie entered the room and stood staring at Sterling with such hostility in his set face that immediately there was an atmosphere of tension between the brothers.

'None of your business,' Sterling said sharply and Rickie came further into the room, his lips set in a straight, thin line.

'Nothing is ever any of my business according to you, is it? But this time you've succeeded in upsetting Mother as well.' He sat down at the dining table, his arms stretched out before him, and Sterling noted that his brother, who was always willing to do battle with words, was taking care that his physical attitudes did not provoke violence. 'What's wrong with you?' Rickie demanded. 'You're power crazed. Taking over the company has gone right to your head.' He glanced up sharply.

'And while you're here perhaps you could answer some questions for me.' He leaned back in his chair, hands thrust into his pockets, another unconscious attitude of self defence, Sterling mused.

'Why are you persecuting the Travers family? First you sack Glanmor without any warning and then if that wasn't enough, you send his brother notice that you intend to foreclose on the mortgage. Don't you realise that Alwyn has a wife and child to take care of?'

'And since when have you been so concerned with the plight of others?' Sterling demanded. 'If you think I'm going to give you explanations you can go to hell!'

'Oh, all very gentlemanly and articulate,' Rickie jeered, 'resorting to expletives now are we?'

'We haven't all had the benefit of a college education as you have,' Sterling replied. 'And if you don't shut your mouth, you'll find my fist filling it.' He clenched his hands, moving forward a pace, but as Rickie jerked backwards in his chair, Sterling's anger suddenly faded.

'I have to foreclose on that mortgage, don't you understand?' His hands fell to his sides.

'Oh, what's the use?' He moved towards the door and without another word let himself out into the starlit night. All around him were the scents of the gardens he had known ever since childhood and he breathed in deeply, wondering how it was that everything changed so drastically and suddenly.

He was no longer the beloved son, safe and secure in the shadow of his father but was now the breadwinner and being balked all along the line by the very ones who should be putting their faith in him. He sighed softly. The time was come to leave childish things behind, he was a man and would shape his own destiny.

In the morning, the sun was bright and warm as he set off from the Mackworth Arms and drove away from the town, bypassing the copper company and crossing the river towards Foxhole. Taking the winding road towards the Kilvey Deep, he reflected on the fact that it would not be pleasant facing Alwyn Travers, but since there had been no reply to the letter his solicitors had sent out, the only possible course Sterling could take was to speak to the man face to face.

The winding-wheel of the mine stood out against the sky as Sterling drew the Ascot to a halt on the dirt track that served as a roadway. There was a shed near the gate and a man holding a large hound on a chain poked his head through the door.

'If you've come to see the boss he's not here.' His voice was harsh and from the broken nose to the battered ear, the man looked every inch the pugilist he undoubtedly was.

'If you mean Alwyn Travers he's certainly the one I want to see,' Sterling replied in a hard voice. 'Where is he?'

The man's bulk filled the doorway of the shed. 'What's that to you, who are you, anyway?'

'I'm Sterling Richardson, owner of the copper company. Tell Mr Travers that I must speak to him,' he said smoothly.

The man gave a short laugh. 'That's rich that is, you're the very one the guv don't want to see. Clear off before I set the dog on you.'

Sterling climbed down from the Ascot and moved closer to the man, who seemed taken aback by his persistence.

'I want a civil answer to a civil question.' Sterling spoke evenly. 'If Mr Travers is not here, then where is he?'

The dog growled low, baring ferocious-looking teeth, and Sterling allowed his hand to move slowly and carefully towards the animal's muzzle. The hound sniffed suspiciously but after a moment sat back on its haunches as though satisfied that Sterling posed no threat.

'Don't you start no trouble here.' The man was less certain of himself now. ' 'Cos gent or no gent, I'll bust your nose for you.'

'I shouldn't try it if I were you,' Sterling smiled and brought his fist upwards, catching the man a clip on the point of his jaw. At the same time he raised his knee sharply, right into his opponent's groin. The dog began to bark, leaping around the small shed as though anxious to escape, and as the man fell writhing to the floor he howled loudly, adding to the confusion.

'Alwyn's up there, in his house, now for Gawd's sake clear out of here will you?'

Sterling drove the Ascot away from the mine and up the track that led to a tall house settled between the hills. The last thing he wanted was a scene with Alwyn Travers on his home ground, but there was nothing else for it, he could not be allowed to get away with his foolish defiance.

The green hills were scarred with the black of coal dust and great slag heaps rose towards the sky, man-made mountains of waste from the rich coal seams, dark and brooding against the morning sky.

Sterling approached the house and lifted the knocker and shortly afterwards the door was opened by a small spare woman with tired lines around her pale eyes.

'May I come inside?' Sterling was already in the small hallway. 'If you would tell Alwyn that I'm here?' He moved into the parlour and though resentment of his action was clear in the woman's face, she obeyed him. Sterling stared around, noting the heavy brass ornaments and the fine carpeting. Travers might be up to his neck in debt but he did not believe in going without his creature comforts.

'What do you want here?' Alwyn was a taller man than his brother Glanmor but his face bore the same ferrety look. His eyebrows straggled untidily across his broad nose so that he appeared to be permanently frowning. 'I don't want the likes of you on my property so why don't you just clear off?'

Sterling shook his head. 'Your man tried violence. It doesn't

189

work, so do yourself a good turn and just listen to me and that way no one will be hurt, all right?'

Mrs Travers came to stand beside her husband, her hand resting on his arm in a cautionary gesture.

'Get on with it then.' Alwyn Travers rubbed at his thin moustache nervously. 'Say your piece and then go.'

Sterling allowed himself a small smile. 'That's fine by me. All I have to say to you is that I am foreclosing on the loan my father made you. You can keep this house and I shall make you a grant of compensation so that you will not be entirely without means. I can't say fairer than that.'

'You can't take the mine away from me,' Travers blustered, his face red and angry. 'It's been in the family for generations, it's always belonged to the eldest son, you can't do it, do you hear me?'

Sterling moved towards the door. 'You've been given ample time to repay me or even make a start on bringing down the balance and this you have not done so I've every right to take the mine and I intend to do just that.' At the door he paused. 'If I were you, I'd sell this house, buy something smaller, move away from the area, right away.'

'Is that a threat?' Travers moved forward, raising a fist angrily, and Sterling put out his hand and held the man at arm's length.

'Now don't go making things any worse,' he said evenly. 'Just think, you are not coming out of this too badly, are you? It's quite obvious you couldn't run a Sunday school outing let alone a business. Eventually you'd have had to get rid of the mine to pay your debts anyway.'

As Sterling left the house and walked towards the Ascot, Alwyn Travers stood in the doorway shouting abuse at him.

'I'll get even with you for this, however long it takes me.' His face was mottled, his eyes bulging from his head, but Sterling ignored him, he was a bag of wind, nothing more. And yet there was a nasty taste in his mouth. He wondered if there had been some other way he could have handled the affair but then, Alwyn Travers owed him the money which Sterling needed if his own business was to survive.

There was no point in having a conscience about it, he told himself bitterly, that luxury was reserved for people like his brother Rickie who thought that championing the cause of the workers was his role in life. And so it was, Sterling thought ruefully, just so long as there was something in it for Rickie Richardson.

'Hell and damnation,' he said to himself, but his words were carried away by the soft breeze sweeping down from the hills.

The public bar of the Cape Horner was smoky, the air fetid with the smell of stale tobacco. The hubbub of voices was deafening for it was a warm day and the sailors, coming from the ships in the dock, were thirsty.

At a table in the corner, Rickie sat with Glanmor Travers on one side of him and Will Owens on the other. Facing him was a motley assortment of men, men with stained shirts on their backs, some of them wearing no boots. They were the dregs of Sweyn's Eye, beggars and thieves and villains, each and every one prepared to do murder for a few shillings.

Rickie leaned forward. 'All you need to do is speak to the coppermen,' he said slowly, anxious to impress. 'Tell them that the changes being made will put some of them out of a job, for new labour will be brought into the town, men who know all about steel. And it will be cheaper labour too, the Irish poor who will take low wages and be glad of them.'

'And what's in this for you?' A man with a thick body and huge arms poked his head forward. His eyes were glittering and Rickie felt he would not trust him in an alleyway on a dark night.

'Well, Cullen,' Rickie paused, knowing that the interest of the men seated around him could quickly turn to scorn. They would not swallow any tale about his concern for the workers, they would laugh in his face. He decided to tell them the truth, or at least some of it.

'It's like this. I want to bring Sterling Richardson down and for reasons of my own which I intend keeping to myself.'

'I suppose that means you want a bigger share of the sheckels.' Cullen smiled thinly, leaning back in his chair, his arms folded across his big chest, and Rickie sighed with relief, it was obvious he'd said the right thing.

'Pay us something on account and we'll be on our way,'

Cullen said in his harsh voice. He watched carefully as Rickie counted out the shillings and then lumbered to his feet, sweeping up the coins with one huge hand.

Rickie felt more at ease when they had gone; he turned to Travers, who had a doubtful look.

'Not sure we should have brought the likes of Cullen into this.' Travers kept his voice quiet as though fearful of being overheard.

Rickie shrugged. 'It will be all right, you'll see. The man will do anything so long as he's paid.'

He turned to look at Will Owens out of the corner of his eye. This was the one he was not sure of, he was more cunning, more subtle than Cullen, and Rickie felt instinctively that Owens was not to be trusted.

'What do you think of Cullen, Will?' Rickie asked affably and watched the expression on the youth's face, carefully trying to read something from his eyes and the set of his mouth. Will Owens shrugged his shoulders, toying with his mug of beer, swirling the dark liquid round and round, deliberating before giving his reply.

'I agree with Glanmor,' he said at last, 'Cullen is not the sort of man I'd like to pin my hopes on, there's too much of the villain in him for the man to be trusted with anything.'

Unaccountably, Rickie was irritated with the answer Owens gave him. 'And do you think you could do better?' he demanded, his voice rising. Owens faced him squarely, his eyes dark and unreadable, but his knuckles were white as they gripped his beer mug.

'You asked for my opinion and I gave it,' he said shortly. 'Do you want me to lick your boots as well?'

Travers thumped the table before him with his glass. 'Let's drink up and get some more beer in, I've got a thirst like a camel.' He looked from Will to Rickie and back again and some of the tension eased.

'Well, I just like to know where I stand.' Rickie spoke truculently and leaned back in his chair. Inside he was burning with anger, this young guttersnipe was daring to square up to his betters and that was something that stung. He would need watching, Rickie thought moodily, he was the sort who would smile as he stuck a knife into his own mother.

'Well, have you found out anything of use yet?' He spoke to Will Owens without looking at him and the youth's eyes flickered with interest.

'As a matter of fact I have,' he said quietly and he looked carefully toward Glanmor Travers. 'This concerns you too and you're not going to be pleased.' He moved his chair forward and placed his elbows on the table, bending his head, wanting to be heard above the noise without raising his voice.

'Mr Richardson is going to cause trouble over a loan given to your brother some time back, Glanmor,' Will said. 'Heard him talking about it to Ben the works manager. It seems the mine will belong to your brother once the legal rubbish has been dealt with.'

He looked at Rickie, who carefully kept his feelings to himself. He was taken aback that Owens had learned something that he himself had only known since yesterday.

'He's supposed to be going out to the mine today,' Will Owens continued. 'Going to offer your brother some sort of compensation, a sop to his own conscience if you ask me, Travers.'

Will Owens was enjoying the effect his words were having upon the two men, especially Glanmor Travers who had turned quite pale.

'Mr Richardson needs that mine,' Will continued. 'Have his own supply of coal then won't he? He'll be independent, he's not soft.' There was a grudging admiration in Owens' voice that grated on Rickie.

Glanmor took a deep hissing breath. 'The bastard!' he said. His eyes were narrowed and his face white and angry. 'Well that's it then, he deserves everything he gets.'

Rickie felt a glow of triumph, trouble was brewing and about to boil over and all he'd had to do was to lay out a few shillings.

'Right then, let's get down to some serious talking, shall we?'

193

Chapter Nineteen

It was pleasant in the small office, the sun shone through the open window and a soft breeze drifted in bringing the scent of roses from the bush outside. Mali sat at the old carved wooden desk, the account book open in front of her, not thinking of her work but about Sterling and his vow that he loved her. He must have been teasing her, she decided, for she had not set eyes on him for almost a week.

She looked down at the neat columns, trying to concentrate on her work, and thankfully the figures were all properly balanced. Only one thing spoiled the pleasure Mali found in her work and that was the fact that the laundry was losing money.

'Good morning, my dear.' Mr Waddington came into the room, taking off his silk scarf and placing it on the coat stand near the door. 'I'm not feeling very well today so forgive me for arriving late.' He sat down in his own chair and leaned back against the hard leather, and as Mali looked at him in concern, she saw that his cheeks were pale, his mouth drawn down at the corners.

'Tell me the worst, Mali my dear, how do the accounts balance, are we at least breaking even?' He sighed softly and his long slender hands placed together were blue veined and delicate and they were trembling.

'I'm sorry,' Mali shook her head. 'It's not at all good I'm afraid, even though we have the volume of work coming in the prices you charge are too low, Mr Waddington. You see what with fuel becoming so dear, not to mention the wages to the women, you are paying out much more than you can afford.'

He rubbed his eyes tiredly. 'What do you suggest?' He seemed to have shrunken into himself and Mali chewed her lip worriedly for a moment.

'I suggest that firstly you put up your prices, they haven't changed at all in ages. You see you're still charging the same for starching and pressing as you did three years ago and it's losing you money.'

She looked down at the figures before her. 'I'm afraid you are going to have to cut back on your working force,' she said reluctantly. 'I know it will be hard on the women but you simply haven't the funds to employ as many as you are doing.'

'Oh dear.' Mr Waddington sighed once more. 'Now how do I decide which people should go? I can't bear to upset any of my ladies. And I know the customers won't like paying extra. All the same I'm sure you're right.'

Mali looked up at him. 'I've given it a great deal of thought,' she said, 'and although the boilerhouse uses all the hands you employ the other departments are needlessly full of women. The checking could be done by the packers as they put the linen into piles and the ironing by half the staff you have there now.'

'I suppose there's no alternative. Yes, I'm afraid I'm going to have to let the older women go, people like Aggie, who are not able to pull their weight any more. Sad though it is, I can't afford to carry them any longer.'

He smiled though there was no light in his eyes. 'Make me a cup of tea my dear, and have one yourself. We have some unpleasant tasks to complete and so we might as well refresh ourselves before we start.'

By the afternoon, Mr Waddington had made out a list of the women who were to be given notice of dismissal. He went round the laundry himself, handing out the papers with a few words of regret for each employee he dismissed. Mali saw a change in him, even since the morning his eyes were lacking lustre and his skin had taken on a grey tinge. She did her best to reassure him that everything would be all right.

'You'll see, Mr Waddington, when you have cut your costs things will be better and if we impress on the women that they must be moderate in their use of soap and paper and string, your expenditure will fall even further.'

As she left the laundry later, Mali was surprised to see a

group of women gathered outside the gate. Sally Benson pushed her way forward, her face twisted with anger, her jaw jutting belligerently.

'So you think you're the boss now, do you? Five minutes in the office and you do just as you like, you little slut,' she said. 'I'll bet you think it's very clever getting people like Aggie the boot, and then it's me next, eh?' She jabbed her elbow painfully into Mali's ribs.

Suddenly Katie was beside Mali, her voice full of indignation as she shouted at Sally Benson. 'Hey, now stop that or you'll get the back 'o me hand for sure. Go on home now and leave us to do the same.'

Sally Benson punched Katie hard in the face and the Irish girl fell backwards against the wall, her hand to her nose which had begun to pour with blood.

'You're on your own, my fine madam,' Sally said smugly. 'Don't look for no one to protect you for Big Mary's gone off home, it's just you and me.' Her hands were on her hips, her smile triumphant as she looked down at Mali scornfully.

'Cat got your tongue then or are you wetting yourself with fright?' She grasped the front of Mali's blouse, twisting it between her big fingers so that the material tore from neck to hem with a loud rending sound.

Mali felt anger growing like a racing tide within her. It seemed suddenly that all the pain and loss of burying her mother and the tears she had not even begun to cry since that terrible day in the winter when she had walked beside the fish cart to the graveyard were boiling up inside her like a volcano. Before she knew what she was doing, she had bunched her hand into a fist and lashed out at Sally's sneering face.

She saw the girl's mouth start to bleed even as she hit out again and again, unable to quench the need to strike out at something or someone until Sally fell to the ground whimpering like a baby.

Mali felt dazed as if all that was happening was unreal, it couldn't have been she who had stood there pounding at the other girl with such venom. She rubbed her face as the rest of the laundry women crowded around her, cheering and clapping her on the back. And then Katie was clinging to her, nose still bloody, eyes red.

'You showed her a thing or two sure you did, Mali, and I'm proud of you, it was about time someone put down that bully for she's been torturing us all for long enough.'

Mali pushed her way out of the crowd of people. She wanted only to get away on her own, her head was pounding and there were tears running down her cheeks; she felt no jubilation, she simply wanted to run and hide.

She was dimly aware of an automobile drawing up beside her and of an arm pressing protectively around her shoulders. She looked up in surprise, unable to believe the evidence of her own eyes.

'Sterling,' her voice sounded far away, 'what are you doing here?' He was helping her into the seat of the Ascot then and she was being driven away from Canal Street and tears were still running unchecked down her cheeks.

But slowly a glow of warmth began to fill her being, she leaned closer to Sterling's broad shoulder, revelling in the knowledge that he had come to her when she most needed him. Love was like sunlight filling her being so that she could hardly breathe and she realised she was coming alive, truly alive, and it was as though, since Mam's death, she had been withdrawn into her own little world where nothing could really touch her.

She did not know where Sterling was taking her, he was guiding the automobile through the back streets of the town but it did not matter, all she knew was that he was at her side and she trusted him to take care of her. He drew the Ascot to a halt a few minutes later at the back entrance to the Mackworth Arms.

'Come on.' He took her arm, 'we must get you cleaned up, you look as though you'd been hit by a steamroller.'

For the first time, Mali became conscious of her appearance. Her blouse was hanging from her shoulders in tatters and there was blood on her hands, though if it was Sally Benson's or her own, she could not tell.

The long corridors of the hotel were hot and stuffy and Mali prayed that no one would see her like this. Sterling's hand was firmly holding hers as she followed him into his room. The carpet was thick and lush beneath her feet and on the beds and windows were heavy drapes hanging in rich folds. From the harbour she heard the plaintive hooting of a tug and suddenly she wanted more than anything to belong, really belong to someone.

'There, lie down on the bed, I'll send for something for you to drink, perhaps a brandy is what you need.'

'No,' she shook her head, 'just come and hold me, Sterling.' He sat beside her at once, taking her in his arms, brushing the tangled hair away from her face.

'Sweet little Mali,' he spoke softly and she turned her lips towards his, waiting, wanting his mouth upon her own.

A stream of pure emotion ran like fire through her veins, she clung to him, feeling the warmth of his body against her breasts. Her heart was pounding so fast, she could hear it like the rush of the ocean in her ears. She didn't know who moved first but she was lying back against the pillows, her eyes closed, her breath mingled with his.

His hands were tender as he removed the torn blouse, he kissed her shoulder and his mouth was warm and passionate. He explored the softness of her breast with his tongue and flames of desire swept through her, she could not think of anything except the new sensations that were possessing her.

They lay close together on the bed, naked now and for a long moment, they looked at each other with joy.

'You're perfect, Mali,' he breathed, 'so beautiful I can hardly believe you're real.' He cupped her face and his mouth was upon hers, his tongue probing, exciting new awareness in her and she responded by tentatively reaching out and touching him. She felt him shudder and knew with a feeling of happiness that she had the power to rouse him to passion. His breathing was ragged and his body tense and strong.

'Come to me,' she whispered shyly and he rose above her so big and powerful that she closed her eyes in ecstasy. She felt him touch her thigh and he was so gentle, his fingers sensitive, and she loved him so much that she could not bear it.

He came to her slowly, careful not to give her pain, and she wound her arms around his bare back, pressing him closer, knowing that he was her destiny, he was making her his own and now she would never be free of him, would never want to be.

The clock on the wall ticked away the hours. Outside the air had grown cooler and darkness was wrapping a soft mantle over the town. Mali woke in Sterling's arms and she leaned on one elbow, looking down at him, loving him, wanting his passion again.

She kissed his mouth and he awoke, staring up at her with his clear blue eyes alight. He put his hand behind her head and drew her down to him, his mouth on her nipple, his tongue hot and passionate. Mali whimpered with delight and clung to his strong neck, holding him close to her.

'I want you, Sterling,' she whispered and she was suddenly held fast while he was thrusting into her.

This time she felt no pain, only intense joy and happiness. Her body responded to Sterling's as though from some inborn natural instinct and together they moved in rhythm, lost in each other, having no existence outside this room.

Later, as they lay drowsily in each other's arms, Mali thought she had never known such happiness. She reached up and touched Sterling's cheek and laughed as she felt the roughness of his chin.

'You need a shave,' she said softly, 'but you are still the most handsome man in all the world.' He lifted her hand and kissed her fingertips gently.

'It's getting late,' he said, 'I must take you home.' He rose from her side and stood tall and beautiful, like a marble sculpture in the moonlight that shone now through the window.

Mali felt suddenly cold, she had not thought of going home, but of course she would have to resume her normal life even though everything in her cried out that the entire universe was turned upside down.

Tonight, she would sleep in her own bed and tomorrow go to work in the office, try to help Mr Waddington sort out his problems.

'What's wrong?' He began to dress and she watched him, unable to look away. She brushed back her hair from her eyes and Sterling came to sit beside her on the bed, buttoning up his shirt quickly. 'You're very quiet,' he kissed the tip of her nose, 'not sorry are you, Mali?'

Suddenly her arms were around his neck and she was kissing the warmth of his throat. Sorry? This was the best thing that had ever happened to her.

'Of course I'm not sorry,' she whispered and he held her at arm's length, staring down into her face, though in the moonlight she could not see the expression in his eyes.

'I suppose you're afraid to face your father. Well don't worry, Mali, I'll be right there beside you, we'll speak to him together.'

He rose to his feet and finished dressing. 'Look, I'd better go and find you something to wear, your blouse is ruined.' He came and kissed her mouth. 'And no one is to see what a beauty you are beneath your clothes, Mali, only I am to have that privilege.'

She warmed to the possessiveness in his voice. 'Where will you find me a blouse at this time of night?' she asked with a smile and he shook his head.

'You don't know me, Mali, I get everything I want, or haven't you noticed? Don't you fret, you'll have something decent to wear and then I'll take you back home.'

When he'd gone, Mali wandered around the room, staring out at the moonlit harbour where the tall masts of the sailing ships gleamed silver. She felt so happy and so deliciously tired and deep within her was the knowledge that she belonged to Sterling, though it was hard to believe that a man such as he would want her.

She sat for a long time, near the window, watching the streets grow slowly empty at last. She glanced up at the clock on the wall and a tiny feeling of anxiety grew within her – where was Sterling, why did he not come to take her home? She wandered to the door and stood looking down the corridor, which seemed to stretch away endlessly, silent and empty. She felt tears burn her eyes and told herself not to be silly, he would return, of course he would.

She lay on the bed, remembering his warmth and passion and the closeness they had shared, he could not have been deceiving her, could he? She began to search her mind, had he actually spoken words to her of love?

She did not think so. She turned her face into the warmth of the pillow, shutting her mind to the traitorous thoughts that wormed their way into her imaginings.

But when the clock struck midnight Mali knew, with despair eating at her like a canker, that Sterling was not going to return. This then was his way of letting her know that it had meant nothing to him, she had simply been an hour's amusement. She should have been wise enough to realise that it was simply a case of the boss and the working girl, had she not heard the same story often enough?

She looked around for something with which to cover her shoulders and finally took a scarf from Sterling's wardrobe. It concealed most of the torn blouse and she hugged it to her, breathing in the masculine scent on it and a feeling of pain encompassed her.

The corridors were long and empty and dimly lit and it seemed as though everyone in the world was sleeping except for her. She ran down the stairs and out of the back entrance and she was in the street, the softness of the night folding around her.

It seemed strange and unreal walking along the roads beneath the light of the stars. She kept to the back streets, afraid she might meet someone she knew.

As she walked back home, the air grew thicker and the old familiar smell of sulphur drifted towards her. She heard the singing of stragglers from the Mexico, and the happy voices served only to make her own loneliness more acute.

As she opened the door, she saw her father rise from his chair near the fire and turn towards her; at his side was Rosa and her sharp eyes roved over Mali in almost malicious amusement.

'And where have you been until this time of night, you little fool?' Davie said harshly, 'don't you know it could be dangerous wandering abroad at this hour? Why you might meet with some of the sailors from the docks, foreigners who do not understand our ways. You would be taken for a whore walking the streets alone.'

'I'm tired,' Mali replied, 'can't we talk about it in the morning, Dad?' She saw Davie hesitate and then suddenly Rosa moved forwards.

'*Duw* look at this, she's been having a rough and tumble with some young boyo by the looks of it.' Rosa pulled at the scarf, revealing Mali's torn blouse. There was silence in the room and then Davie spoke to her softly.

'Has any man laid a hand on you Mali Llewelyn, and I'm

asking for the truth, mind.'

'I was in a fight at the laundry,' Mali said in exasperation. 'Sally Benson got hold of me but she came off the worse, Dad.' She moved towards the stairs and Davie held up his hand.

'On your mother's grave now, Mali, have you been with a man?' His face was set and angry and Mali felt fear rise up in her throat. If she spoke the truth then Davie would be after Sterling like a shot and yet how could she lie?

'Yes,' she said desperately, 'I've been with a man and if you wanted your daughter to be an angel then you shouldn't have set such a fine example by bringing a woman of the streets into my mother's house.'

She had time to see Davie's stunned look before she rushed up the stairs to her room. She stood gasping at the window, staring out into the star-studded night. The summer air was thick with the scent of flowers and Mali took a deep shuddering breath.

'Sterling, how could you betray me this way?' she whispered in anguish.

Suddenly her bedroom door swung open and Davie seemed to fill the room with his anger. As Mali backed away from him she saw that his thick leather belt was swinging in his hands.

'You are going to cop it now, girl,' he said harshly. 'I'm going to teach you a lesson you'll never forget.'

Chapter Twenty

As Sterling left Mali and hurried along the corridors of the hotel, his thoughts were on the warmth and wonder of the way she had responded to his love. She was beautiful and innocent, everything a man could want in a woman. He smiled to himself, knowing that a union between himself and the daughter of one of his coppermen would shake the society of Sweyn's Eye to its foundation. But damn them all, he would be proud to have Mali as his wife.

His house was almost ready for occupation now and he could just see himself carrying Mali over the large marble steps into the hallway. He imagined her green eyes, wide with wonder as she saw the silk wallpaper and the fine carpets, most of which had come from the storerooms of Plas Rhianfa.

His thought turned almost inevitably to Bea; he was grateful for her help with the decoration of the house and even more grateful that she had turned down his proposal of marriage. How wise she had been to see their relationship for what it really was.

As he left the back door of the hotel, a figure stepped out of the shadows and Sterling turned quickly, his hands clenched into fists. The man moved forward and Will Owens was illuminated in the light from the gas lamp that arched over the gateway.

'I think you owe me some money, Mr Richardson.' He sounded agitated and it was clear that his pay was not the only thing he had come for.

Sterling thrust his hand in his pocket and took out ten shillings.

'There's something else isn't there?' he asked flatly. Owens nodded, licking his lips, his eyes fixed on the money.

'There's trouble up at the works, one of the new furnaces blew up when the men were installing it.'

Sterling felt cold. 'Anyone hurt?' he asked harshly, hardly noticing as Owens took the shillings from his hand. The young man nodded, twisting his hat between his fingers as though reluctant to speak.

'Get on with it man.' There was a cold feeling growing in the pit of Sterling's stomach. 'Tell me what happened.'

'It's terrible, old Sam Herbert was on the night watch, blast caught him fair and square, dead he is, stood no chance you see, blown to pieces.'

Sterling took a deep breath, it felt as though fingers of pain were squeezing the breath from him. He'd known Sam for years, remembered him working in the copper when Sterling himself was no more than a child.

'Any other casualties?' God, how had such a thing happened? he asked himself, And yet from the stern tone of his voice, no one would have guessed how shaken he was.

'Yes, sir, one man with his hand blown away and another with injuries to the head, both of them been taken to the infirmary though old Sam's remains, such as they were, have been taken to his widow in Copperman's Row.'

Sterling was silent for a long moment. 'I deliberately got the engineers to install the furnaces after the last shift had finished so that it could be done in safety and without disturbing the men. Now what I want to know is how did the damned furnace blow if it wasn't even in use?'

Will shook his head. 'I don't know about that, perhaps the engineers were trying it out or something, anyway, it's a bad do all right.'

'I must get up there at once, see for myself.' Sterling moved towards the gateway and Will Owens spoke up quickly.

'Perhaps it would be better if you waited until daylight, sir,' he said evenly. 'It could be dangerous to go up there now.'

'What do you mean, dangerous?' Sterling asked suspiciously but Will's face was hidden in the shadow and Sterling could not see the expression in his eyes.

'I just mean that there's a crowd gathered at the gates, Mr

Richardson, like a mob of wild animals they are and they're calling for blood.'

The words were a challenge to Sterling's courage and both men recognised them as such. Sterling stared at the man for a long moment with derision in his eyes, knowing that Owen did not give a tuppenny damn for his safety.

'Well they can bay at the moon if they like, I'm not afraid of them, but the first thing I'm going to do is to see Mrs Herbert.' Sterling's voice was harsh.

The Ascot was standing outside in the back alley and Sterling started it up, feeling coldly angry. Someone had been incompetent or worse and if it took all night he was going to find out the truth. He drove out into the street and headed up the hill towards the works. He gave no thought to Will Owens who stood at the curbside glowering at the departing auto-mobile.

As he drew near to Copperman's Row, he saw a crowd of women gathered outside the cottage where Sam had lived. As he drew to a halt, the women turned shawl-covered heads and a deep, hostile silence fell.

The kitchen of Sam's house was neat and clean, the brass shining, the floors swept and the furniture smelling of bees-wax.

'Mrs Herbert,' Sterling said softly. The old woman was sunk into her chair with her three daughters around her, a bewil-dered look in her eyes. 'Mrs Herbert, I can't tell you how sorry I am to hear of Sam's death. I won't rest until I find who is responsible for the accident, if that's what it was.'

'Mr Richardson, he's out there, my Sam, but they won't let me look at him.' She pointed to the back yard. 'Good thing it's summer, I'd be worried about him lying in the cold under that sheet.'

Sterling squeezed the old woman's hand, unable to think of any words that could bring her comfort. Her eyes looked towards him pleadingly.

'It can't be right, can it Mr Richardson, Sam can't be dead? Why he went off from here after his tea to do watch on the works and bright as a button he was then.'

Sterling rose and moved through the crowded room towards the door. One of Sam Herbert's daughters followed him.

'Your mother will be given compensation of course,' Sterling said softly. 'I realise it won't make up for her loss but at least she won't have to worry about money.'

'We don't need no charity Mr Richardson.' The young woman raised her head proudly. 'We take care of our own and Mam will not go short.'

Sterling left the Ascot at the curbside and walked the short distance to the works. His mind was racing as he tried to sort out what could have happened, was it a genuine accident or had the furnace been tampered with?

He heard the hubbub of voices before he reached the copper company buildings and as he strode to the gates, looking quickly round him, he saw that – outwardly at least – there was little sign that anything untoward had happened. It was true that some of the slates were off the roof of one of the sheds but apparently the explosion had been dealt with swiftly and no fire had spread.

The crowd fell silent except for one man who, as Sterling came forward, murmured '*bradwr*' in a harsh undertone. Sterling shouldered his way to the steps of the gatehouse and stood there, looking down at the men. His eyes roved over the crowd and he caught a glimpse of Glanmor Travers in the background; at his side was Cullen, a known villain who would do anything for a few shillings.

Anger raged within him as Sterling realised with a deep certainty that the explosion had been no accident.

'I want to know what's happened here tonight.' His voice rang out loud and authoritative and the men shifted uneasily, looking at each other, their faces shadowed by the jutting peaks of their caps. 'Isn't anyone going to speak up?' Sterling demanded and one man stepped forward.

'Aye, I'll tell you, boss,' he said. 'Them new furnaces are no good, not like the old calciner furnaces, can't trust them foreign things, and me, I'm not going to work on them. Been a copperman all my life and not scared of nothing but I'm not risking getting killed just to put a few more bob in your pockets.'

'Anyone else like to speak?' Sterling asked loudly. 'What about you Cullen, and you Travers, neither of you are coppermen so what are you doing here at all?'

There was a loud buzz of voices and the men seemed to move apart, leaving Travers isolated in a circle of suspicious faces. He looked round him desperately but Cullen had melted away into the darkness. It suddenly became clear to him that he was alone and his ferrety face turned pale.

'Sam Herbert and my father Joss Travers were cousins, everyone round here knows that. I've a right to find out what happened, haven't I?' He moved nearer to Sterling, his jaw thrust forward belligerently.

'Look here, an old man has died and you're asking damn soft questions.' Glanmor Travers seemed to pull himself together. 'What you are going to do about these furnaces is more to the point. Copperman or not, I don't want to see more injuries in a works than a man would get going down the pit.'

Voices rose in loud assent and a sea of faces turned to Sterling, waiting for his reply. He lifted his hand for silence before he began to speak.

'This man who purports to care about your safety is the one I gave the sack to some months back,' Sterling said. 'He's here to make trouble, to see you all in the same boat he's in, up the road, fired, jobless with wives and children going hungry. What's more he has a personal vendetta against me and so his word is not to be trusted.'

One of the men edged closer. 'That may be true, sir, and I don't like the look of the fellow myself nor of that riffraff he brought here with him but the trouble is none of us trust the new furnaces, see.'

'Don't be fools, men, the new furnaces are to replace the old cracked ones, does that sound as if I want to put you in danger? It would have saved me money to keep the old furnaces going instead of putting out hard cash for replacements, can't you see the sense of that?'

Travers spoke up again, sensing that the men were being swayed against him. 'All very fine and noble of you I'm sure, but bosses never did anything for the sake of the workers so why should we believe you now?' He paused, waiting for his words to sink in before continuing. 'Why not put in new English furnaces instead of the foreign ones, did you get them on the cheap, a job lot that someone wanted to be rid of? We all know that the company is struggling to keep its head above water so don't try to deny it.'

'I am denying nothing,' Sterling said evenly. 'Indeed the fact that the company is losing money only serves to emphasise the fact that I need to be more careful in taking decisions. Have I laid any men off yet? No, and I won't do so unless production falls even lower. You've got to pull with me, all of you if you want to keep your jobs, is that understood?'

'Balderdash.' Travers' voice rang out harsh and aggressive, he was losing his temper, realising that events were going against him. 'I think you are a liar, Sterling Richardson, and worse, a murderer of old men.'

The pent-up distress and anger that Sterling had felt ever since he'd known of the explosion built into an insupportable load and before he knew it, he had leaped from the steps and had caught Travers around the throat, forcing him to his knees.

'You can put your fists where your mouth is,' he said loudly, 'or admit that you were in on this so-called accident. You're a chemist and would know full well how to set off an explosion.'

'That's right Mr Richardson,' a voice called out behind him, 'give the man a pasting. He's been snooping round here for a couple of nights, he can't be up to much good.'

Suddenly Travers lunged forward, catching Sterling off guard. He was on his feet and would have made a run for it but the men closed in around him, hemming him within a tight circle.

'Fight, you lily-livered coward,' one of the men called and Travers, like a cornered rat, swung out a fist in the direction of Sterling's head.

'You'll have to do better than that.' Sterling moved back easily, out of harm's way. 'You're so good with the mouth, let's see how you feel when I close it for you.'

Glanmor Travers staggered back clutching his face. He spat and blood trickled down his chin, he whimpered and moved further away and Sterling suddenly had no heart for the fight.

'Get off home,' he said shortly, 'and never let me set eyes on you again if you want to go on breathing.'

There were cries of disappointment from the crowd who had hoped to see a blood bath.

'Get off my property.' Sterling gave Glanmor a push and the man staggered away towards the gates, pausing for a moment to look back, and his face was a white oval in the light from the lamp above the gatehouse.

'You'll pay for this one day, Richardson, I'll get you back, I swear it, even if it takes me the rest of my life.'

Sterling stared at him coldly. 'At the rate you are going, it may just take you that length of time.' There was a roar of laughter from the men as Travers vanished into the darkness and Sterling turned to them.

'Now go back to your homes and leave it to me to find out what happened here tonight. And another thing, don't let rabble rousers the like of Travers and Cullen influence you, they are nothing but scum, they have no sense of decency. If there's anything you are not sure of that you'd like to ask questions about, just come to me, all right?'

'Your brother was with them too, Mr Richardson,' a voice from the back of the crowd called. 'Saw Rickie Richardson large as life, I did, coming out of the sheds just before the explosion.'

Sterling felt himself grow tense. 'Who is that?' He peered through the darkness as one of the boys from the rolling mill came reluctantly forward. Sterling grasped his shoulder in a fierce grip.

'Jed, it's you. Now I know you for an honest lad but think hard, you're sure it was Mr Rickie that you saw?'

The boy nodded. 'Yes, I'm sure Mr Richardson, he came out of the sheds alone and then I saw those other two men come out after him, slipped past the gatehouse in the shadows they did but my Mam had chucked me outside while she had a row with Dad and I had nothing to do but look around me, that's how I saw the three of them.'

'Good enough.' Sterling felt sick even though he smiled at the boy. 'As I said, leave it all to me and get off home to your beds. I'll speak with you again in the morning and perhaps we can sort it all out.'

'Why don't you get the bobbies up here, boss?' Jed pushed back his cap and scratched his head. 'I've heard they can find clues even in ashes.'

Sterling smiled. 'You've been listening to too many stories, my boy. Go on, off with you.'

Wearily Sterling walked back to where the Ascot was standing outside Sam Herbert's house. He saw to his dismay that the headlamps had been broken and that there was glass all over the road. He sighed heavily; who could blame the people for being angry when one of their own was dead and two more injured?

He managed to drive the automobile back through the town – he knew it must be past midnight but he could not wait until morning, he had to have it out with his brother right now, tonight. He would wring the truth from Rickie one way or another.

It was bright moonlight as Sterling drove along the roadway leading to Plas Rhianfa. As he drew nearer to the house, he saw that there was a light in one of the upstairs windows though the lower rooms were in darkness. He moved around to the back of the great building, knowing that some of the servants would be still up and about.

'Master Sterling, you did give me a fright, knocking the door like that and walking in so unexpected.' Carrie was wiping her hands on her apron and she nervously tucked a stray hair behind her ear.

'Is anything wrong, are you sick or something?'

Sterling forced himself to smile naturally. 'Sorry to upset you, Carrie. No I'm not ill, I'm just looking for Rickie. Is he here?'

'Why bless you your brother's been in bed these few hours since, had some sort of sick headache, he did, said he wanted nothing to eat and wasn't to be disturbed until morning.'

'I see. Well if he should be about, don't tell him I'm here, I'll surprise him.'

Sterling made his way quietly up the stairs. He did not want to awake his mother and have to answer the barrage of questions she would undoubtedly throw at him.

He opened the door of his brother's room and looked inside, sighing heavily as he saw that the bed was empty and had not been slept in. He sat down before the dying embers of the fire, feet stretched out before him, drinking in silence.

His childhood had been a good one, he'd had few problems then and did not realise that, so soon, he would be responsible for the running of the company. He stared into the small flames that rose from the ornate grate and wondered where the closeness that brothers were supposed to share had gone, or had it never existed between himself and Rickie? It was difficult to say.

After about an hour, he lit a lamp and as he blew out the lucifer, he heard a step on the landing, and Rickie came into the bedroom.

'Good night to you, Rickie. Where have you been until this hour, courting some lovely young girl or planning to blow up more of the furnaces?'

Rickie paled visibly and his hands were trembling as he thrust them into his pockets.

'I don't know what you're talking about,' he said quickly. 'What's all this about blowing up the furnaces?'

'You mean to say you didn't know?'

Sterling's irony was not lost on Rickie, he flushed and looked away. 'Well I did hear some talk about it in the town but I don't see why you should start accusing me.'

Sterling moved closer to his brother and stared at him as though he had never seen him before. His brother's face was weak, his mouth drawn down at the corners like that of a petulant child, but then perhaps it was not entirely his fault, he had not been allowed to face the world like a man but had been shut away in some namby pamby school all his life.

'You were seen,' Sterling said coldly. 'Seen leaving the works shortly before Travers and that ruffian Cullen left, and just before the explosion occurred. What do you expect me to think?'

Suddenly Rickie turned on him. 'Just leave me alone will you, I don't want to look at you or see you or talk to you. I hate you, don't you understand that? I've always hated you and even if I have done the things you accuse me of, you've got no proof or you'd be here right now with a constable.' He turned his back on Sterling and his voice was low. 'Just get out of my room, do you understand, leave me alone.'

Sterling had driven halfway to town and was almost at the

door of the Mackworth Arms when he suddenly remembered he had left Mali waiting for him in his room, He sighed softly, she would understand when he explained things to her. Such a lot had happened to him in the last few hours, he had learned that Mali loved him and that his own brother hated him. All in all, it had been quite a night.

Chapter Twenty-one

Dean Sutton sat in the dining room with the warmth of the early morning sun on his face, waiting for his groom to put in an appearance. It seemed that Gray had something urgent to tell him that couldn't wait until Dean had breakfasted.

There was a knock on the door and then Gray entered the room his blond hair sticking up around his head, his eyes alight with self importance.

'There was an explosion last night at the copper works,' he said breathlessly. 'Sounded like the clap of doom it did Mr Dean, and sparks shooting high into the air as though the end of the world was coming, terrible it was.

'My Mary, Big Mary as some calls her, she was like a heroine, ran into the gates of the copper works with no thought for herself, just to see if there was anyone hurt.'

'And was there?' Dean wished that Gray was less of a raconteur and more of a plain-speaking man for there was no hurrying him and Dean was impatient to know exactly what had occurred.

'One dead sir, poor old Sam Herbert, too old he was to be working really but he was kept on to make tea and suchlike and be night watchman whenever he felt like it, which was most nights because poor old Sam had the gout and couldn't sleep anyway.'

Gray paused for breath and Dean rose from his chair and moved to the window, staring out into the sunlit gardens. He had spent less time than he should have on the business of the copper works of late because he had been involved in setting up a chain of drapery stores across the country, and very successful they were proving to be. It seemed that however poor, most women had a taste for fripperies and a new bonnet.

'Two men injured as well, helping to install the new furnaces they were,' Gray continued. 'One lost a hand and the other will be off his rocker for the rest of his life I spects with half the furnace inside his brain.'

'What a God awful thing to happen,' Dean muttered, 'is someone trying to spike our guns, I wonder?' He was thinking out loud more than asking a question but Gray was only too ready to answer him.

'No doubt of it, sir, those furnaces don't explode, not when there's nothing boiling away inside them they don't. No, some one put a stick of dynamite in there, and the poor sods putting the furnaces together copped it.'

Dean wondered what had been going on up there at the works. Though he was not very keen on the changes Sterling wished to make, and doubted the young man's ability to implement them, he did at least feel that he would recoup the money he had invested in the company.

He had decided to step in only if things went badly wrong and that they seemed about to do now. Perhaps some time he would have to take a look for himself, but not today. This morning he was going to see Bea again, they were going out for the day and he would treat her to some fresh sea air at a small secluded bay a few miles along the coast.

They had planned to take a picnic and Dean glowed when he thought of the way Bea had warmed to him recently. And yet she was still subdued, much of the time, her eyes dull, her laughter noticeably lacking. He'd tried to bring her out of herself and on rare occasions he had succeeded; then she had seemed for a brief instant to be almost the high-spirited Bea he had always known.

'What's going to happen, Mr Dean?' Gray was still hovering, waiting for some reaction, and Dean turned to look at him, eyebrows raised.

'Well, I'd say it's all up to the young Mr Richardson to sort out,' he drawled. 'Though if you can find out any more about the incident, Gray, I should be very pleased to hear it.'

Later, as Dean drove the horse and trap away from the

house, he looked down towards the town and saw the familiar main street stretching away like a crooked question mark against the surrounding landscape. Further away, on the other side of the valley, lay the copper works, huddled darkly against the yellow line of the river Swan. It was strange, Dean mused, how he had come to love this place that was as different from his own wide-spread country as a mouse was from an elephant.

He knew that if Bea would marry him, he would be content to settle here for good, build up his own empire, bring up his sons to follow in his path. So some might call him a shopkeeper instead of a man of industry, but he had decided long ago that he would not put all his eggs in one basket.

It was only a short drive from Dean's home to the large old house jutting out of the hillside where Bea Cardigan lived. In the early morning sunshine the bricks were mellow, almost gold, and the turrets on the roof gleamed green, the copper strippings eroded by the rain that fell more in this country of Wales, Dean thought, than anywhere else in the world.

Bea was ready and waiting and the basket of food was being carried out to the cart by the maid who seemed so attached to her mistress.

Dean had deliberately cultivated Bertha, buying her sweets, bringing her ribbons, knowing that she was in her mistress's confidence. It did no harm to keep the servants sweet, they could be very enlightening when it came to the affairs of their betters.

'Bea, honey, you look very charming today.' His words were an understatement for Bea looked good enough to eat in a soft summer skirt and a blouse that revealed her smooth arms and throat. He resisted the urge to take her in his arms and kiss her, for she would run like a startled filly if he did not move carefully.

'And you look very handsome, Dean.' Bea smiled with her lips but there was no light in her eyes. She sat demurely beside him while Bertha straightened her mistress's skirts before climbing into the trap herself. Dean made a mental note to speak to the maid for now the time seemed right to start questioning the girl about what was troubling Bea.

Dean knew he had a persuasive tongue when he wanted to

turn on the charm and he had softened the maid up very nicely; he felt sure she would trust him now.

'Isn't it a beautiful day, Bea?' he said as he jerked the reins, startling the horse into movement. Bea smiled up at him but her eyes were hidden by the brim of her hat and he could not see the expression in them.

'Yes, beautiful.' She echoed his words but there was no animation in her voice. Dean was genuinely worried, he had realised that women had moods and periodic sicknesses that sent some of them off into a swoon but with Bea it was different, it seemed her very spirit had been broken.

He glanced at her sideways and saw the smooth line of her cheek and love for her swelled powerfully inside him. He knew he would kill for her if anyone threatened her.

The curving road at last led them to the little bay that was sheltered beneath the jutting rocks. Tall trees overhung the sand dunes and down along the small, worn footpath was the rolling sea, blue and shimmering in the warmth of the sun.

'Come on, Bea, honey.' Dean lifted her down from the trap. 'You can take off your pumps and dig your toes into the warmth of the sand. Perhaps later you'd like to paddle in the sea, they say salt water is good for horse's hoofs so it must be good for your little feet.' He laughed and Bea allowed herself a smile but she freed herself from his arms almost immediately and turned to Bertha.

'Can you manage the basket or shall we let Dean carry it for us?' She spoke lightly but her voice cracked as though she was on the verge of tears. Bertha shook back her hair and picked up the basket easily.

'There's no need to worry, Miss Bea, I carried so many coal scuttles when I was a kitchenmaid that this basket don't seem like nothing.' She held it before her and made her way across the sand. Bea took Dean's arm and followed more slowly.

'Are you not well, honey?' Dean asked anxiously. 'You're so quiet lately, not your usual self at all.'

Bea's eyes stared out across the blue stretch of the ocean as though seeing pictures that were exclusive to herself. She was locked in her own world where no one was allowed to penetrate.

'I'm all right, Dean, just under the weather, that's all. You know I had a bout of fever some time ago that left me a little weak.'

Dean did remember the weeks in the heat of June when she'd been confined to her bed, very well indeed. He had not been allowed to visit her for James had been very strict about that sort of thing, old-fashioned even. There was no place in an unmarried lady's bedroom for an outsider and Dean had been forced to abide by James's wishes.

He had contented himself with sending fruit and flowers almost every day, realising more and more that Bea meant everything to him. His only wonder was that he'd let all these years go by without giving voice to his feelings. No doubt he had been too busy building his life, making his future as secure as possible, which was one of the reasons why he had branched out into shops in latter years. Security was something that meant a great deal to him.

He believed that the turning point as regards his feelings for Bea had come on that day months ago when he had seen how attracted she was to Sterling Richardson. Determination had grown within Dean not to give her up without a struggle. But happily, she seemed to have got over her infatuation, certainly she never spoke of Richardson or appeared to have much to do with him these days.

'There's a lovely spot over there just among the rocks,' Bea said gently. She sank gratefully onto the blanket Dean spread for her, looking up at him with limpid eyes.

'I'm sorry, I get so tired these days, I don't know why.'

As she leaned against the warm stones looking up at him Dean was swamped with tenderness. He sat beside her, taking her hands in his.

'Let me take care of you, Bea,' he said urgently. 'I'd make no demands and you'd be mistress of your own home. Please don't answer me right now, just think about what I've said.'

'It's sweet of you to offer me marriage, Dean,' Bea said softly and he leaned towards her, resting his cheek gently against hers.

'I'd be very honoured if you would think about it,' he replied.

Bertha was a little way off, looking among the rocky pools, but Dean knew that the maid was keeping a watchful eye on her mistress. He liked that. Bertha loved Bea as he himself did.

'But Dean, you don't know anything about me.' Bea's voice broke and he resisted the impulse to draw her into his arms. 'I'm not what you think.' She continued to speak, though each word seemed dragged from deep inside her. He put his big hand gently over her lips.

'To me, you're the sweetest, loveliest creature that ever walked on this earth,' he said earnestly. 'I love you, Bea, can't you understand that?'

She shook her head wearily. 'Don't speak of it any more now, Dean, let me just enjoy today and think about the future when I'm feeling stronger, will you?'

'Of course honey, I brought you out here to give you some sunshine and some peace. Why not lie there in the sun while I go and look around the headland, see what's over there?'

It was an excuse of course to leave her alone. He moved away and stared out to sea; faintly on the horizon he could see the coast of Devon lying softly against the cloudless sky. He kicked at a stone buried in the sand and his eyes were misted with tears. He had never thought of himself as a soft man and yet here he was all keyed up over Bea Cardigan.

After a while, he retraced his steps and saw that Bea had been persuaded to go down to the water's edge. Bertha was holding her arm and the young girl screamed excitedly as a wave covered her shoes. Dean stood watching them and a determination built up within him to find out the root of Bea's unhappiness and if possible to tear it out.

They ate cold chicken and thin slices of bread and afterwards drank wine in the shelter of the rocks, for the sun was high now, beating down upon the golden sand with a fierce intensity. Bertha began to snore and with a smile, Dean moved nearer to Bea, taking her slim hand in his own strong fingers.

'It could be like this all the time you know, Bea honey,' he said softly. She leaned her head on his shoulder and sighed.

'That sounds very tempting, Dean. I think I would enjoy being your wife but just give me time to think, wait until I'm stronger and then perhaps by the autumn I'll be able to give you an answer.'

With that, Dean knew he had to be content but he felt sure that she would eventually agree to marry him and in the meantime he would begin refurbishing the house, bringing it up to the standard a lady like Bea would expect, for he readily admitted that just so long as he was comfortable, he had made no efforts to improve his surroundings.

They would need a nursery wing later on, he thought warmly, and his fingers clasped Bea's more tightly. Yet he would not rush her, he told himself, his thoughts and dreams and hopes he would keep to himself, for the time being.

Bertha opened her eyes and looked around her anxiously. She sat up brushing her skirts, taking off her shoes and tipping the sand out of them.

'Are you all right, Miss Bea?' she asked. 'Not getting too hot are you?'

Bea smiled. 'I'm feeling very well, thank you Bertha, and if it is a little hot that's only to be expected at high summer.'

Bertha got to her feet at once. 'I'll bring some water to freshen you.' She took a bowl from the picnic basket and began to make her way down to the water's edge.

'I'll come with you,' Dean said. 'Won't be a minute, Bea, you just stay in the shade, all right?'

'Go on the two of you,' Bea said with a wave of her hand. 'You are treating me as though I was a child. I won't shrivel up in the heat, don't worry.'

'Here, give me the bowl.' Dean reached out a hand but Bertha shook her head.

'No sir, I've got me boots off now and I'll be able to go further into the water than you would. Don't want to spoil them nice shoes, do you?'

The breeze was blowing in from the sea now, soft and gentle, bringing with it the tang of salt. Dean watched Bertha's stocky figure as she ploughed through the sand in front of him and tried to think of the right words to broach the subject of Bea's troubled manner.

'You know I'm very fond of Bea, don't you Bertha?' He felt that the words were inadequate but he could not voice his innermost feelings to a servant. 'I know there's something bothering her and I want to help her if I possibly can, I would do anything for her and she can't go on the way she is now or she will be really very sick indeed.'

Bertha turned to look at him, her eyes were anxious and she

was biting at her lip worriedly. 'I don't know what's the right thing to do, sir,' she said. 'I can see Miss Bea is not herself for she used to laugh a lot and enjoy ordinary things and now she's so sad all the time and I fear she'll go into a decline.'

'Well trust me, then,' Dean said persuasively. 'You can't speak to her father or you'd have done so already, so you've got to put your faith in someone. Who better than me who thinks as much of your mistress as you do?'

Bertha sighed heavily. 'All right, sir, I've got to talk to someone 'cos I've been that worried, it's making me sick too. I'll tell you the little I know and I can only hope and pray I'm doing the right thing.'

Dean felt jubilant. 'Of course you are, Bertha, I can help Bea and someone must before it's too late.'

Bertha put the bowl down on the sand and the water sucked and washed around it as though trying to push it over. Bertha rubbed her hands on her skirt and looked out across the sea as if even now she was not sure of herself.

'I know she was in love with Mr Richardson.' Her voice was halting, hesitant, and Dean stood back feeling as if he'd been dealt a body blow.

Dean well remembered seeing the affectionate way Bea had once looked at Sterling but he thought all that was over with now.

'What makes you say that, Bertha?' he asked without betraying any emotion. She glanced up at him quickly as though sensing something of the turmoil within him.

'I accompanied Miss Bea to Mr Richardson's new house several times,' she said and her dark eyes were unreadable. 'And to the Mackworth Arms,' she added slowly.

Dean heaved a sigh of relief. 'Well then, that's not so terrible is it?' he asked with forced brightness. 'Nothing improper about visiting a friend so long as Bea had you for company.'

He saw Bertha purse her lips and felt she was about to go on but then she glanced back to where her mistress was seated and her shoulders seemed to straighten.

'I'm sure it's nothing,' she said quickly. 'I just felt there had been some sort of silly quarrel between them,' she said lamely. 'I know Miss Bea does not wish to keep company with Mr Richardson these days.'

Dean frowned in bewilderment. 'But surely you would have heard them quarrel?' he asked and Bertha's eyes slid away from his. She shook her head.

'I don't know sir, it was very crowded up at the new house sometimes what with workmen and such. I think the row may have been something to do with the decorating and all that.'

Dean smiled. 'I suppose such things are important to a lady, though I can't see why myself.'

He caught Bertha's arm. 'Is that all, are you sure you're telling me everything?'

The young maid's face was suddenly wary. 'Yes that's all, sir,' she said. 'I'd best get back to Miss Bea. See, she's looking out for me.'

Dean watched her run up the beach and followed more slowly. There was something about the girl's explanation that did not ring quite true. And yet, in her weakened state perhaps Bea saw normally trivial happenings in a more serious light.

'You've been a long time.' Bea was holding out her hand to him, and smiling he went to her side. Her face turned towards him was lovely and fragile, the face of a woman who could do no wrong. Whatever the truth of the story Bertha had told him, of one thing he was sure: Bea was blameless. And the thought of Richardson giving her even one day's pain made his gorge rise. The day of reckoning with Mr Sterling Richardson was coming, he decided, and it was coming fast.

Chapter Twenty-two

The summer sun was shining in through Mali's window as she awoke to the sound of the church bells ringing through the still morning air. She sat up quickly, brushing back her tangled hair. Her heart was beating swiftly for she had been dreaming that she was standing before the deacons being harangued because of her lustful association with the copper boss. Her hands trembled as she pushed the patchwork quilt to one side, stepped out of bed and stood for a moment before the window looking down at the streets outside.

Children were scrambling about in the cobbled roadway playing with a hoop, and the breakfast smell of salt fish overpowered even the stench from the copper works. The Catholics were going to mass, faces bright and fresh washed, the women with shawls covering their hair in spite of the warmth of the sun. All in all it was an ordinary Sunday. But not for Mali.

She washed in cold water from the china bowl on the marble-topped table and dressed quickly, trying to push the pain and turmoil of her thoughts into the background of her mind. Today she would clean the house from top to bottom, polish the brass, wash the floors and to the devil with what Dad would say about resting on God's day.

From outside, she heard Dai End House playing hymns on his accordion and the haunting melodies filled her with re-newed sadness; she sank down on the bed, her hands over her face, and the tears slipped between her fingers, salt and bitter.

She loved Sterling, loved him so much that it wrenched and tore at her being. She had thought for one magical night that he returned her feelings but then he had simply walked out of her life and left her alone and deserted in the room at the Mackworth Arms.

She had hoped again briefly that there was some justification for his absence when she heard from Katie about the explosion at the copper works. But then she counted up the hours and realised that he'd still had time to come to her at the hotel and he had chosen not to. She had been a fool even to imagine that she could be anything to him but a flossy, a night's diversion.

There was no point in wallowing in bitterness, she told herself briskly, she must go downstairs, cook Dad his breakfast. He was sure to be hungry as he inevitably was after a Saturday night spent drinking.

She bit her lip. Davie had not been the same to her since she'd returned home with her blouse torn and confessed to him that she had been with a man. Her back still ached with the bruises inflicted by the strong leather belt her father had used on her. Worse than the beating was the fact that her father had condemned her without a fair hearing. But then how could she ever justify what she had done? She, like many a woman before her, had fallen in love with a man who was merely trifling with her.

She had been a gullible fool and should have heeded Katie's warning, for hadn't the Irish girl told her that men like Sterling wanted only one thing from a working girl and that was to bed her. She must have appeared naive, even stupid, believing that he really cared for her. Well, she had learned her lesson now and would not be caught again.

She hurried down the stairs and into the kitchen and took her apron from the line, tying it firmly around her waist. There was the fire to light and the ashes to riddle and sticks to fetch in from the yard all before she could boil up the kettle for a cup of tea.

She stood for a moment in the silence of the sunwashed room. Since her mother had died, there had been nothing but change and Mali knew she could never go back to being the girl she once was.

She longed for her mother in that instant, ached to be comforted, held in warm caring arms. She needed a kind voice to tell her that she had not been a bad girl, simply a foolish one.

223

But there was no point in wanting what she could not have. She must be strong, stand on her own two feet, for she was alone now.

She set to work and soon had the fire glowing behind the blackleaded bars of the grate. She carried the kettle to the back yard and filled it to the brim for Dad liked endless cups of tea when he had salt fish for breakfast. At the other side of the hob, she put the fish on to boil and wiping her hands in her apron, she went outside and strolled along Copperman's Row.

She looked at the familiar cobbled road as though she had never seen it before. Dai End House was sitting in his doorway, his hair slicked down, his collar shiny white, and he played his accordion as though he was in love with the instrument.

The children had vanished from the streets now for soon they would be scrubbed and dressed in Sunday-best clothes and sent off to church or chapel with Bibles under their arms, each one of them eager to earn for their goodness a small picture of the Lord suffering little children to come unto Him.

Mali told herself she was growing vinegary and bitter but for all that, the chapel at Pentre Estyll would not see her today, or any other Sunday for that matter.

A policeman came into sight wheeling his bicycle, his face red, for the day was growing warmer. Her heart dipped as she realised that the man walking beside him was Sterling Richardson. He was hatless and was wearing a light jacket and he looked so handsome that pain exploded within her like a thousand fragments of shattered glass.

Hurriedly, she returned to the cottage, slamming the door behind her. It took her a few moments to regain her breath for her heart was pumping as though she had been running.

She heard sounds of movement from upstairs and knew that Dad was rousing himself. She hurried to the hob and stirred the salt fish but her mind was not on her task.

'Sterling.' She whispered the name softly, reliving the way he had held her in his arms, taken possession of her so tenderly that she could have pledged her very life that he loved her. Suddenly tears were brimming over and running down her cheeks.

The stinging cold of the water she dashed on her reddened eyes seemed to bring her to her senses. What use was crying?

What was done was done. She set out the plates for breakfast, determined to act as if nothing was wrong.

Davie came into the room and stood staring at her uncomfortably. He moved to the fire and peered down into the pot.

'Ah, there's lovely that smells, Mali.' His tone was conciliatory, for they had not spoken to each other in days. Mali turned to him, smiling tremulously, and he rubbed at the roughness of the bristles on his chin, his green eyes not meeting hers.

'There's something I've got to say to you.' He stood stiffly now, hands thrust into trouser pockets. Mali shook her head pleadingly.

'Don't go on at me about how bad I am, Dad,' she whispered. 'I can't bear it if you scold me any more.'

'No, it's not that.' He coughed in embarrassment. 'And I'm sorry I took my belt to you, Mali, first time in my life I ever hit you.' He shook his head to and fro, his brow furrowed, and Mali went to him, her arm around his big neck, silent in her anguish, longing for comfort from him.

After a moment, he put her away from him. 'I got to tell you, Mali.' He swallowed hard. 'Rosa is coming to live with us. It's only fair, mind, for I've made her promise to stay off the streets, see.'

'What?' Mali could hardly believe her ears. 'That no-good flossy living under my roof, oh Dad, how could you?' Mali sank down into the kitchen chair as Davie put his fingers warningly to his lips.

'Hush, she's upstairs now, getting dressed.' Davie had the grace to look sheepish. He moved over to the window and stared outside though it was clear he was seeing nothing.

'A man gets lonely, Mali,' he said. 'Not only for bedding a woman but for a lot of other things besides. Try to understand, will you, girl?'

'It's "girl" again now is it?' Mali felt her anger grow and rise within her so that she could hardly contain it. 'And don't talk to me about understanding because I'll never understand how you could put a flossy in my mother's place.'

She swallowed hard. 'What else is Rosa going to give you but bedding, tell me that? Is she going to cook and clean for you and wash your clothes? Well I'll say this for you, Dad, you don't waste no time in comforting yourself with whatever is going, a woman any man could buy for a few shillings. Is that what you are going to bring into this house as your wife?'

'That's enough.' Davie's voice was harsh. 'It's my choice and I'll stick to it and if you don't like it, there's the door.' He turned swiftly as she gasped in horror. 'I don't want it to be like that, Mali, but if you make me choose then it's got to be her. Look,' he spoke pleadingly, 'you'll be gone soon anyway, married to some respectable boy, if you don't spoil your chances that is. I'll be alone then or haven't you thought of that? Your husband won't want me hanging around that's for sure.'

Mali picked up her shawl and draped it over her shoulders. 'Right then, get that whore out of bed and let her cook the breakfast and bring in the coal and sweep the floor.' She could hardly see, so blinded with anger and pain was she. 'I'm going out to think things over.' She paused in the doorway. 'And don't worry, I'll find somewhere else to live for it's certain I won't share my kitchen with that – that prostitute!'

Once outside, she hurried away towards the canal and so did not see Sterling go to the door of the cottage and knock loudly. She was blind to everything but her own outrage and pain and it was as though the whole world had turned against her.

She sat for a long time watching the sunlight dancing on the turgid waters of the canal and so absorbed was she in her own thoughts that she failed to see Katie come up alongside her and settle on the grass, legs straight out in front of her.

'What's wrong, Mali?' Katie's soft voice startled her and Mali looked up quickly, unable to conceal the tears in her eyes.

'Ah, love, what is it?' Katie's voice was low. 'I've never seen you cry before, not even when your ma died.'

Mali swallowed hard. 'I don't know, Katie, perhaps it's all my fault but there's so much gone wrong I don't know if I can explain.'

'Well take your time, there's no one hurrying you and that's for sure.' Katie pushed the shawl from her head and her red hair gleamed rich and bright in the sunlight.

'Dad's brought Rosa to live in our cottage,' Mali said at last. 'Going to stay with us for as long as she keeps off the streets, isn't that just fine? A whore for a mother, a flossy who has known nothing but men since she was twelve years of age.'

Katie was silent, plaiting the fringes of her shawl together, her hands busy, her eyes staring downwards.

'Well don't you think that's awful?' Mali demanded, amazed that her friend wasn't lifting her eyes to heaven in horror.

Katie shrugged. 'There's worse things than that, Mali, and sure I tink Rosa only put the tin hat on things. There's something that hurts you much more than that now isn't there, do you want to tell me all or are you goin' to let it fester like a sore inside your guts?'

Mali's shoulders slumped. 'Yes, there's more,' she said. 'Much more, but I don't know how to say it.'

'I don't think you need to, I can read it in your eyes, you've lain in Top Meadow, or somewhere like it and with that boss man Sterling Richardson.'

Mali did not attempt to deny it. She shook her head dumbly and it was some moments before she could speak.

'I believed he loved me.' Her voice seemed to come from a great distance. 'When he took me in his arms it was all so . . .' she shook her head helplessly. 'Well, I thought he meant to marry me. I should have had more sense.' She threw a piece of twig in the water and watched it spinning aimlessly in the slowly flowing water.

'If sense came with love there'd be no one making fools of themselves,' Katie sighed. 'This happens all the time, Mali, you're not the first and sure won't be the last to be taken in by a handsome face.'

The two girls stared at each other for a long moment and then Katie put her arm round Mali's shoulder, hugging her close.

'I should have put a stop to it when I saw Mr Richardson driving you away in that fine automobile of his. I might have guessed he wouldn't take you straight home, not him. But why did he run out on you so quick then?'

Mali closed her eyes. 'He said he was going to get me a blouse, this was after . . . after we'd been together.' She lifted her head and looked desperately at her friend.

'But Katie, while he was with me, he was so wonderful, I can't tell you what it was like.'

'They can put on a fine enough act when they want something.' Katie spoke sadly. 'Offer you the sun, moon and stars if it gets them what they want.'

'I expect you're right,' Mali said softly. 'At any rate he didn't come back even though I waited till well past midnight.'

'Just a minute,' Katie said thoughtfully, 'wasn't that the night of the blow-up in the works? For sure you couldn't expect him to turn a blind eye to something bad like that. He had to leave you, don't you see?'

'I've thought about it a hundred times or more,' Mali said, 'and he had plenty of time to come back, hours and hours. If he'd wanted to explain to me that night he could have, the Mackworth Arms is not the end of the earth.'

'But Mali,' Katie's hand was upon her shoulder, 'when men have a cause to fight for they forget their women, we are only part of their life, though to us they are everything. I'm not excusing him, for didn't I warn you away from the man myself? But I think you are being too harsh. Listen to him, wait for his story to be told and for sure you'll feel different about him then.'

A small glimmer of hope came alive in Mali's heart. It was after all only two days since the explosion in the works, there had been a great deal of coming and going behind the company gates. Why, even Davie had been laid off shift for a time while the sheds were put to rights. She sighed heavily and then suddenly smiled.

'At least telling you about it has made me feel better.' She lay back on the grass, her hands behind her head, the warm sun beating down upon her face.

'I can't say I'm happy exactly but I feel more content now to wait and see if he comes for me.'

Katie was silent and Mali turned to look at her, for the first time really seeing her. The Irish girl was pale and there were dark circles under her eyes.

'What about you?' she asked softly. 'How are things between you and Will?' She saw Katie shake her head.

'I'm a worse fool than ever you'll be, Mali for I know the man is using me, coming sniffing round when he wants his oats and leaving me alone when he's had enough. Treats me like a puppy dog so he does, a pet to be put in a kennel when he grows tired of it.'

'I'm thoughtless and selfish, so wrapped up in my own problems that I've not considered yours,' Mali said regretfully.

Katie shrugged. 'I think soon it'll come to a head, either I'll tell him to go to hell and back and see if I care or *he*'ll give *me* the boot.'

She pushed back her hair. 'I think he's caught in some mischief, he's been so ill-tempered lately that he's been bitin' my head off whenever I open my mouth and I'm the bigger fool for worryin' about him.'

Mali laughed suddenly though there was little humour in her eyes. 'It seems we're both barking up the wrong tree, Katie,' she said. 'I think it would be better if we were to forget the pair of them, put them right out of our minds. How's about if we go for a walk somewhere, have our tea in that little shop near the beach, it's open on Sundays isn't it?'

'Hey listen to the rich girl, got that much pay out of old Mr Waddington did you? Well I bet you're blessing the day you started on at the laundry, you've risen to office girl from boiler stoker and put Sally Benson in her place in just a few months.'

Mali smiled. 'Well it's you I have to thank for the job, if you hadn't persuaded Big Mary that I was worth taking on I'd still be at home twiddling my thumbs now.'

Mali rose to her feet and brushed the grass from her skirts. 'I am grateful to you, Katie, though I don't suppose it's ever come into my mind to say it before.' She hugged Katie's arm. 'I'll treat you to tea as way of a thank you.'

Katie did not protest and Mali was pleased for she knew her friend gave most of her money to her father. No one seemed to be buying fish at the moment, the weather was too hot and folks were eating cold meat and summer foods. The most that the inhabitants of the area would stretch to was a salt fish for breakfast on Sundays.

Katie laughed suddenly. 'Saw Sally Benson yesterday, forgot to tell you, she's got a beautiful shiner, her eye looks as though she's put boot blacking on it. Did her good sure enough, you punching her like that, didn't expect it from you, thought you were too weakly to be any threat to her.' Katie shook her head. 'She's had it coming for some time and I wasn't the only one happy to see her put down. That girl's been bullyin' us all off and on ever since she came to the laundry. But be careful Mali, she's got it in for you now and if she can, she'll spite you back, you can be sure of it.'

'She's the least of my worries,' Mali said softly. 'Come on, let's go and get that tea.'

As Mali and Katie had sat talking on the banks of the canal, Sterling was retreating from Copperman's Row, his face dark and set, his hands thrust deep into the pockets of his trousers. He walked down towards the docks and stood staring at the ships bobbing on the tide, the tall masts pointing to the cloudless sky.

The stink of fish permeated the air for the fish market was open, the catches made recently by the fishermen waiting on the quay ready to be bought by the traders. But business was slow and under the heat of the sun the seafood became dried up and unappetising.

Sterling sat on one of the iron bollards, staring over the busy docks. As usual they were a hive of bustling activity, with Chinamen walking beside dark-skinned Africans, and on the largest quay, mountains of coal were being loaded into the innards of the ships. Such tasks were a necessity, even on the Sabbath.

As well as sailing vessels, there were steam packets berthed near the shore and further out in the bay the small craft moved restlessly on the incoming tide.

Sterling tried to recall word for word the conversation he'd had with the woman who'd opened the door to him. He asked her politely enough if Mali was in and she'd shaken back her untidy overbright hair and put her finger on her lips.

'Hush, don't take offence sir, but Davie will go mad if he knows you've come calling. You've upset his daughter right enough and there's no hope of Mali seeing you, none at all. Not that she's here mind, no, gone out galivanting she has, with a friend. Not saying if it's a fine young bucko or no but I 'spects it is.'

Sterling had pushed open the door, entering the kitchen

unasked, and unless Mali was upstairs or out back then the woman was speaking the truth.

'Leave my girl be, Mr Richardson.' Davie had risen from his chair, his face red with anger, his great arms folded across his chest. 'Don't want nothing to do with you she don't. Anyway, it's not right, master and the daughter of a worker, getting together, 'tisn't natural.'

Sterling had backed out of the kitchen then, anger filling him so that he could scarcely see.

The young woman had glanced up at him and there had been something sly in her expression.

'Just don't bother with her any more, no better than she ought to be,' she whispered. 'She's told me things that would make your hair curl. Anyways, you let her down somehow didn't you? No keeping anything from me there isn't.'

Sterling saw a gull wheeling overhead and tried to think calmly. He did not altogether believe the word of the young woman for she had struck him as an unlikely sort of companion for Mali. Yet there was an element of truth in what she'd said, he had not returned to the hotel that night in time to take Mali home. And yet surely she could have asked him for some explanation before condemning him.

He rose to his feet impatiently, he had more important things to occupy his mind than trying to gauge the way a woman might be thinking. If Mali wanted him she knew where to find him, but one thing was for sure, he would not be the one to search her out.

Chapter Twenty-three

The days passed into weeks and Sweyn's Eye took on the mantle of early autumn. The soft western hillside, which a short time ago had sported fresh green leaves, was now covered in a riot of red and gold. Dead foliage began to carpet the drowsing earth, scattering in small gusts blown by the keen edge of the easterly wind.

In the town it was a grey Monday morning. Rain swept down from the hills and the streets were misty and lustreless, the inclement weather keeping the inhabitants of the huddled houses cloistered at their own hearths.

Only the copper works straddling the banks of the swiftly flowing river showed any sign of activity. Sparks shot skyward as though in defiance of the full-bellied rain clouds, and green sulphurous smoke mingled with the dismal drizzle.

Inside the sheds it seemed more hot and breathless than ever for the rain kept the smoke low and it caught at the lungs of the copperworkers like darts of flame. Here the air was heavy with the spurts of steam forced from the open-mouthed furnaces and vapour rose high to linger damply among the wooden struts supporting the roof.

Davie was feeling more than a little tired as he wielded his ladle, his great muscles bulged and the veins stood out achingly proud. He discharged the load with his usual skill and it gave him satisfaction to know that when the copper settled, the coin-like slices would come from the mould neat and even.

Davie's stomach rumbled with hunger. Yet again Rosa had forgotten to put him up a box of grub. He was becoming used to it now but sometimes he longed for the days when Mali used to pack the food, he had eaten well then.

He felt a momentary pang of unease. Mali was still determined to move out of the cottage in Copperman's Row even though in the few weeks that had passed since he had brought Rosa in to live with him, he had hoped that things would settle down. He had tried to persuade his daughter that nothing need change but now he could see how wrong he'd been, everything was different now that Rosa was mistress of the little home.

The brasses were dull, the floor stained with grease and debris. Mali, for the most part, kept to her room, unwilling to speak to the woman who she felt had replaced her mother.

And Mali, his beloved daughter, was growing beautiful, tall and proud, more like her mother every day. Jinny had been a fine woman, no mistake about it, but a man needed more than memories to warm his bed.

He moved away from the mould for it was time for him to have a break. He pulled his shirt over his head and the flannel was soaked, the red turned dark like blood with his sweat.

His chest gleamed bronze in the flare from the furnace and he scarcely felt any cooler than he had done before. Rosa was taking all the sap out of him, he mused, she was a girl far too young for an old ram like himself. He was one man trying to make up for the dozens she'd had before, he thought, and was surprised at his own bitterness.

At first, it had not bothered him that she was a flossy. She was young and needed to fill her belly any way she could but he was fast coming to the conclusion that she had loved her work and now that it was taken away from her, missed the excitement of searching for men who would pay for what she had to offer.

The knowledge was beginning to eat away at him, eroding the sweetness he had found in Rosa when they'd first met. He was nothing but an old fool, he told himself, but he was caught in a trap now from which there seemed to be no escape.

He took a draught of beer from the bottle beside him. Rosa had not put up any tea and to Davie's taste, ale was a poor substitute, and the work was as drying as a desert in far Arabia. Well, he could not have everything, he supposed, and there were not many men of his age who could boast of bedding a wench young enough to be his daughter.

He rose with a sigh and took up his ladle once more. He could not sit around mooning all day, that was not what he was paid for. He fell into the circle of men, feeling like a beast tethered to an invisible cord. Dip and move and tip the burden and back round again to the furnace, surely hell could not be a worse fate than this?

He longed suddenly to be out under the skies however grey, breathing fresh air into his guts. He felt restless and strangely uneasy. It must be the result of going without breakfast, he told himself impatiently.

He glanced over his shoulder and saw that Will Owens was now at the back of him. His uneasiness increased but he told himself that the young man had grown up a little in the past months. Doubtless he still sang songs for the boss and yet there was a new strength to Will's features, a hardness in his eyes, a fresh confidence to the set of his shoulders, perhaps he would turn out all right after all.

Will Owens did not meet Davie's eye. 'Keep up your stride,' he said in a harsh tone. Davie moved forward more quickly, knowing that he was at fault and had come dangerously close to the glowing ladle.

He felt as though he had been working for hours, moving round and round in an everlasting circle. God damn it, he would have to get out of the sheds, find another job, something that would give a bit of life to a man instead of this everlasting heat and stench.

There was a bustling at the door of the sheds and glancing up, Davie saw Sterling Richardson enter. Rain dripped from the loose-fitting overcoat he wore and the huge goggles over his eyes gave him a strangely threatening aspect. Davie tensed, he felt that this man was responsible for Mali's unhappiness and for that alone Davie longed to put a big fist in his face. But he must be fair, he had heard that there had been a fight outside the laundry between Mali and some other girl and Mr Richardson, far from being responsible for Mali's torn blouse and dishevelled appearance, had driven her away in his car. Davie had no proof that anything untoward had happened after that. True, when accused, Mali had turned on him angrily, said she'd been with a man, but that might have simply been a gesture of defiant fury. At any rate, she barely spoke to him these days, like a stranger she'd become and it hurt him deep inside.

Davie sighed, he had thought of giving the boss a hiding just in case he had laid a hand on Mali but what useful purpose would that serve? It would put Davie out of his home as well as out of a job and so he bit on his temper hard.

Mr Richardson was in his shirt sleeves now for all the world as if he was going to do an honest day's graft, he who had never lifted a shovel in his life. Yet he was not soft, Davie gave him full credit for guts.

'Morning, Davie.' Sterling stood beside Davie now, his eyes level. 'Hope your family are well.'

Davie nodded, touching the forelock of damp hair that clung to his brow. 'My girl's doing fine, office worker now she is, but I 'spects you know that.'

Sterling glanced away. 'Don't take that tone with me, Davie,' he said harshly and Davie felt rage flame through him.

'Then keep away from my girl, is it?'

The two men stared at each other for a long moment in silence and both knew that Sterling could have the last word if he wished.

'How would you like to try a new job?' Sterling spoke at last. It was clear that Mr Richardson meant to ignore the clash between them and Davie took a deep breath, determined to follow suit.

'What job is that?'

'Manufacturing zinc wire, it would mean an increase in wages.'

'Sounds all right to me.' Davie tried hard to keep the excitement out of his voice, it didn't do to appear too eager.

'That's settled then, you might as well finish off your shift here and then tomorrow go into the foundry, I think you'll find the work not quite so arduous.'

He moved away along the rows of furnaces, stopping to talk to a few of the other men and Davie turned back to the furnace, dipping his ladle, lifting it with renewed energy, knowing that after this shift, he would not be doing it again.

'One of the chosen then are you?' Will Owens' voice grated on Davie and he glanced over his shoulder quickly, his temper rising.

'What's it to you, you cocky young swine?' he said. 'Don't you think you'd have jumped at the chance if it had been offered to you instead of me?'

Will Owens was not deterred. 'But it wasn't offered to me, was it? Must be a reason for it, something the rest of us don't know about. The boss gives you a way out of this hell hole on a plate and better wages to boot and you've got the nerve to call me a songbird. Well I say there's something here that stinks to high heaven.'

Davie emptied his ladle, suddenly weary of the fight. 'Get back to work, boyo,' he said, 'jealousy won't get you anywhere, so shut your mouth for now and if it's quarrelling you want, I'll see you outside, later.'

As the morning wore on, Davie grew more and more exultant, he was to have a rise in wages. He could buy Rosa some fripperies and perhaps a little gift for Mali, something that would bring the smile to her eyes once more.

Matters would soon right themselves, he thought hopefully, Mali would grow used to Rosa and perhaps begin to show the girl how to keep house, for she'd never been given the chance to look after a place of her own and so couldn't be blamed for not living up to Mali's idea of cleanliness.

As if he had brought her to the works with the force of his thoughts, Davie looked up and saw Mali standing uncertainly in the doorway.

'Hang on boys,' he said to the men around him, 'I'm just going to see my little girl for a minute, won't be long.'

Davie was glad that Mr Richardson had long since left the sheds for the last thing he wanted was a meeting between the owner and Mali. He had sensed the mutual liking between the two of them but surely now Davie'd issued yet another warning, the copper boss would keep his distance?

'Hello, *cariad*,' he said, 'what are you doing here?'

Mali smiled up at him and she seemed more like her old self than she had been in a long time.

'There's a silly question,' she said. 'What do you think this is I'm carrying, Scotch mist?' She held the package out to him.

'There's some food for you Dad, I've been awful to you letting you go without these past weeks and I'm sorry. Been worried about you the last few days, seen you growing thinner, I have. But I'm going to make it up to you.'

He looked down at her and love for his daughter welled inside him. She looked sweet and fresh in her neat blouse and plain skirt.

'*Duw* that looks nice, *cariad*.' He had drawn aside the paper and was looking down at a brown, crusty pie. 'Smells like angel food, my mouth is watering.'

He smiled at her. 'How's work then and how come you've been let out to see me?' Mali's eyes shone with pride.

'Mr Waddington leaves it mostly to me to see to the office these days. He's not so well, chest is bad you see and he trusts me to carry on while he's away.'

'Good girl,' Davie said, 'I'm proud of you.'

He thought of telling her his own news about the new job but then perhaps Rosa should be the first to know. His daughter was an independent woman now; he burned with pride.

'I'd best get back *cariad*,' Davie said, 'I'll eat the pie on my next break but for now I'd best work or the other boyos on the gang will be calling me a shirker.' He waved to Mali and watched her walking away. Her steps were slow, without spring, and he wondered if she could be sickening for some illness or other.

He was soon back into the swing of his work again, dipping his ladle into the burning, molten copper that swirled like a blood-red river, shimmering with a heat that almost scorched his face as he carried his burden, straining, to the mould.

But he felt lighter in spirit than he'd done for some time, for Mali was softening, perhaps even beginning to accept Rosa as part of the household. He looked forward to going home after his shift and telling them both that tomorrow he was to be moved into the foundry.

What happened then was never clear to him, for one minute he was walking along, keeping his place in the circle of men and the next there was a warning cry from Will Owens behind him.

It was as though a mule had kicked him in the back, sending him sprawling onto the wetness of the floor, his arms spreadeagled, his face in the dirt.

Then came the pain, searing, agonising; he heard a hoarse voice cry out and knew it was his own. There was the awful stench of burning flesh and the cloth of his trousers was suddenly aflame.

His voice rose to a scream as the pain flared through his crotch but his throat was thick with the shock and he could scarcely breathe. He prayed he might lose consciousness but he was acutely aware of the hard floor beneath his chest and the sea of boots that were suddenly standing round him and the appalled, unbelieving silence of his fellow workers.

'Jesus, get a doctor someone,' a voice above him said. Davie's eyes glazed over as sweat from his brow ran into them. He seemed to be enveloped in fire from head to foot, he was afraid to move, terrified of what he would see. One of the men held a bottle to his lips and it smelled of gin and he drank from it deeply, praying for the pain to lessen.

But the agony did not go away and after a while, he reached out and his fingers did not encounter flesh but fastly cooling metal that was settling into his body, swiftly becoming part of it.

He felt his eyes roll back in his head. 'Help me, for God's sake help me.' He thought he shouted the words but they came from his lips in a series of small moans that sounded unintelligible even to his own ears. Yet someone heard and understood for the next moment, a large fist crashed down upon his head and Davie fell into deep, merciful blackness.

He did not know how much later it was when he opened his eyes, perhaps hours, perhaps days, but he did know he was in the infirmary. He was lying on his stomach on a crisp clean bed and outside, he could hear the rush of the tide upon the beach.

Voices were speaking at a great distance. Dimly, he saw shadowy white figures, he heard a word spoken crisply and firmly and tried to understand it.

'Amputation.' The voice died away as he moved his head. It sounded again, much quieter but still clear enough for him to hear it.

'Not much else to be done, the poor fellow's scarcely a man any more.'

With a terrible dread, Davie remembered the pain in his back and running through his groin as the metal bit deep into his flesh. Panic flared within him and suddenly he was vomiting uncontrollably.

He felt someone place a cool hand upon his forehead; his mind cleared and he felt again the searing agony of the molten copper running over him. He tried to get up but gentle hands pushed him back against the pillow.

'What's happening to me?' He stared at the nurse whose long veil hung over her cheeks, concealing her expression. She held a small cup containing medication and put it carefully against his lips.

'Just take this, Mr Llewelyn,' she said softly. 'It will ease the pain and help you to sleep.' She seemed to be smiling at him encouragingly but he turned his head away and looked through the window.

'But I don't want to sleep, it's still daylight.' His voice was scarcely more than a croak and the nurse shook her head at him.

'Don't try to talk, you've had a very bad shock, you need to rest so that you'll recover all the more quickly. Now, take this medicine for me, there's a good man.'

Davie drank the bitter liquid and lay his cheek against the pillow, exhausted with the effort. The pain in his back was intense, it was as though flames were licking over him.

'I'm going to die,' he said in a whisper and the nurse took his fingers in hers, smoothing the back of his head with infinite gentleness.

'You will be all right, so there's no need to go feeling morbid, I won't have that sort of talk in my ward, do you understand me?' She rose to her feet and smiled down at him, smoothing the creases out of her stiff apron.

'You'll soon be asleep and that's the best cure we know for healing the body. It will take a bit of time, but we'll have you sitting up and feeling sprightly before long, don't you worry.'

When she had gone, Davie turned his head and looked along the row of beds stretching away down the ward. It was deathly quiet, a place where only the very sick were housed.

'Sweet Jesus, what's to become of me?' He sighed wearily and lay his head on the softness of the pillow. Almost of their own accord, his hands began to fumble beneath the bedclothes and his searching fingers encountered heavy bandaging on the lower part of his body. He remembered then, the half-whispered word 'amputation'.

'Oh, God, not that,' he said and like a baby, he began to cry.

Chapter Twenty-four

The sun was pale and weak, peering intermittently through the grey, scudding clouds. High winds swept the branches of the trees as if trying to shake free the last few remaining leaves. From within the warmth and comfort of the Canal Street Laundry office, Mali sat staring through the small window into the yard.

She sighed heavily. Ink ran from the nib of the pen in her hand, blotting the clean page before her, but she did not notice.

Her mind turned again and again to the first time she'd seen her father after his terrible accident. When one of the copper-men had come to fetch her, telling her that Dad had been taken to the infirmary down on the beach, she could not believe it. Only a few minutes before, or so it had seemed, she had been giving him his grub pack.

She had known at once that Davie's wounds must be serious for it was rare for any copperman to be taken to the infirmary, the workers preferring to treat their burns with a mixture of beets soaked in vinegar.

Mali had almost swooned clean away when she'd walked trembling into the long ward. Her father was lying flat on his stomach and the face turned towards her seemed shrunken, chin and nose jutting forth in a cruel caricature of himself.

She had felt tears hot and bitter pour down her cheeks but it didn't matter for Davie couldn't see her, couldn't see anyone, he was in some limbo of his own, the edges of his mind blurred with constant medication.

Afterwards, the doctor had told her gently that Davie would never walk again for one of his legs had been so badly damaged that it was beyond medical skill to repair. But worse, the copper had burned and eroded so badly that although Davie would live, it would be as a eunuch.

Some of Davie's tew gang had been waiting outside the hospital and one of them, Mali thought it might have been Will Owens, though she could not be sure, had blamed the accident on Sterling Richardson. Apparently, there had been some angry words spoken between the two men, leaving Davie upset. He had seemingly lost his concentration which was a dangerous thing when working molten metal, and had stumbled backwards.

The story was jumbled now in Mali's mind. She sighed, all she really knew was that Davie still lay in the hospital almost a week after the accident, not speaking or moving, just existing, kept alive by dedicated nursing.

Rosa visited Davie day and night, talking to him softly, holding his hand, trying to coax some response from him, but she did not know, and Mali could not tell her, that she would never be a wife now, at least not Davie's.

The door of the office opened and a gust of cold wind scattered leaves into the room. Mali glanced up to see Mr Waddington, smiling down at her.

He looked cold, his silk scarf exchanged for a fine woollen one that covered his throat and clung to the bottom half of his face so that he looked like an egg in a cup, Mali thought with a glimmer of amusement.

'Holding the fort, my dear?' He closed the door and moved towards the fireplace. 'I'm sure you are doing extremely well on your own but I do feel that at a time like this, I must at least try to pull my weight, for you've enough on your plate as it is.'

'You shouldn't be out of bed, Mr Waddington,' Mali chided him. 'Your chest won't be cured if you insist on going out in all weathers.'

Mr Waddington sat down at his desk with his scarf still around his shoulders. He seemed much thinner and his face was colourless, almost parchment-like.

'Let's have a good hot cup of tea, shall we dear, and afterwards we shall look at the books together for I fear we are still losing money. Ring the bell, there's a good girl.' He stared at her intently.

'You are not looking hale and hearty yourself, Mali,' Mr Waddington said gently. 'I know what's happened to your father is terrible indeed but if the will is strong then the flesh will heal.'

'You're right, of course,' Mali replied, for how could she place her own burden of knowledge on Mr Waddington's frail shoulders?

Sally Benson brought in the tea, carrying with her the distinctive scent of the packing room of hot well-ironed linen and suddenly Mali felt nostalgic, wishing herself back in time to when she had never lain with Sterling Richardson, never tortured her mind with regrets and reproaches and more, before Davie had been scarred by the copper. But could she have changed anything, anything at all? She doubted it.

Sally put the cups on the desk with a sniff and a baleful look in Mali's direction. She still held a grudge and doubtless always would but she was too wary, now, to give voice to her thoughts.

'Ah, that's lovely.' Mr Waddington drank deeply. 'Just what the doctor ordered. Close the door carefully behind you, there's a good girl,' he said as Sally Benson left the room.

'I've been looking over the books very carefully,' Mali said gently, 'and I'm afraid the laundry is still not making a profit.'

Mr Waddington looked even more tired as he stared down at the figures in the big red ledger. After a moment, he shrugged his shoulders.

'I know what the trouble is,' he said tersely. 'I need new equipment, the old boilers are worn out, take too long to boil the water, so using up costly fuel. I need an infusion of cash. A hundred pounds or so would do it,' he mused. 'Perhaps I could raise it in the bank by mortgaging my house but I'm getting old Mali, and fearful of taking risks. I expect I shall simply have to sell out in the end.'

Mali's heart sank, she needed the wages Mr Waddington paid her for she was now the sole breadwinner and a great deal of her wages were spent on Dad. It was true that sometimes Rosa came home with a few shillings and it wasn't difficult to guess how she'd earned them and Mali couldn't blame her. But the girl never offered any money for her keep and even if she had, Mali would have been too proud to accept it.

Mr Waddington put down his cup. 'But I've not come here to talk about my problems. No, I thought you might be able to make use of an afternoon off. Get your coat and nip away sharply and I'll keep an eye on things here.' He glanced round him. 'Though you have everything so well organised that there's nothing very much for me to do. I expect you've made up the wages as usual?'

'Yes, I've seen the incoming bills as well, they're all filed away.' Mali rose and drew on her coat though she did not relish going home to the cold empty house in Copperman's Row one little bit.

The wind blew loudly along the street and furrowed the waters of the canal. A small boy noisily chased his cap along the pavement so that at first, Mali did not hear anyone behind her.

'Hey you, wait a minute.' Sally Benson was tugging at Mali's arm. She still wore her laundry apron and the wind whipped her hair untidily over her face.

'You're very thick with the copper boss, aren't you?' She did not wait for an answer but spoke again at once, an unpleasant sneer on her face. 'At any rate when we had that fight he was quick enough to take you away in that fancy automobile just in case I pasted you one.'

Mali felt so beaten down by the events of the past week that she had no spirit to match Sally's spitefulness. She pulled her arm away impatiently.

'Just leave me alone will you?' she said tiredly.

'Leave you alone, is it?' Sally put her hands on her thick hips. 'No my fine madam, I'll not leave you alone. Pay you back I will for hittin' me and for getting Aggie the boot.'

Mali sighed and began to walk away but Sally's next words stopped her.

'Mr Richardson likes his oats, so I hear.' She laughed harshly. 'Had 'em with you I dare say. One thing's for sure, he don't clean up the little messes he leaves behind him, no, my Mam has to do that. She's a midwife, didn't you know? Did a little bit of work on a lady by the name of Miss Bea Cardigan, she's from one of them big houses up on the hill.'

'So?' Mali felt her throat constrict. 'What's all that got to do with me?'

'Just letting you know that servants gossip to my Mam and by all accounts, your rich boyfriend is a right villain. Father of the poor lady's babba he was and left her in the lurch once he knew of her trouble. Come to my Mam to rid her of the unwanted bundle.' Sally laughed cruelly. 'And he don't want you for anything except to get up your skirt so you needn't go puttin' on any airs and graces to me.'

Mali forced herself to walk away and made her way un-seeingly past the Mexico Fountain. She hurried along Green Hill, clasping her arms around her stomach feeling sick, wanting only to get indoors and shut herself away from the world.

By the time she let herself into the house, she was trembling and as the smell of rancid fat drifted towards her, she retched and was forced to go outside to the privy. She leaned weakly against the whitewashed walls, trying to regain her breath.

When she was feeling slightly better, she changed from her good clothes into an old skirt and blouse and set to work on the house. Lifelong habits came to her aid and soon she had a cheerful fire burning in a shining grate. When the water was boiled Mali washed the soiled floor, scrubbing hard so that the accumulated grime disappeared. But it was only after an hour's intensive work that the kitchen looked more like its old self.

Mali sat down with a cup between her hands and enjoyed the blaze of the coals, watching as the flames danced and quivered, and she sighed with weariness.

In spite of everything, Mali could not find it in her heart to blame Rosa for leaving the greasy dishes in the sink or for the thick dust that had lain undisturbed for days on the furniture, for the girl devoted her time to visiting Davie at the infirmary. She sat with him for hours on end, trying to talk to him and awake some response.

Thoughts of Davie were too painful for Mali to dwell on and so she turned her mind to the problems of the laundry. If only she had the money needed to help Mr Waddington, then she might be able to save the business for him. She had seen ways of economising on small things like soda and soap and new scrubbing boards to replace the old worn ones that tore at the sheets instead of cleaning them. But most of all, savings could be made on the organisation of the delivery of the linen.

At the moment, it was quite a random affair. The errand boy took out the horse-drawn van, moving from one end of Sweyn's Eye to the other haphazardly. This wasted valuable time and Mali had worked out a more sensible rota which she had not yet shown to Mr Waddington.

Her idea was to call on a given area on the same day and at the same time every week, both collecting and delivering the laundry. This would do away with the necessity of making several journeys to the same place and folks would soon become used to the new method. She sighed, what was the point of thinking about it? All her small ideas put together were not enough to save the laundry from closing.

She was startled by a loud knocking on the door and when she opened it Dai End House was standing on the step, cap twisted in his hand. He smiled at her in embarrassment as Mali stepped back to allow him indoors.

'Saw you come home early, I did, *merchi*,' he said, 'thought I'd just tell you about the collection.'

Mali pushed the kettle back onto the flames. 'Collection, what do you mean, Dai?' She stared at him in bewilderment as he stood at the table and emptied his pockets. He spilled coins everywhere, they fell onto the floor and Dai grinned apologetically.

'All us from the Mex have been puttin' together for Davie, a whipround just to show we're thinking of him. There's money from the crowd at Maggie Dicks too, goodhearted lot they are even though none of them are coppermen.'

Mali felt tears burn her eyes. 'There's kind of everyone,' she said quickly. 'Tell them thank you from me and from Dad. Will you have some tea, Dai?' She moved the kettle so that the water hissed through the blackened spout but Dai End House shook his head.

'No tea for me, *merchi*, you know I likes my ale too much to spoil my gullet with tea. Now if there's anything you want doing, man's jobs round the house or anything, just let me know and I'll get a gang over here so quick you won't see my feet move.'

He left her and she heard him whistling plaintively as he walked away down the street, and she bit her lip as she looked down at the hard-earned money he had brought her.

The coins amounted to five pounds, a good sum, more than some men would earn in two weeks, and Mali was touched and grateful for the gesture. She swept the money into an old tea tin and put it on the shelf, knowing that the day might come when she would be very glad of it.

She was just about to change from her damp skirt and blouse into fresh clothes when there was another knock on the door. Wearily Mali rubbed her hand across her eyes and brushed back her tangled hair, wondering who else would be coming to call on her. She was in no mood for talking to neighbours, however well intentioned, and she only hoped that whoever it was would not stay long.

Her heart almost stopped beating when she opened the door and looked into the windy street. Her face felt suddenly hot as though it had been slapped and she stepped back a pace instinctively.

'Sterling.' Her voice was little more than a whisper. He moved past her into the kitchen and Mali stared at him in anguish. He stood tall and elegant, his bright hair falling across his forehead, his deep blue eyes taking in every detail of her appearance. In spite of everything, all she longed to do was to rush into his arms.

'What do you want here?' Her cold tone revealed nothing of her feelings.

'Mali, I want help.' He made a move to take her hands but she shook her head wildly.

'No, don't touch me!' She pushed back a strand of tangled hair and stared up at him, loving him so much that the pain of it swamped her senses. He stood upright, his eyes bright and hard. He thrust his hands into his pockets and stared at her for a long moment in silence.

The tension between them was almost tangible. Mali closed her eyes briefly and the sensation of lying in his arms enveloped in his love was so strong that she felt almost faint.

'Then you won't listen to any of my explanations,' Sterling said in a hard voice. 'We must talk, Mali, surely you realise that?'

'Why talk?' she said fiercely. 'Do you think words can right the wrongs you've done me and mine?'

247

He looked away from her, shaking his head. 'Mali, what happened to your father was an accident, a terrible, awful accident but I had nothing to do with it.'

She wanted to believe him, to go and put her head on his shoulder and cry out all her hurt and pain, but she could not.

'Did you and Dad have words about me just before it happened?' she asked more quietly. Sterling stared at her, his eyes clear.

'Yes, we did, Mali, I can't deny that, but it didn't end there.'

She took a deep breath and turned her back on him, closing her eyes, refusing to hear any more even though he was explaining that he had offered Davie a new job away from the copper.

'Don't say another word.' She spoke in a hard voice. 'You wanted me for one thing only, used me as you did that poor lady, Miss Cardigan.'

His hands were on her shoulders, turning her to face him once more and his eyes were lit by anger so that they appeared deep violet.

'What are you talking about?' His grip on her shoulders tightened. 'Bea Cardigan is an adult woman and what happened between us was over before I'd made love to you.'

Mali bit her lip, even now he would not admit that he was the father of Miss Cardigan's child and that he had done wrong by her. 'Just go,' she said. 'There's nothing more to say, I don't think I ever want to set eyes on you again.'

'Oh, don't you now.' He pulled her to him and Mali struggled uselessly for a moment. He was so close that their breaths mingled and their hearts seemed to beat together as one. Slowly but surely, his lips moved to hers and clung. Mali ceased to fight and lay quiescent in his arms. Love seemed to flow between them, enveloping them in a mist of emotion. She was sinking into a great whirlpool which was carrying her ever downwards.

Mali became aware then that his lips were not tender but savage and bruising. Fool! The word rang in her mind and she pushed against Sterling so fiercely that he released her. She moved away from him and stood behind the table, that formed an effective barrier between them. He stared at her, his eyes cold now like blue ice. Mali rubbed at her lips, trying to erase the sting of his kisses. He had treated her like a woman of the streets and if he had intended to wound and hurt her he had succeeded.

'Will you just get out of my life and leave me in peace?' She spoke bitterly, resisting the temptation to cry out to him that he loved her, must love her for she had given herself to him body and soul. Pride came to her aid and she straightened, smoothing back her hair, her face set, her lips pressed together to stop them trembling.

He moved to the door and then paused, his hand going to his pocket. He drew out a package and dropped it on the table.

'Don't plan on refusing this,' he said, 'it's compensation for your father's injuries. It is not charity but comes from a fund set up for cases such as these.'

'Cases such as these,' Mali repeated after him, 'and money is supposed to make up to my father for all that's happened to him, is it?' She paused and there was contempt in her eyes. 'Isn't there any humanity in you at all?'

He was opening the door when he spoke his voice was curt. 'There will be an enquiry into the accident and you can be sure that the blame will be placed squarely where it belongs. Does that satisfy your need for revenge?'

'Take your blood money and go,' she said, stung into anger once more. She was on the verge of tears but she would not reveal one hint of weakness.

'It's not yours to return,' he replied. 'Your father works for the copper company and if he refuses compensation then that's entirely up to him but I believe he will show better sense than his daughter.'

Mali remained silent as he left the house, there was nothing more she could say. As the door clicked quietly shut, she put her hands to her face, feeling empty and alone.

'Sterling, come back to me.' She whispered the words, knowing that now he would never hear them from her lips.

A coal shifted in the grate and Mali knew she must build up the fire, anything to keep herself occupied. Soon she would go to see Dad again and she must try to appear cheerful even if he didn't recognise her.

'But he will know me, he must,' she whispered desperately. She made herself some tea and the hot fragrant liquid soothed her a little. Reluctantly, she turned to look at the package Sterling had left on the table.

Several bundles of notes fell onto the scrubbed boards and Mali realised there must be at least a hundred pounds there. Not much to a man like Sterling Richardson but enough to keep herself and Dad for more than a year. She put the package away inside the old tea tin with the rest of the money. She must talk to Dad, tell him of the kindness of the neighbours and of the generosity of his boss. The first part would be easy enough but to speak of Sterling would break her heart.

She picked up her coat and let herself out into the street. Dai End House was playing 'Eternal Father Strong to Save' on the accordion and Mali's lips quivered. But then she was composed once more, nodding to Dai, passing the time of day with him just as if her world had not broken into fragments all around her.

Chapter Twenty-five

Dean Sutton sat in the smoky bar of the Cape Horner feeling uncomfortable and more than a little conspicuous. He was too well dressed, his large hat and the fur collar on his overcoat making him the object of curiosity. He was very much aware of the riff-raff in the bar eyeing him speculatively, doubtless thinking him easy pickings. Well, just let one of them start and they would soon learn differently.

He looked out of the window at the russet leaves blowing along the ground and his mind drifted to Bea Cardigan. She was a lovely, gorgeous butterfly and just as delicate. If she would only allow him to, he would take care of her for the rest of her life, he would cherish and cosset her and make sure that she was never hurt again.

As the time had passed since that beautiful day they'd spent together on the beach, Dean had become more and more convinced that there was something he didn't know. It had been all very well for Bertha to say that Bea and Sterling Richardson had quarrelled but there must have been a damned good reason for her to turn against the man so completely that she had shut him out of her life.

His hands clenched into fists as he thought of what he'd like to do to Richardson. He'd become cocky of late, his hopes raised no doubt by the small success he was having with this zinc wire. In all probability, it was simply a flash in the pan and would not bring any lasting profit to the company.

Dean drank a mouthful of whisky and put his glass down on the stained surface of the table with an impatient gesture. It had indeed been a mistake to meet Rickie in this grimy public bar, he mused. Here they would stand out like a boil on a flea. He glanced at the large clock on the wall telling himself that if the young man did not show up in the next few minutes he would leave.

The huge fire roaring in the grate beside Dean's chair flared up in the draft from the suddenly opened door. Dean sighed and glared up at the new arrival.

'About time you came,' he said briskly. Then he noticed the boy was not alone, Glanmor Travers was with him and a young dark-haired fellow who by the cut of his clothes was one of the copperworkers.

'Not late, are we?' Rickie spoke pleasantly but Dean would not trust him as far as he could see him. He might find it expedient to throw in his lot with the younger of the Richardson brothers for the moment but that did not mean he would harbour the viper in his bosom.

Rickie took a chair and drew it gratingly towards the table. 'This is Will Owens, the one my brother thought was his songbird but he was working for me all along.'

'Is that so?' Dean looked away from the boy with complete lack of interest. The young whippersnapper was the sort you could buy for ten a penny, not worth a light.

Travers the chemist was a different kettle of fish, he thought with some satisfaction. Although the man had his own personal axe to grind, at least he would use a little intelligence in working out his revenge. He was pleased now that he'd waited, this promised to be a very interesting meeting.

'You know of course that Sterling is branching out into coal?' Rickie said, leaning back and folding his arms. 'Already taken possession of the Kilvey Deep and it won't stop there, believe me. He's got his teeth into something that will pay, not only as a sideline but to provide coal for the copper and steel works.'

Dean stared at the boy with raised eyebrows. 'So?' he said, impatient with the histrionics, wanting to get down to the real reason for such an unlikely crew getting together.

Rickie smiled slowly and leaned forward conspiratorially. 'I've thought of getting the men out against him but they're past that now, they can see that the new foundry is paying out good wages. And so, more drastic action is needed. I think I'll leave it to Glanmor to outline the plan.'

There was a sudden silence at the table while Travers looked at Dean as though trying to get his measure. Around them, the sounds of the public bar ebbed and flowed like the tide, there was the chink of glasses and the raucous voice of the landlord and Dean waited, wondering what sort of ideas this chemist might have to offer.

Travers leaned closer and his voice was so low that Dean had to strain to hear it.

'The Kilvey Deep is the mine with the Cornish beam engine,' he said slowly. Dean shook his head, resisting the urge to tell the man to get on with it. Travers narrowed his eyes and leaned even closer.

'If there was to be an unfortunate accident, say the beam became jammed or exploded because of a blocked valve? The result would be that the entire chain of pits from the Kilvey Deep down through the Landore Copper Pit and the Big Andrew would be flooded in a matter of hours.'

Dean put his elbows on the table and pressed his fingertips together, displaying an outward calm while his mind raced, trying to gauge the effect this action would have on Sterling Richardson. Rickie was there ahead of him.

'Without coal, the works could not operate, no one can make copper or zinc without furnaces. At the moment, the stocks of fuel are fair but they would be used up long before the mines could be made operational again.'

Dean stared at him. 'And what good would that do us? We both stand to lose if the profits fall.'

'Only for a time,' Rickie said triumphantly, 'then we could buy Sterling out at a very low price.'

Dean suddenly saw why he was being allowed to participate in this little scheme of Rickie's. The boy did not have the necessary sheckels to buy out an empty beer barrel.

'There's one flaw,' he said. 'What would we use for coal ourselves?'

Rickie smiled, though there was no warmth in his eyes. 'Strange you should ask, did you know that the small slants just outside the town boundary are being outclassed by the larger pits and the owners are desperate for capital investments? Small the seams may be but rich enough, and all ours for the asking.'

'And what if Sterling decides to import coal from another area?' Dean challenged. Rickie shook his head.

'Time is of the essence. When my brother realises how low his stocks have become it will be too late to do anything about it. If he fails to deliver his orders on the due date, he will be out of business.'

Dean was silent for a long moment, staring at the men seated around him, and they waited anxiously, as well they might, for his reaction.

'It seems to me that I'm taking the entire financial risk here,' he said slowly. 'What if your plan fails, I'm down in the gutter while you, Rickie, will be still sitting pretty.' He shook his head. 'I don't know, this needs thinking about.'

Rickie smiled and folded his arms across his chest. 'We can go ahead without you, Dean,' he said softly, 'and we will if we have to. Don't forget, you stand to make more than any of us. If we are successful, you'll have the biggest share of the copper company.'

The prospect was a pleasing one, Dean thought to himself, and he could well afford to put out a little cash for his shops were doing well. He wasn't really going to risk a great deal, all he would actually be doing was to buy into some of the smaller mines, nothing illegal. This man Travers would shoulder the blame if anything went wrong.

'All right,' he said at last, 'I'll finance the deal.' He saw Rickie exchange relieved glances with Glanmor Travers and knew that in spite of his brave words, Rickie had been worried in case the funds he needed would not be forthcoming.

'There's been some heavy rainfall of late and the pump has been working overtime trying to keep the pits clear,' Travers said. 'And so I suggest we go ahead as soon as possible.'

Dean nodded. 'Fine by me, I'll leave all that to you.' He glanced at the three men, bags of wind all of them though perhaps Glanmor had a little more backbone than the others. Dean rose from his chair abruptly.

'I'll leave you to it, gentlemen.' His voice was heavy with sarcasm. 'But keep me informed, won't you Rickie?'

He went outside and the wind gusted around him, lifting the

brim of his hat, but Dean scarcely noticed the cold, he was exultant, he must go to visit Bea at once. Yes, he would enjoy telling her that Sterling Richardson was going to get his comeuppance.

While Dean was thinking of visiting Bea, she was sitting on the edge of her chair in the drawing room, making a pretence of drinking tea. Seated on the long scroll sofa was Victoria Richardson, her hair slightly dishevelled by the wind that whined and moaned in the branches of the trees outside. The room was silent for neither of the women could think of anything to say and Bea was too weary and too low in spirits to make a great effort at small talk. Victoria put down the fine bone china cup and sighed softly.

'I do hope, Bea, that you don't object to your father and me becoming... close?' She drew her skirts round her legs and her eyebrows were raised anxiously as she waited for a reply.

'You and Daddy have your own lives to lead,' Bea said softly. She did not add that it was time the couple were married, for it might help right the wrong that had been done so many years before.

She would probably never reveal to Victoria that she knew the truth, knew that Sterling was James's son and her own half brother. Nor would she ever be able to forgive, she thought bitterly.

She still ached to be in Sterling's arms and even after the awful events that had taken place since, she could not forget the times she had lain with Sterling and known his love.

Her one great sorrow was that she had been forced to forfeit the joy of bearing his child and she still suffered nightmares about her visit to Mrs Benson.

'I know we are old enough not to need approval,' Victoria continued, 'and yet I would like you to be pleased for us, Bea.' She pushed back a dark strand of hair. 'Of course, we shall wait a while before we marry, at least a year, for I must abide by the period of mourning for poor, dear Arthur.'

'Yes, of course,' Bea agreed though inside her there was a jeering voice that said concern for the proprieties was surely misplaced in such a situation. Mrs Richardson and James

255

Cardigan were only resuming a relationship after all, not entering into a new one.

It was with relief that she saw her father come into the drawing room. She rose from her chair, trying to conceal her eagerness to escape, and kissed his cheek as she passed him by.

'I think I'll go down onto the beach for a while,' she said lightly. 'I'll take Bertha with me so there's no need to worry.'

James looked at her anxiously. 'But I do worry about you, Bea, you are still very fragile. I'm sure you don't realise how badly that fever you contracted affected your health.' He came to her and pressed his lips against her hair. Bea closed her eyes, feeling that old familiar guilt wash over her. It had not been a fever, her mind cried. But how could she put into words the truth of her illness? She would break her father's heart and he would never get over the fact that his folly as a young man had resulted in such tragic consequences for his daughter.

She smiled at her father reassuringly before entering the hall and calling to Bertha to bring her outdoor clothes.

'Where are you off to, Miss Bea?' The young maid held out Bea's good woollen coat and helped her to do up the buttons.

'Just down to the beach for some air, perhaps you'd like to come with me?'

Bea had always been grateful for Bertha's help and support when she needed it so badly. She'd contemplated telling Bertha the entire truth but the fear of Sterling learning the secret of his birth always held her back.

'Here, Miss Bea, put on your hat and then I'll tie a scarf around your head. We must keep you warm, no good getting a chill is there now?'

Bea came back to the present and smiled down at the young maid. 'I'm tougher than you think, Bertha. Come along, let's get out of this house, it's beginning to give me claustrophobia.'

It was cold on the beach, the wind whipped the sand into small dust storms and Bea wondered at the wisdom of her decision to take a walk in such inclement weather. All the same, the rolling pewter sea gave her a sense of peace and she stared outwards, absorbing the wash of the waves, closing her eyes for a moment, trying to calm her racing thoughts.

It was a bitter pill she was being asked to swallow, accepting Victoria as her stepmother. Once her father and Victoria were married, the house would not be Bea's domain any longer. No doubt changes would be made in the decor for a new broom always brushed clean. But worse, Victoria would always be present, there would be no escape from her unless Bea virtually became a recluse in her bedroom.

She took a deep breath of the salt, tangy air and thought of Dean. He did truly love her, and though she would never feel for him the way she did for Sterling, at least he would be good and kind to her. They had a great deal in common, she told herself, he was a fine man underneath the blustery front he assumed.

'What would you do, Bertha?' Bea spoke her thoughts out loud. 'Would you marry one man while you were in love with another?' She glanced at the maid who was struggling to keep her hat on her brown curls.

'I'd forget that Mr Richardson for a start,' Bertha said explosively, 'no good that man, treated you cruel he did and if I was to see him I'd tell him so to his face.' She picked up a stick from the sand and snapped it between her fingers vengefully.

Bea pressed her lips together to prevent herself from leaping to Sterling's defence. Of course, Bertha thought Sterling had simply left her to her fate, she had no idea of what the real truth was and never would have.

Bertha's excited voice broke into Bea's unhappy thoughts. 'Look, there's Mr Dean now, he's coming to find you.' She took off her hat and waved it wildly. 'He's seen us, he's coming this way, how romantic. See how big and handsome he is, marry him why don't you, Miss Bea, he loves you and he's rich too.'

Bea smiled. 'Don't be mercenary, Bertha.' But she watched Dean carefully as he drew closer. His hair was blowing over his brow for he had given up the unequal struggle to keep his broad-rimmed hat upon his head.

'Come here, you silly goose.' He wrapped his arms around Bea, holding her close to his warmth. 'You shouldn't have been allowed to come down here, not in this cold wind, come along, I'm taking you home.'

Bea smiled up at him as he wound the edges of his topcoat around her thin frame as though to protect her from the soft drizzle that had just begun to fall.

257

'Very well, we'll go home.' She allowed him to take her back along the beach and across the slip to the roadway. He held her hand, leading her up the hill towards the house. So suddenly that she gasped, a great pain seemed to clamp around her heart and she staggered a little.

'If I can just rest a little,' she gasped. 'I'm sorry, it's so silly of me.'

Dean's big arms scooped her up as she fell against him and then Bertha was beside them both, crying out in her fear and distress.

'What's wrong with her, Bertha?' Dean asked sternly. 'Come on, tell me the truth about her illness.'

Bertha took a great gulping sob. 'She was having his babba, there now that's the truth!' she cried. 'Had it taken away from her by the midwife. Treated her bad, Mr Richardson did, and I hate him for it.'

Dean tried to calm himself, first things first. 'Come on, let's get her home,' he said flatly.

Just as they reached the house, Bea's eyes flickered open. Bertha was already in the hallway shouting on the top of her voice.

'Mr Cardigan, come quick, Miss Bea's been taken queer.'

'I'm all right,' Bea protested. 'I just need a rest, that's all, I was foolish to go out on a day like this. Put me down, Dean, I really do feel better.'

'Maybe you do honey, but I think you should go straight to bed and have a hot toddy. Try to sleep, you're as white as a sheet.' He set her down but he was still holding onto her slim shoulders, concern written all over his face. Bea smiled at him reassuringly.

'Thank you for caring about me, Dean,' she said in a whisper, just as her father and Victoria Richardson came hurrying out of the drawing room.

'What is wrong Bea, you look dreadful, my dear.' Victoria put her arm around Bea's waist. 'Come along, let me help you to your room. James, you must send for the doctor, this girl is sick, you've been neglecting her.'

Bea allowed herself to be led up the stairs but on the landing, she stopped and looked back at Dean.

'Please come up to see me when I'm safely in bed,' she said and it cut her to the quick to see how his face lit up.

'Bertha, bring your mistress's nightclothes.' Victoria seemed to be taking charge and Beatrice was too tired to argue. She lay under the warmth of the quilts and sighed with relief for her very bones seemed to be aching.

Obediently, she sipped the hot toddy that was placed on a tray before her and after a while, she really did begin to feel better.

'Please don't let me keep you,' she said as Victoria plumped up the pillows for the hundredth time. 'I'm sorry to have made such a fuss, I feel as right as rain again now.'

'I'm not going until the doctor has seen you,' Victoria said forcefully. 'Now you just lie there quietly and leave everything to me.'

In little over an hour Dr Thomas stopped his horse and buggy in the driveway and it was Bertha who let him in. She bobbed him a curtsey and took his coat and looked up into his face intently.

'I think there's something about Miss Bea you should know,' she said quietly and stood on tiptoe to whisper in his ear.

Dr Thomas was smooth and efficient and completed his examination very quickly. He sat down on the bed, taking Bea's hand in his own.

'You are a sick girl,' he said gently. 'Bertha has, quite rightly, told me about your visit to Mrs Benson.' He shook his head.

'You did a foolish thing Bea, you know that don't you?' He rubbed his chin thoughtfully. 'I wondered why you had not come to see me again and it was remiss of me not to call on you.' He rose to his feet. 'It's not my place to pass judgment, Bea, but let me just say this, you are a very lucky girl to have survived the sort of operation you chose to undergo.'

Bea could not meet his eyes, her fingers plucked nervously at the edge of the bed cover and after a moment's silence the doctor continued to speak.

'Your blood is poor, very poor, and you will need feeding on plenty of lamb's liver and all kinds of undercooked meats to build up your strength again. Worse Bea, you will never now be a mother.'

He left her then and went downstairs to where his old friend James was waiting. Beside him stood Dean Sutton and the anxious look on his face told its own story.

'I'm afraid Bea will remain in delicate health all her life,' the doctor said slowly. 'She will never bear children for an infection has run riot through her system, doing God knows what damage. I'm sorry.'

Bea was sitting up in bed when some time later Dean, a smile on his face, entered the room. She held out a trembling hand to him and he took it gently as though he was afraid she might break.

Bea tried to speak but Dean shook his head. 'Don't say anything, I know it all and it makes no difference to me, I still want you to be my wife.'

Bea's breath caught in her throat, in spite of everything he still loved her. Somehow the knowledge helped to ease the dreadful ache within her. And as she went into his arms, she could have sworn that Dean Sutton, the big tough American, had tears in his eyes.

Chapter Twenty-six

The Sunday bells were tolling out through the stillness of the morning. The streets of Sweyn's Eye were empty for the weather was cold and wintry, sharp with the bite of early frost, and bare branches pointed bony fingers at the overcast sky.

Mali sat within the warmth of the kitchen drying her hair. The fire was cheerful and meat sizzled in the oven. Everywhere there was an air of order and peace and to an onlooker it might seem that everything was well. But Mali was heavy-eyed for she had not slept at all in the long dark hours of the night.

Wakeful, she had taken out her fears and examined them minutely. She argued with herself, presenting reasons and excuses for the changes that were happening within her, but at last she faced the dreadful possibility that she might be with child.

She rubbed harder at the long dark strands of her hair, pushing away the unwanted thoughts, turning her mind instead to the problem of Rosa. Each evening the girl spent hours transforming herself from an ordinary woman into a flossy. She painted her face and drenched herself in cheap perfume, leaving the house in Copperman's Row with a defiant toss of her head.

Yet Mali had formed an almost grudging respect for Rosa for she always brought something home with her for Davie, a basket of goodies, a bright scarf, anything that might bring him out of his apathy.

The back door was suddenly pushed open and Mali looked up quickly to see Katie's cheerful face smiling at her.

'I've just been putting washing on the line,' she said, shivering, 'sure, as if I don't see enough dirty linen down at the laundry to last me a lifetime.'

Mali nodded in the direction of the kettle. 'Make us some tea, Katie love, while I dry this mane of mine, I swear it gets thicker each day.'

Katie moved towards the fire. 'Your hair is lovely and the way you put it up on the back of your head suits you well. You look so much the lady on times that I'm afeared to talk to you lest you're not the same Mali who's always been my friend.'

Mali laughed shortly. 'Have I changed that much?' Her tone was rueful as she watched Katie pour the tea, glancing at her over the cups, her face thoughtful.

'Well, you're thinner for sure and your eyes are that sad but it's only to be expected after what's happened to your dad. Is he getting any better now?' She returned to her seat, warming her fingers on the cup, holding it to her lips and drinking gratefully.

Mali shook her head. 'No, he still does not seem to recognise me. Just stares he does as though he's seeing things that to the rest of us are invisible.' Her voice broke and at once Katie put her arm around Mali's shoulder.

'There and sure aren't you entitled to have a good cry for all the things you've been through these past months, it's not a year since your mam died, didn't have time to get over that, did you, and now this has to happen.'

Katie bit her lip and her hair hung over her face, partly concealing her eyes. 'Do you know how your dad was injured? There's some sayin' it's all my Will's fault and I can't believe that.'

Mali sighed heavily. 'There's one thing's sure it's not your fault, Katie, so don't you go worrying about it. I don't suppose we'll ever know the truth of it.' But her heart was full of anger for she had been told that Will Owens had intended to injure Davie, albeit not so badly and that he had tipped his ladle quite deliberately. She wound her hair up in a towel and drank some of her tea, sipping it slowly, enjoying the warmth against her throat.

'He scarcely bothers with me now.' Katie's voice was low. 'Seems to be great pals with some toffs, so he does. Only comes to me when he wants something and me too soft to turn him away. Why can't I be strong and finish it once and for all, Mali? I know that he's nothing but a waster and yet I love him in spite of that. It's got so bad, he'd rather be with them gents than with me.'

'What gents?' Mali asked, though she was not the least bit interested in what Will Owens chose to do, it was just that Katie seemed so forlorn and needed to talk about him. Mali understood the feeling only too well, she had often longed to pour out her anguish over Sterling but some inborn reticence had always prevented her from confiding fully in anyone.

'Oh, he's been seen down the Cape Horner with the younger Mr Richardson and some other men, all of them dressed to kill and drinking like fish. Wonder what's eating him up I do sometimes, he's that moody and yet when he takes me in his arms I believe all his lies about loving me.' She smiled sadly. 'What fools we girls must be to listen to such fairy stories.'

Mali lifted the teapot and refilled both cups. 'How's Sean?' she asked, deliberately changing the subject, and Katie's face was suddenly wreathed in smiles.

'He's gettin' that big you'd hardly know him. Got teeth he has now and uses them on everything and everybody, a fine boy he'll be for sure when he grows up.'

She fell silent then and Mali realised how long it was since she'd been inside the Murphy household. Her life had changed so drastically in the last months, and when she looked at herself in the glass, she hardly recognised the old Mali Llewelyn at all.

'Are you off to chapel today?' Katie asked and it was as if both girls needed to fill the silence that had become a little strained. Mali shook her head.

'No, chapel is not for me, not these days, Katie, I have so much work to catch up on and Sunday is the only day I have to myself.' She looked round her. 'Rosa treats this place like a dosshouse and I'm the one who has to clean it up after her. I've tried talking to her but it's no use, it goes in one ear and out the other.'

Katie looked aggrieved. 'Tell the flossy to get out then,' she said with a flash of anger. 'She's having free board and lodge here and she's not so daft is she? Give her her marching orders for sure she deserves them, for isn't everyone in the row talking about the men she has bringing her home at nights?'

'I know she's not very careful about her reputation,' Mali agreed, 'but Rosa has lived the life of a flossy since she was twelve years old; I feel a bit sorry for her myself.' She saw Katie's eyebrows shoot upward and could not help but laugh at her friend's outraged expression.

'All right, there's no need to tell me again how soft I am but for now, at least, Rosa stays and the neighbours will just have to lock up their husbands if there's any danger of Rosa getting hold of them.' She leaned forward and lifted the teapot.

'Here let me fill your cup again, you still look half frozen. Why don't you sit nearer the fire?'

'Sure I'm fine,' Katie said. 'But it's you I'm worried about, you need some colour in those cheeks of yours, you don't get enough rest. Now let me do a bit of work for you, what if I peel some spuds?'

'Don't worry, everything is in order,' Mali said, shaking her head. 'And don't go bossing me, Katie Murphy, I'm not one of your little brothers, mind.'

Katie laughed. 'An' don't I know that, sure I saw you wid me own eyes punching Sally Benson to the floor, so I won't bother to quarrel with you myself.' She put down her cup. 'I'd best be gettin' back home now though I'm grieved to be leavin' you all alone, the trouble is Dad'll be hollerin' all down the row for me if I don't move myself. Look, Mali, what if I come wid you to the infirmary tomorrow night, if you want company that is.'

Mali smiled warmly. 'I'd like that very much Katie, and don't fret about me being alone, Rosa will be home for her dinner I expect, once she's spent a bit of time outside Maggie Dick's or the Mexico Fountain – drumming up trade I dare say. Rather her than me on a cold day like today.'

Katie laughed. 'Sure an' you're a wicked devil, Mali Llewelyn, and to look at you anyone would think that butter wouldn't melt in your mouth.'

Katie moved towards the door. 'Right then, see you in work tomorrow and then I'll come wid you in the night to visit your dad. Sure you'll be all right now? You know you'd be more than welcome to have dinner with us.'

Mali shook her head. 'Thank you all the same Katie, but I've still a lot of work to do here. Anyway,' she added smiling, 'it's much quieter than your house.'

Katie nodded her head vigorously. 'Sure an' isn't that the truth. See you tomorrow.'

It was silent in the kitchen now, even the church bells had stopped ringing. Mali opened the door and stood staring along the empty row. She wondered how she was going to cope when the time came for Davie to return home. It would be almost impossible to work at the laundry and to look after him but perhaps he would improve once he was out of the infirmary, she thought hopefully.

A little later, Mali was carving the joint of beef with great difficulty for it had always been Davie's job, when Rosa came in through the door, holding her hat on her head, her ragged fur collar hanging untidily over her shoulders.

'Damn me it's a terrible day, the wind is enough to blow the knickers off you. There's a lovely smell, makes the mouth water it does and I'm starving, didn't have no breakfast today.' She sat at the table, still wearing her coat, and Mali could smell gin on her breath.

'Davie's much better,' Rosa said, nodding firmly so that the bright plumes on her hat waved to and fro as though they had a life of their own. 'Spoke my name, so he did, he knew me, you see, said my name quite plain. He's going to be better soon, my Davie is, then I won't have to go round the street no more.'

Mali leaned forward eagerly. 'Are you sure, Rosa, he really recognised you?' Her heart lifted with hope as Rosa nodded her head emphatically.

'Yes, I told you, he said Rosa plain as anything. Going to see him, later are you?' Rosa pulled off her hat and threw it onto a chair. 'God, where's the dinner, I'm so hungry my belly thinks my throat is cut.'

Mali picked up her coat. 'Get your own dinner, I'm going down to see my father,' she said lightly, almost laughing at the look of comic dismay on Rosa's face.

As Mali hurried past the canal, she drew her coat more tightly around her, for the wind was keen. She stared up at the shooting sparks from the copper works and waved her fist at them. 'You haven't won,' she said to herself, 'my Dad is getting better.'

When Mali entered the infirmary, she was greeted by a smiling nurse who knew her at once.

'Miss Llewelyn, good news, your father is much more his old self today and his back is healing beautifully. Go along in, he'll be pleased to see you.'

Davie was propped up against the pillow. He still looked thin and gaunt but his eyes were clear and he attempted to smile when he saw Mali.

'Dad, thank God you're better.' Mali put her arms around him and he felt fragile beneath her hands.

'I want to come home Mali,' his voice was painfully weak. 'Tell them you want to take me home, I can't abide it here any longer.'

Mali took a deep breath, 'I'll speak to the doctor later, Dad,' she said. 'But for now, rest, there's a good boyo.'

By the time she was ready to leave the infirmary, Mali was exhausted. 'See you tomorrow, Dad,' she said gently. 'And I'll ask the doctor about you coming home, I promise.'

Davie looked as though he was about to cry. 'See that you do, my girl,' he said with as much energy as he could muster.

The walk down the ward seemed never-ending and by the time she reached the double doors, Mali felt as if she was wading through cotton wool. She paused just outside and closed her eyes for a moment. The world was spinning away from her; she was falling down into a deep black pit and it seemed there was nothing she could do to save herself.

When she opened her eyes, she was lying on one of the beds in a small side room, a doctor was bending over her and the nurse who had spoken to her earlier was watching with a strange expression on her face.

'There's silly of you to go and faint like that,' she said sympathetically. 'But then your dad's accident has been a terrible strain on you hasn't it, *cariad*?'

'Would you like Nurse Evans to bring you a drink of tea, perhaps?' The doctor was smiling kindly and Mali shook her head, wanting only to get off home.

'I feel so foolish,' she said, 'there's nothing wrong with me, nothing at all, except that I haven't been eating very well.' She spoke almost apologetically. 'I'll be all right in a minute.' She attempted to swing her legs to the ground but the nurse put a restraining hand on her arm.

'You do know about your condition, don't you?' she said, staring at Mali curiously.

'Condition, what do you mean?' Mali stared at her, knowing that her worst fears were about to be realised.

The doctor exchanged glances with the nurse. 'I'll leave it to you to break the news, Nurse Evans, and perhaps afterwards, the young lady would like that cup of tea.'

'What is it, what's wrong?' Mali asked when the doctor had left the room. A feeling of dread was creeping over her and she leaned back weakly against the hard pillows.

'You are about four months gone. I mean you're having a baby, didn't you even suspect, Miss Llewelyn?' She spoke kindly but the words seemed like spears flung into Mali's heart. She stared around her anxiously as though seeking a means of escape.

The blood seemed to pound in Mali's head. She covered her burning face with her hands, closing her eyes tightly, trying to swallow the tears that formed a hard lump in her throat. It was pointless to panic, she must try to be calm and rational, crying would solve nothing at all.

Yet it was so bitterly unfair, she had given herself for one night only to Sterling Richardson and now she was going to bear his child.

'Here my dear, drink this tea.' Nurse Evans had left the room and returned without Mali even noticing and now she put a hand on Mali's shoulder in a comforting gesture. 'It's been very hard on you with your dad so sick but you must begin to look after yourself, no going without decent food. Your baby will need nourishment and only you can provide it.'

Mali drank the tea, grateful that it provided an excuse not to reply. At last she put down her cup, realising that the nurse was staring at her curiously. She was no doubt wondering about the father of the baby but that was Mali's secret and no one would hear the truth, not from her lips.

'I'll come tomorrow to see how Dad is,' she said, brushing down her skirts. 'He wants to come home, you know.'

Nurse Evans smiled. 'I'm sure he does and if he continues to make progress then it shouldn't be too long.'

Mali found herself out in the cold once more, staring across the sands, grey now under the cloudy sky with a dark sea running swiftly shorewards. How on earth was she going to manage to support herself and Dad now? And soon her condition would start to show, people would gossip and doubtless the deacons would want to call her before the *Set Fawr* to impress upon her the sinfulness of her ways. But nothing mattered against the worry of earning money enough to put food in their bellies.

Mali stood for a long time staring out to sea and slowly an idea formed in her head. At first it seemed impossible and yet after a time, she knew it was her only lifeline.

She began to walk home back along the winding street, past the shops closed and shuttered and past the busy chapels full of people in their Sunday-best dress, calloused hands holding hymn books, singing praises to God as though their lives were one long bed of roses. But she must not become bitter, Mali reproved herself, she would be strong and face up to the consequences of her own actions, not blaming anyone but herself.

Tomorrow, she would take the money Sterling had given her, blood money she still felt it to be, and give it to Mr Waddington in exchange for a share in the business. And then she would begin to make all the alterations that she felt were necessary to bring the laundry to a peak of efficiency. It was a risk, God knew it was, but the alternative was to live fairly comfortably on the hundred pounds for a year or at the most two, and then to be responsible for a young child as well as an invalid father and no money coming in.

Her steps were more certain now as she made towards home. She felt pangs of hunger inside her and somehow a softness seemed to fill her as she thought of the child she was carrying. Her hand unconsciously went to her stomach, fleetingly, and she felt a momentary lifting of her spirits. They would be all right, all of them, she Mali Llewelyn would make up to the unborn child she carried and to Dad for the harsh way fate had dealt with them. She would make the Canal Street Laundry the most successful business in Sweyn's Eye even if it meant doing the washing herself.

She stepped out along Copperman's Row, her head high,

and high it would remain, she told herself fiercely. Even when her condition became obvious to everyone, she would still keep her pride for she would one day pay back all Sterling Richardson's 'compensation' and then he could go to the devil for all she cared.

Immediately she opened the door of the cottage, the smell of burning meat overlaid by the sickly stench of gin caught at her, making her retch. She looked around at the disordered room and saw with disgust that the remains of a crude meal of bread, and chunks cut from the meat, were still on the table.

She closed the door moving further into the room, looking around her despairingly. Rosa's dirty washing lay on the floor near the sink in amongst debris from the meal. All the cleaning that Mali had done was wasted effort and she knew she could not go on like this.

The house was empty and silent and Mali felt a scream rise in her throat and she took deep breaths, trying to calm herself. But Rosa would have to go, and when Mali next saw her, she would give her the order of the boot in no uncertain terms.

She sank down then in her chair, staring at the almost dead fire and after a moment, she put her head down on her hands and wept.

Chapter Twenty-seven

As Sterling drove the Ascot towards the Kilvey Deep, his thoughts were on Mali and the strange way she had behaved towards him, almost as though he had committed some vile crime. He was puzzled by her reference to Bea Cardigan. All right, so he'd slept with her but that was Bea's wish and in any case, as he'd told Mali in no uncertain terms, it was none of her business. He wondered how Mali had come to hear of the brief affair – servants' gossip he supposed, for there were not many families in Sweyn's Eye who weren't related to each other in some way or other.

He had been taken aback by Mali's uncompromising attitude and concerned too, for she had looked pale and thin, with large violet shadows beneath her beautiful eyes. She was deeply affected by her father's accident, which was only natural, and yet her bitterness against himself was something he had not expected.

He drew the automobile to a halt and climbed down swiftly. The coal dust crunched beneath his feet as he moved forward to the engine house, where he was pleased to see the beam engine was working perfectly.

At first, Sterling mused, the miners of the Kilvey Deep had looked upon him with suspicion – he was a hard-nosed man who had deprived Alwyn Travers of his livelihood. But as the weeks passed, he had been – albeit grudgingly – accepted as the boss man, the rightful owner of the pit, the one who paid their wages and a darn sight more promptly than the old boss had done. And so easily was allegiance changed, Sterling thought ruefully.

'Morning, sir.' Ceri Morgan touched his cap respectfully. 'Rain's still causing us trouble, keeps the pump working full stretch.'

He was a young man, this Ceri Morgan, and Sterling had taken a liking to him from the start. He had an open honest face, dark-eyed and with the thick hair and stocky body of the Welsh, and a pleasing way of looking at Sterling as though he really saw him and not just a wage packet.

'Morning Ceri, the weather is bad, more rain fallen in the last weeks than all through the year, I think, but the beam engine can cope, can't it?'

'Oh, yes, good engine this, cope with much worse weather than we've been having. Which is lucky for the pits further down the mountain.'

Sterling looked around him searchingly. Everything was well maintained, the machinery greased and operating smoothly. He saw Ceri Morgan watching him and smiled his approval.

'You look after things pretty well in here, can't fault you however hard I try.' He smiled and the Welshman nodded.

'Got to be fussy, something as simple as a blocked valve could lead to an explosion that would blow me to kingdom come. I'm fussy, all right.'

When Sterling left the engine house a few minutes later, he hurried across the yard to the small office. The old manager was not unlike Ben, he thought wryly, managers seemed to be a dying breed, now, for instead of gentlemen with waxed moustaches and spectacles, owners seemed to be employing rough tough youths who would beat the living daylights out of anyone who dared to disagree with the boss.

Alwyn Travers himself had briefly engaged such a man and a guard dog to boot, but it had done him no good. Sterling smiled wryly to himself as he remembered the encounter; thank God he was young enough to stand up for himself or right now he would be sitting twiddling his thumbs instead of looking over his latest acquisition.

He spent only a short time studying the figures for the last month for he could tell at a glance that production had improved dramatically, due no doubt to the bonus he had offered as an incentive for the man who brought out the most coal.

He had concluded the business more quickly than he'd thought and as he left the mine, he felt somewhat at a loose end. Just the same he was pleased with the progress he had made over the last few months. For a start, the bank balance was certainly much healthier now he had taken the mine over.

The production of zinc wire had exceeded all his expectations, too, selling as fast as he could manufacture it. Sterling felt a sense of pleasure as he contemplated his future. For the moment at least, the copper company was in the clear.

Plas Rhianfa was still being held as surety of course, but fairly soon now the profits he was making would more than cover that debt.

As he drove into town, the streets were full in spite of the inclement weather and he had to concentrate on guiding the Ascot through the maze of horse-drawn vehicles. He would have to head back to the works soon but on an impulse, he decided to stop off and see Ronnie Waddington.

The old man had not been very well and had been confined to bed for the last few days. Sterling felt quite concerned about the older man, who had been a close friend of his father, Ronnie being of a similar age to Arthur Richardson. And only yesterday Sterling had heard his mother say she had taken a basket of delicacies to try to tempt the invalid into eating a little.

He drew the Ascot to a halt and even from the large house near the Strand he could smell the hot steamy odour of the laundry. He supposed it was natural for Ronnie to want to live near his business premises, it was very convenient for him, but give Sterling the fresh air of the western hills any day.

The maid opened the door and recognising him stepped back. 'Come in sir, I'll tell Mr Waddington you're here.'

Ronnie was looking decidedly pale and there were huge dark circles under his eyes, but his smile was cheerful enough.

'Come in Sterling my lad, you've just caught me.' He indicated a chair and gestured for the maid to bring in another cup.

'I've been back to the office today, can't take too much time off you know, put too much of a strain on young Mali

Llewelyn and since her father's accident, she's been looking under the weather herself.'

He paused and looked up at Sterling from under bushy brows. 'How is Davie coming along?' He did not wait for a reply but hurried on. 'It's a dismal situation and from what Mali tells me her father has lost the will to live. Do you know yet how the accident occurred?'

Sterling took the tea the maid offered him and smiled grimly. 'I've got a very good idea.' He stirred sugar into the hot liquid, seeing not the tea but Will Owens' cocky face. There was no proof to be had of course because no one knew what had really happened.

The story was that Davie had stumbled backwards, tipping Will Owens' ladle over, but in view of the known bitterness between the two men, it did not seem at all likely.

'How's business?' Sterling deftly changed the subject and Ronnie Waddington shook his head, frowning. 'Not too good, though Mali has proved herself invaluable in many ways and has made my position much clearer. I still need to make a great many improvements if the laundry is to survive.'

He rose to his feet. 'Talking of which, I suppose it's time I was getting back, I've had quite a long lunchtime as it is.'

There was a sudden ringing at the doorbell and Ronnie shrugged impatiently. 'Who is this now?' He smiled ruefully. 'I tell you, my boy, it's very tiring being in a sickbed and I'm thankful to be out of it, the visitors you get are no one's business.'

The maid ushered a girl into the room and she stood in the doorway with the odour of the laundry emanating from her clothing.

'Yes, Sally, what is it?' Ronnie adjusted his glasses and stared at the girl whose close-set eyes were taking in every detail of the room.

'Big Mary sent me, sir.' She bobbed a curtsey. 'It's them papers they wanted in the office, I'm to ask you can I have them.'

'Just a minute, I'll go and get them. I'm glad Mary thought of reminding me, I'd quite forgotten all about them.'

Sterling rose to his feet. 'I'll be away then, Ronnie,' he said affably, 'glad to see you on your feet again.'

He was tinkering with the Ascot when the girl came out of the house. She stood staring at him for a moment and at last he looked up at her questioningly. He had recognised her at once, she was the girl who had been involved in the fight with Mali.

'You're Mr Richardson aren't you?' she said ingratiatingly, and he returned her gaze coolly.

'Yes, I am, what of it?' He gave his attention once more to the Ascot, wondering what Sally Benson was waiting for. She came nearer and stood beside him.

'Too snooty to talk to the likes of me, aren't you?' Her tone was derisory now and Sterling straightened, wanting only to be rid of her.

'That's right,' he said flatly. 'Why don't you just run along back to your work? Mr Waddington doesn't pay you to hang around.'

'Well I know something about you,' she said nastily. 'Me mam is a midwife, see, clears up little troubles for ladies, she does. Miss Bea Cardigan from a fine house up on the hill came to see Mam and the talk is you're the father of the little babba she was havin'.'

Sterling looked at her closely, suddenly giving her all his attention, and he saw a pleased smile twist her lips.

'Thought that would get you,' she said. 'Awful to let her down like that, you might be rich but you're no gentleman so me Mam says.' She stepped back a pace as though suddenly afraid of the look in Sterling's eyes, and without stopping to say any more, she hurried away down the street.

He stood looking after her for a long moment and was unaware of Ronnie Waddington's presence until the older man put a hand on his arm.

'Anything wrong, dear boy?' he said in concern and Sterling forced himself to smile.

'No not wrong, not really, but there is something I want to check up on. Can you tell me where that girl lives?' He pointed to Sally's disappearing figure and Ronnie nodded.

'Just along the road in Canal Street, not a couple of minutes away. Is there anything I can help you with?'

'No,' Sterling answered. 'There is something I have to do for myself.'

It was about half an hour later when Sterling drew the Ascot to a halt outside Bea's house. He was in full possession of the facts now, for he had confronted Mrs Benson and frightened her into telling him the truth. He realised at once that the child must be his, but why had Bea not confided in him?

He frowned grimly. Another thing, Sally Benson had doubtless told Mali the whole gruesome story, which accounted for some of her anger and bitterness towards him.

Bertha let him into the conservatory and there was a look in her dark eyes that told Sterling she knew the truth. Everyone had known it except himself, he thought bitterly.

'Sterling, how good of you to come and see me.' Bea's voice was light, insubstantial and he was appalled to see how frail and ill she looked. She sat down with a small sigh and the thin hands, clasped in her lap, were trembling.

'Bea, why didn't you come to me, tell me you were in trouble?' Sterling said without preamble. 'Do you think you had the right to go to Mrs Benson like that without even consulting me?'

Bea's face grew even paler and deep shadows etched themselves under her eyes.

'You've found out,' she said in a strangled voice. She bit her lip and looked away from him as though ashamed and Sterling felt an almost overpowering sense of pity for her. Before he could move towards her she spoke again.

'Sterling, I'm going to be married to Dean Sutton,' she said slowly. 'Please, won't you just forget everything that passed between us and leave me to enjoy what I may of my life?'

So that was it, she found it inconvenient to give birth to his child when she was planning to marry someone else. And yet there was a pleading for understanding in her eyes and he could not ignore it. He moved to the door.

'Then I can only wish you every happiness,' he said formally. 'Goodbye.'

Outside, he took deep breaths of the cold air, telling himself that what Bea did from now on was none of his business. And yet the sadness in her eyes haunted him and suddenly he wished to God that he had never become involved with Bea Cardigan.

It was late afternoon and Mali was sitting in the office waiting for Mr Waddington to return from lunch. All day she had been trying to pluck up the courage to tell him of her proposition and the fact that she had been more busy than usual had not helped matters.

She pushed the ledger away from her and covered her face with her hands. She felt slightly nauseous and even though she knew the reason for her state of sickliness, she still could not quite believe that she was going to have a child.

They had been very kind to her at the infirmary, telling her that Davie could be kept in longer than necessary if she was unable to manage, but she knew how much he wanted to come home and she could not deny him that. And so it was imperative that she speak to Mr Waddington today.

She sighed and rose to her feet and stared out into the coldness of the yard. The trees were all bare now, the branches standing out against the sky like skeleton fingers, and Mali shivered. But it would be spring again when her baby came, she thought with a mixture of apprehension and joy.

The door opened but it was not Mr Waddington as Mali had expected. It was Big Mary, carrying a tea tray.

'I wanted to speak to you, *cariad*,' Mary said, putting the tray down on the desk. 'Now please do not be offended but it's just that I'm worried about you, see?'

Mali felt her colour rising. 'Why are you worried, Mary, I'm fine,' she replied quickly. 'Dad's accident was a terrible shock of course but I'll get over it, I'll have to.'

Mary folded her huge arms over her ample stomach and stared at Mali, shaking her head gently. 'You can't hide it from me, girl.' She spoke firmly. 'Now come on, don't try to pull the wool over the eyes of Big Mary, you know that I'm on your side, always have been. Perhaps I can be of help.'

'What do you mean?' Mali stumbled slightly over the words as she watched Big Mary pour the hot fragrant tea.

'I've seen it in your face for some time now, *cariad*, you're going to have a baby,' she smiled. 'I doubt if anyone but me has noticed it, mind. And none of my business of course but you need to take care of yourself at such a time, see a doctor at least.'

'What will I do, Mary?' It was a relief in a way to talk to someone older and wiser. 'I'm so tired all the time and soon I'll have Dad to look after, I just don't know how I'll manage.'

Mary smiled widely. 'Don't take on so, there's always ways to work these things out. When you've had the child, you could find a good girl to mind it for you. As to your dad, he might get strong and well again once he's home, but face one problem at a time, see.'

Mr Waddington entered the office bringing with him a gust of cold air. 'Did Sally Benson give you the papers you required?' he asked, taking off his coat and seating himself in his chair.

'Yes, thank you sir.' It was Mary who spoke. 'And there's a good fresh pot of tea there to warm you up.' She left the office then, closing the door behind her, and Mali knew the time had come to speak to Mr Waddington.

'I'd like to put some money into the business,' she said. 'I have over a hundred pounds. It's Dad's compensation and as far as I can see it's the best way of investing it.' She saw Mr Waddington nod approvingly and was encouraged to go on.

'It's enough to buy some new boilers, which will be a good start. Then I mean to reorganise things, make everything work more efficiently.' She paused. 'If you'll let me.'

He leaned forward and took her hand. 'My dear girl, I'm more than willing, indeed, I'm delighted. You've become indispensable to me, don't you know that? I couldn't manage without you now.'

'Then you accept?' Mali said incredulously and Mr Waddington clasped her hand more tightly.

'I think you'd make me an admirable partner,' he said. 'You have youth on your side as well as a good fund of common sense. And you have a flair for business that is rare in a woman, and so I accept gladly.'

Mali smiled at him gladly, excitement rising within her. She had done it, persuaded Mr Waddington to take her into the business. Then her heart almost stopped beating as she remembered there was something else she must say. It was only fair what Mr Waddington knew exactly what he was taking on.

'I can see by the expression on your face that a confession is coming,' he said with a merry twinkle in his eye. 'Don't say another word for I need you whatever your responsibilities may be. You see my dear I've no family, no one at all, and I'm getting old and tired so I can only thank God for sending you along.'

Mali stared at him in bewilderment. 'But you don't understand, Mr Waddington . . .' she began and he held up his hand for silence.

'I understand more than you think, my dear, after all I've grown to know you since we've been working in the office together. I knew there was something troubling you even before your father's accident.' He paused and sighed. 'And it doesn't matter one jot to me, all I care about is your welfare and the fact that my laundry will survive. Now you have the rest of the day off and tomorrow too if you like, and don't worry about our little deal, I shall call into my lawyer's office on the way home, which will be a good excuse to have a drink instead of returning to an empty house.'

Mali stared at him in dumb gratitude, her heart so warm that it seemed to fill her being. Impulsively, she leaned forward and kissed Mr Waddington's thin cheek.

'You won't be sorry and that's a promise,' she said softly.

When Mali arrived home, she was surprised to find Rosa sitting beside a glowing fire and for once the kitchen was neat and tidy, the table freshly scrubbed and the floor swept. Thankfully Mali sank down into a chair and closed her eyes for a moment, simply enjoying the silence and warmth and familiarity of the little room.

She had meant to tell Rosa off in no uncertain terms for her slovenliness and here she was acting like a reformed character, which was just as well, for Mali did not feel she would have the strength to face a quarrel, not just now.

'I've been down the infirmary.' Rosa's voice broke into her thoughts and Mali reluctantly opened her eyes. Rosa was staring down at her hands, a strange expression on her face, and suddenly Mali was uneasy.

'What is it, is Dad worse?' she asked, her heart beginning to beat rapidly. Her hands were clenched so tightly against the arms of her chair that the knuckles showed white. She breathed a little more easily as Rosa shook her head.

'No, it's not that, it's just that tomorrow, they're sending Davie home.' The silence stretched long and empty and Mali felt fear mingling with her relief. She did not know if she was strong enough to face Dad every day, knowing that his life was in ruins.

Chapter Twenty-eight

Davie stared out of the bedroom window into the shadowed court below and the voices of the children playing in the cold cobbled street made the house seem silent and empty, closing him in. He lay back on his pillows, not quite sure where he was. He knew he had been sick for a long time for he well remembered lying in the infirmary with the nurses and doctors fussing over him. And he must still be sick, for see how his hands, old man's hands, trembled incessantly.

He felt he should rise from his bed, for surely he must be going to work in the copper, otherwise he would have no wages to buy bread for Jinny and their baby Mali. He pushed back the bedclothes and saw that he was bandaged heavily and gasped as though a jug of cold water had been flung into his face. Memories teased at his mind but he pushed them away, falling back into bed, weak tears running down his cheeks.

Time passed slowly and he heard a movement downstairs, so he wasn't quite alone after all, Jinny was there looking after him. He pushed himself upright once more and though his arms trembled, he managed to maintain his balance. He was sitting up straight, staring at himself in the mirror, or was it himself?

This creature confronting him was old and grey, a man without life or substance and Davie felt nothing but disgust as he stared at the reflection wavering before his eyes.

The thought crept into his mind and grew larger, dominating him, and he knew it was the goal to which he must put all his strength. He must try to remember what it was.

There were footsteps on the stairs and then the door opened

but it was not Jinny who came to him, this was a girl with straight bright hair and plump breasts, and she was smiling at him as though she feared him.

'Davie, why aren't you resting? It's me, Rosa. Don't you know me now that you are properly awake?'

Something stirred in his mind but he did not want it to be roused so he shook his head. He felt ashamed suddenly, wishing to hide himself, wanting this girl, this stranger, to leave him alone, but she was pushing him back into bed, bringing water to wash him as though he was a baby.

'I'll get you some nice dinner soon, Davie love.' She smiled and brushed back his hair. 'It's rabbit stew, your favourite, and you must eat it all up and grow strong again for Rosie.'

He turned his face away and stared at the wall and a line of black dampness caught his eye, taking his mind off the nearness of the girl. He stared at the damp patch, making up patterns in his head and he thought he could see the devil. Yes, there was his beard, and his cloven hooves, and Davie was suddenly too tired to think any more.

She went away, closing the door softly behind her, and he sighed with relief. But soon, it seemed, she was back. Smiling down at him with blank eyes. He obediently ate the food she spooned into his mouth for he knew he must grow strong to face the task he had set himself, but what was it? The thought that had been so clear eluded him now.

'There, you'll be well and strong for me, soon, Davie boyo.' She put her cheek against his and he looked away from her pink smoothness with difficulty, she had been sent by the devil to try him, that much was clear.

'Get thee behind me Satan.' He whispered the words so that she would not hear them.

'What did you say? Oh speak to me Davie, tell me you're feeling better.' He looked up at her briefly, afeared of her.

'I'm getting better,' he said, his voice hoarse, and the words were like a lesson repeated, without meaning or substance. He must humour her or she could inflict pain, terrible pain, even now he felt a burning in his back and legs and in his vitals.

'I'm getting better,' he said again and saw the woman smile so he knew she was pleased. He heard her footsteps hurrying down the stairs and he groaned as he lay back on the pillows.

'Jinny.' He spoke his wife's name, wanting her, needing her strength. But she did not come to him.

When he next opened his eyes, darkness had fallen but the gas light was on, throwing a soft glow over his bed. He saw the bowl of soup standing thick and unpalatable on the table beside his bed. He stared upwards and memory came like flood water.

Jinny was gone, he had married her and filled her belly with child and in the bringing forth of his daughter, Jinny's light and joyfulness had been extinguished for she had never recovered her strength after the difficult, tearing birth. The doctor had made it abundantly clear that there must be no more babies and Jinny had cried bitterly, feeling she'd failed her husband. But it was his fault and Davie knew it in spite of well-meaning neighbours talking of the will of God.

At first their marriage had been one of passion and love and laughter, they had enjoyed each other, but then Jinny had begun to miss her farmland home on the green slopes of the valley twenty miles removed from Sweyn's Eye, and though she returned home on visits, it was not enough and she became thinner and some of her joy and laughter vanished. Until she had learned that she was to have a child, then her cup of happiness had overflowed and the next few months were the happiest Davie had ever known.

As the years had passed and their child had grown up to womanhood, Jinny had become weaker, as though her role in life was ended, and so it was that the lung disease had found a ready victim, taking Jinny with such ease that Davie had known his wife no longer wanted or needed to live.

He saw the door slowly open then and his eyes were riveted on the vision entering the room. He felt warmth and happiness burst inside him as he reached out his arms to her.

'Jinny,' he said softly and she drew nearer to him, taking his hand in hers, rubbing his cheek, kissing the top of his head, and there were tears spilling down over him.

'It's me, Dad, Mali.' Her voice trembled and Davie's image of his wife wavered in his mind and disappointment was hard and cold as stone lying upon him, crushing him.

'Mali.' He said her name and she sat carefully beside him, looking up now into his face, her eyes, green like sunlit pools, staring into his.

'You are going to be well, Dad, quite soon now, for I'm going to look after you.'

Her voice was strong and vibrant, so alive that it hurt Davie's senses for he was half shadow, ready to move through the gates of this world and into the next. He knew his daughter would never willingly relinquish him to the darkness for which he craved and so it must be done in secret; his escape from the soft prison of his bed needed cunning.

He was aware of Mali kissing his cheek, he felt her love but he did not know the words to speak to this girl whose strong hold on life seemed to anchor him. He smelled the soft clean smell of her and as her silken hair touched his hands, he knew that she too must be released from the burden that was himself.

'Rosa's making you a cup of tea, hot and sweet as you like it, Dad,' Mali said gently.

He heard her words distantly for he felt as though his sight was fading and he knew that reality must not be allowed to draw too close.

He lay back against the pillows, staring up at the ceiling, and he felt he knew every line of it, every crack formed a pattern for him to study. At his side he heard his daughter sigh and felt her distress but he could not help her, how could he when he could not even help himself?

He must have slept then for dawn was creeping into Sweyn's Eye when he awoke. He heard a milkman rein his horse, calling to the creature loudly as though to waken the dead. Boots were ringing against the cobbles, men going to work in the copper sheds. Davie raised his head a little, feeling the heat of the furnace on his face, lifting in his mind's eye the weight of his ladle, tipping with skill and strength as befitted a man, a whole, living man.

His daughter brought him breakfast, slops, bread soaked in milk, baby's food. But he ate it willingly enough for today he meant to carry out his plan of escape and for that he needed to be clever.

'Will you be all right with Rosa for an hour, Dad?' Mali asked. He noticed then that she was very smart in a thick coat that seemed to hang loose from her shoulders as though it was several sizes too big for her.

She brushed back his hair and he chewed on some bread, not

wanting to make the effort of replying to her question. She moved away from him at last, carrying the tray awkwardly.

'I shan't be long, Dad, just got to get some books to work on at home, right? The doctor is coming to see you later on today and we must have you looking your best for his visit so I'll give you a shave.' She was making an effort to smile. 'You could do with a real good scrape, that beard of yours is growing almost down to your knees.'

He tried hard to listen for the banging of the door but he was very tired, he wondered if there had been some medicine put in with the bread and milk, something that would make him sleep, for his eyes were closing, the sounds of the street outside fading into the distance and he could not fight the weariness that washed over him like the sea over pebbles on a beach.

Davie roused himself from the dream that he was on a ship with the wind rising and the sea running swift and deep against the bows. He could feel the waves pounding, hear the wind screaming but perhaps the noises were only inside his own head.

But then there was Jinny's voice and she was calling him to come to her but he could not see her through the storm. He sat up abruptly and the taut burned flesh of his back tugged at him painfully.

Jinny was buried in the cemetery, he remembered now that she lay quietly at rest beneath the tree growing on the slopes of Kilvey Hill. She was removed from the stench of sulphur, hidden behind the bulk of the mountain.

He realised now that the pounding he'd heard was the rain on the window and he thought fretfully that the downpour would undo all the good work he had done on the grave. The rain would be turning the soft banks into slurry and the power of the wind and rain combined might even be enough to disturb Jinny's resting place.

It took him a long time to find a pair of trousers and when he did, they hung on his thin frame like washing on a clothes line. He sat on the edge of the bed for a moment, exhausted with his efforts, and then he folded his thick leather belt around his belly and took a deep breath before hoisting himself to a precarious but upright position.

The stairs were steeper than he'd remembered them, dark

and full of shadows. He was fearful of going on but he could not return to his bed and become a lifelong prisoner.

He moved downwards one step at a time, sitting awkwardly on the thinness of his haunches, trying to ignore the searing pain that racked his body. He was determined to go to Jinny, for only she could want him the way he was.

There was no one in the kitchen but he could hear voices outside the open front door. Slowly he made his way past the table, scrubbed and white, glowing up at him like dead bones. And then he was in the yard and the rain was tumbling down upon his bare head as if God himself was crying tears, Davie thought.

The wind was high and Davie moaned as he suddenly realised that he could never make his way to the cemetery unaided. His face crumpled and he remained still, not knowing what to do next.

It was the soft neighing of a horse that gave him his answer. Outside in the lane was Tom Murphy's fish cart and there was Big Jim standing patiently between the shafts. Now Davie could go to the graveyard, travelling in the same manner as his Jinny had done. He took the broom from against the wall and tucked it beneath his arm using it as a crutch.

He did not notice the stink of fish or the coldness of the silvery scales clinging to his clothing. As he struggled, with jerky, ungainly movements into the cart he trembled with weakness. But as soon as he got the reins in his hands, he clucked his tongue and reluctantly, the animal moved forward.

Through the wind, Davie heard Jinny's voice encouraging him, urging him on, and he did not notice the spiteful rain beating down on his unprotected head. His nightshirt was soon clinging to his thin body but it was not an unpleasant feeling.

He drove between the slag heaps and down to the river, taking the bridge easily for he felt a new power in him, a fresh strength now that his goal was in sight. The hill rose above him, the craggy summit shrouded in mist. 'I'm coming Jinny.' He breathed the words and laughed as the wind lifted his damp hair from his forehead.

He drove Big Jim now as if he was young again, he felt he

was going courting, a lover hurrying impatiently to meet his girl. He would soon be lying with his Jinny and she would hold him in her arms and soothe his pain. They would cling together as they had done in the first, happy years of their marriage, they would never be parted again, not for the whole of eternity.

He lifted his head triumphantly as the gates of the cemetery came into view.

'I'm here, Jinny,' he cried.

Marble headstones stood out sharp and grey against the wet grass and drunkenly, wooden crosses leaned over as though bent beneath the battering rain. Davie stumbled down from the cart and moving forward, slowly, painfully, he gave Big Jim a slap.

'Go home boyo,' he said softly. 'I've no need of you now.'

He did not see the large Richardson vault, the resting place of the rich and dead, he saw nothing but the hill and the tree and the ground beneath which his Jinny lay.

He slipped once and fell, and hot irons seared his flesh. A stream of water rushed by him, covering his hand with mud, but he scrabbled in the wet earth and managed to rise up on his one good knee.

'Be patient, Jinny,' he whispered but he knew that she would hear him. He moved forward slowly, his thin hands sinking into the mire. The hill rose steeply upwards and Davie paused, gasping for breath. A boulder rolled towards him, bouncing against his shoulder and then he was face down in the mud, gurgling as some of the slurry went into his mouth and coated his eyelashes so that he could scarcely see.

He rubbed at his face then and struggled onwards and the tree, Jinny's tree, was torn up by its roots, bending towards him, like a tooth half drawn from a gaping mouth. The branches stretched out in his direction, skeleton hands, trying to reach towards him, to ease him forwards, nearer to Jinny. He edged forward, inch by inch, his clothing heavy with mud, hampering, taking his strength.

At last he was beside her grave and the earth was being washed away, he pushed at the mud with shaking hands and sighed in contentment.

'I'm here, Jinny, your Davie's come to be with you.' His voice was lost in the moaning of the wind and tiredly he lay his cheek against the sodden earth, closing his eyes as though in sleep.

Above him, the mountain shuddered as though settling deeper into its foundations. The rough stone wall on the high bank creaked and groaned like a live creature in distress and Davie stared up at it, his vision blurred.

There was a sharp, cracking noise and the wall split asunder. Slurry pitted with heavy rocks bore downward, unable to withstand the weight of the rainwater.

Davie saw the avalanche coming towards him and smiled, suddenly lucid. 'Jinny,' he said and then a deep, eternal blackness overwhelmed him.

Chapter Twenty-nine

Will Owens was strolling along the street in the direction of Green Hill, keeping a sharp lookout for Katie. He did not want to go calling for her, she would get ideas about him then, start planning a wedding, go on at him about buying a pretty little ring and like hell he would! He had not seen her for several days now for she seemed to have changed of late. She was not half so willing and eager to fall into his arms the way she used to be. And the strange thing was it hurt.

He became aware quite suddenly of the local youths standing leaning against the wall of one of the houses. They did nothing menacing, just stood and stared and yet Will felt the hackles rise on the back of his neck. He held his head high, stuffing his hands in his pockets. He would show them he was not afraid of them, or of anything under the sun, he told himself stoutly.

He knew he was being blamed for Davie Llewelyn's accident but he had done nothing wrong. Llewelyn had only got what was coming to him, surely everyone realised that.

He was the one who had started the whole shebang. After all, when he had dropped a sket of molten copper onto Will's legs he had thought it a great lark.

Mind, he had not meant to tip up his whole load of blistering hot copper onto the older man, Will thought angrily, it was just that Davie had stepped back at precisely the wrong moment and had collided with him, an accident, that's what it was.

Davie Llewelyn was home from the infirmary and back in his own bed, badly enough injured though, so it was being said round the public bars. But that was nothing to do with him, Will mused.

It had been wrong of Mr high and mighty Richardson to give him the sack, suspending him, that's what he called it, but to every copperman working for the company it meant that Will was to blame for what had happened. He gritted his teeth, that was just one more reason for getting his own back.

He wished that Travers would get a move on with his plans for blowing up the Kilvey Deep, at least then Sterling Richardson would know he had enemies who could hit back. He was so sure of himself, so secure in his rich little world that he thought nothing could touch him. Well soon he'd learn differently.

Too late Will saw a tall youth step out of a shop doorway directly in his path. He made to grasp the boyo by the throat but suddenly his arms were caught from behind and twisted painfully.

'What's this, what do you want with me?' Will asked roughly. 'Got hold of the wrong man, haven't you, I haven't done anything, don't know you from Adam.'

A blow caught him in the pit of his stomach and as Will doubled over, gasping for breath, his vision blurred with the pain, he felt another blow catch his chin and he was knocked sprawling to the ground. He doubled over, curling himself into a ball for protection but a booted foot aimed straight for his kidney and with a yell, he rolled over, lying on his back looking up at the grey sky.

His heart was pumping madly, he should get up and run he told himself, otherwise, he would have the living daylights kicked out of him. He was too late, two or three youths were on him, hitting out with fist and boot indiscriminately. Will felt blood run from a cut over his swiftly closing eye and tasted blood in his mouth. His body was savagely and repeatedly kicked so that at last, a darkness swamped him and he lay still.

He dimly heard a voice talking excitedly above his head.

'Jesus, we've near kilt him, that's not what Mr Richardson wanted, let's get the hell out of here.' To his relief, he heard the pounding of footsteps receding into the distance and he lay panting, trying to breathe though the pain in his chest was agonising.

After a time, he managed to push himself up onto his knees, nearly fainting with the pain in his stomach. He leaned against the wall, easing himself into an upright position, gasping as he felt his ribs begin to throb. He was a right mess and no mistake and lucky to be alive. If those thugs had beaten him a little harder he would not be here to feel his aches and pains, he told himself angrily.

Sterling Richardson, he was behind all this, Will thought savagely. He might have known that someone with money had put the local bully boys up to giving him a beating. Anger burned low in his gut, he would get even with the copper boss if it killed him. He remembered, with a feeling of satisfaction, of the plan formed by Glanmor Travers to blow up the Kilvey Deep, and his anger began to abate a little.

If he kept his eyes and ears open and used his head, he reasoned, he might just be able to get Sterling Richardson to the engine house at the right time, at the very moment of the explosion.

He was meeting with Travers and Rickie later that evening but it would be as well to keep his mouth shut about his own little idea. Rickie might just balk at the thought of killing his brother.

Will began to move slowly and painfully along the road, trying to make up his mind where to go. If he returned home in this state, his Mam would have hysterics and would doubtless insist on calling in the constable and Will did not want to draw attention to himself in any way, not right now.

'William!' He heard a voice calling to him frantically. He looked up and saw Katie running towards him, her arms outstretched, her eyes swimming with tears.

'Oh, my darlin' what's happened to you? Jesus, Mary and Joseph, you look as though a tram has run over you.'

'I'm all right, I've just had a tussle with some cocky young bastards that's all.' He spoke abruptly, though he was beginning to see a way out of his dilemma. If he went with Katie to her home he could at least clean himself up a little before facing Mam.

It was as though she was reading his thoughts for Katie took his arm and drew him along the road towards Market Street.

'Come along home with me, I'll see to your cuts and bruises so I will. Sure you can't go home to your mammy looking like that now can you?'

It was comparatively peaceful in the Murphy household, there was only Mrs Murphy sitting in the kitchen with the youngest child in her arms.

'It's all right Mam, don't fuss,' Katie said as her mother rose from her chair in astonishment. 'Will's had an accident, he'll be all right when I've cleaned him up a bit.' She drew Will towards the sink and gently began to wash the blood from his face.

'Don't make too much noise, now,' Mrs Murphy said as she subsided into her chair once more. 'The boys are asleep and I need the rest so for God's sake try not to wake them.'

Mrs Murphy watched her daughter attending to Will for a moment in silence and then as Katie wiped Will's wounds, peered intently at his face.

'Looks like someone's given you a fine beating to be sure; made enemies by the look of it, Will Owens.' Her tone implied that she could understand why, though when she had finished speaking, Mrs Murphy folded her mouth into a straight line as though she meant to say no more on the subject.

Instead, she changed her tack. 'Poor Davie Llewelyn, that accident has changed the man out of all recognition, lost his mind so he has. Did you know he's gone missing now?' Her attitude to Will was hostile and he felt his hands clench into fists, he'd had about as much as he was going to take. Katie's fingers were gentle on his cheek as a warning not to allow her mother to goad him and he made a conscious effort to relax, but Mrs Murphy's voice continued relentlessly.

'Funny thing, our horse and cart went missing for a time, wondered if Big Jim had strayed to look for grazing or if poor Davie had driven him, though where would the man go? He's got no relations round here, that I know of.'

Katie spoke up, obviously trying to change the subject. 'There, Will, you look a new man so you do. The cold water has brought down the swelling on your eye, don't look too bad at all, sure you don't.' Katie's eyes were twinkling and Will knew she was happy to see him even under such circumstances.

'I'd better be getting off home then.' He rose to his feet and stared down at her and somehow a softness seemed to come over him, he wanted to take her in his arms and hold her close, kiss her shining red hair and thank her for taking care of him. He must be going soft in the head, he thought abruptly, the sooner he got himself out of here and away from Katie's blue, beseeching eyes the better.

'I'll see you round some time, Katie,' he said as she went with him to the door. He thrust his hands into his pockets, feeling suddenly awkward. He had never been beholden to anyone for a kindness before and it gave him a strange sensation in his gut. On an impulse, he drew Katie towards him and kissed her soft willing mouth. She responded to him sweetly and he held on to her for a long moment before releasing her.

'Thanks for everything,' he said gruffly and then he was striding away down the road, wanting to kick the dust of Green Hill from his shoes as quickly as possible. He was a fool to let a woman, any woman, get so near to him. Katie was a good sort but then so were millions of other women. That didn't mean he wanted her like a millstone around his neck, did it?

As he left the narrow maze of courts and terraces behind him and drew nearer to the town, he heard the engine of an automobile. He looked around just in time to see Sterling Richardson riding past in his gleaming Austin Ascot, sitting high in the seat, lord of all he surveyed.

All Will's anger and bitterness returned. You had to do people down before they did it to you, as this afternoon's little episode proved. He stopped walking and stared round him; it was growing dusk, the winter evening closing in. He might just as well go to the Cape Horner, to keep his appointment with Travers and Rickie and have a mug of ale before he returned home.

As Sterling drove slowly along the road, his attention was suddenly caught by someone waving a bright silk scarf at him from the pavement. He drew the Ascot to a halt and pulled off his goggles.

'Ronnie! What are you doing out in the cold night air, you should be indoors. Come along, you can treat me to a drink of whisky and hot water, take some of the chill out of my bones.'

When they were both seated in the cosy living room, Ronnie drew off his glasses polishing them nervously with the end of his scarf. He coughed in embarrassment and Sterling wondered what on earth was wrong with him.

'I had to talk with you,' Ronnie said at last, 'been wanting to get in touch but I never knew where to find you.' His smile was rather strained. 'Busy man you've been of late Sterling, but then you've much to do I don't doubt. I'd better ring for that whisky, you do look a little cold.'

Sterling could see that Ronnie was nervous and it puzzled him. He waited patiently while the maid brought the drinks and built up the fire, and then leaned forward in his chair.

'Is there anything wrong?' he asked. 'You seem a little on edge.'

'Well, nothing's wrong, no, it's just that I wanted to talk to you about Mali Llewelyn.'

Sterling felt himself grow tense. 'What about her, is she ill?' he asked quickly. 'And you know if there is anything I can do to help financially, I'll be only too happy to oblige. She need never know that I've been involved.'

Ronnie shook his head. 'No indeed, on the contrary dear boy, Mali is coming into business with me. Under her management the laundry will flourish, I'm sure of it. Once the initial problems have been overcome, she will make us both a fortune.'

Sterling stared at him in surprise. 'You are taking Mali Llewelyn into business with you?' he asked. 'Are you sure that's wise? After all she's simply an inexperienced girl.'

'You underestimate her,' Ronnie said softly, 'Mali learns quickly, knows the books inside out and she has good ideas, she'll be an asset, don't you worry.'

'This is all very interesting, Ronnie.' Sterling tried to speak affably though he still did not know what the older man expected of him. 'But it really has nothing to do with me, has it?'

Ronnie leaned back in his chair and took a sip of his hot whisky and his hand was holding the glass so tightly that his knuckles gleamed white.

'Sterling, I've known you a long time and you might very

well feel I should mind my own damn business but there's something I must tell you.'

Sterling wondered if Ronnie was ever going to get to the point. He waited in silence and after a moment the older man sighed.

'There's no easy way to put this. Sterling, Mali is expecting a child and I'm damn sure it's yours.'

At first the words did not sink into Sterling's consciousness. He stared down into the flames of the fire, watching as a log fell between the bars in the grate, sending up a blaze of sparks.

'Oh, she's told me nothing,' Ronnie went on. 'I guessed at her condition and she did not deny it and I guessed about you, too. I saw you drive her away that day in the summer when she was involved in a skirmish outside the laundry gates. There's no one else in Mali's life and so I put two and two together, you see.'

Sterling rose to his feet abruptly, unable to believe the evidence of his own ears. Mali expecting a child, it just didn't seem possible. But Ronnie was a man who would be sure of his facts before bringing anything like this out into the open.

Suddenly a strange anger began to burn inside him. It seemed that other people knew more about his business than he did. First Bea Cardigan had excluded him from her life, going her own way, doing just as she liked, letting all and sundry know about what had happened and now to cap it all, here was Ronnie Waddington confronting him with this titbit of information.

'I appreciate you talking to me.' Sterling did his best to conceal his true feelings. Ronnie had certainly meant well and he couldn't blame the older mean for recent events. 'But now I really must be going,' he said and Ronnie rose to his feet at once, his face creased with anxiety.

'Oh, dear, I hope I haven't done the wrong thing, my boy,' he said.

'Not at all, I'm very grateful to you for putting me in the picture.'

He left the house and started the Ascot, his mind a turmoil of angry thoughts. So Mali thought she could manage without him. She was going in to partnership with Ronnie Waddington but how did she expect to bring up the child? Foist it onto some inexperienced girl, no doubt.

He drove along towards Copperman's Row and the doors of the cottages were closed against the cold instead of standing open as they did in summer. Yet he felt that curious eyes were watching him as he drew to a halt outside Mali's house, rapping hard on the wooden panel, waiting impatiently for her to let him in.

Her face was pinched and drawn and when his eyes roved over her, he could see the thickening of her waist and the soft swell of her stomach beneath the heavy skirt and he knew without a shadow of a doubt that the child she carried was his.

He walked past her and kicked the door shut with his foot and her eyebrows lifted coolly as though he was a small boy who had got out of hand. Her hair was pinned up on the back of her head and she appeared more mature than he'd ever seen her before.

'What are you doing here?' Her voice was light like a summer breeze and he wanted to shake her hard. She moved towards the fire, her hands folded across her stomach as though in protection of her unborn child. Behind her the brasses gleamed and the hob was blackleaded until it shone, a witness to Mali's industrious nature.

'Mali,' he spoke her name softly, 'I know about the child. Why didn't you tell me yourself? Surely you owed me that much.'

She did not look at him, her eyes seemed to search the distance as though seeking a reply to his question.

'I don't owe you anything.' Her voice fell coldly into the stillness of the kitchen. 'What did you ever do for me except bring me grief?' She turned her face away and all he could see was the soft line of her cheek and the long dark shadow of her eyelashes. He caught his breath sharply.

'Mali, have you considered the advantages I could give the baby? Don't turn your face from me, just listen to me for a moment, can't you?'

'The baby is mine, do you understand, mine!' She spoke in rising anger. 'Now get out of this house, go and leave me alone, I just can't stand any more.'

He moved towards her and reached out his hand but she struck it away furiously.

'The baby is mine too,' he said gently.

'And you'll not take it away from me!' she cried. She lashed out at his face, her small palm stinging his cheek. He took her hands and held them tightly.

'Try to calm yourself, Mali. You are doing no good to yourself by getting hysterical.'

'Hysterical?' she echoed. 'What should I be like with you threatening me and my father out there somewhere sick and ill and perhaps freezing to death in some ditch.'

He stepped away from her, appalled. 'I'm not threatening you, Mali, and I didn't know about Davie,' he said, 'I had no idea he was missing. Look, I'll do all I can to help, I'll get a party of men to search for him at once.'

'Talk, that's all you ever do,' she said, quiet now. 'Promises are easily made and just as easily broken especially by the great Mr Richardson, copper boss. Leave me and mine alone, can't you? Don't you understand that my father would be walking round a whole man now if it weren't for you?'

'You don't know what you're saying.' Sterling made a move towards her but she shook her head at him.

'No, don't touch me. It was to put money in your pocket that my father worked in that stinking hell hole of yours in the first place.'

Sterling stepped away from her, feeling a sudden pain.

'All right, I'm going.' He left the cottage, stepped out into the coldness of the night, and stood for a moment staring back at the glow of light coming from the window. And suddenly he knew just what it felt like to be all alone in the world.

Chapter Thirty

The Sunday bells were ringing through the cold morning air and down the row, Dai End House was playing 'Rock of Ages' on his accordion but Mali simply sat near the fire, her hands lying idle in her lap, her head back against the warm wood of the rocking chair, her eyes closed.

Rosa was busy at the stove as she cooked the rabbit she had fetched from the market last night and even though Mali knew she should be helping her, she was too weary and dispirited to rouse herself.

'Here.' Rosa's voice was rough and ungracious but when Mali opened her eyes and looked up she could see that the girl had made her a cup of tea. Some of it was slopped into the saucer and it was far too strong for Mali's taste but she took it and made an attempt to smile.

'Thank you, Rosa.' It was clear the girl was trying to be helpful.

Mali sipped the tea and its warmth gave her a measure of comfort. 'It's lovely,' she said appreciatively and Rosa sniffed.

'You look terrible.' Rosa spoke without preamble, her eyes resting on Mali's ashen face. 'Think you should see a doctor, find out what ails you, I wouldn't want to catch nothing nasty. Your mam died of the lung disease, didn't she? Perhaps you've got it too.'

Mali shook her head without replying and Rosa sat down near the table, pouring herself more tea into which she spooned liberal amounts of sugar.

'I know you're grieving over Davie and well, so am I but then he'll be found sooner or later and dead he'll be, I just feel it in my bones.'

Mali rose from her chair, almost spilling her tea as she slammed the cup down on the table.

'Don't talk like that, he could be wandering around lost, or off his head with pain, you don't have to look on the black side do you?' Her tone was anguished but Rosa paid no heed.

'Might as well face it, he'd be better off dead would my Davie, can't live as half a man, I bet he wanted to die.' She had tears in her eyes and Mali shook her head, unable to dispute the truth of her words.

'You haven't answered my question,' Rosa said after a long silence, 'are you sickening for something?'

Mali shook her head and returned to her chair. 'I suppose you might as well know first as last, I'm going to have a baby,' she said and the words fell into the silence like pebbles in a pool.

Rosa's mouth dropped open, she stared at Mali, looking her up and down, and then she chewed her lips as though to give herself time to think.

'Jesus Gawd!' She rose from her chair and went to the fireplace, lifting the lid of the pot and stirring the rabbit stew with intense concentration. Mali sank back and watched her, waiting for some other reaction, but there was none.

'Is that all you're going to say?' she asked dully and Rosa turned, her face flushed from the heat of the fire. She licked at the spoon and added more salt to the stew and then stood with her hands on her hips.

'I knew you'd been up to something, in the summer it was when you came back home here with your blouse all ripped and you told Davie a pack of lies about a fight with one of the laundry girls.' She shook her head.

'My Gawd but you've been very good at foolin' us all since then. Good thing Davie isn't here to know the shame his daughter is bringing on the fine name of Llewelyn.' Rosa was gathering strength, her voice rising, her outrage and anger ludicrous in the circumstances.

'Take his belt to you, he would, injured or not. Well at least I'm honest about bein' a flossy, you does things on the sly and gets caught for it and it just serves you right, that's what I say.'

Mali was stunned into silence, she had not expected sympathy or indeed wanted it, but she certainly had not anticipated Rosa's reaction would be so extreme.

There was a sudden rapping on the door and then it was pushed open and Katie Murphy stood in the small kitchen wearing her Sunday-best clothes, for she had been to early mass. She moved from one foot to the other, her face pale and shadowed, her red-gold hair escaping from under her hat.

'I've something to tell you, Mali,' she said, 'but Jesus, Mary and Joseph help me for it's powerful hard.'

Mali stared at her friend and in that moment she knew that Davie was dead. She fetched her coat from the back of the cupboard and slipped it onto her shoulders.

'It's my Dad, isn't it, he's been found?' She heard Rosa give a strangled gasp and then Katie was nodding her head, her eyes downcast.

'Mr Richardson sent the men from the copper works out searching for your father and one of them came to ask Dad questions about our horse, as though Big Jim could tell them anything. Seems someone saw the horse and cart down at Dan-y-Graig the day your dad went missing. Dai End House and my Dad have gone there now, see if they can help.' Katie came forward slowly to take Mali in her arms.

'I'm that hurtin' for you but perhaps 'tis best after all.' She paused. 'Now where do you think you're going?'

Mali untangled herself from Katie's grasp and walked purposefully towards the door. 'I've got to go down there,' she said reasonably. 'Got to see for myself, you can understand that can't you?'

Katie sighed. 'Yes, I suppose so. Then I'll come with you if go you must, but put a hat on your head for it's that cold out, you'll catch a chill.'

Mali turned to Rosa. 'You can come if you want to,' she said grudgingly but the girl was white-faced and trembling. 'No,' she said quickly, 'don't want to see him dead, I'll remember him the way he always was when he loved me.' She began to weep then, loudly and copiously, and Mali, unable to offer any comfort, stepped out into the coldness of the day.

Church bells were ringing as though in honour of Davie's departure from this life, Mali thought as she stared up at the mist shrouding the mountain. She knew she should be crying just like Rosa but in a curious way, all she felt was relief.

'It's a long enough walk,' Katie said gently, 'are you sure you feel up to it?'

'I'm feeling all right, don't worry about me.' She had needed to tell Katie about the coming baby, had welcomed the comfort and sympathy her friend offered but she found being treated as an invalid was becoming a little wearying. Katie took her arm now, clinging to Mali tightly as they crossed the new bridge that spanned the swiftly flowing river. Mali paused for a moment to look downward. The water was green, the colour of Dad's eyes, and Mali put her hand over the roundness of her stomach, wondering if the baby would look like him.

'What's wrong?' Katie asked anxiously and Mali realised that she was staring absently into the distance. She shook her head.

'There's nothing wrong, I was just daydreaming, that's all,' she said abruptly. She looked at the Irish girl anxiously. 'There's no need for you to fuss over me, Katie, I'm a big girl, remember, big enough to get myself into trouble and find my own way out of it.'

Katie squeezed her arm. 'I'm not fussin'. I'm just determined to look after you, that's all.'

The road winding round the hill seemed longer than Mali remembered, perhaps it was because she was heavier now and her legs ached a little. It could simply be that she dreaded arriving at the cemetery and yet no one had forced her to come. No one except herself, she thought grimly, but it was the last thing she would ever do for Dad and she should not be afraid of a little discomfort.

A pale sun shone through the mist, warming the countryside into life. Mali stared around her for a moment, knowing nothing but a great emptiness. She turned to Katie then and felt a renewed gratitude for her friend's company, bitterly regretting her own churlishness.

'I'm sorry I was grumpy,' she said, 'and I shouldn't have dragged you down here, especially as you're wearing your Sunday best. Look, your boots are all muddy.'

'Tush, as though that mattered,' Katie sighed. 'Anyway, I've no one to care a tuppeny damn what I look like now, I've not seen William since he took a beating the other night.' She put her hand to her mouth as though regretting her words and Mali looked at her curiously.

'Will took a beating, why?'

Katie shrugged. 'No reason why you shouldn't know, I suppose. Some of the local boys gave Will a fine old beating. To tell the truth, they're saying it was no accident but that my Will did it on purpose to pay your dad back for sketting his legs some time ago.' She paused and swallowed hard.

'Mali, I know Will has his faults but I don't think he'd be so wicked. Anyway, paid back he was sure enough, had to bathe his poor eyes I did.' She smiled. 'Had to send him back to his mammy looking respectable or she'd have a fit.' She paused, rubbing at the suspicion of a tear on her lashes.

'Mr Richardson suspended him but Will wouldn't work in the sheds now anyway, not with all the men against him. Thought well of your dad, Mali, so they did, all of them.'

Mali heard Katie's words but nothing made any difference any more. Davie was dead and he had suffered so grievously, losing his manhood to the copper. She closed her eyes in sudden pain. What matter who was to blame? Perhaps it was Will Owens as people had said, and perhaps it was Sterling's harsh words to Davie a few minutes before the accident. Now she would never know.

'Come on, we're nearly there,' she said flatly. In silence then, they walked the rest of the way to Dan-y-Graig. Katie clung to Mali's arm as though to give her all the support she needed and Mali's heart warmed a little. Kate was a real friend and it was a shame that she had thrown herself away on a waster the like of Will Owens. But then who was she to judge when she had made such a mess of her own life?

At last the gates of the cemetery came into view. The sun was shining more brightly now though the air was cold and the ground damp with melted frost.

'I'm not at all sure you should be doin' this,' Katie said as they walked through the big gates. To the right was the small chapel built of heavy stone, grey and squat in the pale light. On the left was the church, grander and taller with ornate stonework above the curved windows.

Mali stood quite still for a moment, taking deep breaths, hesitant now that the moment had come. Katie grasped her arm even tighter and together they made their way between the marble headstones.

The noise of men's voices reached towards them and Mali stared around her, seeing how different everything was. The wall that had sheltered her mother's grave was gone. And there was no tree, just a huddle of stones and mud where the hill had slipped into the cemetery.

The men fell silent, leaning on their shovels, and as Mali approached one of them stepped forward, touching his cap.

'It would be better if you did not look now *merchi*,' he said gently. 'Why not go home and wait until Gerwyn the undertaker has done his job?' He blocked Mali's path and she smiled at him, knowing he meant well.

'I must see him,' she said, 'he's my Dad.' She moved up the hill with Katie still clinging to her arm and she could feel the Irish girl trembling. And yet Mali herself was not afraid, not now the moment had come.

The men fell back, heads bowed, and Mali stared down into the wet soil, her eyes unwavering.

Davie's hair was matted with clay, his head was arched back as though he was sucking for air. Had he died at once, Mali wondered, or had it been slow and agonising, a terrible darkness filling windpipe and nostrils, shutting out the good clean air? But he was gone now, his spirit no longer within the distorted body. Dave was reunited with his Jinny.

Beside her Katie was saying prayers, eyes closed, face white and drawn. Then, quietly at first, one of the coppermen began to sing 'Bread of Heaven' and slowly the other men joined in until a chorus soared upwards in triumph, tenor and bass in harmony rising towards the mountain top and it was so beautiful that Mali could not bear it.

A light drizzle began to fall and Katie tugged on Mali's arm. 'Come on, I'll take you home,' she said softly and Mali nodded, for there was no more to do here in the graveyard. She did not feel the rain on her face for it mingled with her tears.

The return journey did not seem to take very long and soon Mali found herself turning the corner past the Mexico Fountain.

'You are not going home yet,' Katie said firmly, 'sure you can come into my house and have a bit to eat, you won't do

301

yourself nor the little babby any good by starving.'

Dai End House had returned to the open doorway, his hands manipulating the accordion with gentleness, drawing soft haunting sounds from the small musical instrument.

'We men want to take the responsibility for burying your dad proper like, Mali,' he said without pausing in his playing. 'No job for a girl and we'll do it all quick and quiet like in view of the circumstances. Gerwyn the undertaker knows what we want and no expense spared, Davie Llewelyn shall have the best.'

Mali could do nothing more than nod but Dai seemed to sense her feelings of gratitude for he inclined his head and then closing his eyes concentrated once more on his music.

It was good to be in the warmth and the noise of the Murphy kitchen and even Tom seemed amiable, his voice gentle as he chided his sons.

'Come sit down my little colleen,' he said kindly to Mali. 'Rest a bit and Mammy will give you something good to warm your belly.'

Katie went upstairs to change from her Sunday clothes and returned a little later wearing a skirt that was darned and patched and kept only for working in.

'I forgot to tell you,' she said, 'Big Mary sends you kind thoughts, I only remembered about it when I put on me old skirt.' Katie sat down near Mali and smiled at her. 'Mary says the laundry needs you so hurry back.' She sighed. 'I think it might be better for you to be in work rather than sittin' at home alone just now.'

Mali nodded. 'You're right, and tomorrow I'll be back at my desk whatever happens.'

Katie appeared doubtful. 'Perhaps that's a bit too soon, for sure you need a little time to get over . . .' she paused and shook her head. 'Well it's up to you sure enough.'

Jess Murphy banged a plate on the table. 'Come on Katie, stop babbling and help me bring in the food, it's only bread and cheese but all home-made, fresh and good. There's a couple of cakes in the tin, you can bring them out later.'

It was pleasant to simply be one of a crowd, to sit and eat the fresh crusty bread and drink hot sweet tea out of a cracked cup and simply not have to think of anything at all, and Mali felt the tension that had gripped her all day slowly ease away.

After they had eaten, Katie placed little Sean on Mali's knee and smiled down at her. 'You just hold the babby and Mammy and me will do the washing up. Soon the boys will go up to bed and then we'll all have a bit of peace.'

Mali looked down at the plump little boy in her arms and for the first time realised that she wanted her baby, he would be a boy, she felt sure of it, he would be handsome and fair, with dimples in his cheeks.

Suddenly, she was very tired, the events of the past days seemed to catch up with her and she could scarcely keep her eyes open.

'Katie, I think I'll go home now,' she said softly. 'I'm very grateful to you for all the hospitality you've shown me, and I don't know what I'd have done without you to keep me company at the cemetery.'

Katie went with her to the door. 'Are you sure you'll be all right on your own?' she asked. 'For sure I'll come and sleep down on your kitchen floor if you want someone with you tonight.'

Mali shook her head. 'No, it's all right, Rosa will be there, though I expect she'll have a few hours in the public bar of Maggie Dicks or the Mexico Fountain before she comes home.'

Katie frowned. 'You want to tell her to get out, especially now, there's no reason why you should have to put up with her, no reason at all.'

Mali rubbed at her eyes tiredly, dusk was falling and she felt as though she wanted to crawl into her bed and sleep the clock around.

'I suppose you're right but I'm too tired to think of anything now, I'll talk to Rosa in the morning, I promise.'

It was cold in the street and from down the row, Mali heard a woman singing soft and beautiful. Other people were happy, she thought tiredly, families were together wrapped in the warmth of well-lit kitchens; it suddenly seemed that she was the only one in the whole world who was alone.

She opened her door to darkness. The fire burned low in the grate and Mali knew that if she hurried, she could save it. She threw off her coat and put some sticks into the dying flames, watching them kindle with a sigh of satisfaction. When she lit the gas lamp, all at once the room seemed transformed and Mali did not feel quite so alone.

She placed coals carefully on the sticks and coaxed the flame by fanning it with her hand. Soon the fire glowed into life and Mali sank back on her heels and sighed. She looked around her at the untidy kitchen. Dishes lay greasily in the sink and the table could do with a good scrubbing, she decided, for there was salt spilled in the crevices between the wood and tea stains marred the whiteness of the boards.

It did Mali good to be occupied, for her feeling of tiredness had disappeared. Perhaps all she really needed was to be alone and instead of pitying herself for her solitude, she should be grateful, at least she had a roof over her head which was more than many folks could say.

A new thought struck her then. This cottage she was so fond of was Sterling Richardson's property, he could tell her to leave at any time he chose. She brushed back her hair wearily, she could not dwell on such thoughts, not just now, she would face those problems when she came to them. It was just like her mother used to tell her, 'Sufficient to the day is the evil thereof.' It sounded like words from the good book, only Mali could not be sure.

She filled the kettle and put it onto the blazing fire. She would have some tea and then go to bed.

As she sat at the table a little later, with a cup in her hand, she wondered what was different about the small kitchen. She looked round curiously and began to realise that none of Rosa's possessions lay cluttering the room as they usually did. That was strange, very strange. She lifted her head and sensed that the house was well and truly empty of everything connected with Rosa.

Mali hurried upstairs and into the bedroom, pulling open the cupboard, moving aside Davie's clothes; she went to the chest of drawers but the tattered fur collar, the dingy battered hat and all the rest of Rosa's possessions were gone.

Slowly, Mali descended the stairs and returned to the kitchen. She did not blame Rosa for running out, she understood that Davie's death together with the news of the forthcoming baby was all too much for the girl to take in her stride. In a way

304

it was a relief to have Rosa off her hands.

A sudden suspicion entered Mali's mind. She moved to the dresser and lifted the tea tin, holding it close to her for a moment, taking a deep breath before prising the lid open.

The tin was empty, not a farthing remained. All the money collected by the men from the Mexico Fountain together with the hundred pounds compensation had vanished. Mali dropped the tin to the floor with a clatter.

'Oh, Rosa, how could you?' she said and the words fell into the silence like a cry.

Chapter Thirty-one

Sterling knew that the new order for zinc wire should have made him the happiest man in Sweyn's Eye. If he could fulfil the demand from Coopers, which was a huge industrial company situated about twenty miles away from town, then he would be solvent once more. He would be in a position to discharge his debts and to expand the zinc foundry so that it would be a real money-spinner.

And yet there were memories lurking in his mind, thoughts of Mali Llewelyn, her green eyes wild and accusing, her soft body changed by the child she carried within her. But her accusations had been unjust, without foundation, and anger overrode any other emotion as he thought of their last encounter.

He rose from his chair and stared out into the cold January day and sighed heavily. When he had sent out his men to search for Davie Llewelyn, he had not expected them to have found him in such terrible circumstances. He had been dismayed to hear of Davie's death and the manner of it was too horrible to think about.

He moved restlessly from the window, perhaps a walk in the fresh air might clear his head. He drew on his coat and glanced towards Ben. 'I'm going out, keep an eye on things.'

Ben smiled and the ends of his waxed moustache lifted. 'That new order is going to make us rich,' he said. 'Going to celebrate with a nip of something warming are you Mr Richardson?'

Sterling paused, Ben's words bringing to the surface the triumph of his success. He smiled. 'We do seem to have turned the corner, Ben,' he replied.

Outside, the wind was keen and a rim of frost covered the cobbled yard, coating the rooftops of the huddled buildings so that it appeared to have been snowing.

He strode out briskly, looking up as the sudden burst of sparks from one of the chimneys illuminated the dullness of the day. The stink of sulphur pervaded the atmosphere and Sterling suddenly wanted to get right away from the Richardson Copper Company.

It had dominated his life in this last year since his father had died, he ate it and slept it twenty-four hours of every day. And his brother Rickie, who might have been helping, did nothing but frequent low bars, consorting with villains who would cut a grandmother's throat for the price of a pint of ale.

He felt a fierce and burning resentment against his brother. If Rickie had pulled his weight, taken his share of the responsibility for the business, then Sterling might have had more time to live his own life. Instead he had been either cooped up in the office poring over books or attending auctions or chasing orders.

He turned the corner of the buildings and came upon the banks of coal that usually towered high into the air like miniature mountains. To his dismay, he saw that the stocks were alarmingly low. If he did not see to replenishing them at once, there would not be enough fuel to last through the winter months. Yet he was sure he had sent off the order as he usually did at the end of each month. What could have gone wrong?

He returned quickly to the office and Ben looked up startled as Sterling entered the small room, slamming the door behind him.

'Ben, check on last month's coal records,' Sterling said quickly. 'Either the suppliers have let me down or I forgot to send in the order.'

Ben glanced through the books swiftly and efficiently. 'Ah, here we are, I remember now. Mr Rickie came into the office, told me that you wanted to give the contracts to some of the smaller pits outside town by way of a change. Only trouble is there's no note of any response from them.'

Sterling sat on the edge of the desk. 'Rickie came here telling you what I wanted done?' he said incredulously. 'Since when

307

have I confided in him or when has he shown an interest in the business for that matter? You should have checked it out with me, Ben. In future don't listen to anything my brother tells you.'

Anger was hot within him; Rickie must be up to something. Well he could just keep his nose out or he might have it pushed out.

Ben was looking crestfallen, staring down at his books, his mouth drawn into a straight line.

'I don't suppose there's any real harm done,' Sterling said more calmly. 'I'll get some supplies over from the Kilvey Deep. The last thing we want now is any hitches,' he added. 'Without coal we wouldn't be able to supply Coopers with that zinc wire.'

He felt uneasily that he should find out what Rickie thought he was playing at, coming into the office out of the blue and issuing instructions the way he had.

'I'm going to take the rest of the day off,' Sterling said decisively. At the door he turned. 'Remember, Ben, don't take any further orders from my brother, is that understood?'

Ben's face was long. 'Right you are sir, I did think it strange at the time.' He shrugged. 'But Master Rickie is family . . .' His voice trailed away and Sterling nodded abruptly.

'I understand, Ben, but it mustn't happen again.'

As he drove the Ascot up the hill, Sterling glanced towards the place where his new house now stood, ready for occupation. He was sick of his room at the Mackworth Arms and yet somehow he did not relish the thought of living alone as much as he once did. But it was time he moved in, for the house needed warm fires to light the rooms or they would become damp.

It did not take him long to reach Plas Rhianfa and it seemed a long time since he'd driven through the huge gates and along the winding drive to the great mansion that dominated the skyline. It gave him great satisfaction to know that the old place would remain in the family, the order for zinc wire would see to that.

He drew the automobile to a halt and climbed down from the driving seat. He stood for a moment drinking in the sight of the house where he had been born. One day his son would own it and he relished the thought.

Sterling walked round to the back of the house, towards the stables. He might as well enter by the rear door, he did not want his arrival to be announced by his mother's delighted greetings, so giving Rickie a chance to get away before they could talk. Foxy whinnied softly from the stable and, smiling, Sterling moved to rub at the animal's ears.

Voices speaking low from somewhere inside the wooden building made him pause, there was something in the half whispers that alerted him. He moved silently round towards the doorway and edged inside.

Through the gloom, he saw three men, one of them his brother Rickie, seated on boxes, heads bent forward.

'It will finish him,' Rickie was saying in triumph. 'It's worked out even better than I'd thought for without coal the order for this new zinc product he's been making will go down the drain.'

Sterling could see now that Will Owens was facing Rickie and to his brother's right sat Glanmor Travers, his face eager, his close-set eyes gleaming. The three of them were hatching some nasty little idea to put him out of business, obviously, but what was it?

'I set the charge like you told me,' Will Owens was saying in a low voice. 'The whole shoot should blow sky high.' His voice held a bitter satisfaction.

Sterling tensed. Suddenly his mind was crystal clear: the men had mentioned coal and an explosion, and all at once their conversation made sense. They meant to put the Cornish beam engine out of action and so flood the chain of pits from the Kilvey Deep right down into the valley.

He stepped out into the open so suddenly that the three men turned and looked at him as though he was a ghost. It was Owens who spoke.

'Jesus Gawd, he's heard the lot.'

'Yes I heard the lot, damn you,' Sterling stared at Rickie angrily, and a fine brother you turned out to be.'

'Brother?' Rickie's voice was loud and contemptuous. 'You're no brother of mine!'

Sterling's fist caught Rickie square in the mouth and he staggered back against the wall, blood running from his cut lip.

'What have you done, you bastard?' Sterling said harshly. 'Where have you set this charge?'

Rickie spat blood into the straw and wiped his mouth with the back of his hand. 'Find out.'

Sterling's anger was growing with each minute and he caught Rickie by the throat. 'Tell me what I want to know or by God, brother or no, I'll beat it out of you.'

He jerked Rickie to his feet and the two men stared at each other for a long moment.

'That's just it,' Rickie gasped at last, 'you are not my brother.'

'What game are you trying to play now?' Sterling's grip tightened on Rickie's throat.

'It's true, you are not Arthur Richardson's child.' His voice was rising hysterically. 'You are a by-blow conceived from a sordid little affair between our mother and James Cardigan.'

From behind him Sterling heard a strangled gasp and turning, he saw Victoria standing in the doorway, her hand to her throat, her face white. By the expression in her eyes, Sterling knew deep down in his gut that what Rickie said was true.

'Mother,' he said softly, almost pleadingly, but she looked away from him.

'Good heavens! I could hear the sound of you shouting from the house. Please boys, stop this fighting, I will not have it.'

Sterling saw her mouth move but he did not hear her words, there was a great bursting pain within him and it was as if the foundations of his life were rocking beneath his feet.

He hit Rickie again and again in an unseeing rage. 'It's not true, it's just filthy lies!'

He heard Victoria cry out behind him. 'Someone help me! James, I must fetch James.'

Sterling's vision cleared a little. James Cardigan his father, surely it could not be? He was a Richardson, he had been born in wedlock, brought up as beloved eldest son, yet in a moment all the security of his childhood had been wiped out with a few bitter words.

But he was still the man Arthur Richardson had brought him up to be, he reasoned, and it was he alone who had saved the company from extinction. And no one, nothing, could change the man he had become.

He gave a low growl and threw Rickie away from him and the younger man lay amid the straw moaning.

Glanmor Travers seemed suddenly spurred into action for the next minute he was through the door and running for his life. Sterling let him go but he knew he must marshall his thoughts, undo the harm Rickie might have done. It was Will Owens who had planted the charge, he was the one who must be dealt with now.

'Owens, where is the charge planted and what time is it to go off?' He stared menacingly at the younger man but Owens returned his look, his lip curled in scorn.

'Do you want to try to beat it out of me, too?' he asked fiercely.

Sterling tried to control the impulse to wipe the smile from Will Owens' face. This situation needed cunning, not strength.

'I'll give you a hundred pounds if you show me where you set the charge.' His voice rang out loud and clear and Owens' eyes flickered with greed.

Rickie stepped forward quickly. 'It's too late!' he cried. 'Don't be a fool Owens, you'll never get there in time. Keep your trap shut if you know what's good for you.'

Sterling pushed Rickie aside. 'Two hundred,' he said desperately. 'Just think what you could do with that sort of cash.'

He could see Owens hesitating. What he didn't know was that the man wanted Sterling's death even more than he wanted the money and the only way to get him on the spot at the time of the explosion was to pretend to go along with him.

'Right, it's a deal,' he said harshly and Sterling smiled in bitter triumph at his brother.

'You see, Rickie, you haven't won, not yet.'

Rickie seemed to go wild then, he flung himself at Sterling, attempting to punch and hit him, his face contorted with rage.

'Nothing belongs to you, by rights it's all mine, I'm the true heir to the company, the house, the lot. Why should you get away with it all?'

Sterling shook him off scornfully. 'Have you ever done a day's work in your life? Your only contribution has been to lord it around the town and enjoy the money which I've earned by the sweat of my brow. Whatever the truth of my birth, everything is mine because I've earned the right, do you understand?'

He strode out of the door and Will Owens followed him to where the Ascot stood at the front of the house.

'Get in,' Sterling said shortly and after a moment's hesitation, Will obeyed.

Sterling drove as though all the demons in hell were chasing him. The Ascot screeched around a corner as the automobile left the road and bumped onto the rough pathway that led across the hills.

Sterling glanced at Will Owens who was clinging to the sides of the seat, his face pale, his hair blowing back from his brow. He looked scared to death. Serves him right, Sterling thought angrily, he should be horsewhipped for the part he'd played in planning to blow up the Kilvey Deep engine house.

'Don't you realise what it will mean in terms of human life if the pump should fail?' he asked sharply and Owens remained silent, glancing at him through half-closed eyes. Sterling concentrated on his driving, attempting to force more speed from the small Ascot.

'You deserve all you get for that beating you arranged for me.' Will Owens had to raise his voice to be heard.

Sterling frowned. 'I arranged no beating,' he replied tersely. 'If I wanted to hammer you, I'd do it personally.'

'But I heard the gang of youths mentioning you by name,' Owens protested, 'Mr Richardson they said, as clear as you like.'

Sterling smiled grimly. 'There are two of us,' he shouted, 'which one do you think would be afraid to meet you face to face?'

At last the Kilvey Deep came into sight. Owens took a watch from his pocket and gave a strangled cry. 'Stop, we're too late, I don't want to die!' He threw open the door, his face contorted with panic.

He took a great leap from the moving Ascot and fell to the ground, tumbling down the steep hill with sickening force.

'Damned fool!' Sterling grated the automobile to a halt and ran towards the spot where Owens lay, quite still now, his head against a large boulder.

There was the sound of galloping hooves and then James

Cardigan was climbing from his horse. He came towards Sterling and looked at him questioningly.

'I think he's dead, God help us,' Sterling said. 'James, we'll talk later but I must find that explosive before it's too late.' He ran towards the engine house, unaware that James was following him.

And then everything seemed to happen at once. The wall of the engine house appeared to lift upward and outward so slowly that Sterling could scarcely believe it. A great deafening rushing sound filled the air and dust, thick and heavy, mingled with a shower of small stones that fell like raindrops to the ground.

Sterling felt James make a grab at him, holding him tightly. Slowly, as if in a nightmare, Sterling saw the wall of the engine house collapsing in on itself. Huge segments were falling around him. James threw his body protectively over him and then there was a great choking blackness and Sterling knew no more.

Chapter Thirty-two

In the streets of Sweyn's Eye chaos reigned as warning sirens from the coal pits echoed through the hills and down in the valleys. Shopkeepers closed shutters and, still wearing aprons, hurried towards the coalfield, knowing that some disaster had come upon the town.

In the office of the Canal Street Laundry, Mali lifted her head from her books and the child moved within her womb as though sensing her fear. Mr Waddington rose to his feet and patted Mali on the shoulder.

'There, be calm now, no use upsetting yourself,' he said, 'I'll go and see if I can find out what's happening.'

Mali managed to smile up at him. He had been unbelievably kind to her in the last few days. He had attended her father's simple funeral, standing holding her arm, giving his support as Davie was lowered into the grave beside his wife Jinny, and Mali did not know what she would have done without him. Mr Waddington had been even more considerate since she had told him of Rosa's treachery in running off with the money.

'That doesn't matter,' he'd said. 'All I care about is that you are here to help me. You are like the daughter I had and lost and if I may, I shall try my best to be, if not a father, then a guardian to you and to the child when it arrives.'

Mali watched now as Mr Waddington opened the door and walked slowly to the gates. He was joined almost immediately by the women from the laundry, some of whom had menfolk working in the pits.

Mali could hear him telling the women that they must leave at once, not to mind the work, and her heart ached for the ones

314

who would most certainly have lost loved ones.

Sally Benson stopped at the door of the office and there was a strangely triumphant look on her face.

'I've some news for you,' she said excitedly. 'I've been talking to the maid from the Cardigan household and a real rumpus there's been up there, so Bertha says. And it appears that Sterling Richardson is Master James's natural son, there's a scandal for you. Gone chasing off to the Kilvey Deep now, both of them.' She smiled spitefully. 'Thought I'd be the first one to tell you, knowing how fond you are of Mr Richardson.'

Mali sat in stunned silence after Sally Benson had hurried away to join the other women at the laundry gates.

'It isn't true, this can't be really happening,' she whispered and even as the full import of what Sally had said sunk into her mind, she was rising to her feet. She drew her coat over her rounded body and hurried outside into the coldness of the day.

Mr Waddington came hurrying towards her. She stretched out her hand and he took it in his own. 'I must get up there,' she said, but Mr Waddington was gently hushing her.

'I've heard all about it and I've sent for the pony and trap.' He tried to smile. 'Don't worry too much, there's a good girl. No good ever came from jumping to conclusions. These stories are always magnified, you know that as well as I do.'

She scarcely heard him as he took her arm, helping her up into the swaying seat of the trap. She drew her coat more closely round her swollen belly as though to protect her child from the awful images that had begun to torment her mind. She could imagine Sterling lying injured, perhaps calling for help, and she could not bear it.

The terrible noise of the sirens seemed to be inside her head along with Sally Benson's words that were dancing crazily through her thoughts.

Sterling Richardson was James Cardigan's son, it hardly seemed credible. Then Bea Cardigan must be Sterling's half-sister. Mali struggled to sort things out in her mind. Miss Cardigan must have somehow learned the truth for that would make sense of all that had happened later. And it must have been she who had broken off the relationship with Sterling.

Mali felt an overwhelming sense of protectiveness towards Sterling; perhaps everything he had worked for might now be cruelly snatched away from him. But nothing mattered, she told herself, nothing except that he be alive and well.

'That young Rickie is tied up with all this, you mark my words,' Mr Waddington was saying. 'Never did like the boy, eyes too closely set, always a sign of a sly nature. Mixes with some real villains he does too, but they will all be brought to justice, never fear. Ah, we are nearly there, hold tight, my dear, the road is a little bumpy just here.'

It was not very long before the slag heaps came into view and Mr Waddington was hard put to keep the trap on the roadway for the throng of people had grown increasingly large. Already at the pit head there was gathered a huge crowd of onlookers. Most of them were women with shawls over their heads, standing silent and tense, watching the rescuers bring out the injured and the dead.

'This is terrible indeed.' Mr Waddington tied his scarf more tightly around his throat. 'And I imagine there are other pits all along the hillside with similar scenes to this taking place above the coal face. The water rises so quickly, you see.'

It was as if he was simply voicing his thoughts out loud, but in any case Mali was not listening. She had caught sight of Victoria Richardson kneeling on the ground, her face contorted with grief, and Mali's heart almost stopped beating. With steps that seemed to move with nightmare slowness, she went forward. Her mouth was dry and her hands felt icily cold as she clenched them to her sides.

She stopped still then, staring down at the limp figure hastily covered with a coat. Her eyes met those of Sterling's mother and it was as though the two women recognised that they were caught in the same tragedy.

'They've not found Sterling yet,' Victoria whispered. Her tears gushed afresh then and she held a handkerchief to her face. 'James, my poor James.'

Mali moved woodenly away, her eyes searching the crowd, praying she would catch sight of the familiar tall figure, the golden hair and clean-cut features that were so dear to her. Let him only be alive so that she could tell him she was sorry. Explain that she did not really blame him for Davie's death, the words had been spoken in anger and pain.

A few of the rescuers, shopkeepers and miners working

316

together, were placing the dead in rows along the ground. Some of the fatally injured were colliers caught in the blast, blackened faces shining as though they still sweated over their labours. Many more were still trapped down in the seams, unable to move because of the gushing water that was swiftly drowning the mine.

Mali stepped forward, approaching what was left of the engine house with trepidation. The blast had ripped the thick walls apart as though they were paper and the tangled remains of the beam engine lay among the stones. She moved away abruptly and saw as two men lifted a body from the perimeter of the debris, the head was lolling backwards, the eyes staring sightlessly at the sky. Mali clutched her hands to her breast as though she could stop her heart from bursting with fear and then with a sigh, she saw that the hair was dark, not gleaming gold like Sterling's.

'This is no place for someone in your condition, *merchi*,' one of the men said kindly. He was wearing a barber's apron and there was an open blade jutting out of his top pocket. Mali looked at him dumbly and he shook his head at her before beginning to move away. It was then that Mali recognised the face of the youth the men were carrying, it was Will Owens. He did not appear to have a mark on him and yet it was clear even to Mali that he had been dead for some time.

She put her hand to her mouth. 'Poor Katie,' she murmured and then she turned away for there was no time to be spent crying.

She scrambled over a heap of boulders and stopped to watch the rescuers inside the shell of the engine house, lifting a great stone from a man's chest.

'*Duw*, it's Ceri Morgan,' a voice said, 'and he's still alive. Come on, boyos, let's get these boulders shifted.'

Hope lit in Mali's heart. If one man had survived the blast then surely Sterling could be alive too! She turned to look frantically around her, it was as though she could sense him near.

The crowds were growing by the minute. Mali saw Bea Cardigan on the arm of the tall American, Dean Sutton, and both of them were ashen-faced as they helped Victoria Richardson to her feet. Bea was crying even as she attempted to lead the older woman away but Victoria was shaking her head and Mali knew that the woman was afraid she might yet learn she had lost a son.

Mali felt an arm encircle her waist and she turned to see Katie staring at her with wide, frightened eyes. 'Terrible, so it is,' she said, 'there are so many dead and I'm frightened 'cos I can't find my William.' Mali folded her friend in her arms and they clung together desperately. Closing her eyes in pain, Mali knew she must speak, tell Katie the truth, for what good was it to live in false hope?

'He's dead, Katie.' She whispered the words but by the way the Irish girl stiffened in her arms, she knew she had heard them.

Katie suddenly began to sob, deep, heartrending sounds that tore at Mali's heart. The Irish girl clutched her rosary and lay against Mali's shoulder as though for comfort. Mali felt unutterably weary. Perhaps she should offer to go home with Katie and yet how could she leave the Kilvey Deep until she had seen the last of the dead laid out for inspection?

'Look out there!' There was a cry from behind them and Mali pulled Katie clear just as a huge chunk of the engine house wall fell slowly downwards, sending a shower of dust and stones over the place where a few moments before they had been standing.

'God, there's no hope for anyone left inside the engine house now.' One of the men who had been digging in the ruins rubbed the dirt from his eyes. 'Crushed like bugs they'd be, poor sods.'

Katie tugged at Mali's arm. 'Come on home, there's a good girl, I've lost Will and I couldn't bear to lose you too.' Katie's face was streaked with dirt and tears and Mali looked at her pityingly.

'I must stay, please try to understand, Katie,' she said softly.

'Mali, come here, I must talk to you.' Mr Waddington was clambering over the stones, his face drawn and grey. 'Sit here for a moment with me my dear, that's right, on this flat stone.' He coughed a little and Mali stared at him, fearing that he had bad news.

'Look,' he held out a torn coat, 'Mrs Richardson believes it

318

belonged to Sterling. I think you are going to have to be very brave, my dear.'

She held the cloth to her cheek and felt the roughness of the material rub against her skin. He was not dead, she could not, would not believe it. She shook her head.

'It's going to be all right,' she said softly, 'I'll just wait here but please, you go home, you look so tired.' She closed her eyes, clinging to the coat, trying to shut out the sounds all around her. There were women crying, and among them her dear friend Katie. But Mali must be calm, she must wait and not give up hope. Although it might be fanciful, it seemed then to Mali as though Davie and Jinny were sitting there right with her, giving her comfort and strength.

It had been at Mam's funeral that she'd met Sterling, a year ago this month. The weather then had been bitterly cold as it was now, but Sterling had illuminated the day with his presence. He had set some spark alight in her and Mali realised that she had been in love with him from that moment on.

And yet many months had gone by before her love had come to fruition. She had found joy lying in Sterling's arms but her happiness had been short-lived indeed.

She had believed many bad things about him, she had thought him hard and callous and all the time she had known nothing of the truth about him, judging only by what she saw on the surface.

And yet, Mali reasoned, the love that had blossomed that cold day in January had never really altered. She carried within her Sterling's child and for that she would always be grateful.

He had been rightly angry with her because she had not told him that she was expecting his baby and had not gone to him for help. She had thought herself too proud to ask anything of him and yet if he were only here now she would throw herself at his feet and take any crumbs he cared to offer.

A movement at her side caught her attention and she looked up to see Mr Waddington scrambling away from her. Her heart began to pound as she realised that the last of the dead and injured were being laid on the cold hard ground.

Slowly she forced herself to stand. Her legs were trembling but she must go forward. She still clung to Sterling's torn coat, clutching it in her hands as though it could bring him near to her. She stumbled a little and a soft ray of sunshine illuminated the place where she stood. Her eyes grew wide and unbelieving as she looked towards the crowd of rescuers.

He stood tall and proud, his hair begrimed with coal dust but with the gold still shining through. His shirt sleeves were rolled above his elbows and along one arm there was a great gaping wound. But he was among the rescuers, not the dead and injured, Sterling was alive and well.

Mali took a deep shuddering breath and for a long time, so it seemed, they both stood and stared at each other, the sunlight shining upon them like a benediction. Afterwards, Mali did not know who made the first move but then he was coming towards her, taking her in his arms, holding her close.

She put up her hands wonderingly to touch his face, stared into his violet eyes, wanting to drink in every detail of his appearance.

'I love you,' she whispered. 'God how I love you.' She stood on tiptoe and pressed her lips against his and his mouth was tender, telling her all that words could not.

She swayed a little and then Sterling was sweeping her up into his arms. He held her so close that their heartbeats were as one and suddenly the child within her moved as though feeling the great love that flowed between Mali and Sterling.

He looked down at her, and there was so much tenderness in his face that Mali put her head on his shoulder and wept.

'Hush now, it's all right,' he said softly. 'Nothing will ever separate us again, I'm taking you home.'